Marilee the Wild

Marilee jumped to her feet. "Stay away from my horse, and from me. Bed down with you tonight? I'd rather sleep with a snake."

She watched his face go stiff, his eyes take on a more sleepy look. "Reckon you'd do that, too, was you short of men."

Trembling, she said, "Man, *man?* What makes you think you're a man, Joe Langston? The gun you wear? The rapes you can force on a woman? You'll always be just what you are right now—an unschooled animal, no better than a hound whelp."

Marilee the Woman

Slateblue icicles, his eyes stabbed back at her. Pivoting his horse, he trotted it across the clearing and paused at a tall wateroak dripping gray moss from its branches. She watched him ride off into the trees without once looking back. Marilee kept staring after him, trying to stab him in the back with her eyes, wishing with all her heart that she could kill him like that. Wishing with all her fiery soul . . .

MARILEE

CON SELLERS

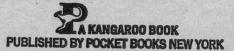
A KANGAROO BOOK
PUBLISHED BY POCKET BOOKS NEW YORK

Distributed in Canada by PaperJacks Ltd., a Licensee
of the trademarks of Simon & Schuster, a division of
Gulf+Western Corporation.

Another *Original* publication of POCKET BOOKS

POCKET BOOKS, a Simon & Schuster division of
GULF & WESTERN CORPORATION
1230 Avenue of the Americas, New York, N.Y. 10020
In Canada distributed by PaperJacks Ltd.,
330 Steelcase Road, Markham, Ontario.

ISBN: 0-671-81211-4

First Pocket Books printing April, 1978

Trademarks registered in the United States and other countries.

PRINTED IN CANADA

For Redroses, my luck

(With thanks to Ted Fehrenbach for invaluable research via his histories *Lone Star* and *Comanches*.)

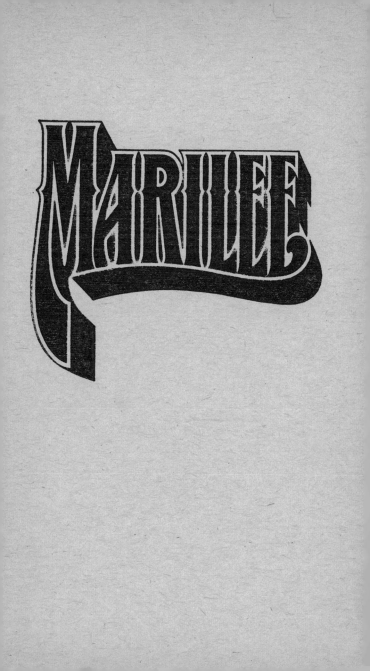

Chapter 1

A patch of silvering burned away and a corner broken off one end, the cracked mirror gave back the wavery reflection of a strange woman. Marilee didn't really know her anymore. The ball gown was too rich, glaringly bright against the peeling walls of the slave cabin.

Spreading wide skirts meant for hoops, she did a slow and graceful pirouette before the salvaged glass, her head tilted to one side as she listened for the piano and violins, the deep and carefree laughter of adoring swains backgrounded by the more subdued, flirtatious, and sometimes envious murmuring of girls.

There had been the melodic tinkling of crystal goblets, scents of violets and roses and even some of that daring new musk from Paris. And if she danced out near the veranda, framed by wisteria vines and sentineled with cane chairs, there was always the drifting bluesmoke of cigars and the creamy blooms of Cape Jasmine bushes flinging their rich perfume about the garden, spendthrifts made drunk by heady moonlight.

Listening now, she heard only the soughing of tired wind through loblolly pines, the echo of it mourning around the stark and blackened chimneys of Bradburn. Other than

1

those early, impossibly exultant drums and bugles, it had been a long time since she'd heard music; lonely ages had gone by since she moved gaily in her wine-colored gown across the gleaming ballroom floor, laughing and laughing.

Did anybody laugh anymore?

Certainly not Marilee Bradburn; she couldn't even remember smiling. She tried it now, bending close to the mirror. The expression was more like a grimace on her thin face, her teeth too white against a face tanned as any mulatto. Well, she thought, a quadroon anyway. And her hair—loose and shaggy long, tied back with a twisted bit of rag.

Back in the old times, the good times, Marilee had often worn it in pigtails like a pickaninny or in a bun upon her neck, much to the despair of her mother, who couldn't understand how hair got in the way of riding. But for the formal parties, Lucinda had always done up the silvery mass into an intricate coiffure of ringlets and curls. And Marilee's mother had always said the same thing: "Now you look like a lady."

Mama, she thought, the imitation smile fading from her lips; sweet and fluttery, her mother had never grasped what was happening to the South, to Bradburn itself, and wouldn't try. Shaking her head, Marilee backed from the mirror and forced her mind to other things; she didn't want to think of Mama wasting away. She would think of Lucinda, then: as long as she was trying on the ball gown —the only gown left—she might as well bring back the maid fixing her hair for the soirée.

Patient, worrisomely moral, where was Lucinda now— doing for some other mistress up North? Or, more likely, trudging the roads looking for something, anything, like all the other bewildered free Nigras. If she found her way back to Bradburn and peeped into this cabin, Lucinda might remember the ball gown, so frivolous and lacy, but she'd be shocked to see Marilee looking this way. Her young mistress had been worn down by work she was never meant to do—field hand labor—and Marilee's pampered skin was now burned by a merciless sun, and her hands. . . .

Not daring to look closely at her callused hands, Marilee hid them in the voluminous folds of her skirt and tried harder to slip into the childhood game of Let's Pretend. Glowing, fresh from a hot bath that was sinfully delicious after a long ride to the hounds with Daddy and her brothers, she was leaning back in the brocade chair and wearing only her thin chemise. Of course this horrified Lucinda.

"I swear, Miz Marilee, yo mama come in here and catch you thisaway, she whup me good for helpin' you be so shameless."

"Lucinda, you know very well Mama never whipped anybody--and besides, it's too hot to wear petticoats."

"Set still, now--you worse'n a wiggle worm. How you speck me to get yo hair done proper?"

"*I* don't much care. I'd rather be on a fox hunt tonight, instead of simperin' with a bunch of giggly girls."

"And young genmun, too. Reckon Mister Robbie Dee acomin'."

"Oh, pooh! Robbie Dee Crownover thinks he's already a sure enough grownup, too biggity to pay attention to me."

"Reckon he might, did you act mo like a lady, 'stead of hootin' and hollerin' through them woods. Yo mama know you come in ridin' straddle agin?"

"And don't you tell her, either! Sidesaddle is for prisses like Sue Anne and that silly Charlotte, who always plays like she's faintin'. In the woods, they'd fall off first time the horse got out of a walk, fall right on their tender little—"

"Marilee Bradburn, don't you put your mouth to that word! Yo mama wash it out with lye soap. Now you cover up them naked knees and quite wigglin'."

Blinking, Marilee ran her hands over the gown's sagging skirt. Lucinda was free now, even though she hadn't wanted to be, driven off with the other house servants and field hands when the first Yankees came. Lucinda had been so proud of her in this dress, with her hair up and stately, as proud as Daddy himself. Even though having the gown brought up all the way from New Orleans was Mama's idea, Daddy had been happy over the change in his little tomboy. At fourteen, a young lady was supposed to look and act the part, so she would interest eligible young planters like Robbie Dee Crownover.

Backing away from the mirror, Marilee sank back upon the crude bed with its cornshuck mattress and closed her eyes, seeing Robbie Dee as he'd been, what seemed about a thousand years ago. Tall against a hot-blue summer sky, he moved gracefully as a Kentucky thoroughbred without putting it on. That kind of style was bred in the bone, and Robbie Dee carried his blood lines well.

He laughed easily, the corners of his cornflower-blue eyes crinkling as he looked down at her, strong hands gentle upon her tiny waist as he guided her in a waltz or cupped to give her a leg up on her horse. It didn't matter that he was five years older; he treated her almost as equal as Daddy and the boys did.

But that silly Charlotte Maddox was always calling her "child," since Charlotte was a full sixteen and had already been to Atlanta and New Orleans and thought nobody but a Bradburn or a Crownover was good enough for her. When Charlotte wasn't having the vapors at convenient times she was using all her feminine wiles on Elliot Bradburn and Robbie Dee—only she never captured either one.

Dry shucks crackled as Marilee propped her elbows on the mattress and smiled. Robbie Dee didn't have any notion of getting married right off, which was just fine with Marilee. They had fun following the hounds or just going lickety-split through the woods and across the fields, jumping everything that got in their way. And once, on a sticky afternoon, they'd gone swimming in the Homochitto River, casual as if her mama were chaperoning them from the bank.

She kept on her petticoat, and Robbie Dee seemed embarrassed in a silly pair of cotton drawers that came clear down to his knees, hurrying into the water before she could get more than a glance at his lightly haired chest. It had been very exciting, swimming close to a man who was practically naked, a man who wasn't one of her brothers. They'd laughed and splashed and chased a dignified old bullfrog until they had to flop out in the shallows at a sandbar that looked like a bed of white diamonds glittering in the sun.

"Your eyes look like green diamonds, too," Robbie Dee said.

"Emeralds, you mean. I saw pictures of them in a book."

4

Shaking water out of his bronze, curly hair, Robbie Dee said, "That's something else about you, Marilee. You ride like a man and shoot like a man—you even read books like a man."

"I'm not a man, though." She sat up, riverwet making the petticoat cling to her body.

This time his voice was roughened, as if he had a catch in his throat. "No, you sure ain't."

And it seemed perfectly natural for him to take her in his arms and kiss her, but it was different from the quick pecks on the cheek he'd given her before. Robbie Dee's lips were soft and warm, and her breath got all tangled up with his. Marilee was acutely conscious of the way her nipples had gone funny-stiff and were pressing through her thin, wet shift into the slippery flesh of his chest. When his tongue parted her lips and eased into the gasping of her mouth, she knew a scampering of little mice feet up her back and a wild, shaky excitement tingling along her inner thighs. Robbie Dee felt so *good* against her body, his hands sliding down over her shoulders, sliding across her slim hips.

Then he suddenly pulled away, breaking the kiss and pushing her back forcefully. His eyes were cloudy as he stared at her, and Marilee could see a pulse throbbing in his tanned throat, a beat that matched the one in her own.

"Didn't I do it right?" she asked.

Robbie Dee chewed his lower lip and frowned. "Too damned right."

"Then what—what's wrong? Let's do it again."

Water purled off him as he stood up and slammed through the shallows, his hands crossed in front of his belly. His voice floated back to her: "Get dressed, Marilee."

His back to her, he yanked on his breeches and shirt, stuffing his wet body into clothes as if he were ashamed of it. He oughtn't to be, she thought, realizing that Robbie Dee Crownover's body was downright pretty.

Dressing more slowly, she wished her own was as nicely put together, that she was maybe full sixteen years old and developed like Charlotte Maddox, that her breasts were bigger and bolder. If she were a filly, she'd

5

consider herself off in the rump, too, not filled out enough.

But Robbie Dee was sneaking looks at her anyhow, peeping from beneath his thickly curling lashes when he thought she wouldn't notice. So Marilee took her time getting back into her dress, teasing him because she had just learned she could, and when he laced his fingers to give her a leg up, she leaned her body against him.

Practically hurling her into the saddle, he said sharply, "Now you just stop that, Marilee. You ain't never been a flirt, and this ain't the time—or the place—to start." Then, atop his own horse, he muttered, "For a little old shirttail gal that don't even know what it's all about, you sure can make a man go clean out of his head. It must be just naturally born into some women."

Tossing her head, Marilee said, "Whatever are you talkin about Robbie Dee? Just because you don't have the gumption to kiss me like that again—"

"Hush," he said fiercely, "just you hush now," and spurred his big gelding into a lope up the path, leaving her to smile after his broad back. She was beginning to understand, but only vaguely, what it was like to be changing from a girl into a woman.

Restlessly Marilee stirred on the bed, sitting up and drawing her fingers through her hair. It was all so long ago and far away, and she was having trouble bringing back Robbie Dee's face exactly. Oh, she could see his eyes and the little squint marks at their corners and it was easy to recall the stubborn set of his mouth when he kept telling her no, no, he wouldn't make love to her that way until after they were married. He'd made her sorry she tormented him so, but now she wished she'd done it more, driven Robbie Dee past the point where he'd stop being a gentleman and take her like he would some high yellow slave wench in the quarters.

Eyes closed, she had to strain to put together his whole face, to make the parts match properly. She could smell the intriguing mansweat of him, and her fingertips knew the silker feel of his skin, but his image kept fading, wavering like her own in the cracked mirror, blurred around the edges and distorted by time. She remembered other parts of him—the eager swelling of his manhood in his breeches, the pulsing of it when she drifted her hand over

6

it and made him gasp. But all that had caused was for him formally to ask Daddy for her hand in marriage.

Aloud, she whispered, "Damn it, Robbie Dee—*why* didn't you make love to me?"

Now he never could. Robbie Dee Crownover, captain, Confederate States Cavalry, was buried somewhere near Richmond. And since their engagement party, when she wore this very gown and he'd been so dashing in his gray uniform with the gold sash, Marilee had seen her betrothed only twice. Each short leave, he'd been more determined to cling to the old and honorable ways, even though his eyes were sunken and the uniform patched, and Robbie Dee didn't laugh much.

After the war, he insisted; they'd be married after the war, when everything was back the way it used to be, had to be again. Until then, their bodies could only long for each other, and they had to make do with lingering, hungry kisses.

"You should have," Marilee whispered. *"We* should have, because it's all gone now—Bradburn and the music, the flowers, even the horses we rode through the woods. Everybody is gone, Robbie Dee—you and Daddy and my brothers, Mama, too—even Lucinda and the rest of the slaves. I'm the only one left, Robbie Dee—and I'm not much anymore—half starved and scared and feeling sorry for myself."

Bitter tears welled in her eyes, and angrily Marilee brushed them away. The time for crying, for mourning, was long past, and she was being stupid, trying to reach back and catch a handful of dreams. What was it Lucinda used to say—"Pour peas in one hand and wish in the other—see which 'un gets full quickest."

Pushing herself off the bed, Marilee wished she had some chickpeas to put in the pot. But the little garden she'd been scratching out wouldn't bear for a month or so yet, and she'd have to get by just as she had all winter, through foraging in the woods. Draping the useless skirt of the ball gown over one arm, she stooped to feed fat pine splinters into the castiron stove.

Some of the rabbit stew was left, and maybe her snares would have another cottontail for her tomorrow. Wild onions hung drying from the rooftree, and poke greens added some taste to the rabbit, but she was woefully low on salt. Her body craved fat, too; there was a dab of oil to be gotten from boiling mudcat skin and heads, but only enough to simmer the fish itself. What she desperately needed was rich, fat pork, and though she'd caught sight of some pigs gone wild, they were too wary for her crude traps and she had no gun to get them with.

Flint and steel struck sparks onto the pitch wood, and the pine kindling flared into dancing life, making its resiny, suppertime smell. Closing the stove door, she wondered if she could trade the ball gown for some salt. Maybe some Yankee soldier would want it for his woman up North. God knows they were taking everything else they could lay their hands to, anything somehow left over from what they didn't burn or loot during the war. And Yankees always had plenty of provisions.

Crouching in the brush, she'd seen a long, dusty column of bluebellies winding down the road toward Doloroso Crossing. Some of them would probably stop off there, while the rest went on to Woodville. Like hardshell locusts carrying the plague of defeat with them, they were spreading out through the entire South, stripping the land bare.

On Bradburn, there was nothing left for them to steal, burn, or run off—only this miserable little cabin left among the ruins, this slave shack once occupied by Uncle Bluegum and his wench. So no Yankees had come back this way yet, but they would; Marilee was sure of it. She wasn't so certain what month it was, or exactly how long it had been since General Lee surrendered at Appomattox, but it hadn't been too long back. One of the Jenkins boys had limped up to tell her the news, the only Jenkins boy left from the overseer's family down to the Allison Plantation. And he'd warned her to stay hidden as best she could, because the damned bluebellies were raiding and raping, and to top it off, they'd brought *nigger* troops with them.

Standing back from the heating stove, Marilee fingered the lacy material of the gown and thought that surely she could find one who knew something of courtesy, some farm boy who'd exchange salt and perhaps even a piece of fatback bacon for a dress to send home to his lady love. She had nothing else to trade; Northern cavalry had caught Blackburn unprepared, before they could bury the silver, mainly because Mama had insisted on carrying on as if there were no war, as if Daddy would come riding home at any minute, with the boys cutting didoes on their horses around him.

Nobody could make Mama believe any different, even after Colonel Wayne Bradburn fell at Corinth and his older son was lost under the rubble of Vicksburg. No, not even when young Darrell Bradburn came crawling home to die holding the festering stump of his right arm and was buried out yonder in the family graveyard, marked now with the hoofprints of Yankee horses.

Loretta Elliot Bradburn continued to smile wanly and cling to her daily routine, only faintly puzzled at the lack of servants, rolling bandages torn from sheets and petticoats and finally from dresses and curtains. She was still piling up bandages when bluecoats stripped the big house and set it afire, and Marilee had to drag her mother protesting from the flames.

Moving the half-filled pot of rabbit stew to the front of the stove, Marilee wondered if perhaps that hadn't been best for Mama, the way she caught herself in a better time and stayed there, not accepting death and change and loss. She'd died in the same fashion, quietly wasting away, the shell of a lady beneath a grimy patchwork quilt that might have been the finest of linen sheets, died planning the ball she would give when the colonel came home. All the best families would come, of course—all the way from Cottage and Rosedown plantations in Louisiana.

The dryleaf rustling of her tired voice said, "Marilee, you be sure to have Lucinda fix your hair properly, you hear? Really, you must be more of a lady."

And Marilee whispered back, "Yes, Mama."

A true aristocratic plantation lady could never have scraped out the grave for Mama, not even one who'd had to learn something of work during the last years of the war. But somebody had to bury Mama, and there was nobody else. It took the best part of two days, because the shovel had its handle broken short, and blisters swelled and broke to bleed through the rags wrapped around Marilee's hands.

But it was done at last, and she couldn't cry when she packed the black loam of Bradburn upon her mother's frail corpse, its fragile stillness without a coffin, wrapped only in the old quilt. Marilee couldn't cry because her tears had been used up for her daddy and her brothers and the man she was to have married someday.

She couldn't weep for Mama or for the South itself and would not cry for Bradburn, because the plantation was still alive. The house was dead, but the soil, the vast, rolling acres of its land, was alive beneath her knees. It lived through her, as it had through four generations before Marilee, through the strong men and determined women who carved the plantation out of wilderness and breathed spirit into it.

Bradburn had been here before Mississippi was a state, the blood of its founders spilled by Choctaw arrow and tomahawk. Wars could not kill this land; men could not slay it—not so long as a single Bradburn remained. And Marilee was still living, somehow holding her flesh together in order to hold the land. It was her reason for not fleeing to Jackson or down to the coast, where there were kinfolk who might be better off and would care for her. She owed a debt to the shades of all those who had gone before and meant to pay it.

Some way, she would bring the land back into production. Somehow, the big house would rise again from its ashes, grander than ever before, white-columned and stately. Once more, a thousand candles would blaze from faceted crystal chandeliers, while the orchestra played and rosewood tables were piled high with the lavish hospitality of Bradburn.

Some way Marilee thought, staring into the dented tin pot that held her thin and watery supper.

Somehow, she swore.

Chapter 2

She didn't hear him coming, because the neglected yard had weeded over and the Johnson grass muffled the slow beat of the horse's hooves. The hounds had been first to go when food got short, so they weren't there to growl warning.

The first she knew was when he spoke behind her, his voice rough and scratchy as his stubbled face when she whirled in shock to see him there.

"Well now," he said, leaning indolently against the doorframe. "Looks like I found me a little Reb gal all by herself, dressed up real pretty and with supper on the stove for me."

Taking a step backward, Marilee stopped, lifting her chin with a bravado she didn't feel. "I—I'm waiting for my husband. He'll be back any minute."

The man scratched his unshaven cheek, blue forage cap cocked back on his head. His eyes darted around the cabin, taking in its bare walls and shabby bed, skipping past the rough-hewn table and its stools. Then he ran those muddy eyes over her, his mouth twisting. "That so? Don't see no man's clothes about. I figure if you had a

11

man, he's probably stinkin' in a ditch somewheres, with a bunch of other dirty Secesh."

He was the first Yankee she'd seen up close since the night they'd torched the big house and barns. Then they'd all seemed hardfaced and hateful to her, but there was something different about this one, something worse. At least the Yankee lieutenant who'd ordered the destruction of Bradburn had apologized for having to do his duty and half-heartedly tried to stop the looting. But this one. . . .

Uniform stained and slovenly, oiled pistol at his belt, he kept one hairy hand upon the hilt of a cavalry saber, beady eyes never still. There was a feral aura about him, a watchful kind of hunger that chilled Marilee.

"You ain't got a man," he said, "and that won't do, for a pretty gal like you."

Fighting to keep the terror out of her voice, to hold it even, she said, "You're welcome to share what we have. It's not much, just rabbit stew."

He moved lazily toward her, spurs clanking dully, and she could feel the hotness of his eyes reaching through the frilly satin gown, probing at her breasts and sliding down over her tensed stomach to search slyly across the joining of her thighs. "Oh, you got more'n that to give away. Ain't been no troops around here for a long time. I scouted the land pretty good and didn't see no sign. That means you ain't been bothered lately and could easy have something hid out. Like gold, or maybe some silver service, the family jewels."

Carefully, she shook her head. "Your army didn't leave us anything."

He was closer, so that she could catch the rancid scent of him, the whiskey odor. Lip curling to show her a wet gold tooth, he said, "All you Reb bitches got something hid, waiting 'til you think it's safe. Buried stuff or hung it down the well on a string. No—wouldn't be down no well —a fancy dress like that would come from where it's warm and dry."

Helplessly, Marilee's hands fluttered up to the plunging neckline of the dress. "I—this didn't burn when the house did. It was h-hanging out back to air. Look—you can have the dress."

Not a tall man, but thick across the shoulders and heavy in the legs, he grinned wolfishly. "Know I can have it—ain't nothing to stop me from taking it—or anything else I want."

She measured the distance to the door. If she could get around the table and circle him, make it outside and into the woods, he'd never catch her on foot. Marilee's body tensed, but he sensed her panic and eased to one side, blocking her.

"Guess I can make you show me your hiding place later, after I give you what you been needing, out here all by your lonesome How long's it been since you had a man between your legs gal?"

Backing until she felt the heat of the woodstove against her legs, Marilee shook her head dumbly from side to side eyes pleading with him, top of the ball gown squeezed in her tight fists. "P-please—I never—"

Stubby fingers fumbling, he unbuckled his sword belt and tossed it rattling upon the table. As Marilee crowded herself against the wall, the man unbuttoned his blouse and dropped it. His shirt was gray with dirt, and her eyes went wide as she saw the animal hair that covered his matted chest and even crawled up over his shoulders.

"Been wanting to get me a fancy Southern bitch," he said, licking at thick lips, "but never had a chance afore. Too busy guttin Johnny Rebs, but now—"

Marilee knew how small a bird felt, mesmerized by the slow eeling of a water moccasin, every instinct screaming at her to fly. fly, but unable to move. One word was a dull, staccato tomtom inside her head: no-no; no-no! They'd ripped all else from her—family and the man she would have married, her horses and the music—all the good things that had made up her life, the life she was born to. Carrion crows in countless swarms, they had picked clean the helpless body of a prostrate South, until only the bones were left.

Now this last gloating scavenger was here to rob Marilee Bradburn of her final and most precious possession, her virginity. Incongruously in this moment of terror, her mind shrieked out at Robbie Dee Crownover: *See, see! You should have done it with me, you, not this slobbering Yankee bastard. Is this what you saved my maidenhead for, Robbie Dee?*

Deep inside her belly, a cold snake of fear coiled its a serpent whose scales were glittering flakes of ice.

women killed themselves, rather than submit; she'd heard about those heroines all through the war. Some didn't have to; the Yankees or scalawags did it for them, cutting the shamed white throats after they'd raped them over and over again.

Lips gone dry and powdery as brick dust, a pulse beating in her throat, and her heart pounding erratically, Marilee put out shaking hands to fend off the man. "Please don't. I—I lied. There is some silver, and if you don't—don't hurt me, I'll take you to where it's hidden."

She hadn't realized he was so close. The cannonball exploded against her cheek, a full-handed slap from a horny palm that fired off crazy white lights behind her eyes and staggered her along the wall to collapse across the bed.

Dimly, she realized he was sitting beside her, working off his boots, shifting his weight upon the crackling shuck mattress to slide down his breeches.

"Know you were lyin'," he grunted, "but there's plenty of time for the silver, after I get me some of that high class meat. You're about to find out what it's like to have a real man mount you, instead of some limp-dicked gentleman."

Shaking her head in an attempt to clear it, feeling the blaze across her cheek where he had slapped her, Marilee instinctively drew up her knees. She saw his thing, ugly and swollen with veins writhing around its obscene horror, the puffed, blunt knob threatening.

As he swung up on the narrow bed to kneel at her legs, Marilee kicked out blindly, fiercely, and her bare feet slammed into flesh with a gratifying thump. But as she hurled herself up to claw at his eyes, the man slapped her again and again, rocking her head back and forth. The back of her head struck the wall, and she tasted salt blood inside her mouth.

Her eyes couldn't focus, and the cabin walls undulated sickeningly. Bonelessly, she lay inert as he tugged and pulled to draw the gown over her head, the lovely, wine-colored ball dress that had made her look so grown up, that made Marilee Bradburn the envy of all the other girls that night, especially with Robbie Dee's hand upon er tiny waist. He was so handsome and dashing, and he ⁱ looked at her the shaken, hungry way he had that ⁱⁱⁱng afternoon in the river.

14

"Damn," the man grunted, his hands digging at her naked breasts, her bare thighs. "Damn if the hair on your quim ain't the same color as your head, all silvery and shiny."

When he cupped it, his fingers cruel, the pain lanced up into her quivering belly and Marilee gasped. The stubble around his mouth sandpapered her face as he sought and found her open lips. Twisting her lower body against that hurtful grip between her thighs, Marilee hooked her fingers into his greasy hair and fought to lift his head back.

But his teeth raked her cut lip, and his tongue, thick and slippery and long, jabbed wetly into her mouth. Panting for breath, she felt his bushy chest crushing her breasts, flattening them painfully.

"That's the way, you bitch," he hissed into her mouth. "I like a woman with some fight to her."

Trying to lock her knees tightly together, she found them forced apart by his forearm, and when she rolled to get away from it, the man's leg was there like a pry bar. Suddenly she could breathe again, but only because his avid mouth was clamped onto her breast, ringing the sensitive mound with sharp teeth. Oh, God! His tongue was whiplashing her nipple, making it stiff.

Marilee's scream rattled despairingly around the cabin walls, and he chuckled around her breast. But when she beat at the sides of his head with clenched fists, he snarled and struck her again. This time her chin flew up and her eyes rolled back into a furry sheeting of midnight.

Then he was poking at her, hunching himself between her veed legs, lifting her knees and spreading her wide. Dazed, she didn't feel much at first, only the insistent ramrod motion of him. But when he penetrated, when that awful part of him forced itself deeply into her secret place, Marilee knew the spearhead of sharp agony.

She didn't realize she was crying out, that she was sobbing brokenly with each grinding thrust that jolted her violated body and rattled the bed against the wall. Impaled, Marilee writhed upon the thing that was ripping her apart, struggled weakly to slide herself from the plunging rhythm of it.

"Shake it, wench—yeah, yeah—shake it. You really know how to give it back to a man, don't you?"

Forever.

It went on forever and ever, an eternity of being covered, pierced, soiled. There was no escape, no strength left in her to fight, and his hairy, sweating weight bore her down, crushing any resistance that might have been left to Marilee.

But far back in an impossibly untouched somewhere, hidden deeply in some yet pure corner he hadn't been able to reach, an ember flickered. As he rutted upon her, the spark was fanned, and grew slowly, burning more angrily moment by terrible moment until it blazed whitehot, and Marilee knew it for what it was.

It was hate, so pure and refined that even its outer edges were razored, and the core of it a roiling cauldron.

Whinnying, the man jerked atop her, digging his blackened fingernails into the softness of her buttocks to loose the final degradation within her flesh. She felt its fountaining, just as she felt the seepage of blood down her inner thighs, but it could not flush its filthy torrent over that special core of loathing.

Like any other sated male animal, he rolled off her, sweating freely, the musk of him thick and cloying in her nostrils, the stain of him forever upon her belly.

Marilee lay there upon her back, realizing that she had been crying all the time, that tears had channeled into the corners of her bruised mouth to mingle their sea taste with the blood flavor already there. She didn't want to cry, to give the dirty beast beside her the satisfaction of conquering her spirit as well as her body. So she focused upon the little white flame deep inside and tried to warm herself at it.

Listening, she heard his rasping breath slowly subside and thought how different it would have been with Robbie Dee, how lovely and sweetly overwhelming her first experience would have been with a man she loved. Gentleness; there'd have been a slow, adoring tenderness and giving— not that animal pounding, with no more devotion than a stallion showed to a mare led to him for breeding. Less than that, she thought; if a mare wasn't in season, if she wasn't ready to be bred, the stud couldn't force her.

Was she forever ruined, now that she had been raped, her private parts torn asunder without love? Between her closed lids, another slow tear escaped to find its way down her hollowed cheek.

"You're some piece," the man said beside her, his corded and furred thigh touching her own. "Even if it was your first time, and I got me a maidenhead, you're still some piece. When you get it put to you a few more times, you'll like it even better, go crazy for it. Sure am gonna enjoy breaking you in, woman; I'll teach you some tricks you never heard of. That's so when the troop moves on and you get hungry, you can take up a trade. A good whore can always make out for herself."

Marilee turned her head from him, pressing her cheek to the crumpled satin of the gown wadded against the wall. It too was dishonored now, its former glory dirtied, the beautiful memories it had once contained smeared and sullied by what had happened here.

Lifting one knee away from the dull horror of the man's skin, Marilee shivered. He meant to do it to her again; he'd already said so. And she read other hints that told her this hairy animal wanted to keep on using her, to own her as if she were some slave wench who had to do his bidding. For how long, oh, Lord?

Until his troop was sent somewhere else, she thought, and that would take forever. Yankee units were everywhere through Mississippi now, an army of occupation grinding its boots upon the necks of the defeated. They could remain for years and years.

She tried to think clearly, to make her head stop reeling. With a great effort of will, Marilee succeeded, although his hand was roaming again over her breasts. Surely, there couldn't be bluecoat detachments everywhere along the back wagon roads; they'd probably be concentrated at the settlements, more of them drawn around larger towns. It was just possible she might slip through their patrols, but where could she go, how could she hide?

Greatoaks Plantation had also been destroyed, the Crownovers all gone, and it was the closest place. Maybe she could get all the way down to the Maddox land, but that wouldn't do her much good; the Maddoxes were poverty-stricken, too, and couldn't feed an extra mouth. Besides, her presence there might bring down the wrath of this rapist, who'd surely search for her when she fled.

And there was Bradburn. If she abandoned it now, her ancestral acres might die, be taken back by the undergrowth—or worse, be stolen by some Yankee.

"We'll get to that silver pretty soon," the man said, squeezing her breast until Marilee winced.

The nonexistent silver she'd lied about; he'd beat her savagely when he found there wasn't any hidden place, maybe kill her if he believed she was trying to keep it secret. Marilee stiffened, her mind darting about, beating itself against the inside of her head.

"Stew's burning," he said. "Better haul your tail over to the stove and take care of it. I want to watch you walk naked."

Trying not to cringe, but feeling the slither of his eyes over her buttocks, she moved uncertainly from the bed, her groin aching, her thighs sticky. She moved the pot to the back of the stove, wishing she could burn away the ugliness within her flesh, purify herself with flame.

"Turn around," he commanded. "Yeah, that's it, and stop tryin' to hide your quim. Damnedest little cunny I ever saw, with all that funny-colored hair around it. How come you never got married or lost your maidenhead afore now? All you Southern bitches are hot-blooded."

Marilee didn't answer. Her tongue felt around inside her cut lips, but her eyes were dry now. Maybe she could make him forget about looking for treasure, at least for a little while. She tried a smile that hurt her mouth, that hurt her heart more.

Hands tucked behind his head, stretching his nude body without shame, he grinned back at her, the gold tooth glistening. "Uh-huh; just never found you a real man 'til I come along. You took to it like a bitch in heat, and you're all ready to go again, ain't you?"

Miserable, she nodded. "If I—if you'll let me wash myself."

"Use the bucket in the corner," he said, scratching around in the black thicket of his chest hair. "You even start for that door, I'll break your goddamn back."

Somehow, trying to clean herself with him watching was almost as bad as being penetrated by him. The window, she thought, but her only clothing hung by pegs near the bed, and she couldn't run naked through the tangled woods. God, *God;* why had he come along? Why couldn't he have been searching for loot anywhere else?

Please him, she thought; she had to keep him contented and not thinking about Bradburn's silver service, gone these years back in the saddlebags of other raiders. There was no soap, so she scrubbed at her stained thighs with a rag and water, taking as long as she could, her skin crawling, goosebumping in disgust.

"Good enough," he said. "Get your ass back over here and I'll show you something else. You ever ride a horse, wench?"

Marilee nodded again, turning to force her unwilling legs to carry her to the bed.

Stroking himself, the man said then, "Just pretend I'm a horse, and this here is a saddle horn, like them Western troopers use. All you got to do is ride it."

She was a wooden marionette, moving jerkily, the lying smile painted upon her face. Her knees touched the mattress, and she adjusted them to poise above his repulsive body, steeling herself for the pain, the ordeal to come.

His hands were fumbling along her thighs, and the smirk widened his unshaven lips. "Just happened to think how come you still had your maidenhead," he said. "Probably had you a husband lined up, and kept yourself a virgin to strike the bargain. But that didn't stop you from gettin' your pleasure; I just bet you and some of them fancy planters swapped ends all the time. Guess you had that little mouth on more'n one like mine."

Marilee's skin drew tight over her flesh. Did he mean —he *couldn't* mean—oh, no!

"Hell," he said, "and I was goin' to teach *you*, when you're already a whore of sorts. So forget ridin' the horn, you wench. Just bend on down and do what you're used to."

She couldn't move; her body would not respond.

"Do it!" he snarled, and lifted up on an elbow. One hand reached up and caught her flowing hair to jerk her off balance. Her cheek was pulled against his mossy belly, and Marilee retched. Insanely, she clawed at his privates, and he flung her aside with an oath.

Her hip banged into the wall and she staggered, the lip of the iron stove searing her leg. The pot handle was in her hand as she wheeled, as he came roaring off the bed like a maddened bear. The boiling stew caught him full in the face, splattering against his eyes and mouth.

Screaming hoarsely, he pawed at his face, and Marilee wobbled into the table, snatching desperately for the belt there, her hands closing upon the butt of the dragoon pistol. It wouldn't come out of the holster. She yanked violently, and felt it give.

Blindly he hit her in the spine and drove her to the floor, but the pistol came away locked in her fist. She looked up to see bits of meat and rabbit bone dripping from his scalded face, to see that hairy belly creased against the table edge as he jerked the long cavalry sword from its scabbard.

"You bitch!" he hissed. "I'll cut you clean in two, god-damn you!"

Her thumb pulled back the iron hammer of the pistol, and she swung the muzzle up. She didn't tell him to stop, didn't warn him to back off. She didn't want to.

The saber whirled high, and his beady eyes glittered insanely. Centering the muzzle, steadying the pistol in both hands, Marilee shot him in the chest. The slap of the lead ball drove him back across the room, hammered him off his bare feet, and sledged his shoulderblades into the wall.

While the gout of powdersmoke spread and the thunder echoed, he hung there for a long moment, his mouth hung foolishly, slackly open. Then his knees gave way and his back slid rasping down the wall as his head fell forward. The dark blood streamed out of his body as it rolled over onto one side.

The thunderclap died with him, but the smoke eddied awhile, acrid upon Marilee's tongue and smarting her eyes. She stood up, the heavy pistol still aimed down at him. "Damn you," she whispered. "I wish I could kill you again."

Chapter 3

The surrender at Appomattox was over, and most of the Yankee army sprawled some dusty miles behind them when Joe Langston threw the saber into a thicket. Damned fool weapon, the saber; it was heavy and it rattled, and there wasn't no sense riding right up to a man and trying to chop him out of the saddle, when it was a whole lot easier just to punch a hole through him with a ball.

Still, it had been handy in its way, because it was quiet. The bluebellies got took by surprise when the troop cut its way out before they realized what was happening, that every grayback wasn't going to lay down his arms like General Lee said to.

Wiping the back of one hand across his mouth and spitting dust, Joe rocked easily in the saddle, back near the tail end of the hurrying column. Riding flank or rear guard wasn't the right place to be, and the major was welcome to the danger of the point. Joe was happy right where he was, ready to cut off into the brush on his own if they ran into Union troops. He'd been too long at war to act the hero, especially since it was over now, had

21

ended when the general handed over his sword to that black-bearded, cigar-chewing Grant.

That chunky little man made a point, showing the stately Virginian you didn't have to be an aristocrat to know how to fight. Hell, Joe could have told both of them that right at the start. It didn't take him long to learn that lesson and he'd had him one hell of a mean teacher.

Aristocrats, hogshit—flag-waving slave owners that didn't have no better sense than to ride head-on into cannon, like their blue blood protected them from grapeshot and minie ball. Seemed to Joe that all blood looked exactly alike when it got spilled—Yankee, planter, redneck, or nigger it was all the same.

April sun was warm on Joe's slouching shoulders as he followed the jangle of horses ahead, and the butternut gray of a near-new Confederate uniform rode scratchy upon his back. Lucky thing that dead man was near about his own size when he found him, and with all the mixed-up units milling around Appomattox courthouse, wasn't nobody about to question him or ask where he came from.

Clenching an unlighted cigar between his teeth, he pulled the cap lower over his eyes and grinned. Wouldn't nobody recognize him anyhow—not with his scraggly new beard—and the bluebellies would be too busy gathering up dispirited Rebs to check for one more deserter from their own ranks.

Wasn't like he'd been with them long enough to matter, anyway. It didn't take him long—no more'n two, three months to find out he wasn't going to get in on any of the loot, and there was just too damned many brand-new officers riding herd on him—fuzzy-cheeked younguns fresh down from the North who'd never even smelled powdersmoke before. They sure could spout off about rules of war and military regulations and honor, though—all that pure-D hogshit.

It made Joe happy to change his coat again, just like he'd done when things got too hot for the raiders and both sides took to calling Quantrill and his riders flatout bandits. Didn't take all that much knowhow to slip up across Kansas and draw some bounty money for signing up in a Yankee regiment. A man had to look out for himself, that was plumb sure, and Joe had thought of all the big, rich houses down home where if a man was quick and halfway lucky he could just about make his fortune off silver and jewels and a whole lot of booty he could tote away.

Hadn't been all that much in Kansas; some, that was natural sure, but seemed like hard money went about as quick as it came in, passing from a man's pocket to some whiskey peddler or wiggly whore, before it had a good chance to warm itself. It had been pretty good with the raiders, Joe admitted, kneeing his horse around a bend in the road. Even though Quantrill kept the biggest chunk of whatever they got when they burned a town, there was still plenty to go around.

But later on, when things got a mite rougher, new horseflesh got scarce to find, and damned if they didn't have to take to buying mounts from folks who had them hid out and guarded right good. And after Yankee cavalry took to riding hard after them, with farmers drawing a bead from the brush at any stray rider and even Confederate patrols disclaiming Quantrill's commission, things didn't look too good. The South was about to peter out, and that was for certain sure; a man with a good nose could smell it on the wind.

What with folks putting the name of outlaws and brigands to the irregulars, it was high time a man thought about saving his hide. Joe chuckled, thinking back to how he had presented himself to the Union recruiting sergeant, his face slicked off and hair cut, wearing clothes he took off a scared spitless farm boy. He'd made that limp pretty believable, bobbing along when he walked like a crippled-up rooster, and saying "Yes, sir, no, sir" real polite. The sergeant took him at his word that he'd just come back from the Oregon Trail and meant to do his bounden duty to the Union, by God.

Three hundred greenback dollars in bounty money didn't hurt none, either. He spent most of it in a whorehouse, thinking there'd be a heap more to hand when his regiment rode South to sweep through the plantations Joe hated so damned much.

But what the soldiers that got there during the fighting didn't take wasn't much worth having, and there were all those spanking new lieutenants ordering men around, hollering about the pride of the uniform and magnami—mag-

something toward a defeated enemy. Seemed like there was provost troops everywhere a man tried to slip off and do some scouting around on his own, too.

It just made good sense for a man like Joe Langston to hunt him a new home after he had to bust a provost in the head. The sergeant had been right muley-headed about arresting Joe for taking a gold pocket watch off a nigger. Hell, he ought to have known the nigger took it off somebody else, because that was the way things worked—some took and some got took from; the only color that mattered was the color of money.

So Joe had worked through the woods until he found the dead Rebel with the almost-new uniform. No more'n a boy, he'd been, with the good luck to get himself shot high in the head so no blood spilled over his clothes. From no uniform at all with the raiders, to Union blue, and at last Confederate gray, Joe had made the rounds.

He grunted, chewed his cigar, and patted his full saddlebags. According to the major, they'd all probably be wearing another kind of uniform before too much longer, if they made it across the border. Joe wondered about that, because it seemed like foreign soldiers leaned to getting themselves up too fancy and shiny; made for a good target. But they said the French down in Mexico paid good, and there was a sackful of gold waiting for anybody man enough to take it. There wasn't no place else to go, anyhow—not when both sides had a score to settle with Joe Langston.

He could go home and hide out, probably. Wouldn't take him all that long to cut off through Alabama when they got there, but home hadn't ever been much and likely would be less now. Hardscrabble dirt farms didn't change, except to get harder to work, making bellies leaner and putting croppers deeper into debt to the big planters.

Spitting again, Joe glanced ahead where dust rolled and a gentleman planter was leading a die-hard bunch of losers from one war into another. The only thing that made sense about wars was the chance they gave a man to get a little something for himself, instead of sweating and grinding out his life on a patch of poor ground nobody else wanted.

Even with slaves, the Langston place would have had

24

a hard time making a living for the family; without them, it was work from can't-see to can't-see, and nothing to show for it but calluses. It seemed to Joe that his pa never looked up, that he worked and walked and sat at the table with his back bent over and his head down. His ma wasn't much better, wordless and skinny, and the other younguns—well, they took off like birds soon as they got their feathers and couldn't nobody fault them for it.

A sharp whistle floated back over the column, and horses started turning off into the brush on both sides of the road. Joe shoved his own mount through a tangle of berry bushes blooming pinky-white and into a deep patch of pine saplings. Cloaked by the thick green needles, breathing their spices, he looked to his saddle gun, that spanking new Spencer repeater the Yanks had issued him.

It wasn't likely the bluecoats would sense anything wrong, even though road dust was still hanging yellow in the air. They were all flushed with victory and not setting a watch for some Reb detachment doing its best to keep out of sight. The war was over: hurrah, boys, hurrah. Even though news didn't travel fast, and little bunches of men here and there might not get the word for a spell yet, that kind of celebrating attitude just might let his column slip on west and south without trouble.

"Boy," his pa had said, "trouble ought to be your middle name, 'specially, you keep suckin' up to them quality folks in the big house. That ain't goin' to get you nothin' but the Lord's own grief, because you just a white nigger to them. Best you know your place and stay to it."

Peering through needled branches and hoping the rest had enough sense to stay in deep cover and keep their horses quiet, Joe watched the road and had to admit that his pa had been right. That's just what he was to saucy, golden Miz Susanna—just another stud, only one more hard whang to sport herself with, and it didn't make a good goddamn whether he was white or black. But back then he wasn't near smart enough to see it; he was a good-looking youngun just feeling his oats and knowing his manhood. From the first time Miz Susanna put that small, soft hand into his own, Joe Langston saw fairytale dreams opening up for him. He was in love.

Now Joe's bearded lips twisted and he ground the word

between teeth solid and white as a good working hound dog's—*love*. Spencer across his knees, his eyes were narrow as he watched the road, as his ears picked up an oncoming rattle of horses and equipment. Two artillery pieces came bumping along, their bronze tubes dull in the sun, caissons rattling along behind. Men with them were hooting and hollering, cutting didoes around the lumbering cannon and waving their hats.

Easing his Spencer back, Joe sat easy and rubbed at his fresh beard. Like the major said, it was going to be a big help to them, the war being over and done with. But it was a shame not to bust those Yanks from ambush, cut them down and take their horses. Those were mighty fine animals, hard-muscled and sturdy, yet with light-boned legs that said they could run—bigger necks than Joe had ever seen on anything but work plugs, too. 'Course, they'd been fed a heap better than Southern horses. He stared after the group as it clattered past. It was a long way from Virginia to Texas and the border; might be he'd still get him a chance at one of those Yankee horses.

Dust came filtering through the trees and laid more dirty gray icing along the pine trees before the major whistled again. Joe waited a spell before nudging his horse out to join the gathering column. Four years of fighting had bred slow caution into him, and he'd be glad when they took to one of the little-used side roads and cut across country. It wouldn't do to get drilled by a bullet anytime, but especially not now, when there was so much waiting for him in Mexico.

He settled into reverie, trying to picture the flashing-eyed señoritas down there, silver combs high in their midnight hair, their hips beckoning and slim, brown legs dancing. One of Quantrill's men had been to Mexico and told them about the women down there. Squatting around a hundred smoky campfires, Joe had listened and dreamed of dusky girls with smooth skin and ripe mouths.

He was sick to death of lying, high-class bitches, tired of whores and faded-out farm women with hardly any meat to them. In fact, he hadn't had a woman for a while now, and might as well quit thinking about any, except those in Mexico. They'd be traveling too fast and hard for dallying. Joe grunted; might be a hooraw was they to run across some leftover *quality* woman huddled in a big white

house somewhere. It would be worth his time to lag behind and see to her. Too damned many gentlemen in the
bunch, though. If they were to find somebody like Miz
Susanna, the major and his kind would scrape and bow
and tell each other what a fine lady she was. Given time,
Joe would show her she wasn't any different than a high
yellow doing it for a sack of peppermint candy.

Somebody was riding close to him, stirrup to stirrup,
and Joe glanced over at a boy who couldn't be more than
fourteen, fifteen. Even through the coating of dust on the
youngun's face, he could see the paleness there. He saw
the rip in the boy's jacket, just below the shoulder, and a
stain, spreading itself like a dark flower.

"Got any water?" the boy asked.

"For your gullet or that hole in your arm?"

"Both, I reckon. Picked me up a saber cut when we
broke out of Appomattox." He said it proudly.

If they'd been on the dry plains of Kansas, Joe would
have told the youngun to go to hell, but there'd be plenty
of creeks ahead, and cold springs in the hills. He unslung
a canteen and passed it over. "Welcome to it, boy. But you
need whiskey to slosh over that cut, and I ain't totin' any."

Pulling thirstily at the mouth of the canteen, the boy
lowered it and looked a question at Joe. Joe said, "Go
ahead," and the kid poured some over his sleeve before
stoppering the canteen and handing it back.

"My arm was gettin' some hot," he admitted. "I'll make
out all right when we stop tonight, can I find me some cob-
webs and good mud. Don't recollect seein' you afore."

"Ain't been with this bunch afore," Joe said. "Name's
Langston, Joe Langston from Alabama. Figured it wasn't
such a good idea to give up, and that talk the major gave
decided me for sure."

Clumsily, the boy reached across and gave Joe his hand.
"Howdy; I'm Timmy Santee, South Carolina Mounted
Rifles."

"Not long, I expect."

Timmy used his rein hand to squeeze his elbow, and
Joe thought the wound was giving the boy hell. "Long
enough. Pa kept me close to the house until I slipped off
about six months back."

"Picked you a bad time to join up, whipped as we was
even afore then."

"Couldn't join up afore. It was my pa, but I reckon I showed him I was old enough to hold my own."

They rode in silence for a while, then Joe said, "How come you ain't goin' home? Your place burned down?"

The boy shook his head and cradled his left arm in his right hand, letting the reins go slack on the horse's neck. "No use goin' back now; I'm just a private soldier with nothin' to give, nothin' to show. Major Ainsworth says there's a real chance in Mexico for fightin' men, a chance for glory and gold. When I *do* turn for home, I mean to be a somebody."

Taking a small sip from the canteen, Joe slung it back on the saddle. "Trade you my part of the glory for your part of the gold."

Timmy Santee straightened his narrow back. "Takes both, I expect. Hear tell there ain't nothin' left in South Carolina, and I just can't go home with my tail atween my legs, with nothin' to offer—"

When the boy broke off, Joe said, "Got you a girl waitin'."

Face brightening, Timmy said, "I sure have. We're goin' to get married soon as I get back from Mexico. Left a letter with one of the men givin' himself up; he'll see it gets to her. May will understand. That's her name—May Endicott. May—" he rolled the name hungrily in his mouth, tasting the flavor of it—"she's pretty as springtime itself. Got hair kind of yellow-orange, like honeysuckle, and smells just as good."

For a long time they were quiet again, and Joe stole quick glances at the boy. So damned young, but war either grew them up fast or cut them off in the bud. "Glory and gold," Timmy Santee said, like he could wrap hard money in a halo, and bring it all back tied in a pretty ribbon to his girl—if she hadn't took off with somebody else. If he made it back at all; no matter what the major said about the ruckus in Mexico, it was still a war, and not a quilting bee.

Six months the boy had been in the army, and all of that while the Rebs were falling back, short on rations and ammunition and everything else. All they were doing then was trying to keep their tail out of a crack, and Joe wondered how much Timmy had learned about fighting. It was one thing stalking a deer or fox squirrel through the woods, and something else when whatever you were hunting had a gun. Just about any country boy could draw a pretty good bead on table meat, but damned few could use a short gun. And a boy like that might just wait that split second too long and get his wishbone busted.

Shrugging, Joe figured it was none of his business; he'd have enough to handle taking care of himself. He let his horse drop back a mite, so Santee wouldn't act like he'd made a bosom friend, and slumped deeper into his saddle, dozing a little. Plenty of cornmeal and fatback in the saddlebags; some tobacco, too; salt and dried field peas. There was a blanket and ground sheet tied across his pommel, plenty of ammunition for the Spencer and his special pride—that pretty Colt revolving pistol. When he took it off that knocked-in-the-head provost. Joe'd never seen more than two, three of the newfangled short guns, but it shot quick and certain. It was the best thing he'd come out of the war with, about all he had to show for four years—except maybe the slickness to use it fast and true.

A rifle cracked up ahead and to the left flank; Joe's head snapped up. Was that some fool Yankee celebrating, or had the major run into a picket that knew men wearing gray weren't supposed to be carrying weapons, that all arms should have been stacked back there at the courthouse?

Joe didn't do anything but come alert all over; he didn't have to check his guns because both of them rode with rounds in the chambers and hammers eased down. A touch of his legs woke up the plodding horse, too; they were ready for just about anything.

No other shots, no warning whistles, and the column kept moving at the same pace, but now Joe saw it turning off the main track, saw the erect figure of the major sitting at the crossroads to look out for any stragglers.

When he turned past the man, Joe saw something else —the sprawled figure of a bluecoat face down in the dust, fallen on his own long rifle. Must have been a green recruit, Joe thought, to challenge a whole column of cavalry. Well, he wouldn't ever get to be an old soldier. The major had dropped him in his tracks. But nobody had turned out his pockets.

One look at Major Ainsworth's gaunt, set face told Joe

it wouldn't be any use to climb down and rifle the body, either, so Joe rode on. Ainsworth was one of *them,* no doubt raised in a big white house, house servants scooting to his beck and call, looking out over his rich fields of cotton and passing the time of day with a fine-looking woman by his side. That kind of life gave a man all kinds of set ideas about right and wrong and honor.

Only planters with full bellies and straight backs had the time to fret about honor; dirt farmers were too busy scratching out a bare living to be polite and do-si-do about challenges and fancied insults and the like. If somebody did you wrong, you busted his head with a singletree, and if that didn't make it, then you laid for him with a long gun and made the lesson permanent. But not gentlemen; they sidled around each other like game roosters, fighting mostly with words, and sometimes the spat came down to them meeting with pistols under a special set of rules. Didn't make a lick of sense, Joe thought, to give the other man more than an even chance to kill you.

He had to give the major credit, though; wasn't many men would come back to war after losing a foot. Couldn't walk much on that boot stuffed with rags, because the stump pained him, even if Ainsworth tried not to show it. Artillery shell blowed off that foot somewheres around Chancellorsville, hear tell, and he could have been invalided out, gone home to his cotton fields and took care of his wife and younguns, even if there wasn't any niggers left. But seemed like the major was one of them that wouldn't holler quits, even after he kept getting knocked down time and again. He was the muley kind just kept getting back up and coming at you until you flat had to kill him to make him stay down.

Changing position in his saddle, Joe admitted he never understood hardheads like that. If you ran up onto somebody meaner than yourself, or somebody with a bigger stick in his hand, it made sense to light a shuck and get out with a whole hide. There would always be another time and another place, where you could pay back for a whipping.

He squinted at the lowering sun and thought maybe that's what Major Ainsworth had in mind at that. The man was probably hoping to get in his licks later on, get back at the Yanks after Mexico. Joe nodded. Sure enough, because that was smarter than just trying to keep on fighting when the other side had you beat down to your knees. Go to Mexico and get some treasure, hire some guns, gather some men. maybe even worry at the French until they lent a hand along the frontier. There was a heap of land out West, land the Yankees didn't have claim on, and it could be the major and men like him meant to carve them out a piece of it, make a new Confederacy.

Timmy Santee dropped back beside him, but shook his head when Joe reached for the canteen. "Reckon we'll be making camp soon; I can make it 'til then. Had a funny idea, seein' that dead Yank at the crossroads. Expect he might be the last one killed in the whole war. It might make him famous."

"He won't be the last," Joe said, "and if he was, he's just as dead as the first 'un to stop a minié ball at Bull Run."

"I don't know," Timmy said thoughtfully. "Had him a lot of sand, to stand up to the bunch of us thataway. If he brought it off, he'd been a hero."

"Boy," Joe said, "don't you understand a goddamn *thing?* That bluebelly wasn't nothing but a fool, and now he's a dead one. Happens to fools all the time."

Biting his lip, hurt arm stuck in his jacket now, Timmy Santee moved his horse up into the column, and Joe stared after him. Heroes and glory lived in that boy's head, and he was even proud of the wound that might fester and kill him. It wouldn't do to get too friendly with that kind, because Timmy Santee wasn't going to last long in Mexico —if he made it that far.

But Joe Langston meant to last, to survive, to be there when the last shot of that other revolution was fired, with his saddlebags stuffed with gold. Anybody else had best look out for themselves, because Joe Langston sure as hell wouldn't.

Chapter 4

To hide her ravished and shamed nakedness, the bruises turning blue upon her flesh, Marilee wore a ragged dress that had once been owned by one of the plantation slave wenches, a shapeless thing considered not worth carrying along when the girl took the freedom road.

She couldn't look back at the dead man, not just yet, but she gripped his pistol tightly as she slid out the door and into the yard. Dusk was gathering beneath a sunset the color of spilled blood; its eerie stain lingered over the ragged tops of pines and merged with night coolness puddling in shadows growing ever longer.

Shaking inside, her stomach knotted, she moved hesitantly toward the horse tethered to a water oak sapling, hearing it stamp with a jingle of metal and a creak of leather. "E-easy," she murmured, more for herself than the horse as she eased toward its dark bulk.

A finely sculptured head lifted, small ears thrust forward inquisitively, and even in the oncoming twilight, Marilee could make out its great black eyes and the wide shape of nostrils meant to drink the wind. Allowing the horse to sniff her slow hand, to know the scent of her, she untied the reins and led it shuffling behind her to get it out of sight behind the cabin. The trooper who had raped her might be only an outrider, a scout for a group, and she didn't want to be standing in the open with his horse.

Looping the reins around a low branch of a mulberry tree, she gave his soft nose her hand to sample again, then moved gentle fingertips along the high cresting of muscular neck, felt over a glossy hide that spoke mutely of good health. The horse was a stallion, she discovered, amazingly muscled and compactly built, not nearly as long backed and tall as the thoroughbreds she had once known so well. Only about fifteen hands high, she thought, and was pleasantly surprised when she bent to run expert hands over his forelegs, for the cannon bone was oval and fine, not coarsely rounded as she expected. She could feel no splits, those little lumps along the tendons that showed injuries from strain.

This stud was in marvelous condition, and although she would have to wait until daylight, when she could closely check his teeth, Marilee was certain he was young. Even-tempered, too, she decided, seeing how he stood so quietly for inspection, but she could sense the latent power coiled within him, the hot blood eager to fling the powerful body out and away.

The saddlebags: she went through them to discover a store of cornmeal and a slab of bacon, a little sack of salt and another of dried beans. She found a curiously made carbine snuggled into the saddle scabbard, and a bedroll tied behind the cantle with leather cords. A skin pouch contained enough ammunition to fight a small war; there was also a filled canteen.

She couldn't keep one hand from stroking the stallion; no matter what kind of filthy beast the horse's rider had been, the animal himself was magnificent. Marilee admired the lovely shaping of him, the tremendous potential of that wide-barreled, deep-chested body, the beauty of a long wavy mane and tail.

Her caressing fingertips found a fault—the big ugly brand that had been seared into the stallion's left hip, "US"—United States. It was a mark that couldn't be hidden, but might be explained away, far from here where Yankee cavalry might not be so numerous.

Leaning her forehead against the horse's mane, she felt weak and nauseated, because two things knifed through her at once—the delayed reaction to having killed a man and the chill realization that she was going to have to leave Bradburn.

It hadn't been murder; even if the Yankee hadn't been swinging the blade of the saber high over his head, killing him was justifiable. She had punched a heavy pistol ball through the man's naked, hairy chest, and he certainly had it coming. Marilee had killed before, but not a man, and not in fear and revulsion, only caught up in the wild excitement of the chase, thundering behind her father and brothers across the fields, sometimes *ahead* of them.

Deer was meat for the table, especially if the year had been drought-stricken and a poor season for corn. That's when the Bradburns harvested deer like any other crop, thinning the herds and issuing venison to supplement slave diets. They went after black bear, too, but usually when the shaggy beasts had made themselves nuisances by raiding the hog pens and had to be run down.

"Really, Marilee," her mother had said, "it's not at *all* ladylike for you to be handlin' those awful guns and gallopin' around like some wild Creek Indian. Whatever will Robinson Crownover think, or any other acceptable beau? I'm very put out at your father, Marilee, for allowin' you to become so—so downright *masculine*."

Her cheek against the warm and silken neck of the horse, Marilee felt her mouth quiver. Her acceptable beau was lost in the battle-torn ground near Richmond; they hadn't even brought home his body to be given proper burial. Softly, she whispered to the stallion: "You know, you remind me of Robbie Dee; both of you strong and young, powerful but gentle, with good breeding. But I wish he hadn't been so true to his breeding, that *he* had been the first to—to—"

Quietly, the horse stood while her flowing tears dampened his satin hide, while she cried for what might have been, should have been, as she mourned both the past and the bleak future. Marilee cried for a maidenhead that by right belonged to Robbie Dee Crownover, not to that vile, snarling animal who'd savaged her so brutally, who had commanded her to—to. . . .

Straightening her back, Marilee wiped at her cheeks and stepped away from the horse; the stallion swung his head and stared at her. There was a knowing between them, an understanding, and she was grateful for it. The way she felt right now, she could never love another man, never wanted another male animal to put cruel, hairy hands upon her body. But she could love this beautiful stallion, and be loved back by him, in their own special way. That made her feel better, made her feel less alone, as she began to accept the fact that she must abandon Bradburn Plantation.

The last years of numbing tragedy and destruction, the back-breaking labor she had put in trying to hang on, simply to exist, had come to this—down to this terrible moment. Because of that two-legged beast dead in the cabin, Marilee's life had been brought to a single, unavoidable decision, one that would tear out what was left of her heart.

She had killed a Yankee soldier, a member of the enemy army that occupied her beloved Southland, and no matter that he had raped and defiled her; he had worn the uniform of the conquerors, and she would be punished for her act. If she wasn't hung out of hand, Marilee faced the prospect of many long and dreary years in prison— or something worse. The dead man's friends might find her and use her as he had, spreading her nude, helpless body to take their grunting, thrusting turns within her flesh, soiling her once-secret depths again and again with their hotly spurting juices.

"No!" she said aloud, said it fiercely. She would cut her own throat first, or fight them so madly they would have to kill her.

The horse shifted, sensing her tension, and she calmed him. "Stand easy, easy. I'll be back for you in a little while."

She had no idea how close an encampment of bluecoat cavalry might be, but it couldn't be too far. The man had come looking for something to steal, for silver and woman flesh; maybe he'd told somebody which direction he was taking, that he meant to prowl the ruins of the burned-out plantation they'd ridden past. Any time, a search could be getting under way for him.

The body had to be hidden, to give her a little more time, to cover her trail while she rode the godsend horse far into the night and away. She moved quickly to the hut of peeled logs that had once been whitewashed but were now only a hopelessly faded gray, like the Confederacy itself.

Laying the pistol upon the table beside the sword belt still dangling there, she reached down for the clothing her rapist had scattered upon the earthen floor, so hurried in his lust. Teeth clenched against the memory of that swollen, terrifying shaft of veined meat rising, Marilee forced her hands to sort out the drawers and pull them over her trembling legs. Discarding the tattered shift, she felt her skin crawling at the woolen, intimate touch of the clothing that had also gripped the man's crotch.

Although her body tried to rebel at donning the filthy shirt, she fought the thing on, tucking it into blue breeches that had a yellow stripe running down the legs. The man she had killed hadn't been very tall, but she had to draw the belt tight to make the pants stay up. His boots were too big, but they would keep out water, and she didn't mean to do much walking, no more than she would have to. Now she had a horse, a means of escape.

In the pockets she found a penknife with a keen blade, a black twist of chewing tobacco, and three silver coins. There was a greasy wallet containing—her fingers shook as she leafed through it—fourteen greenback dollars, a fortune to her now. She also found a dirty bandanna and some sulphur matches wrapped in oilskin. The jacket would be warm, but she pushed it aside; she'd make do with the ragged coat hanging on the wall peg, because being in complete uniform might call attention to herself and get her questioned as a deserter. Discharged soldiers of both sides still wore bits and pieces of their old uniforms, mainly because that was all the clothing they owned.

But the cap—she'd have to use it to cover her hair. Oh, Lord, her hair, now that her party dress was ruined, her hair was all she had left of the old days, the good times before the war.

"A woman's crowning glory, Marilee," her mother said. "You must let Lucinda take better care of your hair."

And Lucinda said, "Stop yo wigglin' now. You want all them young genmun to think you just some kind of lowdown white trash?"

Catching a handful of her flowing hair, Marilee sawed

at it with the penknife. Dropping each butchered silvery
tress upon the bed as she cut it away, she chopped her
hair short as she could. The cracked mirror showed her a
long-faced boy with jagged chunks of towhead hair sticking up every which way. But when she jammed on the
blue cap, the girl peeked through again, big eyes, her
mouth too full in the lower lip, too sensuous. *Sensous;* she
grimaced.

She'd need something to add to her disguise. A woman
alone in the woods, a woman riding the back roads,
would be fair game to any Yankee or scalawag—those
despicable creatures who were either deserters from both
armies or just draft dodgers sidling around the countryside
to pillage and murder. And rape, she thought; she would
never forget rape.

Wheeling to the table, she used the penknife to cut a
small circle from the leather sword belt, used the point of
the blade to drill two holes in the piece. Another strip
from the belt was threaded through the holes, and she
adjusted the narrow strap behind her head; this time the
mirror told her she'd made a passable patch for her left
eye—that she appeared to be a young soldier who'd suffered a grievous wound.

Tilting the thing away from her eye, Marilee steadied
herself and stared down at the corpse. The man looked
even more evil and uglier in death than he had in life,
his face twisted in that final, unbelieving shock, bits of the
rabbit stew still hanging to his cheeks, and spittle trailing
from his open mouth. Beneath him, the hard dirt floor
was dark with blood, and Marilee knew she couldn't bear
to touch the corpse, that she couldn't stand to know again
the feel of his skin against her own, that sweaty flesh
turned clammy and chill.

But she didn't feel sorry for him; she still hated him.
One of his feet was stretched out to touch the kindling
pile, and the pot she'd flung at him lay nearby. The long
cavalry saber was still in his hand, its point arrowed toward the stove.

The stove, she thought; it might as well be that way as
another, especially since she couldn't drag him out and
hide him in the brush somewhere or throw him down the
shallow well the slaves had used to draw water. Catching
up the pistol, Marilee poked the barrel behind the stove-

pipe and jerked it loose from the chimney. She planted one boot against the stove itself and turned it over onto its side, so that the door flew open and glowing red embers spread themselves, smoking across the kindling so purple and rich with resin.

Stepping back, she picked up her ball gown, letting it hang across one bent arm while she dragged the cornshuck mattress off the bed and laid it over the hissing coals. The striped ticking partially covered the man's body, but didn't reach up to his face.

Staring down at him, at those stubbled lips that had crushed demanding and lusting against her own, at the eyes whose cruel fires had glazed over, she said, "Here—you wanted this dress, damn you. Take it to hell with you!"

The color of new wine, scalloped with dainty white lace, the ball gown fell across his face and shoulders. It was a far better shroud than he deserved, but she couldn't take it with her now. She turned away from the bright tongues of flame that were licking up at the dress, the symbol of everything that used to be.

Marilee stumbled around back to where the horse was tied, clumsy in the too-big boots. As smoke poured from the cabin window, the stallion's eyes showed nervous white, but he stood steady when she drew the reins over his head. Marilee shoved the pistol into her belt, lifted a foot to the stirrup, and placed one hand upon the thick, strong neck where it tapered down into sloping shoulders.

The army saddle wasn't much different from those she was familiar with, and she swung lightly onto it, settling against the seat. When she got away from the fire, she'd take time to adjust the stirrup leathers to suit her legs better, but for now they'd do. The horse stirred beneath her, not edgy or trying to skitter away on his own, but gathering himself for the command of her legs and a touch of the reins.

Gently, she eased him back and turned him with the pressure of her right calf, with just the mere kiss of a rein along his neck. Responding beautifully, the horse moved as a part of her body, and Marilee had to admit that whatever else the dead man had been, he had also been an accomplished rider.

The cabin door spat forth a mouthful of angry red flame as she walked the stallion toward the creek path. At the dark edge of the woods, Marilee stopped him with a word and a jiggle of the bit, to pivot in the saddle and look back. There'd soon be a glow against the night sky, but burning houses were no rarity in the South these days; maybe nobody would even come to investigate this one. If a Yankee patrol did ride up, all they'd find was the blazing pile of a slave cabin; no horse and rider, no woman to dishonor, nothing left to steal.

Guiding the horse along the trail, Marilee wondered where she could go. Even if anyone were left to the south, some surviving member of a family she had once known, she couldn't expect them to hide and protect her. Every village of any consequence was occupied by blue-coats, and certainly every town. There might be sentries posted at major road crossings, on the lookout for Confederates who hadn't given themselves up and didn't mean to.

So going south was out of the question; to the north and east lay even more of the enemy. West, then, she thought, as she ducked to pass beneath the low-hanging bough of a live oak centuries old. A long beard of Spanish moss caressed her face. Some of the weary, battered Confederates passing through since the final defeat at Appomattox had spoken of the frontier—"The only place to get away from Yankees," they said. "Only place folks like us can get a chance to start over."

Texas—she remembered them saying Texas. It was wild and dangerous, but the savages there could be no worse than the one frying behind her in his just reward. Could anyone really start over, be reborn, like the fabled phoenix, from the ashes of a life and culture so completely destroyed?

It had to be possible, because if it wasn't Marilee might just as well have waited back at the cabin for the hangman's rope. Hand-to-mouth living, just scratching in the dirt for food, wasn't being alive. For some, maybe, but not for her; Marilee Bradburn was to the manor born and meant to claim her heritage.

A big order for an eighteen-year-old woman on the run for her life, frightened and confused, and with no clear idea of where she was going or how she would get there. But she had a fine horse under her, weapons and ammunition and food to last awhile. It was more than most Southerners owned, and she could make do.

Reaching the creek bank, she kneed the stallion into the dark waters of the shallow ford, and the horse took it without hesitation. Marilee nodded in appreciation and guided him out onto the far side, where she turned west. She knew practically every inch of the plantation, but beyond its boundary she knew only main roads, and not all of them.

She had seen very little of the world, but there had been a good library at Bradburn—tall, long shelves of leatherbound books that held the world's information between their covers. And there had been tutors those first years, one a prissy lady from Birmingham who spent more time hovering over the boys in the house and the overseer in the fields. After her came a succession of men, pale and reedy and old, rheumy eyes peering through spectacles, their tacky clothes smelling musty. Somehow from each of them Marilee had learned something, if for no other reason than to outdo her brothers. She'd learned to appreciate books and knowledge for the sake of knowing.

"Honey," her mama said, "you are a constant puzzle to me. Ladies don't have to know how to read and write and figure. There are more wifely virtues, and I do wish you would pay attention to them."

Poor Mama, Marilee thought, as she skirted a clump of huckleberry bushes that grew straggling down the creek bank. If her mother had had her way, Marilee might know how to do fancy needlework and play a tune on the harp or spinet, but she'd have no idea of direction or geography. She wouldn't be able to snare a rabbit, much less skin and dress it out, or hit a running deer or scrabble catfish from under a riverbank; if she'd been a simpering, "Yes, ma'am" kind of *lady*, she'd be trying to get through these black woods on a sidesaddle, which was ridiculous.

But there was much to be said for being a lady, too. Her mama had always looked serene and beautiful and had made Wayne Bradburn happy, made him proud of his sweet, calm wife and the children they produced.

Aloud she said, "Someday, Mama, when the good times come again, I'll be everything you ever wanted me to be."

But never a virgin again, never clean inside herself again, never in love.

Topping a small rise where the brush grew low, she turned and looked back at the glow in the sky, where the last building on Bradburn was burning, where a filthy Yankee rapist was burning with it. She didn't even know his name; he'd never said it.

The big stallion stood beneath her patiently, but she could hear him sampling the air and feel the suspicious movements of his head as he stayed alert for the odors and sounds of possible danger. Fine horse, strong horse who might sire copies of himself bred to almost any mare. Staring at the orange sky, Marilee felt a surge of real hope. She had called the stallion a godsend, but he was even more; with any luck at all, this horse was her future, too. He was worth more than the guns and food and clothing he carried. She didn't know what breed he was, but she was certain that his powerful loins carried the means for rebuilding the plantation.

The war had killed countless thousands of horses, and out on the Texas frontier savages had butchered and stolen more thousands. A stallion like this one, if his blood held true, was worth his weight in diamonds; crossed on the wild mares out West, his get would be special and in demand.

With determination, she looked away from the fire and squeezed the horse forward at a walk. Horses didn't see well at night, but this one had a rapid, flat-footed walk that covered ground, and by morning they would be many miles away. She would find him a glade where lush grass grew thick and high, hobble him while they ate and slept. And when she was certain they were safe, she would figure a route for them in her head, calling on blurred memories of all the maps in her geography books. But she would depend more upon her experienced sense of direction, and together they would reach Texas.

Reins loose upon the stallion's massive neck, she stroked his shoulder. "You can't go on without a name," she murmured, "so I'll call you—I'll name you Bradburn. That's it, *Bradburn*, because you're my hope for the future, the hope of the land."

As if the horse understood, he lifted his head and whickered, but softly, softly in the blackness of the April night.

Chapter 5

The major put out night pickets, but Joe Langston managed not to be one of them. He didn't much care for a cold camp, but until the troop was farther along the way to the border, he could see the sense of it. Uncooked cornmeal mush was better than nothing, and he still had a stick or two of jerky left. Better a lean belly than calling the Yankees to you with campfires.

Curled in his blanket with his saddle for a pillow, the groundsheet beneath him to cut out dampness and earth chill, he covered the flare of a match with his cap and relighted the butt of a cigar.

Close by, the kid was sitting up, still messing with his wounded arm. Spiderwebs and black mud might do the job good as anything, Joe thought; but again, it might not. He leaned to whiskey treatment himself, but if anybody had any, they weren't sharing it. Timmy Santee's arm might heal up right good, or it could start to fester and stink; then it was either goodbye arm or goodbye boy, and just as easy both. No skin off Joe's back; every man was bound to take care of his own hide.

"Feels some better," Santee whispered. "Reckon it's goin' to heal."

43

Joe took a slow drag on his cigar and rolled the smoke around in his mouth. "Major means to be gone at first light; best you get to sleep."

"I got a skillet," Santee said. "If we get to light a fire, we can use it together."

"Yeah," Joe grunted, and rolled over onto his side to cut off any more talk.

For a while, he watched the stars hang bright spiderwebs over treetops and listened to horses grazing within a rope corral. If the major didn't run up on some grain afore long, those horses would be crowbait; you just couldn't work them so long and hard without corn. He thought again of the Yankee horses pulling those cannon, fat and sassy as the bluebellies themselves.

Burning low, the cigar singed his fingers and Joe carefully pinched out the stub to tuck into his shirt pocket, saving it for his horse. Tobacco helped worm an animal and kept it going longer.

The air was warm, and from somewhere off in the woods a stray wisp of honeysuckle perfume came floating. Adjusting his neck upon the saddle, Joe closed his eyes and smelled deeply until the sweetness passed, losing itself in horse sweat and man sweat. As a youngun, he'd pulled many a honeysuckle bloom off bushes, nipping the tip of the stem between his teeth to suck out a tiny bit of sweet juice, beating honeybees to it.

Poor younguns didn't get much sweetening, maybe a little sorghum after the cane was cut and ground, but that usually ran out before winter did. Finding a bee tree was cause for a hooraw shared by the whole family, because the honey could be stored a spell, and all the kids played the fool with beeswax, chewing it until the good was long gone.

Wasn't no shortage of sweetening up at the big house where Miz Susanna lived; they had sugar cake and shortening bread, and sometimes she brought along sure-enough chocolates, molasses taffy, and the like. Even the wine was sweet, and Joe'd gotten his first taste of it because of her—a crispy-flavored wine made by house niggers out of scuppernong grapes.

She'd run up on him at the creek, where he had a fish-pole stuck in the bank upstream while he was cooling off in a deeper hole and cutting didoes in water stained

brown by oaks and red dirt. Naked as a jaybird, he didn't
hear the horse coming until he shook water from his eyes
and looked up, and there she stood, outlined against
summer sky.

Right off, Joe knew who she was, even if she hadn't
been sitting that fancy white horse. He'd watched Miz
Susanna Paisley from afar, seeing her carriage pass on the
wagon road, kind of spying on her when she sometimes
rode the cottonfields, holding a lacy parasol over her
golden head. Once he'd slipped up close to the big house
and hid out in a hedge, peeping at her while a wench
fanned her on the shaded front porch of the mansion and
brought her cool lemonade. He didn't know why he took
the trouble, unless it was like his hunger for sweetness, for
the too-quick nibble on a honeysuckle blossom.

Now she sat that white mare, legs hidden in a creamy
long skirt, her oval face shadowed beneath a wide-
brimmed straw hat that sort of curled around and had
flowers on one side. Miz Susanna posed far up on the
steep creek bank and stared down at him bare-assed in the
water. Joe dropped deeper into it, clear to his chin, feeling
a hotness through his flesh that the running creek couldn't
cool, knowing his face was red and damning himself for
that. Wasn't his fault she'd come up on him this way.

He caught the quick, pearly flash of her smile and saw
her twitch the reins as her mare stamped impatiently.
"You're the Langston boy, aren't you?"

Glancing toward his clothes laid across a log on the
near bank, Joe said, "Yes'm, the oldest 'un."

Her laughter was like the tinkle of little silver bells. "I
could tell that. What's your name?"

Before he could answer, he tried to cool his face with
water, and even then his voice didn't sound anywhere near
his own. "Joe."

"Well, Joe—is the water good?"

Damn her; she sat that blooded horse like some kind of
princess and played like she hadn't seen him naked.
"Guess so."

Gracefully, she lifted her skirt and he saw the scalloped
fluffiness of pantaloons, the turn of a delicate ankle as she
eased her foot from the sidesaddle stirrup. He could have
sworn that she drifted to the ground like a leaf, but more
like one of those white puffballs that the wind scatters so

that they float along through the summer air without trying.

Watching her tether the mare to a branch, he wondered why she was deviling him like this, how come she hadn't screamed and galloped off when she saw him buck-naked with his hammer hanging down. Joe didn't know exactly how he felt; it was all mixed up—part shame and part excitement, with a goodly dab of pure scared thrown in. He wanted to scoot on off down the creek and come back for his clothes after she was gone; he wanted to stay right where he was and stare as she climbed down the bank and took off her floppy hat with the flowers on it, as she shook out a sunshine mane of hair unpinned from a bun.

"I think I'll join you," she said, color high in her smooth cheeks and all that shining hair floating over her shoulders like a golden waterfall.

Maybe she hadn't got a good look at him before and had it in her head that he was wearing breeches. Swallowing, Joe forced words through his constricted throat. "I—I ain't decent, ma'am."

As she did things to her bodice, Miz Susanna laughed again, a dainty cascade of music that skipped out over the water and slid beneath the surface to tingle down Joe's backbone. "Oh, I'd say you're a mite better than just decent, Joe."

She was going to take off her clothes. He knew it with a sudden numbing certainty that shook him clear to his gullet. Miz Susanna Paisley was about to show him what he'd been dreaming of for a long time, the naked beauty of her body; she was easing off the long skirt, pulling it down and stepping out of it. And she was just as unconcerned as if Joe was her ornery, gray-headed husband, acting like they'd been doing it for years.

Doing it, Joe thought, and slipped back into deeper water until he could just barely hang on to the sandy bottom with his curled toes; would she really do it with him, or did she only mean to take a cooling dip in the creek, flatout tormenting him with her pure white body? Maybe she acted this way around her housemaids, not caring if she showed herself bare, because house wenches didn't count; maybe she looked on him just about the same, as if he didn't matter, being only a hard dirt farmer.

One petticoat; that was all she was wearing, a pale pink thing that Miz Susanna casually tossed over a bush with her dress. Joe started at the thin shift that covered her upper body, at the frilled lace pantaloons that snuggled long, slim legs. He could see her nipples, see the shape of them pushing stiffly against thin cotton material, and all his skin went tight over his flesh, tight as a bear hide stretched to dry in the sun.

Head thrown back and cheeks pink, the hot sun picking up lights in all that golden hair spread out across her shoulders and down her back, Miz Susanna darted the end of a quick red tongue over her full bottom lip. He couldn't take his eyes off her, and beneath the water felt the throbbing that lifted his erection.

Moving closer to the creek edge, she started to pull the shift over her head, but hesitated. Her voice was lower now, gone kind of husky: "How old are you, Joe Langston?"

It was hard for him to talk. "Goin' on seventeen, ma'am."

"Umm," she kind of purred, and suddenly the shift was gone, whipped away in a single, flowing motion. Her breasts seemed to jump out at him, creamy gourds sticking their pink tips right in his eyes. "That's plenty old enough," she said, her eyes getting darker, warmer. "You ever had a girl, Joe?"

"Sure," he said quickly, his eyes caressing those pale globes, following the marbled shaping of them, lingering upon the swollen nipples.

Her hands lifted slowly to cup her breasts, jiggling them in a way that made Joe's eyes widen and his whang pulse beneath the water. "I don't mean for just kissin' and holdin' hands," she said. "I mean really. You haven't been sniffin' around any of our nigger wenches, or I'd have heard. Do you visit a little farm girl somewhere, some skinny child who wears floursack drawers?"

Bigod, she had no call to tease him, just like she knew he hadn't done it with anybody yet. And it wasn't because he didn't get the chance; there'd been more than one high yellow wench give him the eye when he ran up on them doing washing in the creek; and there was Jessie Faye Robbins always wanting to hold hands with him behind the church house, her palm sweaty and finger tickling.

It was Miz Susanna's fault, he reckoned. She'd married old man Paisley about two years back, and him a dried-out widower near three times her age. Ever since the first time Joe got a clear look at her, it seemed like his wet dreams kind of bore down on just Miz Susanna, and making up to wenches didn't hold much interest for him. Even his brothers had gotten to hoorawing him about not getting any diddling, until he knocked a knot on their hard heads and hushed them. Hell, for all their big talk, he knew they whipped their whangs much as he did.

"No, I don't," he said, thinking he'd be damned if he ever called her ma'am again. "But it ain't because I *can't*."

Her smile brightened, and she used small, neat hands to tug ineffectually at the top of her pantaloons. "Then you're a sure-enough virgin, Joe. I thought all little boys did it soon as they could, to calves or sheep if they couldn't find a girl willin'."

Joe flushed. She talked the damnedest of any woman he'd ever heard. "Well, I never," he said. "I just—well, hell—I just never, that's all." Was she going to come in the water wearing those long underdrawers or stand there on the bank and pick at him all day?

"Then you've been savin' yourself for some special girl," Miz Susanna murmured. "You know, I've seen you slippin' around our place and peepin' at me."

His jaw tightened. "Reckon I go near about where I want to, and it might not be to peep at a married woman."

Even her giggle was husky now, turned scratchy with excitement. "Oh, I'm not that married, Joe. Mister Paisley is old as can be and can't get it up more than twice a month."

The creek current pulled at his ankles, and Joe had to move up on the bottom, his hands crossed in front of his crotch, just in case she could see through the dark water to where his whang was rammed out like a singletree turned sideways.

Miz Susanna kept fiddling with the ribbons of her pantaloons. "Well, now," she said softly, "are you goin' to squat there in the creek forever, or will you come on out here and help me get these things untied? Course, if you're just a scared little old boy and not nearly a man grown—"

Before he could stop himself, Joe was out of the water almost to his belly button. "You ain't all that old yourself, and if you ain't *that* married, how come you got wedded to a man could be your grandpa?"

Her hips were rolling gently from side to side, her

sleek body like a willow branch in the wind, those high, rounded breasts curtsying and bobbing. "There's two kinds of poor, Joe," she whispered. "Your kind of poor, where you don't expect anything else, and my kind—where Mama had to patch my dresses and play like we were still rich as when Papa was alive. You wouldn't understand that genteel sort of poverty, but I reckon it's worse than your own. Mister Paisley wanted him a pretty young wife, and Mama and me wanted to stop pretendin'. Our name was good as his, so—"

When he still hesitated, half in and half out of the creek, she stamped a small, bare foot upon the grassy bank and said in exasperation, "Damnit, boy, I can see your thing anyhow. If you have any sand in your craw, you'll climb on out of there right this minute!"

"I ain't no boy," he said, low in his throat, and splashed up on the bank to stand angry before her, buck-naked and no longer shamed by it. Somehow she knew just exactly how to get him mad, and Joe didn't give a fiddler's damn about his hammer standing out hard and long. But if she laughed at it, Miz Susanna Paisley just might get her pretty head knocked off, even if that meant he'd have to run for it and get clear out of the county.

Her deep blue eyes were wider now, coppery lashes fringing them thick and curly; her mouth looked like a rosebud, only softer and damper. "No, you're not a boy," she agreed, staring down at him. "Give me your hands, Joe Langston. A youngun might be scared to death to put his hands on a married woman, but a horny *man* wouldn't: a *man* has sense enough to reach out for what's offered him, and the devil take the hindmost."

God, but her skin was soft, softer than new cotton and a whole lot slicker; his hand upon her tiny waist, Joe could feel the heat of her searing his fingertips. All of him trembled like a young sapling caught in the high wind of a summer twister. He shook worse when she caught his wrists and moved his hands up to the wonder of her breasts, making him cup them, making him press his palms hard against their points.

"Don't be scared," she whispered, the silken stuff of her pantaloons moving against his aching shaft. "It's nothin' to be scared about, because I can teach you all you'll ever need to know. I'll be proud to show you how to please a woman, Joe Langston."

When she gave a knowing wiggle of her hips, the pantaloons slipped down and she kicked them off. Before she came hungry against him, Joe caught a flash of the hair between her smooth thighs, hair that was fluffy and curly and dipped in sunshine. Then she was in his arms, held tight to him with her nipples digging into his chest, her belly sliding across his own and her red, ripe mouth lifting. There was a rich, wild taste to her lips and through her mouth breathed a flavor of honeysuckle and magnolia and something else—a honeyed fierceness that Joe had never savored before.

Jerking some when her tongue first came sliding between his lips, he caught on and held her tighter as Miz Susanna's teeth clashed and her sharp nails dug into his shoulders. Somehow his tongue knew just what to do, and got itself all tangled up with her lashing one, just like his panting breath. Soft and hot and pulsing, her belly moved over his whang.

She pulled him down to the grass, squirming and heaving as he went with her, as she kept her mouth fastened to his, tearing it away only when he half lay, half crouched above her gleaming white body.

"Be strong, Joe," she hissed, her nails raking his hips and down his thighs. "Be powerful as a stud horse, because that's how a woman likes it. Drive it into me, push it deep and strong, like you mean to tear me wide open. Here—let me guide it—"

He flinched when she took him in her hand, but the need was pounding through him, hammering inside his head and blinding his eyes. Soft and curly, springy and giving, and a magic hot slippery place. . . .

"Ahh!" she cried out. "Oh, yes, Joe—that's the way —hard, hard—don't fret about bein' too quick your first time. Ahh! It'll happen real fast, but that's all right—ahh, yes! Just keep right on, keep right on!"

Moving and moving, locked together as her long legs thrashed, she beat her crotch at him and around him, wrapping him deep and loving, taking all he had and thrusting for more. She was the princess giving him all her castle treasures, turning hotbright day into hotdark night and spicing it with honeysuckle, the syrup of her mouth sweeter than anything he'd ever known, the eagerness of her beautiful body making of him more than he was and showing him the way to be more than he had ever dreamed.

She was experienced and she was wise, because she was right about it happening right off, quicker than a randy stallion that hadn't mounted a mare all year. If she hadn't warned him, Joe might have been shamed to have it happen so quick, but she wasn't about to let him stop anyhow. Miz Susanna kept at him, twisting and carrying on and holding him in the grip of her fine, thoroughbred legs until he was just as strong as before.

This time it lasted a spell, and she kept telling him how to move around, showing him the way to give it back to her deep as she wanted. When she took to crying and biting at his throat, Joe slowed up, thinking he might be hurting her some, but it wasn't so; she was just getting into her own short rows, just reaching her pleasure like he'd gotten his.

They were dripping slick with sweat when she eased off, but she still didn't want to turn him loose and that was all right with Joe. He was starting to understand what the preacher down to the church house meant about the promised land and glory, glory. He was already jammed right in between the pearly gates, and if heaven had anything better than this, the folks up there were sure keeping it to themselves.

A horse stamped and snorted; somebody muttered beneath his blanket, and Joe heard the faint rattle of metal against wood as a picket changed position in the night. They were a far piece from that creek bank where Miz Susanna Paisley and a redneck youngun tried to eat each other up.

Pulling himself deeper into his blanket, Joe twisted his lips. When you got right down to it, he reckoned, the planter's wife had chewed him up and spit him out, only it took him a spell to see just how deep she'd set her little white teeth. Moving his head against the saddle, he scratched at the itching of his new beard and wondered how she had made out during the war. Good enough, he figured; Miz Susanna was one to get her own way and wouldn't let little things like a war and Yankee occupation stand in her path.

Joe felt the chill kiss of gathering dew upon his cheek and turned again, puzzled at his restlessness. Let's see now—Miz Susanna had been twenty-two when she bedded him the first time, and him a short sixteen, instead of the near seventeen he'd lied about. According to the clock, both of them were ten years older now, but he'd piled on a lot of hard and hurting time since the days he thought he was so damned much in love; Joe Langston had been to the well too many times. Hell, he felt old enough to be his own grandpa, not like he was only twenty-six.

And the golden princess from the big white house? Miz Susanna would hold her beauty; she was that sort of woman. That is, if she didn't wear herself out diddling every hard shaft she could get her legs around. She was that kind, too—like any other among her high-class breed.

"You asleep, Joe?" Timmy Santee's voice was low. "Heard you frettin' around. It ain't easy for me, neither."

Hunching the blanket around his shoulders, Joe sat up and felt for another cigar. He had three of them left and would go easy on the smoking until he found some more in somebody's store or somebody's pocket. It was going to be some peculiar, not busting a cap at any bluebelly off by himself, and he wondered how lean times would get before they got down into Mexico.

"It ain't my wound," Timmy whispered. "That's feelin' pretty good, considerin'. I keep thinkin' about my girl, about May, wonderin' if she's goin' hungry or what. You got a girl in Alabama, Joe?"

"No," Joe said, "nor wife either." He thumbnailed the sulphur match under the blanket and ducked to put it to his cigar end. "Maybe none of us got a woman left."

The quiet drew itself out before Timmy said, " 'Spect I have. May and her kinfolk take care of each other, and she's promised to me. She wouldn't have no truck with Yankees."

Drawing smoke, Joe held it in his mouth and savored the taste. "If you say so."

Agitated, the boy leaned closer. "Look here, you got no cause to talk thataway. I know you been to war a whole lot longer'n me, and you're older, but you don't know *nothin'* about my girl."

"All right," Joe said. "Leave it lay. You want a puff of this? Keep the coal hid in your hand."

Coughing, Timmy handed back the cigar. "Obliged."

One more drag, and Joe pinched out the glowing tip and tucked the rolled leaf safely away. What the hell was he picking at the boy for? Let him hang on to the dream long as he could; deviling him about it wouldn't change the youngun's mind. Timmy Santee probably wouldn't live long enough to go home and see for himself, and it was probably best that way.

" 'Night, Joe."

"Yeah," Joe answered and put his back to the boy. That damned whiff of honeysuckle started it, bringing back the memory of Miz Susanna and all her doings. He might be restless because he hadn't had a woman in so long, because he sure enough didn't give a hoot and a holler about what happened to that golden bitch. Anywhere a man went, given the time, he could find him another one just like her, cut out of the same pattern.

Joe expected to get a chance at another Miz Susanna before too much longer, only this time he'd see to it that her nose got rubbed in the dirt, not his.

Chapter 6

The sun was high and warming when Marilee awoke and stretched. She came awake all over, everything about the night before flooding back to raise goosebumps along her arms. The stallion grazed peacefully nearby, not fighting against his hobbles, happy in lush green grass which grew thick as it gathered around the little cold spring.

The man's stink was still musty in his blankets, and she wrinkled her nose in disgust as she climbed from them, extending her arms and flexing her body again. They'd reached the glade before daylight, and Bradburn's nose had guided her to the spring. It was a good place, she thought, ringed by crispy pines and graceful water oaks, a starleafed sweetgum tree claiming squatter's rights at the water's edge.

Marilee wore only the tattered slave's coat, because she'd been unable to stand the crawling filth of underdrawers and shirt and uniform pants she'd stripped from the corpse of the man who had brutally raped her. Pulling the ragged jacket about her sore body, she carried the other stuff to the spring and hunkered down to wash them as best she could without soap. Only after she'd scrubbed at the seams with handfuls of sand, rinsed again, and hung the clothing spread to dry upon a huckleberry bush did she dip herself into the chill waters, working at her body harshly with her hands. She knew she'd never be able to wash away the stain upon her, the dirt left within her ravaged flesh, but she had to keep trying.

Chopped-short hair still dripping, she emerged from the spring and slipped on the coat again. Scraping soft bark from a fallen pine with her penknife, she used flint and steel to get a spark going, then blew it into flame, adding dry twigs and limbs as it grew. Sulphur matches were in the saddlebags, but she was saving them.

Water in the trooper's fry pan—no, *her* skillet now, as everything else the man had owned was hers—to clean it out, and leaving only a film of moisture to float the bacon, Marilee cooked breakfast. Mixing water with cornmeal and adding salt, she couldn't wait for the johnnycake to fry, but gulped down the fatback hungrily. It tasted so good, so rich that she could have eaten the entire slab at one sitting.

Turning the corn cake, she said, "Bradburn—I hope you're enjoyin' your meal as much as me." Calling the horse that didn't quite fit her mouth yet, but it would. It was his name and hers and that of the land she'd fled; it belonged to her daddy and brothers dead, to all the ancestors who had wrested the plantation from wilderness and Indians. When she came riding the stallion back to claim her own, when he pranced before another big white-columned house, his name would be only proper, *Bradburn,* ringing proudly over the land once more.

When she finished the johnnycake and scrubbed the skillet, Marilee filled her canteen with clean water and felt over the clothes she'd spread. They were still damp, so she took a while to curry the stallion with moss pulled from oak trees, rubbing hard at his fineboned legs, talking to him and getting him more used to her. The smell of him was sweet, and in sunshine he was even more beautiful: sleek dappled hide, flowing mane and tail, alert and strong. Beauty and hope and freedom—all packed into that muscled, compact body—and possibly love.

Bitting him and looping the reins over a limb, Marilee gathered her things, rolling damp blankets around the groundsheet where sun could get at them. She thought of love, and its taste was bitter in her throat. She knew a strange kind of gladness that her mother was dead and would never know her dishonor, and again Marilee felt the resentment, the nagging anger at Robbie Dee for not making love to her before that—that sweaty, stinking animal had.

She shook her head. "No, Bradburn—that wasn't making love. It was making hate, and I'm happy I killed your master. How could *he* have a horse like you? But I'm not faultin' you for it—a horse can't help who owns him."

Ears forward, head turned, the big horse watched her with dark, liquid eyes.

"We made about ten miles, I reckon," she went on, stuffing rations in the bags, shaking out the saddle blanket. "That was a long way in the dark, but we had to put distance between us and *them*. You never stumbled once."

She pulled clammy drawers over her legs, put on the shirt, feeling clean now, and Yankee cavalry breeches that had to be doubled around her waist and belted there. She'd wear the ragged coat open and keep the pistol hidden beneath it. Tying the band of the eyepatch around her head, she tilted the patch up on her brow, meaning to keep it that way until she came up on somebody. The forage cap covered her chopped hair, and she was ready to saddle her horse.

Swinging lightly into the leather, she said, "We'll follow the sun, boy. Doloroso has been bypassed, so I guess we'll have to head for Woodville, and that's more to the south, but we'll swing off there and aim for the Mississippi. Daddy and the boys talked about a ferry somewhere around Fort Adams."

The sheathed carbine was comforting against her knee as she moved the stallion gently out through the brush to find the game trail that had brought them to the glade. It branched off a little-used wagon road that was going in the right direction, and Marilee thought she'd follow until it got too close to the main track.

Bradburn was eager to be away, and she allowed him to work off some of his stored energy before slowing him to a ground-eating walk. The stallion could walk faster than many horses could trot. Good, she thought; they'd cover a lot of miles without tiring at that pace. She hoped she wouldn't have to call upon the coiled power she felt between her knees, but if she *had* to let the horse out, she didn't want him weary. She wouldn't know how much bottom he had until then.

Stirring yellow dust as he went, Bradburn flowed along the road, passing her through scented shade and bright sun. She smelled the wind, and it was laced with the spices of springtime, teasing her with wildflowers and softly uncurled buddings. It should be a time for celebration, as the earth stirred and the young air of April drowned the chill of winter. Slaves ought to be turning black loam in the fields, clucking to mules and singing out to each other. In the big house, Mama would be worrying servants into cleaning and polishing every inch of walls and floors until the wood glistened like mirrors, making the wenches lower the chandeliers and wash every bit of crystal. Then they would air bedding and beat carpets and clean the silver. . . .

Marilee nibbled at her lower lip. The only silver was in her pocket, less than each slave on the plantation would have gotten for "Christmas gif," not nearly enough to buy the calico and linsey-woolsey they'd be given too. Did any of them have new clothing this year or good shoes by old Samuel, master leather craftsman? All those drifting, hungry hordes trudging for the promised land—could the Yankees care for them all? *Would* they?

It was true that some slaves had been mistreated. Marilee had heard whispers of brutality, manacles that ate into ankles and blacksnake whips that scarred backs. Most of that happened to runaways, though, and the best thing to do with a light-footed nigger was take your loss and sell him quick. Only damned fools savaged their own stock, and most planters had more sense. They kept the slaves clean as they could, saw to it they were doctored and well fed. Old ones were given easy jobs, put out to pasture like faithful horses.

And Wayne Bradburn had always been careful about their bloodlines, crossing a proper buck on the best wench. Marilee's daddy had never allowed indiscriminate breeding and sold off any cull younguns. Lord, she thought, left to themselves now they'd have no way to care for their offspring.

Aloud, she said, "*You* could make it on your own, Bradburn. But they can't get by grazing the fields. I wonder what they think about freedom now, if they wouldn't trade it back for full bellies and warm hides."

The horse's head swung right, his ears pointing. She checked him with the bit and sat alert in the saddle, one hand upon the butt of the carbine. Off in the thick woods, muffled sounds faded, and she thought it must have been a rabbit or one of the few surviving deer. Marilee gently squeezed the stallion's thick barrel with both legs, and he stepped out again.

In a while, a little creek cut across the track, and she let Bradburn drink there while she swung down to stretch her legs. She was sore low in the groin, around her privates, and her thighs ached; her breasts were tender from the mauling they'd received. Putting her hand to her mouth, Marilee felt swollen lips where the man's teeth had crushed them, where his heavy slap had bruised them. Kneeling to rinse her mouth with creek water, she spat.

Too wrapped in her own thoughts as she rode the horse around a masking thicket of bayberry, Marilee didn't notice the clearing until she was in it, didn't catch the faint odor of woodsmoke until it was too late. Stiffening, balanced in the stirrups, she made out the cabin crouching beneath mossy oaks, its weatherbeaten grayness blending its shape into the tree trunks. Her eyes picked out a blackened washpot, a pile of fresh kindling, some small animal hides stretched upon the cabin wall, but the only sign of life was an almost invisible feather of smoke curling up from a mud chimney.

Hard dirt farm, she thought. Back of the trees would be a few scraggly fields whose earth was too acid or worked only haphazardly to produce more than marginal crops, or land that had simply been worn out. Folks on a place like this were mostly woods runners, living hand to mouth on what game and fish they could get, the men spending more time making bustskull whiskey than at the plow, their scrawny women worked down to whining shadows. She'd seen their kind before and never understood them, never cared enough to try. As a class, they fell below storekeepers and notions peddlers, a cut under overseers, but they stood above slave dealers and the blacks, although the slaves themselves, especially house servants, contemptuously referred to them as white trash.

Marilee started to turn the stallion, to push him quickly across the yard and away into sheltering woods, when he said from behind her: "Fer enough, Yank. Set real still, else I blow off your head."

He was too close; she could *feel* the rifle muzzle aimed

between her shoulders. She carefully kept her legs away from the horse and swallowed. "I—I'm not a Yankee," she said, calmly as she could.

"See about that," the voice said, words sandpapering against each other. "Won't be nothin', do you reach for that saddle gun. Luther! You got him in your sights? Jesse?"

Off to her left, somebody chuckled. "Spang in the wishbone, Pa."

And from behind an oak tree ahead: "Atween his eyes."

Marilee quivered; there were three of them, boxing her in so that even if she tried to run, one would be bound to cut her down, to drive a ball through the stallion before they could reach shelter in the brush.

"I'm no bluebelly," she said again.

The man behind her had edged closer when he said, "Then you be a scalawag, come nosin' around to rob honest folks. Youngun, too—but nits is bad as lice, I reckon. Step down easy, like you was lightin' on eggs."

There was a cold spot in Marilee's belly, a chill that warned as it grew, but she tried to fight it down. These men were only trying to protect what little they owned, and when they discovered she was neither Yankee nor scalawag, they'd let her go. After all, they were Southerners.

Reins in her left hand and held shoulder high, Marilee kept her right away from her body and the ragged coat. She didn't turn around, but watched two men slouch from cover ahead, rifles at the ready. They were lean as hungry hounds, their eyes watchful beneath shapeless black hats.

The man behind her said, "That's right sensible, youngun. Might be you a deserter from the Yanks, or jes' lookin' to see what booty you can come up on. Made you a mistake, I expect—we can purely use a horse like that 'un, and all your gear."

Lifting her right hand slowly up, Marilee made sure the eyepatch was in place, "I need my horse. They—the Yankees are after me." She flinched as a rifle muzzle poked her in the spine.

"Yanks is after everything, I reckon—that don't mean they can *find* everything."

Closer now, the other two seemed to be stalking her,

wary as if she were a bobcat caught in a snare. Middling young, both of them, and cut from the same shoddy cloth —sparse and matted beards a pale yellow, darkened around thin mouths by tobacco stains; hunched in the shoulders; flat-bellied and barefoot, their toes spread in the dirt.

One of them showed mottled teeth. "Nothin' but a saplin', Pa—only a youngun with one of his lights knocked out. What the Yanks after you for, boy—stealin' that there horse?"

Marilee hung her head so he couldn't look directly into her face, and mumbled, "More'n that. I'm from up the road, and—"

The rifle pushed into her back and she braced against its push. The older man said, "Up the road, hey? Who might you be?"

"My name is Mar—Martin," she answered. "Martin Crownover, from Greatoaks Plantation. Some of you, all of you, must have worn the gray, too. You'll help me get away from the bluecoats."

Now the older man sidled around to peer at her. More stooped, darker in the face and his beard sanded with gray, he was near toothless and sharp-eyed. The bore of his long rifle never wavered. "Say you one of them Crownovers? Ain't so high and mighty now, be you? No more fancy house, no more niggers and the Yanks after your hide to boot. How 'bout that, boys? Looks like we caught us a *gentleman*."

Lowering his rifle butt to the ground, one of them nudged his brother with a ragged elbow. "Luther, you tell this here *gentleman* we wasn't fool enough to wear no Confederate gray and git ourselfs killed so he could keep his niggers."

Luther propped up on his rifle barrel, too. "Why Jesse —don't you know no better than to hooraw your betters? Take off your hat and say yes-sir, no-sir to him, just like you was one of his field hands."

The old man giggled. "Too bad he ain't got a wench or two left. Know somethin', *Mister* Crownover? We had one of your high yeller gals for a spell, and right handy at diddlin' she was, too. But Luther didn't tie her up too good one night, and she lit a shuck."

Luther grunted. "Keep tellin' you, it was Jesse."

"Uh-uh," Jesse said. "You topped her last that night."

"Don't matter," the old man snorted. "Fact is, we been outa' pussy for a long spell, but could be we'll make up for it. If the Yanks want this youngun bad enough, maybe they got a bounty on him, and we can swap him for cash money. Few geegaws and some calico, and we can toll one of them free wenches to the house."

Luther spat a brown splatter of tobacco juice at Marilee's boot tips. She didn't move. He said, "You kill the bluebelly had that horse boy? Guess you slipped up on him and knocked him in the head with a lighter knot."

"Hell," Jesse said, "a gentleman like him? He probably whupped the Yank to death with the Stars and Bars while he was whistlin' Dixie."

Marilee's chin lifted and she glared at them. "You— you white trash! Mocking the flag that *good* men died for—"

The stallion skittered when she was knocked into his flank, but she hung on to the reins as her knees buckled, her hat fell off, and her eyepatch slewed to one side.

"Pa! Looka' there—it's a gal!"

"Damn if it ain't," the old man chortled, his skinny face blurring before her eyes. "A little ol' gal with her hair cut off and her tits jumpin' around like rabbits under that there shirt. Reckon we don't need to buy no geegaws; our new pussy just rode right on up to us."

Marilee put her right hand to her cheek and shook her head. "No—no—please. I have a few greenbacks— don't—" But even as she begged them, she knew it was no use. Heart slamming inside her chest, she couldn't believe it was going to happen again, that her body would be violated, used savagely and ruthlessly. And this time the terrible thing wouldn't be done by just one man, but by three of them. Oh, God—over and over and over, all three of these gloating, crawly animals taking turns between her thighs, forcing their ugly, swollen things into her shuddering flesh, mouthing at her breasts and raking her tender haunches with cruel fingers.

"Look at her shake," Luther said. "Reckon she can shake her ass just as good?"

"Natural," Jessie grinned. "That comes natural to all

them high-falutin' *ladies* in the big houses. They learn it from their nigger wenches. Who's goin' to tie up that horse, and who gets to put it to her first?"

The old man was shifting from one bare, splayed foot to the other, his stained lips jerking. "You see to the horse, Jesse. Your old pa gets first pop at her. Oh, my—it's goin' to do my heart right good to make this 'un wiggle and holler. You, gal—don't look so down at the mouth. You about to get you some real meat for a change, get yourself mounted just like a bitch dog in heat with all us he-dogs scratchin' the dirt and histin' our hind legs."

"Oh, hell, Pa," Jessie said. "You got the yeller wench first."

"Just warmin' her up for you, boy," the old man said, bending to place his rifle on the ground. When he came back up, he was dropping his breeches and fondling himself.

Marilee saw it again—that threatening, monstrous thing ready to dirty her, puffy and veined, a degrading horror.

"Good 'un, ain't it?" the old man chuckled. "Jesse, you take that horse on now—and Luther, get hold of that saddle gun, does she have a mind to try for it. Time you boys take your turns, this Crownover bitch is goin' to be hotter'n a fat pine fire. Careful she don't scald your whangs off clear to the roots."

Jesse's hand caught at the stallion's reins before she could move, but the touch of his skin against her knuckles shocked her into action.

Dipping her right hand under her coat, she snapped up the pistol and laid its barrel across Jesse's cheekbone as hard as she could. He spun backward and Marilee whipped the muzzle around, her thumb pulling back the hammer as Luther shouted something, as the old man tried to leap back and stumbled because his breeches were down around his skinny ankles.

"D-don't, gal!"

Luther still had his rifle, and Jesse was wiping blood from his face with one hand and pawing around on the ground with the other, searching for his own gun. So Marilee fired pointblank at Luther, and the man's weapon flew aside as the ball sledgehammered into his shoulder and thunder blasted around him.

Jesse got hold of his gun and rolled aside, but dropped it when Marilee missed his head by an inch with her next shot. He scuttled away like a turpentined cat, digging at the ground with hands and knees.

Marilee wheeled to aim the pistol at the old man. He held out both shaking hands to ward off the shot, his eyes popped wide and the snags of his teeth showing brown and yellow. Slack lips worked and spittle gathered in their corners.

"Y-you—you won't shoot a poor old man? We was only funnin'—we was goin' to let you go—I swear—"

Gunsmoke swirled around her as she stood with feet wide apart, the big pistol clenched tightly in her fist. At her shoulder, Bradburn only blew through distended nostrils and tensed. "You were going to rape me," she said through clenched teeth. "You rotten white-trash bastards were going to rape me. I think I'll shoot you in the crotch, blow off that dirty thing you're so proud of, so you'll never use it on another helpless woman."

From the ground, his fingers dug into his shoulder and dark blood seeping through them, Luther said, "Helpless. Great godalmighty—*helpless.*"

The old man went to his knees, clawing the air in supplication. "Don't rile her, boy—for chrissakes, don't rile her. Please, gal—"

Marilee's finger trembled upon the trigger. "Lady," she said. "You damned rednecks know how to say it, so *say* it: lady!"

"Lady," the old man gobbled, "lady, lady."

Cutting her eyes from him, she looked at wounded Luther, at crouching Jesse. "Back off," Marilee ordered, and when they inched away, she thrust the pistol into her belt and scooped up one rifle. It made a satisfying smash when she chopped it into the ground.

Luther swayed and held to his shoulder. "Leave us one, lady."

She splintered the stock of another gun and jammed the muzzle into the dirt. The old man wasn't too far from his own weapon, darting hungry eyes at it. "Go ahead," she whispered. "Go ahead and see if you can reach it."

He edged farther back. "D-didn't have no such thing in mind, but guns is hard come by, and we purely need one to hunt meat."

When she drew the pistol again, she thought he was going to cry. She fired into the breech lock of his rifle, and the bullet flung whining pieces of metal and wood in all directions. The old man rolled into a ball, his knees drawn up and arms clasped around his head; his naked butt was obscene and ludicrous. Marilee picked up her hat and eye-patch.

"Starve," she said, and backed to the horse to vault into the saddle.

At the touch of her heels, Bradburn flung himself across the clearing, and as she leaned into the wind of his gallop, pistol warm in her fist, Marilee thought the stallion was glad to be away from the shooting. But he'd stood firm, only flinching at the shots and smoke, keeping his head and holding his nerve. She was proud of him. If he'd bolted, she would have been in trouble, unless she killed all three men; she wasn't sure she could have done that.

Marilee didn't look back, and she didn't let Bradburn full out, but kept him on the bit, still moving swiftly away from that miserable cabin and its more miserable family. Bradburn took a bend in the track at a long gallop, and she slowed him to a trot, then waked him. He shook his head, impatient to be running again, but obeying the reins. Beyond a tangle of blackberry bushes just beginning to put out little green fruit, she stopped the horse to listen. Weaponless and afoot, that bunch didn't dare follow her, but she knew she'd have to be far more cautious about riding up on houses and people. Her mouth twisted—even Southerners.

A reaction set in, and her hands shook as she levered brass casings from the chambers of the revolver and fed in fresh rounds. They'd hated her; it was more than just wanting to rape her. Those half-wild woods runners wanted to humble her, make her no better than themselves. *Fight so you can keep* your *niggers?* they had said. *Not so high and mighty now, you Crownovers.*

"Forgive me, Robbie Dee," she murmured. "Forgive me for using your name and letting those filthy creatures mock it. I didn't realize they hated us so, envied us that much. Trash, poor w-white trash—oh, my God! And you died for the likes of *them*."

Angrily, she brushed at tears and made her back proud

and straight. Reloaded pistol beneath her coat, hat jammed down over her ruined hair, she rode southwest. Mississippi and all the good people couldn't be dead; she refused to believe that.

Chapter 7

When the scouts came easing back through the trees, Joe Langston slid his carbine from its scabbard and checked its lever action, but softly, muffling the metallic sound with his spread hand. There was trouble ahead, he could sense it, feel it deep within his belly.

"Wonder what they run into," Timmy Santee whispered.

"Somethin' we can't get around," Joe answered, and loosened the good Colt pistol in its holster, conscious of the boy watching his every move and copying him.

He watched the stiff-backed major getting the report and saw him nod. With a sweep of his gloved hand, Major Ainsworth circled the troop about him, and the horses walked quietly, the men straighter in their saddles, tensing in anticipation of a coming fight. It was always the same, Joe thought, no matter how many times a man had seen the elephant, how many battles he'd ridden into; his belly still pulled tight and his hide felt naked.

The major eased his stubbed leg in the stirrup and glanced around the ragged circle. "Our scouts have found a camp of scalawags," he said, "murdering scavengers bunched up like so many buzzards. No pickets out, because they think they're safe with no troops around."

Joe rubbed at his new beard. "Might be they are," he drawled. "There's some right bad folks rides with scalawags."

Ainsworth's dusty face tightened. "Buzzards," he repeated. "Traitors and deserters and sneak thieves feeding on the bones of the South. There's not a true soldier among them."

"Don't take a pretty uniform to be handy with a gun," Joe said.

Tired but hard, the major's eyes fixed on Joe. "This isn't a discussion," he said. "This is a military command, and you're a soldier in it. You and the rest of the men placed yourselves under my orders when we left Appomattox, and, by God, you'll *follow* my orders. The war isn't over for this troop, and never will be, until we can walk our land again as free and honorable men."

"Oh, shit," Joe said. "Order away, major."

Ainsworth's lips twitched. "Thank you. Well—it normally would pay us to swing wide of the camp, but it lies directly across our path, and the scouts report considerable loot there—grain and the like. Our horses need that grain, and we'll take whatever else we can use, then burn the rest."

"More like it," Joe whispered to Timmy Santee, "only he ain't said how many woods runners is up yonder."

"He did say they're not soldiers," Timmy breathed, "so we can easy ride 'em down."

"Quantrill wasn't no *soldier*," Joe said, "but he could sure as all billy hell eat up a ragged bunch like this 'un and never even belch."

Major Ainsworth was making his battle plan, fanning skirmishers left and right, moving them slowly in a quiet crescent through a heavy growth of pine saplings, and Joe nodded tacit approval. Gentry though the man was, he knew his business and wasn't hurrying things; the troop would slip up on the camp and surprise the scalawags in their blankets.

"We're in the center," Timmy hissed in excitement.

"Good for us—we'll be the last in." Joe stuck a cigar stub into his mouth, but didn't light it. He watched the major whip his hat against one knee to beat dust off it,

saw the man tidying his worn uniform as if he was going
to one of those fancy balls in a big white house.
Goddamned aristocrat, taking himself clear to Mexico so
he could go on fighting a lost war, so he could walk his
land again as a free and honorable man—*his* land and
freedom, *his* honor. If Joe Langston had anywhere else
to go, damned if he wouldn't turn tail and hunt a hole; he
didn't have any land, and any freedom he'd known he'd
by God earned himself.

Honor? That was a word the gentry used to their own
ends, acting like nobody else had a right to any.

Like Miz Susanna, that honorable mistress of a great
plantation; it was all right for her to diddle a redneck
farm boy because her old husband couldn't get it up more
than once or twice a month. She was entitled to privileges
because she was a blueblood, not just because she was
beautiful and passionate, not only because she was all
silken to the touch and honey to the taste and knew it all.

Joe ran his hand lightly over the smooth butt of his
carbine like it was her leg and thought of all the places
they'd met, not able to count the times he'd slipped off
from his chores to find Miz Susanna waiting breathlessly
for him.

Kind of off-hand, Pa broke a stick of stovewood over
his shoulders for falling behind at the plow, and his brothers deviled him day and night, trying to find out who he
was putting it to. Joe laid for them when they trailed him,
and stomped them good, so they quit following.

They met at the edge of a sugar cane field, with whispery green tops waving over them and a tablecloth
spread in the shade. He'd never seen such good things
to eat and got to like the fruity taste of scuppernong wine
upon his tongue. But she was flavored special, headier
than the wine, more filling than picnic food, and somehow keeping him hungry for more of her.

The creek was his favorite place, because that was
where it happened the first time, when she showed him
what it was like to be a man. When old man Paisley was
to home and she couldn't get out, Joe would go to the
creek and hunker down on the sandy bank to dream. With
his eyes closed, he could feel the satin roundness of her
breasts in his hands, those pink tips pressing eagerly into
his palms. He'd pretend to smell the honeysuckle perfume

of her golden hair, and his body would go rigid with the need to touch her. But Joe never played with himself; he was beyond that, and saving it for her.

When it got cold, Miz Susanna showed him how to get into the cotton crib, and she'd laugh softly as they snuggled down into the fluffy, warm whiteness. That was where she taught him how to drive a woman crazy with his mouth, and every time he did it to her, Joe thought she was going to tear up the crib, flinging that slim, rich body around every which way, so he had trouble holding on to the rolling, heaving mounds of her buttocks.

"Oh, you lover!" she crooned, digging her fingers into his hair and making him a happy prisoner between her slick, fine legs. "Oh, you strong, young lover—yes, yes, darling—that's the way to do it—ahh! *Ahh!*"

And once in a while, she'd do it to him, when she was real hot and excited, not minding that it weakened him for a spell and he had to rest before mounting her whichever way she wanted him to.

They did it in the crib, and shivering under quilts in the frosty woods, winter and spring, summer and fall—did it on the creek bank and down in the water, too. They did it in wagon beds and up in a hayloft, but Miz Susanna never tried to sneak him into the big house, so he could diddle her in a bed with linen sheets on it.

Joe was so much in love that it ached him not to be with her every waking minute of the day, and she walked his dreams at night, turning him restless and muttering on his pallet upon the floor of the Langston shack. And always in those dreams Miz Susanna smiled with him, twisted upon him, and led him by the hand up to the front door of the columned house, across the veranda shaded by purple wisteria and white wisteria. They went inside where all the house niggers were drawn up in a row, bowing and scraping to the new master and the beautiful young mistress nobody could help loving. But nobody in the whole world loved Miz Susanna Langston the way he did.

She had the lunch spread on a snowy tablecloth beneath live oaks—fried chicken and white bread, purple wine and sugar cakes—when he told her about the dreams, told her they oughtn't wait any longer.

"Mister Paisley acts like he's goin' to live forever,"

Joe said. "He's just ornery enough to reach a hundred. So let's you and me run off."

Sharp, perfect teeth let go the chicken leg they'd been worrying. "Joe, Joe," she said. "Where would we go?"

"Mobile, I reckon," he said. "There's work there, I hear tell. I'd see you never go hungry."

Even as she smiled, a tiny wrinkle creased her forehead. Afternoon sunlight lay across her loose hair, jealous of the tumbled gold. Miz Susanna said, "Darlin', I don't doubt that. You're willin' and strong—oh, so strong—and I expect you'd work clear around the clock to take care of me, but—"

Edgy, he waited for her to go on. The chicken tasted dry now, and he put it down to drink some wine. "You could take your mare," he said, "and me a mule. Pa owes me that much."

She caught her lower lip between her teeth, but the giggle broke free anyhow. "Oh, Joe—a mule?"

Stubbornly, he said, "It's a good mule, and we can sell him in Mobile. He'll tote a trunk of clothes for you, and whatever booty you want from the big house. Don't reckon we can take a nigger, though—Mister Paisley would be put out if we run off with one of his niggers."

Miz Susanna stopped laughing. "You're serious, aren't you?"

Joe nodded and finished his wine, turning the fragile crystal glass between callused fingers, not looking at her directly.

She said, "Joe, and you figure my husband wouldn't be put out because I ran off with you, that he cares more for a house nigger?"

"He don't *own you*," Joe insisted, "and he can't put patrollers out after you, like he'd do for a runaway slave. Might be he wouldn't say nothin' to nobody that you was gone. A man don't spread it around that his wife left him."

Gently, she touched his hand; as always, he trembled at the feel of her skin, its impossible softness and warmth. Miz Susanna said then: "You're a very sweet boy, and a wonderful lover, Joe. But you forgot what I told you about different kinds of poor. I just can't live on hoecake and field peas. I *won't*—no more than I'll wear calico and sleep on a quilt. You think Mister Paisley doesn't own me? He sure does—just as much as he owns every field hand

70

on the place. I'm bought and paid for, Joe, and my husband knows I have to stick by my bargain. Don't you understand, Joe? Please understand."

Her hand left his own and began a slow, tantalizing creep up his thigh. She spoke huskily, leaning closer to him so he could smell the scent of her body. "What's wrong with keepin' on like this, Joe? We can meet more often—Mister Paisley's goin' on a long trip up North before long, and we can do it every day, every night. Nobody will ever know, and I'll be so good to you—I'll kiss it for you every time. Ah—I can feel you gettin' hard—you're such a handsome, horny boy—"

That wasn't the only place he was stiff; it seemed like all his body was swollen, the skin stretched thin over his flesh, his bones locked tight. "In Mobile, we could get married. When I get enough money, we could go to New Orleans, where nobody knows you."

Her hand closed over him, deft fingers kneading and caressing. "Forget about that, darlin'. I need you right now and right here. I need to have you inside me, to feel you movin' hard and powerful as a stallion—"

He jerked away. "Goddamnit, I ain't a stud horse! I'm a *man*, and I—I love you."

Reaching for him again, her eyes hot as July sky, her mouth damp and her breasts rising and falling, Miz Susanna hissed, "Then make love to me now! Don't act like some stupid youngun dreamin' of marryin' the princess and havin' the king give you half his kingdom. I bet you never even heard of a princess, because you can't read. But if you had, you ought to have sense enough to know that she screws just like every other woman."

He stood up, shaking like a spooked horse. "I heard tell of a princess, and I never asked for half of no kingdom; I never begged for a damned thing in my life, and I ain't fixin' to start now."

Running, branches whipping at his face and briars stabbing his legs, Joe plunged blindly through the woods, hearing her call after him, her voice insistent, commanding, with a high whine to it that he'd never heard before. The echo of it followed him to clang around inside his head after he'd run until he couldn't and dropped face down onto a pallet of brown pine needles.

It wasn't too bad, not seeing her for a whole week.

Joe drove himself in the fields, tearing at stumps and burning brush and working the mules into a lather, as if he could turn the hardscrabble farm into rich bottom land, like Paisley had. He fell onto his quilts at night, too tired to eat cornpone and collard greens with a little grease in them.

Next week, he took to easing over to the creek and hiding in the brush, in case she was to show up on the far bank, but Miz Susanna never came, and never sent word with one of her niggers that he was to meet her somewhere. Joe sweated with hoe and ax and hurried the mules behind the plow until his pa told him to back off some. But now the nights weren't dreamless, and he fretted himself awake before sunup, holding his hardness and seeing her shining, naked body printed against his eyelids.

A full month went by before it came to him what he had to do. The preachers that hollered fire and brimstone at camp meetings sometimes told about folks in the Bible just up and running off with women, scooping them up and riding off to wed them without giving the women a say-so. It happened all the time in the Bible, so Joe figured that it ought to hold true now. Miz Susanna didn't know her own mind, was all. She appreciated strength, she said, loved it when he handled her rough. She'd see how it was to be once he had her thrown over a mule and halfway down to Mobile.

It took him a few more days, leading the mule to the creek and tying him back in the woods, but at last Joe heard her laughing there and went sliding down to the huckleberry bushes like a fox creeping up on a chicken pen. Parting the leafy branches carefully, he peeped through to see her on the other side of the slow water, her long hair turned loose and capturing the sun, her white body gleaming and beautiful.

Only Miz Susanna wasn't alone on the sandbank. There was a black buck with her, bare-assed and shiny with sweat. As Joe stared, the buck crouched over her nude body, and she reached up to take the black whang in her slim hand, a pecker long and thick as a stud horse carried between his hind legs. It was like getting kicked in the brisket by a mule when Joe saw that, when he saw Miz Susanna's crotch hiking and rolling at the swollen knob, the blackness pushing up into the gold-haired pink whiteness.

Bushes crashed back behind him as Joe jumped into the creek, scattering water, thundering through the shallows and up onto the far bank before he knew he was there. There was a jolt clear to his shoulde when he fisted the buck behind the neck, and he caught a flask of her white, scared face as the nigger grunted and fell off to one side.

There was something in Joe's hands now—a length of dry oak limb that he smashed across the black's head, and struck with it again to wheel the buck over onto his spine. The nigger's hammer stood straight up, but Joe was blind with fury and missed it to land the heavy stick across the sweating belly instead.

She was grabbing at his legs, wrapping her arms about Joe's knees as he slashed the stick at the rolling black. "Joe—Joe! Don't—"

Stunned, crouched now on hands and shaking knees, the slave's nappy head wobbled and a bright string of blood stained the sand.

"Kill him," Joe panted. "I'll beat that black bastard to death."

"No—no—" Miz Susanna coiled around his legs, tearing at them.

He saw the buck's head lift, yellowish eyes wide and frightened. The black said, "Swear it—swear I didn't want to. She made me—she made me do it, get me—get me whupped if'n I didn't do it."

"Get your black ass killed because you did," Joe snarled. "A white woman, you son of a bitch—a *white* woman!" He tried to shake Miz Susanna loose, and thought he had, only to jerk double in sudden, violent pain as she hit him between the legs.

Eyes glazed with hurt, he hung on to the club and glared murder at the stupified black The man tried to get up and run, but Joe had caught him some good licks, and he couldn't make it.

"White man, white man," he moaned. "Afore God, I never meant to."

Miz Susanna was right up in his face then, screaming at him. "Stop it, stop it! He's tellin' the truth—I *made* him screw me! You goddam redneck, you think I'm goin' to do without it because you ran off? Act like you got some sense."

He was sick then, a twisting pain low in his belly that had nothing to do with where she'd hit him. His mouth was dry and he just stared helplessly at her as she took the oak branch from his hands and stepped back.

"That's better, Joe." The light in her eyes was hotly triumphant, exulting. "See? It's goin' to be all right—everything's goin' to be just fine, just fine. Look at me, Joe—look at my body, my breasts, at my mound. You should have known you couldn't stay away from all this, you silly boy. And don't act all high and mighty because you caught me diddlin' a nigger—he's got nice hard meat, too, and bigger than yours. I know all white men put it to wenches every chance they get, so I figure it's nothin' to you if I take on a buck when I'm horny."

One foot reached behind him, then another, both of them shaky. Joe looked at the beautiful body she stood so proud in, at the sunshine gathering of fluffy hair between her spread thighs. He looked beyond her at the head-hanging slave and the softened hammer hanging, at the trickle of blood from the man's head.

Miz Susanna said, running her hands over her hips, over the modeled breasts, "I hope I didn't hurt your pecker, but I had to keep you off him, any way I could. Come on, Joe—grow up—you can take your turn with me, because I sure can handle both of you. Jethro won't care if you go first."

Joe didn't remember running back through the creek; all he remembered clearly was the mocking sound of her laughter ringing after him, like little silver bells, but this time with sharp edges that cut and cut. A branch caught him a lick across the cheekbone and made his eyes water; they kept leaking long after he caught up the mule and rode aimlessly around in the woods for quite a spell.

It was sundown when he turned the mule's head and circled him back for the Paisley land. Sitting awhile in the edge of the woods, he watched candles being lighted in the big house and saw cookfire smoke rising from the slave quarters. He tied the mule and went straight to the nearest cotton crib, the one where Miz Susanna had rolled with him in wiggly, soft warmth. Joe struck flint and steel there, and had a good fire roaring before moving on to the next shed.

They caught him there, as he was working his way toward the big house, meaning to burn down every damned thing in his path. He fought them viciously, happily, tearing into the first startled blacks with a grinning fury that drove them flailing and stumbling before him. The field hands squalled and tried to hold him, not much daring to pound on a crazy white boy, but when the overseer got there, Joe went down from a whop to the side of the head by a whipstock.

When his eyes cleared, a pair of muscled bucks were holding his arms tight, stretching him between them. Rolling his head on his shoulders, Joe could see the overseer standing with his feet set wide and a coiled blacksnake whip dangling from one square-knuckled hand. Light from the blazing cribs jumped and danced over Mister Paisley, tall and gaunt, with a mean gray face. It sprinkled red lights into the gold of Miz Susanna's pinned-up hair and skipped over her pretty white dress.

"Whip him," Paisley ordered. "Give that white trash ten good licks with your whip, Slater. It won't pay me for my cotton, but it'll keep his kind where they belong."

Joe saw the scare in Miz Susanna's eyes, the naked fear that he'd try to beg off by telling on her; he saw something else, too—a coldness that said plain she'd prove him a liar and get more hide cut off his back to boot. Head twisted, he hollered at Mister Paisley: "You better kill me, while you got the chance! You can't whip me like I'm a nigger."

"Show him, Slater," Paisley ordered. "Then haul him off my land."

When the first stroke bit into his back, Joe surged forward in the grip of the blacks and clamped his teeth against the scream that wanted to break out. It hurt; it cut into his hide and laid the meat bare and bloody. But there was a deeper agony in him, one he could balance the whip lashes against, and that helped Joe keep his teeth locked tight.

"Six," one of the blacks hissed into his ear. "Four mo' to go, white boy. You ain't gonna' make it."

Grunting when the next fiery rope seared his back, Joe forced an eye open. The buck hanging on to his right arm was the same one he'd busted with the oak limb, the black bastard who'd jammed his big whang into Miz Susanna.

"Three mo'." Jethro grinned as the firelight jiggled and

a sigh lifted from a ring of black, staring faces. "You 'bout to holler, boy, you 'bout to fall out and beg the man quit."

It was hard prying his teeth apart, but Joe got them open. "Fuck you, nigger."

Blood ran down his backbone and into his breeches, down the calves of his legs.

He took the rest, even the final, spiteful lash that drove him twisting and jerking against their sweaty grip. And he never cried out.

"Tote him crost the creek," the overseer spat. "Chunk him over and leave him be. But first—" the man dug cruel fingers into Joe's hair and bent his face up. "Boy, you keep your ass off in the piney woods, hear? You damn lucky Mister Paisley didn't string you up by the neck. You slip back here, I be first to haul on the rope."

They stumbled him through plowed ground, jerked him this way and that, the buck Jethro chuckling and poking at him. The other nigger eased him down into the creek and fanned cool water up over his ruined back. That hurt, too; anything that touched the flayed skin hurt.

That one said, "White boy, pay good mind. They flat kill you."

Jethro grunted as he stepped back. "Pay good mind— white trash."

Joe lifted his head slowly, doggedly; on his knees in the creek, bent over against the pain, he said, "I ain't about to forget."

And sitting his horse now, Joe Langston could feel again the bite of the blacksnake flash, the contempt of niggers, the old hurt reopening itself like a scab picked off a festering wound. She did it to him. She might have stopped it, begged him off, but she didn't; Miz Susanna protected herself, and her sweaty black stud.

"Goddamn," he said aloud, and as the horse moved under him, as the first spatter of rifle fire broke out ahead at the scalawag camp, Joe heeled his horse and threw him into a dead run at the screen of trees.

He flashed past the major, by the others waiting, and crashed through the brush, stupid blind and raging, reins in his teeth and the carbine ready. Straight at the fight he galloped, head-on for the shouting and shooting.

Dimly, he knew that someone was riding at his stirrup,

loosing the high-pitched Rebel yell, firing as Joe fired, at plunging horses and collapsing tents and scuttling figures.

Putting a ball through a running man, slashing down with the carbine barrel at a bobbing head, Joe caught a look at the rider who'd followed his maddened dash into the enemy camp.

It was Timmy Santee.

Chapter 8

Her saddlebags were stuffed with sundried catfish and
salted rabbit, for Marilee was frugal with her remaining
store of beans and fatback, and she'd spent a lot of time
and trouble gathering supplies from the woods she traveled through. For nearly a week, she'd eaten well and
added to her rations without seeing a soul as she moved
around the little towns of Woodville and Lessley. Now
she wasn't far from the river crossing at Fort Adams,
where it would be more difficult to keep out of sight.

She'd also practiced pitching her voice lower, and
walking with longer, slouching strides, more boylike.
When she was forced to take to the highway and make
for the ferry, she'd be sure to keep her face dirty and
hold it down. The eyepatch would help, and she was glad
she was taller than most women her age, because she had
a feeling she'd soon have to bluff her way through Yankee sentries.

If somebody had found the trooper she'd killed—or
what was left of him—they'd have no reason to suspect
young Marilee Bradburn or even know of her existence.
But if by some twist of fate the bluebellies were really
after her, word probably wouldn't have reached this far.

She felt almost safe as she came out upon the main road and fell in a goodly way behind a settler's wagon.

She and Bradburn had gotten to know each other well; they were closer now, living together as they had, dependent upon one another for food and safety and comfort. It was easy to love the great horse, but Marilee still didn't know his capabilities. How fast and how far could the stallion run, if he were pressed?

Ahead, the wagon clanged and rattled, and she rode slowly in its trailing of road dust, kerchief pulled up over her mouth and eyepatch in place.

Because of the noise the wagon made, she didn't hear them coming until they were close behind her. Glancing over one shoulder, Marilee saw four horsemen in Yankee blue, moving at a slow trot. She forced herself to sit easy, to keep the horse plodding along as if she wouldn't be bothered by the entire Northern army.

The leader pulled up beside her and slowed. "Hello, young fella'."

"Morning," Marilee answered, voice muffled and holding to the g.

"Sergeant Watkins," the man said, bluff and hearty behind his short black beard, "Wisconsin Volunteers. You heading for Texas?"

"Guess so," she mumbled.

"Lots of the boys going west," he said, pacing his rangy mount beside the stallion. "Bunch of unreconstructed Rebs, too, so best you be careful. They'll bushwhack you for wearing the blue, much less for that stud you're riding. Been mustered out long?"

Adjusting the kerchief, Marilee wished the man wasn't so talkative, so nosy. "Since Richmond," she said. "Lost my eye there."

"That's too bad." He rocked along with her, spurred boot almost touching hers. "You didn't get to see 'em give up at Appomattox, then. Most of 'em, anyhow—there was a bunch caught us by surprise and took to the hills. All units are keeping an eye out for 'em, though, and we'll pen 'em up before long."

"Yes," Marilee said, turning her head.

"Good thing they let you have your horse," the sergeant went on. "Funny thing—General Grant let the Johnny Rebs keep theirs, too—figured they'd need 'em to use for plowing. That's a whole lot of horse you're riding, boy. Wonder somebody else didn't get him while you were in hospital."

"I was lucky," Marilee mumbled. "Rode him in myself."

Behind them, other troopers shuffled along, sabers clanking, equipment creaking. Marilee leaned to one side to look beyond the wagon and caught a glint of sunlight upon broad, muddy water—the Mississippi River. Where was the ferry?

"Yessir," Watkins said, "if it hadn't been for Morgans like that one, we mighta' had a harder time with the Reb cavalry. Their thoroughbreds were fast, but when graze got scarce, they weakened quick. The Morgans, though —they just kept right on, fat and sassy as if they were getting plenty of grain and good hay. Ran the Secesh right in to the ground."

Marilee didn't say anything, and the sergeant took off his broad-brimmed hat to wipe at his forehead. "Wish we'd all been riding that breed. Say—what outfit did you ride with?"

Thinking fast, Marilee said, "The—the Fourth New Jersey."

From the corner of her eye, she saw the man put his hat back on and wedge it firmly into place. Then he put one hand on the hilt of his saber. "That right, boy? Now that's mighty peculiar, because the only regiments with horses like that—Morgan horses—were from Vermont and maybe Massachusetts. Pull up there—guess you better show me your mustering-out papers."

Nodding, Marilee nudged Bradburn to the side of the road and turned as if to fumble in a saddlebag. Her heart was racing and her breath turned ragged. The river was so close, but so very wide, its current tremendously powerful, and even if she could make the ferry. . . .

She had to try. Laying the reins left across Bradburn's neck, she legged his barrel and immediately the horse spun on his haunches, lifting his front feet off the ground to swing in an abrupt circle. Clamping both legs into his flanks, Marilee urged the stallion into a burst of speed. His forward leap almost flung her from the saddle, and they were across the road, flying past the wagon with a staccato roll of furious hoofbeats before the Yankee troopers realized she was gone.

Low along the horse's neck, his mane whipping her cheeks, wind whistling in her ears, Marilee rode hard, her crouched body flowing with Bradburn's. Faintly behind her, she heard an outraged yell, but no sound of shots. Down the road she sped, not having to push the horse, just hanging on. The river spread itself before them, wide and mighty, too broad to swim, its currents treacherous.

The ferry—she looked for it, for the log-and-plank dock. If it wasn't on this side, if it was tied up, she'd have to swing south and keep Bradburn pounding down the levee, hoping to get out of range before the sergeant and his men began shooting.

But there it was, bobbing away from the wharf, rocking out upon the river, a long, flat boat of planking laid across tarred kegs, a frail-looking railing around the sides. Lifting in the stirrups, she saw the oarsman manning his long, clumsy sweep at the stern, saw the men and a few horses clustered upon the raft. A strip of water was growing ever wider behind it as the ferry drifted out into the current.

She had to decide right now—to try for the ferry or pull Bradburn left and hope they could get away along the riverbank. And she didn't even know if the horse could jump.

"Come on, darlin'," she hissed into the stallion's ear, "if you miss this, we're dead."

Bradburn didn't hesitate when she gathered him, when she used the strength of her legs to help lift him. Roaring down across the dock, his hooves a clattering drumroll, the horse left smoothly, thrusting powerfully with his hind legs and reaching high with his forelegs.

For a breathless second, they seemed to hang in mid-air above the frothing yellow water—then the stallion's front feet struck planking and Marilee shifted her weight back, shortened him on the bit as he began to slide. But Bradburn got his hindquarters beneath him, practically squatting with his front legs out stiffly, and they skidded just far enough to throw his shoulder into a crowbait horse that nearly lost his balance and went over the side.

"Migawd," somebody said, and another man: "Damned near knocked us all into the river."

Trembling, she stepped down and pushed her horse into the crowd, looking back toward the wharf where bluecoat soldiers were just galloping up. Hands cupped to his mouth, Sergeant Watkins yelled, "You there—ferryman! Turn that thing around and bring him back!"

Heavy-shouldered, arms like tree trunks, the boatman spat a blob of tobacco juice into the water and hollered back, "Cain't! River won't let me."

"Damnit!" Sergeant Watkins waved his carbine in one hand. "Then get outa' the way so I can get a shot at him! That boy's a horse thief—that's a U.S. government mount he's riding!"

Poling harder, the boatman angled his ferry farther into the flowing river, and it picked up speed. "Pay you not to shoot, Yank. Mite crowded on this here raft."

The troopers were growing smaller, but Marilee could hear frustration in the sergeant's voice when he called out, "All right, damnit! But there's troops on the other landing, and they'll be waiting for him when I heliograph 'em!"

A grizzled old man leaned against his mule and said, "What's a helio—helio—whatever the hell he said?"

"A mirror thing to send messages with," the boatman answered, working his sweep with long strokes. "Hey, boy —guess you ain't clear away nohow."

The old man grunted. "Guess you ain't so comfortable in them blue pants, neither. Reckon you'd be easier in gray. When you stole that there horse, hope you knocked the fella' in the head."

Marilee's knees were shaking and she was panting. Hooking one arm around the stallion's neck, she said, "Killed him, I reckon. Ferryman—isn't there any way you can land upriver from the other dock? The Yankees want me kind of bad."

Only one hand on the sweep now, the big man thumbed back a drooping moustache to spit again. "Ain't possible— got to start upriver and angle acrost. Got mules on the other side to haul me back upstream alongside the bank, so I can get back."

Marilee leaned her face into Bradburn's mane. "I appreciate everybody gatherin' around me so they couldn't shoot."

Another man pushed back a shapeless gray hat. "Hell, Gen'l Lee said we was to lay down our arms. He didn't say nothin' about *helpin'* the damned bluebellies."

She could feel the power of the river beneath them, the speed of the raft as the current pushed it inexorably toward the far bank where another contingent of northern cavalry would be waiting for her. She hadn't expected the Mississippi to be so wide, maybe a full mile along here, and it rushed along with a terrible strength.

The old man with the mule said, "Killed the fella, huh? Jellicoe, I 'spect with a little help on that oar, you could swing up near the bank this side of the bend."

The boatman hunched his thick shoulders. "Not *that* near—no more'n a hundred yards or so."

Gray hat said, "Reckon you can try. Them Yanks on the dock can't see around the bend, and if that horse swims like he jumps—"

"Do he, boy?" Jellicoe asked.

"Don't know," Marilee said, "but we sure have to give it a try."

"Get on over here then," Jellicoe said. "Two, three you folks grab on and when I say pull, you pull your guts out."

The old man told Marilee, "Edge him over to the side, right about there. Make room, you folks—sidle around!"

She could see the shore approaching, but still so far away, separated from the raft by a threatening stretch of hissing river. Taking a deep breath, she climbed into the saddle and gathered reins. Bradburn looked down at the rushing water, ears thrust forward, blowing through distended nostrils. She patted his neck. "You can make it, boy. You *have* to make it for us."

The man with the mule said, "After you hit the water, best you come outa that saddle and hang on to his tail."

At the sweep, Jellicoe yelled, "Pull—*pull!* Get ready to jump, boy!"

"R-ready," Marilee called. "Ready as we'll ever be. And I thank you all."

"Might be thankin' us for your grave," the old man grunted, "but it appears like you got no choice."

"Now!" the boatman bellowed, and she squeezed Bradburn's chest with both legs, hard.

The stallion hesitated only a fraction of a second, then hurled himself up and out. They hit the river with a mighty splash, their heads going under dirty water, chill and foaming, to come up spluttering. Catching a breath, Marilee let go the reins and snatched at the wet flag of the horse's tail, kicking both feet and paddling with her free arm.

Bradburn swam powerfully, lunging at the water, hooves churning as he pushed them toward the bank. But the current tore at them, tried to sweep them farther down and around the bend that hid them from waiting troops. The stallion fought the river, battled it with all his strength, head out of the water and nostrils spread wide. Marilee struggled with him, kicking, chopping the water, her hand slipping inch by inch down the wet tail.

Her feet touched soft mud at the same moment Bradburn's hooves found a purchase, and when the stud lunged up on a crumbling bank of sand and clay, she lost her grip upon his tail and fell. One wildly flailing hand caught at something—a slippery root—and she dragged herself erect.

"Go on, Bradburn—go on!"

Hooves tearing at the loose earth, the horse pushed himself up a steep bank, flinging clumps of dirt behind, humping his back and climbing like an overgrown goat. Marilee sobbed with relief as she saw him up on the top, shaking himself with a rattle of stirrups, his sides heaving and his head held proud.

Clawing her way up, boots squishing and slipping in the mud, she reached flat ground and lay there, gasping for air. Oh, God, she thought, they'd made it—they had really made it.

She sat up and wiped water from her eyes. Miraculously, her hat was still in place, jammed down over her ears; she was sodden, and she pulled off her boots to drain water from them. The carbine and pistol would have to be cleaned, soon as she could find the time and dry moss to work with. Her supplies—the cornmeal might be saved, if she could spread it to dry; beans and bacon and dried meat would be all right, but her salt would have dissolved in the river. Somehow, she'd have to replace that.

Weak-legged, she stood up and leaned against the horse's shoulder. "You—you're beautiful," she panted. "Oh, Bradburn, you're the finest horse in the world, brave and strong and smart. You got us onto the ferry and out of the river, and now we're in Louisiana."

Turning, Marilee looked back across the water to her native land, toward Mississippi. "And you'll carry us back," she said. "I just know you'll take us to Texas and bring us back home. I swear I'll make it all up to you then, Bradburn—I swear it."

Back up in the saddle, she looked at the sky and moved the horse into the cover of willow trees, pointing southwest. All the dampness on her cheeks didn't come from the river.

Chapter 9

Kicking out of the stirrups, Joe Langston lit running as his horse swerved away. He jacked another shell into the Sharps and let fly at a skinny man in a Confederate coat, but Yankee breeches. The man fell over, and Joe wheeled to pump another round at a fat man crawling from a collapsed tent.

Horses squealed and reared, and something had already caught fire. When the carbine clicked empty, Joe slicked out the handgun and dropped two men with it; the last one fell in the fire and kicked some. Behind him, somebody screamed, and he spun around, but the wounded man was one of the troop.

Almost as fast as it started, the fight was near about over. A gun popped on the far edge of the camp, and a man yelled hoarsely. A riderless horse galloped by wildly, eyes rolling white.

"Joe, Joe!" Timmy Santee stood straddle of a bedroll, his long saber poked out to hold a scalawag at its point. On the ground, the man lay still, glaring up at the boy. "Joe—I got me one! Look here, I caught me a prisoner."

Taking two long strides, Joe reached the boy just as

Timmy turned his head to grin at him. He saw the scalawag move, the hairy hand coming up with a pistol in it,
and slammed into Timmy Santee, knocking the boy
aside as the gun went off. Deftly, he punched a bullet
between staring black eyes and snapped the shaggy head
back, then hammered another shot into the man's broad
chest, the Colt live and accurate in his fist. When he
whipped back around, Timmy was on his knees, the saber on the ground. The boy was clutching his right arm,
the wounded arm, and new blood was inching out over his
fingers like red spiderlegs.

Before going to the boy, Joe looked all around. All he
saw moving was the major's men, catching up their
horses, turning over bodies with boot toes, rummaging
among bedrolls and trampled tents. He jacked out spent
shells and reloaded his handgun.

He stood over Timmy, pistol hanging loosely at his
side. "Boy," he said, "ain't you got no goddamned sense
atall? What the hell you mean, you got you a prisoner?
You think this was some kind of gentleman soldier battle?"

Face going pale, Timmy squeezed his arm harder. "I
—he said he gave up."

"And you didn't see did he have a gun. That goddamn saber. You dumb youngun, ain't nobody ever told
you not to give *nobody* a chance to kill you? How bad's
that arm?"

"Pretty bad, I reckon," Timmy muttered. "Hadn't been
for you, he'da got me in the belly. I—I'm beholden, Joe."

"You ain't beholden, you're stupid," Joe said. "Here,
I'll take a look at it."

Joe worked the jacket down and slit the shirt with his
knife. "Same damned arm," he said. "Wasn't healed up
yet, and you had to get yourself busted spang in it."

"H-how's it look?" The boy's voice wobbled.

"Won't lie to you none; it's a mess. Ball went on
through, and took some bone, but you ain't bleedin' bad.
Set still while I go find some whiskey; them woods runners bound to have some around."

Kicking aside a tent, turning over a saddle, and stepping across a pair of corpses, Joe found a bottle and uncorked it to sniff. He looked up at Major Ainsworth sitting
his horse above him.

"Drink hearty," the major said. "You deserve it, leading the charge that way. I didn't really expect that of you, Langston."

"I didn't either," Joe said. "This bustskull is for the youngun—took one in the arm tryin' to be a goddamn *gentleman* with a saber."

Leaning to rub his stumped leg, Ainsworth was gray-faced. "There are uses for the saber, but I noticed you're an expert with a pistol. You never said who you rode with during the war, where you learned to use a handgun that way."

"That's right," Joe answered, "I didn't." He brushed past to bend over a body and rip a bandanna from around its neck, to feel in pockets until he found a plug of tobacco.

"Lie back, Timmy," he said, sopping the kerchief in white whiskey and wringing it out. "This is goin' to smart some." Chewing the tobacco, he made a mush of it while pouring strong whiskey into the open wound, eyes going narrow at the fanned little splinters of bone he found there. Fool boy; be mighty lucky if that arm didn't have to come off, and luckier yet did he live through an amputation.

"Uuuhhh!" Timmy grated when the raw alcohol burned into torn flesh, then clamped his jaws manfully against making any more noise. Sweat glistened over his set face.

Joe packed tobacco into the wound and bound it tightly with the bandanna, pouring more whiskey over it. "Best I can do; ain't no sawbones with this troop." Taking a long swallow of the fiery stuff, he passed the bottle to Timmy.

"Better n-not," the boy said. "I'm apt to be sick as it is. Help me up and I can sit my saddle, though."

"You'll have to—looks like the major is in a hurry. I'll catch up our horses."

"Joe—"

"Yeah?"

"I just knew you was a hero. When you took off on the charge, I was right proud to ride with you."

"Oh, hogshit," Joe said. "I was just mad at somethin' else, and cuttin' the fool. Here—let me hist you up. Now you hang on while I find booty for us, before them others get it all."

One body yielded a little hide sack of goldpieces, maybe a hundred dollars' worth—another some cigars. Joe lighted one and went on methodically turning out pockets and emptying saddlebags. He found a sack of corn and hefted it up behind his saddle, looping a strip of rawhide to hold it steady. There wasn't a pistol good as his to be found, but he changed hats with a dead man. Forage caps didn't keep off sun nor rain, but this one had a wide brim and a high crown that would do both jobs.

Another flat bottle of stump whiskey and a pretty good belt knife, half a side of smoked bacon; the scalawags had done right good for themselves. He was squatting to draw a pair of high boots off a gutshot man when the major loomed over him again.

"Pistoling's not the only thing you're good at," Ainsworth said tautly. "You've stripped bodies before."

Joe sat down and pulled on the boots; they fit. He said, "This fella can't use 'em no more, and I can."

"We had to hit this camp," Ainsworth said, "but we take only what's necessary to our mission. We're not scavengers like them—we're Confederate soldiers."

Standing up and stamping one foot at a time to get the feel of his new boots, Joe said, "That right? Better take you a good look around, major. All these boys ain't genuine Stars and Bars troopers; some of 'em's outlaws no better'n these scalawags, and I reckon you ought to be glad to have 'em. The South lost its war usin' genuine soldier boys, and if you mean to win one in Mexico, best you forget saber charges and bugle calls and not turnin' out pockets."

Mouth tight, the major wheeled his horse away to shout orders, shouldering the black gelding among men busy at looting. A fire sprang up, then another. Joe was cramming his saddlebags and using Timmy Santee's for the overflow when he heard Ainsworth call out.

"Quiet, you men—quiet, now! We have no time to bury these corpses, but for the sake of decency, I'll say a few words over them before we ride on."

Joe swung up into his saddle. "You believe that?" he asked Timmy. "No wonder them gentry officers lost the damned war."

The boy was taking off his hat when Joe grabbed his reins and jogged back for the road, hauling Timmy's horse behind him. Out of the brush, he pulled them up. "Look back yonder at the smoke and figure how far off somebody else can see it. Little while ago, he was callin' them buzzards and murderers, now he's sayin' almighty grace over 'em. Bein' dead don't change 'em none, and I don't reckon Bible words will slip that bunch through the pearly gates."

Timmy swayed in his saddle, face white and sweating. Joe uncorked the whiskey and passed. "Take you a good big swallow—here's water to go with it. There—ought to burn your guts so you forget your arm a spell."

Strengthened, the boy walked his horse beside Joe, sitting tall as he could, and Joe shook his head. "If it pains you a heap, cuss out loud—won't nobody mind."

"Reckon I can make it good as anybody," Timmy said. "You don't have to hold my hand or give me no sugar tit. I'm a man grown, same as you."

Watching the boy's pale, strained face, for a moment Joe was back in that plantation yard with flames from fired cotton cribs leaping into a tortured night sky. He was there with his arms jerked wide and held fast by two chunky slaves while the whip chewed into his back. And he knew how Timmy Santee felt, knew what the youngun had to prove to himself. Timmy was just a mite younger than he'd been that night, all of sixteen years old and being blacksnaked like a runaway nigger. He wouldn't give them the satisfaction of hearing him bleat like a gelded ram.

"All right, boy," Joe said softly. "Here comes the troop now—we just got us a headstart on them."

Loping past, Major Ainsworth stabbed at Joe with hard eyes, and Joe knew he'd made a big mistake by calling attention to himself. The major wouldn't forget his face nor his mouth. But if the man got too military, Joe would just peel off from the column and go his own way, Mexico be damned. Like as not, there was money to be found in Texas just as well.

Horses walked on, and Joe counted ahead with his eyes. They'd lost a man or two back yonder, too, and he could see one hunkered over in his saddle. He looked at Timmy. "Time we stop at a creek, I'll wet down your arm again."

"I'll cut it," the boy said. "I'll purely cut it, Joe. Just got to get to Mexico and make her proud of me, bring somethin' home to May. I sure wish I could handle a short gun like you do—be easier to shoot with one hand and grab with the other."

"Now you're gettin' the idea," Joe said. "I'll learn you."

They rocked along in silence for a while, and Joe could smell horse sweat, dust, and the freshness of pine trees. Cigar smoke was good in his mouth, and he smelled that, too.

Timmy said, "What's it like to be with a woman, Joe? I mean sure enough *be* with her. Lately I been thinkin' on that a lot. I mean—well, May ain't that kind of girl, but she was wantin' to, afore I left to get in the war. I could tell she was wantin' to, but I was kinda scared."

Like being belly-deep in a creek, Joe thought; like feeling a tremble run all through you when you stared up at the most beautiful woman you ever saw and saw her fingers opening her bodice so the round, white breasts jumped out. He said, "Everybody's scared, the first time."

Holding his hand over the hurt arm, Timmy said, "Do you have to do anything special? It ain't like a bull mountin' a cow, is it?"

"Somethin' like," Joe said. "Or a rooster topping a hen, only a woman don't run and holler and flutter her wings."

"It lasts longer, don't it? I'd hate to think it got over so quick. With my girl, I'd want it to last a long time."

Joe nodded and chewed on his cigar. "It can do that, too—all depends on you and the woman." With an experienced woman telling him it was all right to be quick the first time, hissing into his ear to keep right on, it would get better. Miz Susanna was right; it just kept getting better and better, until he thought he couldn't stand it being so damned good.

"Does it hurt her?" Timmy asked.

"Damned if I know, boy. Never had me a virgin, and I ain't all that sure I want to try one on for size."

"I just keep thinkin' on it," Timmy said. "Maybe I should of done it with May while I had the chance. Might be a long time now—might be I won't see her again."

Glancing sharply at the boy, Joe said, "You can cut it, remember? It's certain sure you'll get back to your girl, come ridin' up on a fine Mexican horse with silver on the saddle and gold in your pockets."

"Reckon?" Timmy said, and his chin dropped on his chest.

Joe rode close, watching in case the boy tilted sideways out of his saddle, ready to grab him if he did. What the hell was he lying to the youngun for, and how come he was babying him along like he was Timmy Santee's own pa? He saw slow blood oozing down to blot the jacket sleeve and pulled deeply upon his cigar before throwing the butt into the dusty road. That's what came of letting somebody get close to you, so you got responsible for him. The poor little bastard was dreaming of his girl back home, a girl who was probably lying up with some blue-belly soldier right now, wiggling on his big cod like Timmy Santee never lived. Silver saddle and gold in his pockets, hogshit; be almighty lucky if the boy didn't get buried before he got his first peep at Mexico.

About three hours later, he helped the boy from the saddle and stretched him out on grass close to a clear little creek. Filling their canteens with fresh water, Joe made a twig fire and rubbed fatback into a skillet before slicing bacon to fry.

"Guess I don't want much to eat," Timmy said.

Busy sloshing whiskey over the wounded arm, Joe said, " 'Spect you better. Looks like the major is plannin' to ride half the night, and bellies could get flat afore we stop again."

Timmy slowly chewed bacon, sitting with his back against a tree trunk. "We must be gettin' close to Texas."

"Ain't sure," Joe said, "but I calculate we're somewhere in Louisiana. We don't run into a passel of Yanks, might reach Texas in a week or so."

"Seems like it's so far off," Timmy said, cradling his arm, and putting his head back.

Cleaning the skillet with sand and rinsing it in the creek, Joe thought it was no farther than the trails he'd laid since cutting out from Alabama the first time. His back had healed slowly, after that whipping from the Paisley overseer, his ma rubbing hog grease into the cuts and his pa saying nothing except that a man ought to stay with his own kind and keep away from the gentry.

There was a long gun in the shack, and Joe felt bad

about taking it, but the shotgun would bring down enough winter meat for the family after he was gone. He didn't take much else, just powder and shot and a raggedy quilt —and the mule. Ornery and apt to kick a man's head off, was he careless, the mule was long-legged and could hold to the same lope all day long. Joe figured he'd need to cover ground after he did what he had to.

He didn't get a shot until after daylight, when the slaves were being herded out to the fields, and it was a good thing the buck Jethro wasn't being used for stud that day. Good thing, too, that he was out front, strutting biggity ahead of the others. It gave Joe time to charge the old muzzle loader before Slater came galloping up on his horse to see what was the matter.

The first ball took Jethro through the head so fast and hard that the nigger died with a wetlipped grin still on his face. The rest of them ran around like chickens when a hawk sailed over, and there came old blacksnake Slater, whip coiled in his fist, jerking the horse around and hollering what the hell.

Joe got him clean, too, knocking the man off his horse with a neck shot. Powdersmoke rolling around him in the brush, Joe said, "Told you bastards I wasn't about to forget."

Then he lit a shuck on the mule, keeping to the woods all day long and far into the night. He'd never figured on getting to old man Paisley, nor to Miz Susanna, and reckoned he was about even for the scars on his back. Time they put dogs after him, Joe was long gone, walking the mule through every creek and pond he came to, throwing hounds off the scent, staying in the brush and finding what he could to eat.

Because he'd talked to Miz Susanna about Mobile, he didn't head there, but kept on until he got clear down to New Orleans, a ragged country boy straddled bareback on a mule, both of them leaned down by hard travel. But he had the long gun to swap and the mule to sell and sand enough in him to work on the docks, sweating alongside free niggers for nigger pay. Joe Langston made out, and the law never came looking for him—not for the Alabama killings anyway.

Timmy Santee was asleep when the major walked his

horse up. "Can the boy make it?" Ainsworth asked softly.

"Holdin' up right good."

"For now," the major said. "I'm leaving John Mixon here—he's shot through the body."

"The youngun can cut it," Joe said, "unless his arm festers. He can't make it back home by himself, nohow."

"It's sad," Ainsworth said. "No doctor, no medicines— any man badly wounded will have to be abandoned, for military expediency."

"That what you call it?"

The major bent forward to rub his cutoff leg. "I expect the same, if it happens to me. And so do you, Langston. I've heard some whispers about you, about who you rode with."

Joe nodded. "That fella with the red beard—thought I saw him somewheres afore. Got him a mouth under all that hair."

"I don't give a damn about your past," Ainsworth said. "If Quantrill himself was here, I'd make him second in command. We need guns like yours, if we're going to complete our mission. Your peculiar talents are in demand right now, so if that boy can stay in the saddle on his own, you ride out as a scout. I imagine that *you* won't be out looking for trouble and can steer the command around any."

Pulling out a cigar, Joe stuck it in his teeth. "Reckon you imagine right, major. But I just take my turn and no more. *I* aim to get to Mexico, even if none of these other horse soldiers do."

Ainsworth adjusted his hat. "Just so you don't let young Santee become a burden that keeps you from your duty."

"Ain't nobody a burden to me," Joe said, and watched the major walk his horse off, stiff in the saddle, proud as if his uniform wasn't patched and dirty, uppity as if he still owned a big, rich plantation.

"Duty," Joe said, and spat.

Chapter 10

Water was refreshingly cool on her naked body, stroking away grime with flowing fingers, and Marilee luxuriated in the running creek. She scrubbed at her hair and at her flesh, thinking that she would have to find soap somewhere; there'd never be time to make any.

The rivulet was small, the hole she was using as a bath not very deep, but she appreciated the chance to feel clean again. Her clothes were drying on willow bushes, and Bradburn was grazing close by, freed of saddle and bridle, content to stay close to her. Splashing her face, Marilee watched sun-dappled rippling water and saw brilliantly hued dragonflies darting along the surface farther downstream, wildflowers nodding along the bank. Her weapons were safe against a fallen blue gum tree, the carbine propped, pistol lying atop peeling bark.

She felt good, relieved that she had been able to put many miles between herself and pursuing Yankees, proud and amazed at the tireless power, the lasting ability of the stallion that had carried her far and fast. Bradburn could jump and swim; he had blinding speed and stamina; above all, he was smart and honest, giving his all when asked.

Smiling over at him, she lay back and let water caress her flesh. So far, they had enough to eat, and there'd be plenty of rich grass for Bradburn on the way, plenty of game for her. Marilee glanced up at an angle of daffodil sun filtering through a waving canopy of tree limbs and decided she should get moving. Standing up, she waded to the bank and brushed water from her body with her hands, turning slowly so the sun would help dry her.

Something was wrong: off in the brush, a mockingbird stopped in mid-trill and a blue jay cursed. A tingle ran across her bare skin as Marilee sensed the wrongness and looked sharply around at the circling trees, at the stallion with his head thrown high and his ears pricked forward. Bradburn was staring at the blue gum log, and she hesitated for just a moment too long before lunging for the pistol there.

As if he'd vaulted right out of the earth itself, a man raised himself behind the log and slapped aside her handgun. Snatching instead at the carbine, Marilee got one hand on the barrel before it was twisted roughly away from her. She staggered back along the creekbank.

The man was tall and wide across the shoulders, narrow in the hips, and flat of belly. The upper part of his face was tanned, his jaw lighter in color, as if he'd recently shaved off a beard. A long, narrow scar pulled one corner of his mouth up slightly in a cynical grin.

Trying to control her trembling, Marilee crossed her hands over her mound, her shoulders hunching involuntarily in a hopeless attempt to hide her naked breasts. But the man's eyes weren't searching over her exposed body; they were reaching into her own. They were sleepy, hooded eyes of a pale and nearly colorless blue, strange eyes set behind long, black lashes. Marilee caught her breath at the impact of them.

"Pretty picture," he said in a deep, lazy voice that seemed to lift effortlessly from his broad chest. "Right pretty picture." Turning his leonine head without taking those watchful eyes from her, he called out: "Come on in, boys! It's just a naked gal."

Throat constricted, Marilee said, "Please, my clothes—"

"Part Yankee clothes and part rags," he said, propping one boot on the log and grinning wolfishly at her. "You look better without 'em."

"You—you're a Confederate," she said quickly. She might be able to reach the carbine; he didn't have a pistol in his hand. It swung holstered at his hip. "So am I. Please let me get dressed, and I'll explain."

He tilted back a wide hat with his left hand, exposing a wavy mass of long hair glistening blueblack as a raven's wing. "And spoil it for the boys? Reckon they deserve a good look, too."

Tensed, she heard them coming through the brush—two other men in gray, unshaven faces stretched grinning as they approached, rifles swinging in their hands. They all wore butternut, *looked* like Southern soldiers, but were they? Confederates were supposed to have laid down their arms at Appomattox courthouse after General Lee surrendered his sword, but these men were uniformed and armed. They could be outlaws, marauding scalawags using the gray as an excuse to plunder and kill—to rape.

"Whooie!" a redbearded man said. "Ain't she purely somethin'? Slick and pretty as a button. Move your hands, gal—I want to see if'n the hair in your crotch is the same as your head."

Another man sidled around her, a plug of tobacco in his cheek, beady-eyed and smirking. The one at the log still propped a boot casually there, languid and amused. "Funny color, ain't it? Like silver—like she's a good-kept ol' woman, only them tits say she's young and sassy."

Redbeard grunted. "Got her a Yankee horse yonder. Any bluebelly friend close by, gal?"

"I—I'm alone," Marilee said, her skin cold now, gauging the distance between her bare feet and the flung-aside carbine. "I'm running from the Yankees and I'm alone."

"Some skinny," Redbeard said. "Me, I usually like 'em with more meat on the bone—gives a man more to hang on to. But I reckon she'll do." He glanced at the tall man. "You found her, Langston—gives you first pick."

She couldn't believe a man could be so quick. One moment he was lounging at the fallen log, but when she dove for the carbine, he beat her to it by a full arm's length. Crouching, she glared up at him, hating him for what he was, despising them all even as the fear unfolded cold petals deep within her stomach.

"Damned if it ain't the same silver hair," the nondescript man whistled. "Got more fluff to it, though."

Oh, God—wasn't there a decent man left in the whole South, a single gentleman who wouldn't take advantage of a woman alone? This bunch of rabble had found her, far off any beaten track, and she could see what they meant to do with her. Again, oh, Lord—forcing their dirty flesh into her body, hurting and ravishing her, making her filthy all over again. Marilee wanted to be sick, to throw up the breakfast she'd eaten. It wouldn't do any good to plead with them; she'd tried that before with their animal kind—tearful with the Yankee who'd raped her, trying to talk the rednecks out of it. Nothing had helped—only the guns she'd so foolishly left beyond her reach.

"Get dressed," the one called Langston said, and her mouth fell open in surprise.

"Now look here," Redbeard said, "if you don't want to cod her, me and ol' Jessup sure as hell do."

"Yeah, yeah," Jessup said, prominent Adam's apple bobbing. "I ain't had me no nooky since I come up on a nigger wench in Virginia."

Langston held Marilee's carbine. He said, "She's got a horse branded U.S. and Yankee gear to boot. Maybe she got 'em close by."

"Hell." Redbeard spat. "And maybe she screwed for 'em. What difference do it make? I ain't fixin' to let no ass like that get away."

Marilee stayed where she was, hunkered down, glancing back and forth at the men with something like hope rising in her heart. The one with the pale, hooded eyes seemed to get sleepy, going all slouched and lazy, but he said almost in a whisper, "You're fixin' to get yourself dead. Seems you run off at the mouth, Blodgett. Like you done to the major about me."

She saw Redbeard go stiff, but the man carefully kept his rifle at his side. "So that's how come you picked me'n Jessup to scout with you. So's nobody could tell about you and Quantrill and the James boys and all the rest of it. You mean to drop both of us, bigod."

Langston was easy as a cat, but Marilee could sense the coiled snake waiting within the man. He said, "Picked you woods runners because you're careful of your hides —did I want you, I'da left you dead in your blankets.

98

The major knows some about me, thanks to you, but that don't make no never mind now."

Marilee heard Jessup's voice, shaky but venomous. "You want her all to yourself, that's what."

Marilee thought that Langston was smiling, but she couldn't be sure; his eyes weren't. He drawled, "You want her bad, Jessup? Or you got your eye on that fine horse more?"

The quiet pulled itself taut, stretching until she thought it was going to explode in sudden, bloody action. Then softly, Langston said, "Told you to get dressed, gal."

She moved carefully, not disturbing the delicate balance of them, suddenly grateful to the big man. Marilee didn't feel their eyes upon her as she hurriedly pulled on her clothes; they were busy watching each other.

"All right, all *right,"* Blodgett said then. "It ain't worth goin' up against you, just for a piece of ass—not for no horse, neither."

She moved to his side as the tension eased. "Thank you—I'll catch up my horse and be on my way."

Putting those pale eyes on her, he said, "You're comin' with us. There's more behind us."

"But—but *why?* I can make out on my own."

"You know anything about herbs and carin' for hurt folks?"

Marilee frowned. "Some, I guess. But what's that got to do with—"

"Got a boy back yonder needs tendin'," he said. "So I'm givin' you the doubt. Ain't made up my mind whether you're highnose gentry or plain folk. You talk like you come out of a big white house, but you went for this gun like you know somethin' about it. Fancy plantation ladies do their fightin' different. Catch up your horse."

He had her weapons, so she couldn't bolt when she had Bradburn saddled and bridled. He'd said there were more soldiers behind him, and maybe she would be safer in the protection of their numbers; possibly there might be an officer among them, a real Southerner.

"You two go on ahead," Langston said when they were all mounted, and she knew he didn't want the other men behind him.

As they moved through the woods, Marilee kept eyeing him slyly. He was handsome, she thought; not downright pretty as a few men she'd known, not even conventionally handsome as Robbie Dee Crownover, but with a certain wild beauty in his face. His long jaw wasn't quite square, but she'd seen it set and knew the danger that lay just under his skin. She hadn't met another man with such Indian black hair and light blue eyes; thinking on it, Marilee decided there was somewhat of an Indian cast to his features —high cheekbones and an aquiline nose. This Langston's mouth was finely sculptured, the lower lip a shade too full for a man, sultry-looking.

When he opened those lips to put a cigar between them, she saw that his teeth were white and even, and wondered what he would be like if he ever truly smiled, if his somber, sleepy eyes could possibly light up.

This man had saved her from rape; Marilee didn't doubt that for a moment, even though he'd looked upon her with lust himself, been so bawdily casual about finding her naked at the creek. He hadn't let her get dressed right away, because the "other boys deserved a look, too." Yet, when they had been so ready to ravish her, Langston called them off; more than that—he'd dared them to try it.

She glanced at him again as he bobbed loosely on his horse beside her, remembering what the redbearded Blodgett had said about Quantrill and the James boys. Had this man deliberately used her as bait, to draw the others into a gunfight? Or had he challenged them simply to prove his authority over them, his domination?

A locust whirred in a chinaberry tree, and she flinched at its nearness. He'd sneaked up on her without a sound, not even alerting Bradburn until he was up close, and tormented her into thinking he would join the others in raping her. For a terrified few minutes, she'd been certain he wanted her body as much as the others had.

"My—my name is Marilee," she said. "Marilee Bradburn, from Mississippi."

"Joe Langston," he said. "The Yankees really after you?"

"Yes. I—something happened, and I took this horse and ran."

"Good horse," he said. "Better'n anything in the troop. Best you keep a close eye on him. One of them Morgans, ain't he?"

She nodded, glad she didn't have to wear the eyepatch now, that she didn't have to disguise her femininity.

"That's what a sergeant said, just before we outran him and his squad. I—look, Joe Langston, we're ridin' along and talking just as if nothing happened back there. But I don't really feel calm. I know how much I owe you for not lettin' them—"

"Had it in mind myself," he said, cigar clenched between white teeth. "But I never had to rape a woman yet, and if I do, it won't be with a pack. For a minute there, if them others hadn't been out on the flanks—well, you look a whole lot like somebody I used to know. Not a spittin' image of her, understand, but here and there just about the same. Same kind of long, fine legs and high, round gourds. If your hair was gold instead of silverlike, and your eyes blue instead of green—I might have run off them others and topped you good."

Marilee drew a sharp breath. "Then I would have tried to kill you."

He looked at her, nodded, then passed across her carbine. She pushed it into the saddle sheath and held out her hand for the pistol. As Joe gave it to her, she saw his teeth flash in amusement—only a quick smile, but one that seemed to transform his entire face. It melted his iceblue eyes and softened him, but only for a second before the mask settled into place again. Or perhaps the softness was the mask and the hard watchfulness his real face.

Joe said, "That ain't the best handgun around. First change you get, swap it for a Colt. Mean that much to you, gettin' stuck by a man? Must be you still got your cherry."

Angered, she said, "That's somethin' I won't discuss with you, or anyone else." He was arrogant and crude, but an enigma, too, composed of more than his surface parts; Marilee could sense complications in him, baffling and—no, she shook her head in denial—no, not all that interesting. Because he'd saved her from rape, she was making him a figure larger than life.

Obviously, the man was an uneducated redneck, of the same class and cut as the trash who had tried to maul her back at the cabin. Joe Langston was perhaps stronger, with battle-hardened steel in him, and had strange quirks that shifted him from lust to challenge. But he had never been a gentleman and never could be.

They came out into a clearing and Joe pointed to a sheet stretched between saplings. "Yonder's the boss man.

'Spect he wants to talk to you, ask about your horse and guns. Soon's he gets done, I'd 'preciate it did you come see to a hurt boy."

Not escorting her to the man who rose painfully from a tree stump, not waiting for an answer from her, Joe Langston trotted his horse across the camp and left her staring after him.

The thin officer propped himself on a cane, sweeping his hat from his head and making a bow. "Bless me, if it isn't a lady. My pardon, miss, for not walking to meet you. I'm somewhat incapacitated. Wilson—" he gestured with the plumed hat—"take the lady's horse."

"Please don't take him far," Marilee said as she stepped down and handed the reins to a gaping young man. "He's used to me." Feeling awkward in her swaddling breeches and too-big boots, boyish with her chopped hair, Marilee approached the courtly officer, knowing at once that he was one of her own kind.

He bowed over her extended hand. "Your servant, ma'am. I'm Major Fitzhugh Ainsworth, at your service."

"Marilee Bradburn," she said, resisting an ingrained impulse to curtsy. "I'm grateful to your men for findin' me, major."

"Ah, yes," he said, "a lady traveling alone in these perilous times—" Lifting an eyebrow, he said, "Bradburn, Bradburn—might you be kin to Colonel Wayne Bradburn of Mississippi?"

Gracefully as she could, she took the seat he offered as if it were a luxurious chair, instead of an old pine stump. "My father, sir."

"Of course," Ainsworth said, leaning on his cane. "Bradburn Plantation. Your father was a courageous man, and his loss a blow to our cause. I was with him at Corinth. But please tell me, why are you alone in this wilderness?"

Running her hands helplessly over her hair, Marilee said, "And riding a Yankee horse? Circumstances, sir—I was driven from my land by Yankees, fleeing for my life —and more." It was amazing, she thought, how easily she could slip back into the old, patterned ways of speech, the parlor phrasings and cadences rolling deftly from her tongue. Marilee felt good about it.

The major clucked sympathetically. "My condolences, ma'am. The Yankees—" He gestured with his hat.

"They're why this troop is retaining the honor of the Confederacy, why we refused to surrender. I mean to take this command to the court of the Emperor Maximilian in Mexico City, to offer our services against the rabble."

Marilee folded her hands in her lap. "How gallant, how truly Southern. We can never be defeated, so long as there are men like you, Major Ainsworth."

"Thank you, ma'am. We are *not* defeated, and others will come to join us after we're regrouped. With the help of the emperor, a new Confederacy may rise in the Western territories, new strength gathered, and someday——"

"Ah, yes," she sighed. "Our plantations will belong to us again, and life will be as it used to be, as it was meant to be."

Major Ainsworth bowed again. "Spoken like a true daughter of the South, ma'am. I hope you'll allow me to offer my protection."

"Gratefully, sir—most gratefully. I have no place to go, but I wouldn't burden you for the world. One of your men said you have a wounded soldier, and perhaps I can attend him."

Ainsworth hesitated. "The boy may soon be beyond help, but of course you may try. I'll have a man escort you to him, and I hope you'll join me for supper. Poor fare for a lady of quality, I'm afraid, but all I can presently offer. It'll be a delight to share civilized conversation with someone so lovely. It's been a long time."

Marilee rose from the stump and gave him her hand. "I wish——but of course I accept your kind invitation, sir."

"Langston," the major said brusquely, "take this lady to young Santee, and see to it that she's not molested in any way. I'll see to her accommodations for tonight."

Joe Langston only grunted, and strode off ahead of her. Following his long-legged, deceptively lazy walk, Marilee kept her head high as if she were wearing crinoline and lace. For a little while, she'd felt almost as if she were home again, in her own ballroom.

Leaning against a tree, Langston jerked a thumb at a slim figure on the ground, a towhead boy propped against a saddle set in the shade. "This here's Timmy Santee—ma'am. If you mean to dirty your hands, that is."

She frowned up at him. "Joe, what do you mean? I just——"

"See to the boy," he said sharply. "Could be you learned somethin' about doctorin' from doin' for sick niggers on your plantation."

"W-why, yes," she said. "How'd you know that? Mama used to carry me with her to the quarters when—"

"Some field hand got his back sliced to bloody ribbons by your overseer." Joe's eyes were hooded, gone chill. "Hell, I just been gone too long. I shoulda seen it from the first. The major, he knowed right off. Hey, boy—hey there, Timmy Santee, ain't you the luckiest little ol' redneck? You got a sure enough *lady* to look after you."

Unbelieving, Marilee stared at him. "Joe Langston, I don't know what—"

He turned away, his voice coming back to her, flat and hard: "A goddamn *lady*."

Chapter 11

He had to lead her horse from the picket rope, because the big stud would take no foolishness from lesser horses crowding him. Yet the Morgan was docile enough as Joe brought him back to the trees where he'd left the woman tending to Timmy Santee. Tying off the stud in a clump of bushes to keep him busy, Joe loosened the cinch and stood back to watch Miz Marilee of Bradburn Plantation.

She was sitting beside Timmy, talking softly to the boy while she worked off the bandanna wrapped around his swollen arm. Even with her hair whacked off to her ears and sticking up every which way, wearing those floppy clothes and boots made for a man, she was still pretty enough to hurt a man's eyes. Joe couldn't help wondering how she'd look with her hair grown natural down her slim back, and he couldn't keep from seeing her inside his head, the way he'd caught her at the creek.

Sunshine had wrapped her sleek, naked body then, made her shine like she was polished from head to toe; it had reflected off little beads of water on her pearly skin and glittered like a handful of diamonds in the silvered curling of her mound. Joe shook his head, but the picture of that moment wouldn't go away, the long, clean lines of her standing there like a finebred filly.

She was a whole lot like Miz Susanna, too much so. The same be-damned-to-you pride of her and the way she held her head; soft, damp mouth and rosy pink nipples, heat spreading out from her body that you could *feel* clear across a creek. And, of course, this one was a lady of quality, too.

And there was that special silken voice with a little breathless catch to it when she talked to Timmy, asking him if it hurt, how his arm felt. Something like Miz Susanna's, but enough different to be more bothersome.

The boy had jumped awake when she kneeled beside him to touch his forehead, staring bugeyed up at her like she was some kind of storybook vision. Joe listened to Timmy now, heard him being the manly and wounded soldier.

"You—you don't have to do that, ma'am," Timmy said, sitting up with his arm damned near killing him and not willing to show it. "I can make out just fine."

"Sure you can," she said, and Joe watched her struggle to keep her face unchanged when she saw the ugliness of the wound, when she smelled the greenrot stink of it. Ladies weren't used to battlefield stink; they got the vapors and breathed lavender from lace handkerchiefs, or honeysuckle. Oh, hell yes, honeysuckle.

Standing close over them, Joe told himself it was because of the boy and said, "I got some more whiskey to pour in there."

"It'll help, I reckon," she said. "I wish we had some comfrey roots. They might be kind of hard to find, but camphor could do for a while."

"I know camphor trees," Joe said, after one glance at the leaking hole in Timmy's arm. "Ma used to squeeze the balls for juice and put it on burns. I'll keep on the lookout for some." Uncorking the whiskey bottle, he started to splash liquid into the boy's wound, but handed her the job instead.

Breath hissed sharply between Timmy's teeth when the stuff burned into blueblack flesh, and his thin body went stiff; sweat popped out all over his face. When he could talk, he said, "Smarts a mite."

She used her bandanna, still damp from washing in the

creek, to mop his face. "My mother used to say salt was real good for hurts like this."

"I'll get some," Joe said, when she looked greeneyed up at him. She was doing all right, he had to admit; she wasn't going white and ready to puke But he wondered if she could keep it up, how she'd act when that arm got so big its skin would split and drip pus that was more black than yellow.

Women off hardscrabble farms grew up to things like that; the gentry never had to. When one of *them* got sick, here came a real doctor with his black bag lickety-split. Poor folk did for themselves or sent for a conjure woman, or they died.

Oh, sure, the lady of the manor took her herb basket and potions and saw to niggers that got mule-stomped or took with fever; it was no more than the overseer did for the rest of the stock, so it could keep on working. But it made the Miz Susannas feel good, like they were angels of mercy.

Bringing salt back from his saddlebag, Joe poured some into Marilee's upturned palm. The touch of her skin was wondrous soft, but he jerked his hand like he'd caught a hot stovelid, and backed off a ways. The way her face tilted in late sun, the shaping of her cheek bothered him somehow, so he stared at Timmy instead. For days now, the youngun had been off his feed and looked it; not heavy to start with, Timmy's face was sharper and his bones showed through yellowish hide.

Stooping for the whiskey bottle, Joe lifted it and took a swallow. Young Santee wasn't going to make it to Mexico or anywhere else, unless this angel of mercy could pull off a sure-enough miracle. And maybe miracles didn't work, unless the angels toting them wore hoopskirts and hadn't mislaid their wings.

When the salt hit his arm, Timmy shook all over. She said, "You're very brave," and the boy worked up a sick grin, like he was a puppy patted on the head. Joe tried to look back in time at himself on a creekbank, in a cotton crib surrounded by sugar cane: had he acted like that, so damned glad to even be noticed by Miz Susanna?

For more reason, if he had, for something beside popskull whiskey and salt poured into a festering wound.

But both the great plantation ladies managed to hurt like hell.

"Can you find somethin' to use as a clean bandage?" she asked. "I don't have anything except this kerchief, and I think I should change the dressin' much as I can."

Joe said, "I can tear up a shirt I got. You ridin' with us, then?" He couldn't decide which color her eyes were, which shade of green.

"To Mexico? It's as good a place as any, I guess. I can't go back home."

"No rich kinfolk to take care of you?" He thought her eyes were kind of willow green, when the light hit them proper, like soft young willow sprouts.

Marilee said, "No—is anybody rich in the South now?"

"Some—mealy-mouthed planters that sold cotton north, blockade runners that brought in silks and satins instead of gunpowder. Fine, upstandin' gentlemen like that."

He watched her jaw set and she said, "Please bring me that shirt."

Women like her always had that sweet way of talking, even when they were mad. The only time they changed was when they were in heat for some lover, or some nigger buck. Then they had a mouth on them like a Kansas City whore. Maybe the whores were more honest; they'd only steal a man's money, not his pride, and he never heard of a man getting his back torn open with a whip because of one.

Bringing her the old shirt, Joe was careful not to brush her hand, but dropped it on her lap. "I see the maggots fell off'n him. That whiskey'll kill near about anything."

Her hands were slim and steady, but strong as they tore off strips of the shirt. "You're not shockin' me; I've seen maggots before. I took care of my own horses on the plantation, treated screwflies and blowflies and cuts."

"With some nigger moppin' up after, sure."

Eyes going dark as the shiny side of a magnolia leaf, Marilee said, "And you wouldn't have used a slave—if you'd had money enough to buy one."

Timmy Santee said, "Why you pickin' at this lady, Joe? She's been hurt bad as any of us in this war."

"Since her kind brought on the damned war, could be she's deservin' of it. And no ma'am, Miz Bradburn, I wouldn't work no slave if I had one—I'd set him free to look after himself, just like *I* had to. Makes a man a whole lot less'n he truly is, does he have to bow and scrape and do like he's told, right or wrong—even a nigger."

Busily rolling bandages, Marilee was watching her own hands, not slapping at him with those tilted eyes. "Sounds like you wore the wrong uniform, Joe Langston."

"Damn it, I—" He chopped it short because he said too much. She had a way of getting under his skin like a chigger, and already he was wishing he'd just let things happen natural there at the creek when she'd been so naked and him and the others so horny.

If it hadn't been for Timmy Santee needing care, hadn't been for this skinny youngun that had someway got stuck to him like a seed tick, Joe wouldn't be bothered with her now. "All right, Timmy—I'll leave it lay and get the skillet goin'."

Unconcerned as if he'd been just a bug flitting around her, Marilee said, "Maybe you can take some soup, Timmy?"

"Ain't got the fixins," Joe said.

She pointed. "My saddlebags—dried catfish and some wild onions, cornmeal. I can make a passable fish stew for him."

He was standing beside the big stallion before he realized he'd been sent there, not asked to get the stew makings, but ordered, like. She kept getting him mixed up, looking like a boy in her clothes and her hair cut off, but with a mouth and eyes like no boy ever had, with all that clean-limbed thoroughbred body underneath.

No wonder he'd been thrown off track back there at the water; Marilee Bradburn talked like a lady, and acted the part, especially when he brought her to the major; she simpered and posed and carried on like she wore a fine dress and was waving a pretty little fan. But she'd kept her guns close by, and when he eased up on her, when she saw what he meant to do with her, she'd gone for that carbine quick and mean as a riverboat gambler. No wonder he got confused about her and let her off so easy.

But she belonged to *them*, right enough. Guns and Yankee horse set aside, this woman with the cornsilk hair and changing green eyes was plantation born and raised, same as Miz Susanna. He wondered if she'd also married up with a rich man twice her age, or some young beau with lace at his wrists. He wondered if she'd had some sweating black buck act as her stud, picking and choosing from the house servants and field hands.

" 'Spect I'll try to eat, Miz Marilee," Timmy was saying when Joe returned with the food. "You're bein' almighty kind to me."

"Little enough I can do for one of our fightin' men," she said. "Now lie back and get some rest while I do the cookin'. Joe, if you'll stir up the fire and pass me some water—"

He hesitated, then said, "Might's well—mudcat stew'll taste pretty good. We been runnin' so far, ain't had time to fish. Sure you know how to cook?"

A quick glance cut at him, but her face didn't change. "I was alone on our place for almost two years, after the last slave ran off. I'm alive. That answer your question?"

"You don't *have* to fix for us," he said. "Heard the major give you a supper invite."

"And I'll join him later—Timmy needs something to give him strength." She nodded where the boy lay with his eyes closed and head against his saddle, then whispered: "How long has his arm been like that?"

Squatting to poke up a nest of coals, Joe shrugged. "Three days—trouble is, he got hit right where he was wounded afore. His own fault, actin' like a fancy soldier and tryin' to take a scalawag prisoner. Now what the hell would this bunch do with a prisoner?"

She mixed meal with water and brought out a small knife to slice green onions. Joe looked at the sharp little blade and remembered what she'd said she'd try if he'd raped her; she'd had that sticker hid away all the time. He wouldn't forget it.

"But there are rules of civilized warfare," Marilee said.

Joe grunted and laid a stick of dry oak on the fire. "Ain't but one—stay alive. War's over and done with, anyhow."

"Then why are you riding to Mexico with Major Ainsworth, if you don't believe in the rebirth of the Confederacy?"

He settled back on his heels and blinked at her. The more she talked, the more certain he was about her, and didn't know why he kept lallygagging around. If it wasn't for Timmy Santee. . . . "Never heard of anything gettin' born twice," Joe said. "Didn't even believe in it the first time. I'm headin' acrost the border for the same reason most of these outlaws are—'cause we ain't got anywhere else to go, and there's gold down there. Now, Major Ainsworth tells it like the war ain't lost and we're just re-groupin'. Hell, I got sung that kind of lullaby every time we got our tail whipped and had to run from the blue-bellies."

Coming to her feet in one smooth, quick movement, she said, "Major Ainsworth is a gentleman, and that's somethin' you'll probably never understand. Stir the stew and try to get Timmy to eat some. I'll come back for my bedroll."

Joe lifted an eyebrow at her. "He ain't got any candles to put on that stump, nor no snowwhite tablecloth—sure you can eat that plain?"

Watching her walk away from him, Joe found his eyes clinging to the slick way her hips rolled and the easy swing of her legs, the proud way she held her back. She was going off to have supper with a *gentleman,* and it was too damned bad she'd miss out on dark rich wine in a stemmed glass, that sweet and heady stuff too good for a redneck youngun who didn't have sense enough to know it.

He didn't understand gentlemen? Hell, he didn't—better, than they knew themselves. From old man Paisley on, he'd seen enough of the breed to know. What he couldn't puzzle through was what made them all act like the world was hand-whittled just to fit their own notions; and when things didn't go to suit them, they kept stumbling right along, bumping into hard corners like a moonblind horse.

If they called themselves gentry, it didn't matter if they stood master of a cotton plantation or head of a Creole family that barricaded itself behind iron gates and brick walls in New Orleans. The name could be Paisley or Lecroix or something a man was hard put to get his tongue around, but they thought alike and acted alike. And now that their special carved world was knocked to stem-winding hell, and their niggers turned loose, they flat wouldn't admit it could be true.

Yonder sat Miz Marilee Bradburn, howdy-doing with Ainsworth, talking about things and times and places long gone. She had the same blind staggers mark on her, acting the princess when she didn't have no more than a horse stole from a Yankee and not much clothes on her back. And without the clothes. . . .

Joe dragged the skillet off the fire and wrapped its handle in his jacket sleeve. Beside Timmy, he said, "Wake up, boy. Spoon down some of this stuff cooked personal for you by a real lady."

Blinking, struggling to a sitting position, Timmy took the spoon in his left hand, awkward with it. "How come you brought her back, if you don't cotton to her, Joe?"

"To keep from bein' your pa. Go on, eat."

"I think she's so pretty," Timmy said, blowing on the stew before taking some in his mouth. "Prettier'n my May, even, in a different way. But that don't mean I ain't still in love with May. Me and my gal, we're a match—I never even dreamed about no lady like Miz Marilee."

Fiercely, Joe said, "Why the hell not? You think you ain't got a right, or think they don't go to the outhouse same as poor women? If they wipe their ass with cotton instead of a corncob, that make 'em *better?*"

Staring, Timmy said, "I—I reckon not, but I mean, well—"

"I know damned well what you mean. It's what we been learned, that folks in the big white house are some special, and we ain't worth a hoot and holler. You know what makes 'em special, boy? Money—gold to buy niggers and seed and mules, gold to get hold of the best bottom lands and buy pretty clothes to ride their blood horses in."

Timmy tried another spoonful of stew and made a face when he swallowed. "They read books and write letters. I can cipher some, but I never learned to read."

"Ol' preachers hollerin' brimstone can read—that ain't nothin'. In New Orleans, them shopkeepers can even read French. I saw a nigger on the docks readin', but nobody called him a gentleman."

"This tastes right good." Timmy sighed. "But seems like my belly shrunk. You been clear to New Orleans, Joe?"

"Up and down the river, too. North to Kansas and back and forth acrost the South, but never fool enough to travel to Gettysburg. Ol' Marse Robert, that fine gentleman, took a heap of boys up there, but never brought 'em back."

"Joe," Timmy said, "I'd 'preciate was you not to talk

about General Lee thataway. Reckon you better eat this stew—I can't get no more down. And I can't help it none if you're mad at the gentry, but it ain't fair to get red-eyed at Miz Marilee, when she's only helpin' us."

The skillet handle wasn't hot enough to blister his hand, just enough to make him curse. Across the clearing, he could see the angle of her shoulders, the setting sun touching her light hair with red as she nodded and laughed at something the major said. It was a laugh with the ring of little bells in it. Damn them for that soft peal that walked kitten-footed up a man's backbone. They must spend years practicing to laugh like that, learning to roll their eyes and swing their tight little tails.

Behind him, Timmy made a muffled sound, but when Joe turned, the boy said, "It ain't nothin'."

"How about some whiskey?"

"Better not. You mean to watch out for her horse, Joe. Blodgett's been eyein' him—Jessup, too."

"Cain't watch out for *every* damned thing around here," Joe said.

Marilee was rising across the way, holding out a hand to the major. Ainsworth gave her his arm and came hobbling back with her. Joe got interested in eating stew, and the major said, "How you doing, boy? Miss Bradburn told me you ought to have a rest."

Joe watched Timmy's face as the boy's eyes widened. "I can make it, sir," Timmy said quickly. "Swear I can. Don't leave me behind."

Gently, Ainsworth said, "The rear guard reports Yanks on our trail. We have to move fast."

"Major," Marilee said, "you didn't mention abandonin' this boy."

Joe put down the skillet. "The major don't say a lot of things, like he knows damned well Timmy's arm has got to come off, and even if the youngun lives through that, Timmy can't keep up."

Shrilly, Timmy Santee's voice rose. "T-take *off* my arm?"

Going swiftly to the boy, Marilee kneeled beside him, but not before she hissed at Joe: "You're a cruel and vicious man!"

Chapter 12

Maybe she hated other men more—the trooper who had defiled her upon her own land, the white trash who'd also tried to rape her. But if they were all in a horse race, Joe Langston would be running close behind them. How could the man be so heartless, so cold? He might as well have killed this suffering boy himself as to ride off and leave him. Just coming out and saying Timmy had no chance was shock enough.

The dust of the troop's passing still drifted in dawn air, spiderwebbing upon dewdamp leaves, and the creaking rattle of their going had faded. Tucked back into the brush, away from the campsite itself, Marilee had Bradburn saddled and hidden still more safely. But she had no intention of deserting Timmy Santee, even if the Yankees should discover them.

"Miss Marilee," Major Ainsworth had murmured apologetically, "it's my bounden military duty to lead this command to our objective. I realize that the harsh urgencies of war are difficult for a lady to understand, but—"

"You're abandonin' this boy to his fate," she said. "He

fought for you, and yet you intend leavin' him to die alone. It's not fair."

Shfting upon his crippled leg, the major said, "Santee is only one soldier—I'm responsible for many more like him. If we wait, there may be a pitched battle with the Yankees, against superior forces, and more will die."

"Then I'll stay with him," Marilee said.

"Miss Marilee, that's dangerous, and I cannot allow—"

"Allow? *Allow*, sir? I am a civilian and not under your orders."

Pained, he said, "Please, ma'am, I cannot spare men to stay with you, and you do need protection. Perhaps Langston, then, but only for a while. If the lad doesn't linger too long—"

"That, sir, is most callous." She'd faced him defiantly. "I must admit I need help and protection, but I'm certain I can care for myself awhile, and catch up with you when—when I'm no longer needed here."

Major Ainsworth bowed over her hand. "A gallant lady, ma'am. I respect you for your stand." Lifting his voice, he called, "Langston!"

Lazily, Joe Langston had drifted across to them. "The youngun wants to keep his arm. Way I see it, he's right —lockjaw's goin' to kill him anyhow."

"You're to stay here with Miss Marilee until the boy passes on, then rejoin the command."

She saw the hard set of Joe's face as he refused, the flash of anger in the major as he insisted. Then Joe said without even looking at *her*, "Timmy's takin' it like a man, and don't expect nobody to hold his hand. You try and make me stay, major, you'll never see me and my guns again."

Marilee said, "But he's your friend, and you mean to let him die alone!"

Then he looked at her, his blue marble eyes opaque. "Comes his time, every man dies alone."

"Without comfort and kindness—without even sorrow? My God, what kind of men *are* you? Go, go on and leave us!"

Tracing aimless lines in the earth with the tip of his cane, Major Ainsworth muttered apologies and explanations that trailed off. Joe Langton stayed only a few seconds longer to say, "I said my goodbyes to the boy. He understands."

"Does he—does he really?" She wanted to slap him. "That boy worships you, although God only knows why. He *needs* somebody with him, so he won't be afraid."

Joe looked across the camp and she saw his mouth didn't change—that sensuous mouth, with the scarred and cynical twist to it. He said, "Major's takin' his horse and guns. I'da left him the pistol."

Furiously, she said, "So he can shoot himself? Why—why, that's the most terrible thing I ever heard!"

Suddenly, painfully, his hands were on her shoulders, iron-hard and punishing. "Ever see anybody die of lock-jaw, damnit? Hurts a sight worse'n a bullet through the temple, I'd say. Right now that youngun is sufferin' the fires of hell them preachers talk about, and then some. A pistol ball'd be a mercy. Timmy knows there ain't a doctor he can get to, knows he can't ride, knows damned well we can't tote him—and now he knows he's about to die. What can I do for him? What the hell can *anybody* do for him?"

"Let me go," she snapped. "I can do somethin' for him. I can stay with him until the end, keep him company and show him that somebody cares."

His hands fell away from her shoulders. Tall, looming wide and stubborn against the lightening sky, Joe Langston said, "And you're liable to be keepin' him company in hell, do the Yanks find you."

"I don't care!" she hissed at him. "He needs—I believe—" But she was hurling her words uselessly against the air, for Joe Langston was gone.

Now she patted Bradburn's thick neck and warned him to be quiet, before moving back through the brush to where Timmy Santee lay upon her spread bedroll, head pillowed upon her coat and his. The boy's arm, puffed to twice normal size, lay misshapen beside his thin body. His left hand cupped the bottle of whiskey Joe Langston had given him, final legacy from a so-called friend. Marilee sat down beside him.

Timmy said, "Horse all right?"

"I don't think he'll whinny, when the Yankees come—if they come."

116

"Good horse," Timmy said. " 'Spect you was a mite hard on Joe. He ain't a bad feller, considerin'."

"Considerin' what?" she asked. "That he's cold and brutal and without a drop of human compassion?"

He sipped from the mouth of the bottle and sighed. "Took care of me long's he could. The major now, he explained it all to me, but Joe didn't have to say nothin'—he knew I understood." Timmy took another drink and winced as the movement jiggled his bad arm. "Reckon he's a hard man, and got a right to be. Heard them others talkin' about how he rode with Quantrill's raiders and what a cutter he is with a handgun. Seen that myself, when he was droppin' scalawags like flies. You know if he hadn't pushed me to the side, I'd been dead back yonder? Don't know's I thank him for that, though—mighta been better."

Marilee saw that the liquor was loosening Timmy's tongue. She also saw the fever hot in him and the agony he tried to hide. His arm had swelled so much she'd had to cut away the bandage, and nothing had helped—not camphor juice or comfrey root or the whiskey and salt. The infection had had too good a start before she'd gotten at it.

"Some say Quantrill turned outlaw and killed on both sides, but any man with him was bound to be hard and quick with a gun." Timmy's eyes were closed, but he kept talking. Night was closing around them as she poured water from her canteen onto a strip of cloth and bathed his face. "Bet you he done some things down in New Orleans he ain't proud of, too . . . rode the river, Joe Langston did. Had to run off from home time he was sixteen years old . . . never said how come, but you got to credit a man makes it on his own thataway."

Marilee wet another rag and placed it gently upon the ugly, discolored arm. Despite her tenderness, Timmy flinched. After another drink of whiskey he said in a different voice, "May—May?"

She waited, then asked softly, "Who's May?"

Only a shadow now, his face turned toward her. "Why, she's my girl. We mean to be married, soon's I get back from Mexico. . . . Joe said I'll come ridin' a fine horse and sittin' a silver saddle, with gold in my pockets. May Endi-

cott will be waitin', pretty as ever. May, May—ain't that
a pretty name, like springtime?"

"It's a very pretty name," Marilee whispered.

"Back home in Carolina, I reckon that' the best time
of year, in May. Mean to make it back from Mexico then,
so I can marry May in May . . . ain't that funny?" He
tried to laugh and his back arched.

"She'll like that," Marilee said softly.

"Feel like I been hit in the jaw . . . like the hinges
don't work . . ."

Marilee held the whiskey bottle to his lips. "Drink some,
Timmy."

He swallowed with difficulty and mumbled, "Thank you,
ma'am . . . thank you, darlin'."

He was quiet so long Marilee was frightened; a locust
whirred loudly in the darkness, backed by a concert of
crickets. A pair of fireflies winked pale green through the
trees, and Bradburn stamped once upon a carpet of fallen
pine needles. She said, "Timmy?"

"Build us a fine house, May . . . good as any in the
county. Missed you so much while I was gone. . . . Away
down there in Mexico, I used to think about how you'n me
should of done it afore I went off to war . . . but I was
scared to, May. Wasn't I didn't love you and want you so
much it hurt my belly . . . but I never done it with a girl
afore, and I was just plain scared to. . . ."

Marilee tried to cool his face again, but the heat of his
parched skin seemed to burn right through the wet rag. She
gave him more whiskey, thankful that Joe had left a full
bottle, hoping it would ease the boy's pain a little.

Timmy's laugh was a choked rattle in his throat.
"You . . . you know what, May? I asked him how it was,
with a woman . . . ol' Joe Langston, my partner . . . he
didn't hooraw me for not knowin'. . . . Good ol' boy, Joe
. . . I tell you he's a gunfighter? . . . Slicker'n butter with
that pistol, and a hero, too. Rode right on into them scalawags poppin' right and left, clean out in front of the
charge. . . ."

Shivering, Marilee pulled a blanket up around her
shoulders. It was so black around them that the quick on-
and-off lanterns of fireflies were startling, and no wind
shook the pine trees. She jumped when a whippoorwill

cried from a thicket: *Chip married a widow—Chip married a widow!*

Poor Timmy Santee wouldn't marry anybody; he'd never see his beloved May again. Black poison was racing through his tortured body, making him delirious, but not bringing the blessing of unconsciousness.

She wished she could light a fire, but that would call the enemy to them. They needed warmth, for even though Timmy was burning with fever, there were moments when he shook uncontrollably, too. The poor, poor boy; deserted by the only friend he claimed, dying out here in the wilderness while he dreamed of the girl he'd left in Carolina.

". . . Kind of cold," he muttered, and Marilee didn't wait any longer. She spread both spare blankets and crawled beneath them, pressing her body against the boy's, very careful not to touch his disfigured arm.

". . . Gettin' warmer, May," Timmy said. "Never takes more'n a touch of you to make me warm. May, May. . . ."

"Yes," Marilee said softly. "Yes, darlin'."

His good arm was around her shoulder, and she put her face into his neck, the length of herself along him, and didn't draw back when she felt his hand gently cupping her left breast.

". . . You got the prettiest 'uns in the country," he said. "Paired like apples, only soft, soft . . . I love you, May. . . ."

"And I love you, Timmy." It was the least she could do for him—allow him to live out his dream before the final darkness came swirling and he dreamed no more.

". . . I know it ain't right to get naked, but I want to feel your skin all over, May. . . . Oh, my darlin', I'm ridin' off to war and I never felt your skin all over. . . ."

She waited as he held her lightly, gently, and thought this was almost how it might have been with her own lover, if Robbie Dee had only asked. She would have gladly, exultantly, given her virginity to him then, in a tremulous expectancy.

For Timmy, she didn't have the same eagerness; Marilee didn't feel love for the boy, beyond the love of one compassionate human being for another less fortunate. She pitied him for all he was losing, for the sweet romance he'd never know with his faroff May, because

119

Timmy Santee was dying before he had ever truly lived.

Marilee unbuttoned her shirt and gave his hand the bare mound of her breast. Timmy sighed into her hair as he rolled her nipple very gently between shaking fingers, and she was surprised to feel it hardening. Not with lust, she told herself; she had lusted only after Robbie Dee Crownover and been denied. And she wasn't responding out of love; she could never love that way again, after what had been done to her.

But she could allow this dying boy's hands to wander her flesh, make that part of his short life real enough in his delirium. Wriggling from her breeches and underdrawers, Marilee snuggled to him, lying still as he trailed tender and inexperienced fingers across her stomach, then back to her breast. Even bewildered with fever and alternately shaken by chills, Timmy was still afraid to reach out for what he most craved, delaying the moment of knowing. And Marilee couldn't take his hand in her own to place it upon her mound; she couldn't.

". . . Dreamed I rode off without lovin' you," he said into her hair. "Terrible, it was—I kept gettin' the idea I might not come home to you, sweetheart. My . . . your skin is soft as rosebuds, and I want to kiss your breast. . . ."

Because he moaned when he tried to turn over, because the need was so deep within him, Marilee moved up to give him her breast, feeding him its nipple as if he were a child in need of nourishment. As his tongue felt over her and his lips ringed her, Marilee felt something else, a lifting where her knee crossed his lower body. For a stark and brittle moment, terror washed through her, a wave of fear dark and ugly as the thing that had happened to her. But Timmy was murmuring around her breast, and his good hand was roaming slowly down her back. He was only a lad, just a boy who would never see his prime; Timmy Santee wasn't a hairy brute.

And he'd left his love behind; he had never known the richness of her young body, putting it off until the war was over. Like Robbie Dee, she thought. And May was like herself, waiting for a fiancé who would never return, for the deflowering that would be, had been, done by someone else.

". . . May, my love. . . ."

"Yes, Timmy, yes."

She had trouble with his belt; he kept trying to roll over against the monstrous agony of his swollen arm, and she pushed him gently back. Then she had his breeches down and dared to take his thing in her hand. It was slim and throbbing, not frightening at all; she held it tenderly, her fingers caressing delicately.

Like it's a horn on one of them Western saddles, the trooper had said. *All you got to do is climb up there and ride on it.*

His panting breath got mixed up with the runaway thunder of her heart when she carefully straddled him, and she wondered if ever a woman had given herself to a man while being called by another woman's name. Marilee had to force herself to do it; it was an act of mercy, an act of repentance, and yet she had to demand that her hand guide the slender shaft between her thighs.

The first brush of its puffy head sent a chill through her belly, and for a crazy, confused fragment of spinning time, Marilee knew again the loathing she'd experienced at that other thrusting, painful thing. But the boy's hand quested lightly over her thigh, up across one haunch, and his whisper was filled with pleading. So she held his thing firm and lowered herself upon it, inch by slow inch, finding the proper place and choking back a gasp as the hard warmth of him began to penetrate, as she opened the depths of her body to his young manhood.

It didn't hurt. She was surprised at that, and moved her loins experimentally, still not finding pain. Bending over the boy, she clung to him while his body surged and the back and forth movement began. There was no pain, only a knowing that he was inside her, and no loathing or disgust. But there was nothing else, either. She knew only a sense of giving, of pity and sadness because she wasn't his beloved May and he wasn't Robbie Dee. She wanted to cry for all of them, the dead and the living dead.

When the motion hurried itself, when Timmy reached hungrily and quickly up into her flesh, Marilee hurried with him. His cresting was swift then, his belly straining upward against her own, his one arm locked possessively about her waist.

After a while, he whispered, "So that's what it is . . . so beautiful, May . . . so beautiful . . . ."

"Yes," she whispered back, tented beneath their blankets and holding her weight upon knees and elbows as much as she could, to keep her weight from pressing down upon him.

". . . It's like we're married . . . like our weddin' night. . . ."

"Yes," she whispered.

In time, lifting herself from his softness, she knew that his strength was gone, spasmed into her body in that first and last culmination of his boyish passion. She had to raise Timmy's head to give him whiskey and water, and the second time she poured some into his mouth, he had difficulty opening his teeth.

Later in the long night, he mumbled about his home, his words indistinct and jumbled, but she understood he was talking to his pa, explaining why he had to go to war. No more whiskey would go down his throat; his teeth seemed wired together, and his neck strained, its cords standing out like wire under her fingertips. The sounds he made then weren't words, only sounds, and once he cried. She felt the hotness of his tears along her cheek.

Cradling him close, crooning softly to him, Marilee was all the women in Timmy Santee's life—comforting mother, understanding sister, and a girl who'd proved how much she cared for him. When the sweat of him slicked her skin, she wiped at it with cooling cloths; when he shook with cold, she warmed him with her body.

He was breathing deeply and quietly when her eyelids grew heavy and the night hung silently around them in the housing of their blankets. Her head pillowed lightly against his shoulder, her naked body against him, Marilee fell asleep.

Chapter 13

Sunrise fingered damp and cool over her as Marilee sat up, blanket sliding from bare shoulders as she looked first to the thicket where Bradburn had been tied all night. Catching a flicker of tail swishing there, she glanced down at Timmy Santee.

From behind her, Joe Langston said harshly, "Ain't been dead long."

Her face twisted toward him looming tall and dark above her, then back to the boy. "D-dead? Oh, no." Trembling, her hand touched his cheek. "He isn't cold."

"Ain't breathin', neither."

He was right. Marilee said, "No, Timmy—oh, no."

"He can't hear you, but it looks like he passed on happy. Or did you diddle him to death?"

Suddenly conscious of her naked upper body, Marilee snatched the blanket around her, but somehow that made it worse. It exposed the boy's naked limbs, and she spread a corner so he was covered, too. "How did you sneak up on—why did you come back?"

When he drifted closer and around to one side, she

123

could see the shovel he carried. "Got to thinkin' on the youngun, but I didn't figure on you givin' him such a send-off. Couldn't you wait to get somebody else atween your legs?"

Glaring at him, she said, "You—you filthy-minded— you were supposed to be his friend and you deserted him. Yet you have the nerve to scorn me for—for taking care of him."

His mouth was cynical, but she couldn't tell if it was the little scar causing it. "Took care of him all right, but it couldn't do you much good, him a dyin' boy and virgin to boot."

Oh, how she hated him for making her feel guilty, for trying to make her feel unclean. She despised that knowing leer upon his face—*Handsome is as handsome does,* Lucinda had always said. Why would he make something evil and loathsome of what she had given Timmy Santee?

"How could I expect *you* to understand? It wasn't like that at all. He was out of his head, dreamin' about his girl, and it was precisely because he was pure that I—"

She didn't care for the look in his eyes; Marilee Bradburn wasn't used to having anyone look at her as if she were inferior.

"Get out of the way," he said. "See to your horse and fry up somethin' to eat. I come the long way back around, cuttin' yesterday's trail, and didn't see a bluebelly."

She clutched the blanket, refusing to stare at Timmy's body, not wanting to see Joe's disgust. He had no *right*. "Eat? How can you even think of it when—"

"Takes food to live," he said, laying aside the short shovel to reach out. She pulled sharply away and he added: "And I mean to keep right on livin'. You want me to bury the youngun, or you mean to do it yourself?"

As she rose, Marilee took one blanket, stooping clumsily for clothes, going sick when she had to untangle them from Timmy's stiffening legs. A single glimpse of pale, waxen flesh was too much, and she closed her eyes to wriggle awkwardly into breeches behind the shielding blanket. The man was shifting blame. *He'd* abandoned a friend, left him to die, not her. Yet he was trying to make her feel like a—a prostitute.

Did he expect her gratitude because he'd come back to bury Timmy? She could have managed by herself somehow. She had buried her own mother. Walking stiffly, shedding the blanket at the edge of the thicket, she whispered his hatefulness to Bradburn as she untied and unsaddled the stallion. Watering the horse at the spring, she put a loose rope on him so he could graze. Before she left to rejoin Major Ainsworth's troop, she would give him some corn.

Hearing the *chunk-chunk* of the shovel unnerved her, so Marilee got busy cracking dry branches and starting a small fire. She fought the memories of last night as they threatened to overcome her—softly fumbling hand; eager, adoring excitement; the fulfillment of his need. Marilee shook her head as she sliced bacon with her penknife and mixed cornmeal batter; she'd done the right thing, the *only* thing anyone on God's earth could have done for Timmy Santee.

Joe Langston was still digging steadily when the bacon and bread were done. She moved the pan to one side, where the food would stay warm without burning. Keeping her back to him and the grave, Marilee dipped her bandanna in the spring and washed her face. Later, she'd bathe all over, not as she'd scrubbed at her body after the Yankee raped her, but to wash away the lingering imprint of death.

Steeling herself to look around, she flinched at what she saw—Joe dragging the blanket-wrapped body into a shallow hole. Marilee clenched her hands at the muffled sound of dirt being thrown atop the boy and bowed her head until it was done, until the patting down was finished and Joe Langston straightened up.

The sun was higher, and sweat streaked his bared chest, highlighting his muscular shaping. She saw there was little hair, that his skin was strangely white when contrasted to the tan of his arms and throat. When he half turned to lay aside the shovel, she drew in her breath at the pattern of old scars that crisscrossed his straight back. Other marks of violence marred the smoothness of that flesh—a puckered hole at his shoulder that could have been a bullet wound, a gouge above his right hip—but the netting of ugly marks was by far the worst.

Moistening her lips, she said, "I—we ought to say something over him."

His pale eyes mocked her. "You and the major. Go ahead, then."

Desperately, she tried to remember the phrases. "Ah—man that is born of woman is—is of little duration and filled with pain."

"Amen to that," Joe said.

"Wait—that's not all. I can't seem to remember—ah—ashes to ashes and dust to dust—"

"If the devil don't get you, the Yankees must."

Glaring, she said, "Can't you show him a little respect?"

"Buried him, didn't I?" Joe Langston stretched, and she saw the ripple of muscle across his ribcage, over his flat stomach. He left her staring down at the raw dirt mound. When she returned, Marilee found him at the dying fire, eating with his fingers.

"He was a nice boy," she said.

"Should of gone on home, but he wanted to be a somebody."

Marilee took some cornpone and a piece of bacon. "Is that so bad?"

"Anything gets you killed is bad."

She wished he would put on his shirt; his casual nakedness bothered her. "Then why are you goin' to Mexico, instead of home?"

Shrugging, Joe said, "Couldn't go home if I wanted."

"You've worn those whip marks a long time," she said. "Maybe it's forgotten."

From behind lowered lids, his eyes probed at her. "You've seen whip scars afore, I expect. Part of growin' up a fine plantation lady. Mine got laid on as part of growin' up, too—put there so I wouldn't get biggity and try to be a somebody."

"We—I never had a slave whipped in my life, and especially not a white man! You must have done somethin' terrible." Why did he irritate her so?

He munched bread, squatted teetering on his heels. "Terrible depends on who does it—nigger or white trash gets whipped for things the gentry calls their due, or acts like it don't see."

There was no reaching him, she saw. He'd called himself trash, and Joe Langston should know. Finishing her meal, she took the skillet to the spring for cleaning.

Behind her, he said, "Be ready to light out soon. Major's a long way off, and could be them Yanks ain't."

Putting aside the fry pan, she said: "After I've washed up."

"Go ahead, but it won't get the youngun's dyin' sweat off you."

Marilee whirled. "Go on, get out of here! I never asked you to come back, and I sure don't need you. I reckon I can follow trail as well as you."

Standing now, he was putting on his shirt. She noticed that he'd never unslung his pistol, not even while digging the grave. "Suit yourself. Ainsworth is hankerin' for your company more'n I am."

She watched him climb his horse and walk it across the clearing. A crude, impossible man, she thought; someone who couldn't stand the thought of anyone being of higher station in life. Joe Langston was a stubborn, sullen redneck who'd misspent his life resenting his betters, and he probably well deserved the whipping he'd gotten.

At the forest edge he turned in the saddle. "Major's wore to the nub and a cripple, but he can pleasure you more than a dyin' boy."

She spat it at him. "You—you bastard!"

Trembling with impotent rage, she waited until he was gone, then flung off her clothing and stepped shivering into the cold waters of the spring. Splashing quickly, skin going all bumpy, Marilee worked over her body, wishing for soap, any kind of soap—the harsh laundry kind made from suet, ashes, and lye, or the smooth, perfumed bars she'd once been familiar with. What a luxury a hot, scented bath would be.

The stallion blew soft alarm through his nostrils, and she whirled, grabbing first for the shirt to cover herself, then lunging for the saddle and her guns.

"Got caught short again," Joe Langston said. "Let me get atween you and your guns."

Marilee stared hate at him. "What are you—get away from there, damn you!"

His eyes slid over her, pale as a July sky and as warm. "You're prettier'n her, I reckon. Didn't think any woman could be, but you are."

Clutching the shirt to the front of her body, she said,

"Why did you come back? I told you I could find the troop on my own."

Lounging with his back against a sapling, he said slowly, "Came back for you, but waited 'til you got washed. Never did care much for a woman with another man's sweat on her."

"You—you *what?*" Oh, God—were they *all* like this? Did they consider any lone woman legitimate prey? Marilee pretended she didn't know what he meant, that she didn't recognize the hotness of his eyes and the taut readiness of his body. "All right, I'll ride back with you, and—and thanks. If you'll pass me that blanket so I can finish dressing—"

He kept staring. "There's somethin' about you, and I don't know what. Maybe all you ladies got it in common, you and Miz Susanna and the rest of your kind. You give off somethin'—a smell, maybe—a thing that calls a man to warm his hands on you. Guess I know what makes a pack of hounds follow a bitch in heat."

Stooping, Marilee felt for her breeches, keeping her eyes on him. There was no use even trying for her weapons; they were too far away, and she'd seen how snake-quick this man could move.

"No sense tryin' to hide all that pretty body," he murmured. "I'd just have to tear them clothes off you."

She crouched there, fighting down a shudder that threatened to overwhelm her, but her legs trembled anyhow. "I'm not your Miss Susanna, and I'm not any particular *kind*. I'm me, just Marilee Bradburn, and I don't want anything to do with you—especially with *you*."

Maybe antagonizing him was wrong, but Marilee didn't think she could beg off, either; if sheep ran, killer dogs pursued them.

"How come one man and not another?" he asked. "Timmy Santee wasn't no lace-cuff planter, neither."

"I told you why," she said, chilled and so very naked behind the inadequate covering of clenched shirt and rumpled breeches. "The boy was out of his head and dyin', and I—"

Coming away from the tree he'd been leaning against, looming above her, Joe said, "You're all sisters. Hair and eyes different, but inside you're blood kin—plantation ladies choosin' their studs. Well, this time the stud is doin' the pickin'."

Her guns, the shovel—too far away. But there was the penknife, and she dipped into the breeches pocket for it. He was on her before she could open the blade, big hand steely around her wrist, flipping the little knife away. She could smell the sweat of him, the power, and fought blindly against him, naked and twisting helplessly within his grasp.

"Remembered that pocket knife," he grunted, twisting her over onto her back. "Damn, but you're beautiful. Guess a woman has to be a bitch to be so beautiful."

She spat up at him. "You filthy redneck—white trash—" Choking on her rage, Marilee hissed wordless hate at this brute who was overpowering her, his half-naked body blotting out the sun.

When she tried for his privates with a jerked knee, Joe turned it away with his hip, and in horror Marilee saw the thick swelling of his manhood. Squirming, heaving, she battled to free her wrists, to somehow break away from him, but it was no use. He was too strong.

The cynical upturn of his mouth was more pronounced as his face lowered to hers, and Marilee caught her breath, held it when Joe's mouth touched her trembling lips. A lightning bolt seared her mouth and burned far down into her body, far back into her brain. Strangely soft, yet violently demanding, an odd blending of fierceness and tenderness, his lips covered hers, and she shuddered as her teeth were forced apart, quivered at the probing of his tongue.

Struggling for breath, for some kind of equilibrium, she found her head spinning, and her heart slamming like the hoofbeats of a runaway horse. He kept her arms locked above her head, both her wrists clamped in one hand, his grip unbreakable. Oh, Lord—and now his free hand was roaming over her body, caressing her breasts.

Into her gasping mouth he said, "Like young melons, all firm and round—skin like white velvet."

She bit viciously at his mouth, and he pulled back his head, only to bury his face between her breasts. His hand trailed over her hip, over her thigh, and Marilee's back arched as she tried to somehow jerk her body from beneath his. Then his mouth was at her breast, his tongue racing hotly over her nipple, and a strangled cry caught in her throat.

Covering her mound, his hand was warm and strong,

and though she bucked madly, Marilee could not shake it loose. He let go only to fumble at his breeches, one knee prying apart her thighs, and suddenly, oh so powerfully, his distended hardness was pressing at her, pushing itself inexorably into her body.

When she screamed, his mouth came back to cover her own, throttling her sobs, gasping into her lips. Thrusting, burying himself full length into her shuddering depths, he violated her flesh, the private sanctity of her inner self. He moved unhurriedly, penetrating deeply, withdrawing lingeringly, and with a growing terror Marilee felt an alien sensation building inside her.

Different from anything she had ever known, the feeling was first an ember in the pit of her stomach—no, not there—somewhere else, a pinpoint of whitehot something insistently spreading, fanned by her trying to twist away from the impalement of him, by the slow, agonizing caress of what he was doing to her. Marilee gasped into his mouth and struggled more furiously to get away. Joe let go her hands, and used both of his to hold her hips.

Savagely, she hammered at his back, and when he ignored the beating of her small fists, raked at his shoulders with her nails. But that only seemed to spur him on, to increase the pounding, grinding rhythm of him—and the blazing thing within his frantic body burst into ravening tendrils of flame that raced along all her turned-raw nerve ends.

It couldn't be, her confused mind shouted—it simply could not be! She wasn't some yellow wench shamelessly responding to being bedded by her master; she was no painted whore wise in the ways of men. She was Marilee Bradburn of Bradburn Plantation, and she couldn't—wouldn't. . . .

She had no control over herself. Her body squirmed and heaved without directions from her mind, reveling in the bulk of him, in the mansweated smoothness of his chest, in the brute force of him. With every speck of will left to her, Marilee resisted being used, battled against being tamed like a green filly, fought the conqueror of her flesh—but it was no use, no use.

She went spinning wildly off into a nameless somewhere, a place where creamwhite jasmine bloomed, where a warmsoft river carried her whirling gently past sand that had been sprinkled with moonlight. Then the jasmine became lotus, and she drifted among them, gone boneless and mindless and melted into nothingness, the nonbeing of her laved with honey and powdered by starshine. Turned inside out, she saw herself as only pure feeling and felt herself as only utter beauty. Foaming, the summertide river carried her gently to an enchanted sea, where she gave herself up to the lulling rise and fall of glittering waves.

They subsided slowly, slowly, leaving her floating in a tidal pool so warm and comforting that she resented any other movement, especially the tugging that was taking something away from her. Stirring, murmuring a protest, Marilee tried to hold on to the bright bubble, but it dissolved within her fingertips, and she silently mourned its passing.

When she opened her eyes, he was kneeling between her legs, but gone from her body, and Joe Langston was staring down at her with those smokeblue eyes wide in puzzlement, in disbelief. But they shuttered themselves swiftly, before Marilee really had a chance to read them. She realized that she was spread nakedly before him, and drew up her knees, curled herself into a tight ball, denying all she had felt, replacing those tangled emotions with the stark reality of the nightmare itself.

"You—you're one hell of a woman," he said huskily, as if he were having trouble breathing. "All your studs back home must miss you like hell."

Her cheek was against the grass and she would not look at him again. She only wanted him to go away.

"Might as well get dressed," he said, his voice farther off now. "I'd like to stay here and carry on with you a mite longer, but we ain't got the time."

Rolling over, Marilee put her back to him and felt around for her clothing.

"We'll bed down again tonight," he said, "if you ain't got plans for the major."

With her shirt on, hunkered down so that it practically covered her entire body, she said, "You go to hell."

His short laugh was cynical. "Comes down to it, I 'spose I will, but I ain't ridin' to meet the devil—he'll have to come for me. Saddle your horse—this itch atween my shoulders says the Yankees ain't all that far off. If you're just goin' to squat there, I'll saddle him for you."

Marilee bounced to her feet. "Stay away from my horse and from me. Bed down with you tonight? I'd rather sleep with a snake."

She watched his face go stiff, his eyes take on a more sleepy look. "Reckon you'd do that, too, was you short of men."

Trembling, she said, "Man, *man?* What makes you think you're a man, Joe Langston? The gun you wear? The rapes you can force on a woman? Man—don't make me spit! You're trash, just ordinary white *trash*, and I wish that whoever striped your back had beaten you to death like the sneakin', envious mongrel you are."

Slateblue icicles, his eyes stabbed back at her. "What the hell do I envy? The plantation you don't have, the niggers you don't own, the big white house you got run out of?"

"You resent your betters," she said furiously. "Because you're common dirt, crawled up out of common dirt, you hate anybody of higher station, anybody with decent blood in their veins. That's why you raped me, to try and drag me down to your own filthy level, to try and make yourself feel better than you are. But it won't help. You'll always be just what you are right now—an unschooled, sweaty *animal*, no better than a hound whelp."

Muscles flexed along his jaw as he stared at her. "And callin' yourself a lady keeps you from bein' named a whore?"

"I *am* a lady—I'm a Bradburn. You and the Yankees can't take that away from me."

"Can't take anything from you that you give away free," he said. "A bitch is a bitch, purebred or crossed blood. You goin' to saddle that horse now and ride back to the troop with me?"

She was shaking both outwardly and inside, denying the warm glow that still clung stubbornly deep within her flesh. "I wouldn't take another step with you."

"Then stay, damnit!" He strode to her saddle and gathered her guns.

"Are you a thief, too?"

Wide shoulders tense, he stamped over to his own horse. "If you're goin' to be muley-headed and get back to the major on your own, I'll leave these in the fork of that tree over yonder. Wouldn't put it past you to shoot a man in the back."

"I wouldn't waste ammunition on you," she hissed. "It's easier to kill a snake with a hoe."

Astride his horse, he looked at her. "I ain't easy to kill. As for callin' names and rapin' you—I been a spell without a woman, and you were the only slut I'm liable to get close to afore reachin' Mexico. I figured on gettin' some good out of you, and by the way you wiggled and carried on, you got as much good as me. Now I reckon I can wait for a señorita honest about her whorin'. But if Major Ainsworth can't do you much good, I'll let you slip into my blankets."

Feet braced apart, small fists on her hips, she glared up at him. "I remembered somethin' else about the ashes to ashes thing you were so flippant about at Timmy Santee's grave. You no doubt heard it before, but just in case, it goes like this: 'Dust to dust and ash to ash—I'd rather be a *nigger* than poor white trash.' "

Pivoting his horse, he trotted it across the clearing and paused at a tall water oak dripping gray moss from its branches. She watched him place her weapons in its fork, then straighten in the stirrups and ride off into the trees without once looking back. Marilee kept staring after him, trying to stab him in the back with her eyes, wishing with all her heart that she could kill him like that.

Chapter 14

Twice he almost turned the horse's head and went back for her, but poison mad as she was, she might try to put a ball through him. So twice Joe kept right on going, following the beatendown trail of the cavalry troop. When Miss Marilee Bradburn got over her sulks, she'd soon come loping after. She wouldn't stay out in the woods on her own—not when she had a good thing in the protection of Major Ainsworth and the band.

Hell, it didn't mean all that much to her, despite that hurt look in her slanty eyes. She'd diddled the youngun half the night, and it wasn't like she was an honest-to-God virgin. Women like her lost their maidenheads soon as they could get around to it, taking their pick of fancy planters' sons or strong black bucks, or redneck younguns without a lick of sense but toting a pocketful of dreams.

He could still taste the wild honey of her upon his tongue, and he struck a sulphur match to a cigar stub to wash away the flavor of her mouth. Nothing seemed to ease the print of her that he could still feel ground into his body, and Joe shifted uneasily in the saddle because of it. All right, she'd been all silks and velvet, with skin smooth as honeysuckle blossoms and as fragrant. And underneath that sleek tingly hide, she hid a fire that could blaze out and burn deep into a man's flesh; burn deeper than that—right on into whatever passed for his soul.

Twisty and wiggling, her tears warm and salty on his lips, her spiced breath panting into his open mouth, and her fingers raking, raking, while her hips rolled and went *ticktock-ticktock* like a woundup pocket watch—damn!

It wasn't that he was a green and horny youngun caught naked in the creek by a princess from the big house; he'd had his share of women since Miz Susanna, and more. There'd been whores who enjoyed their job, and some camp followers of Quantrill's bunch, and a few times women who'd been without their men so long that they got over being scared real quick.

So why should it make any difference to him because Miss Highnose Bradburn raised such a ruckus about being stuck? She'd liked it as much as he did, moaning and carrying on when she got down to her short rows. Maybe he'd been without womanflesh too long and she seemed a whole lot more than she was, just because he was so hungry.

Ducking under a low-hanging cedar branch, Joe moved his horse at a jog across an open space, and pulled up on the other side to listen. She'd had no call to beat him with words after they diddled, to sting him with whip-lashes that cut near about deep as the blacksnake that scarred his back when he was sixteen years old. And he was seven kinds of a fool for feeling the hurt, too.

I'm a Bradburn, she had said, *and you can't take that away from me.* Like her name meant anything these days; like she was a hoopskirted lady with house niggers jumping to do her bidding; like she'd *ever* been any better than a Langston. That had been hogshit from the start, and the war proved it, but there'd probably always be them that hung on to being gentry because they had nothing else.

Look at Ainsworth and his stumped leg, acting like he had a real command in a real army, instead of a bunch of ragtag troopers wore to the bone and out at the elbows, with as many outlaws among them as soldiers.

Joe legged his horse on through the brush and tried to shake the picture of Marilee from his head. He'd wanted her from the first second he saw her lifting out of the blankets with sunrise lying pink along her pale skin, when he knew damned well that she'd bedded Timmy Santee the night before. For all her talk about being good to the boy in his last hours, it didn't change the fact that she'd diddled him good, and just knowing that had made Joe swell himself hard and aching.

Maybe he'd wanted her before that—when he saw her all silver and white in the creek, her smooth body shining in the sun. It had been kind of like she was him when he was sixteen, and he was Miz Susanna, looking down from the bank. And it was why he hadn't let the others get to her. Thinking back, it might have been a fool thing. Now he had to watch his back; those two wood runners wouldn't forget him doing them out of their pleasure with her.

There might be another problem, when she got back to the troop. If she was to tell the major he'd raped her, then Ainsworth would feel himself dutybound as an officer and gentleman to call Joe out. And that would blow the Mexico expedition all to hell, because Joe'd just have to kill the man and any others that stood with him.

Could be Marilee wouldn't say anything; she wouldn't want it known that she'd laid with two men, one after the other. She might be smart enough not to talk about it to anybody; he'd have to wait and see.

Pulling up again at a wagontrack, Joe turned and listened but didn't hear her following. She couldn't miss the trail, he thought; even a plantation lady ought to strike the trail without trouble. But there was the feeling he had about bluebellies being somewhere close by; his instincts had kept him alive and he didn't fault them now. Prowling Yanks might be atween him and Marilee, searching for the Rebs that wiggled through their net at Appomattox. Damned fool woman and her stubborness! Joe's belly knotted as his mind's eye pictured her stripped naked and surrounded by grinning troopers. All that pure silvery hair, the perfect skin that tickled and burned a man's fingers at the same time, her clasping velvet cup. . . .

Teeth savage around his cigar, Joe rode on. The first flashing-eyed señorita he ran into would wipe away the feel and taste of Marilee Bradburn, the first loose-legged, laughing Mexican girl would make him forget all about the plantation *lady* without a plantation. The major could have her and welcome.

An hour along, Joe laid up in the bush, leaned forward

to press fingers into his horse's nose and guarantee him staying quiet. The horsemen were greenhorns, clattering along, joshing and paying no attention to the woods. He watched them pass, fresh and shiny in new blue uniforms, and thought it was damned lucky their war was won for them and luckier yet they wouldn't run across the troop. With no scouts or flankers out, they were going the wrong way, just skylarking along and blind to the trail. One cantering along in the rear was a lieutenant just out of school, and Joe gave serious thought to easing up behind the man and clubbing him off the fine horse he rode. It was near about good as Marilee Bradburn's stud.

When the dust settled, he eased across the track and slid through the woods, keeping to the tall timber. Marilee could damned well find the way by herself, if she was so almighty better than him. She'd gotten a good horse by herself, and guns with him, and she never said how. Stole the bunch, most likely, leaving some bluebelly officer sleeping in a bed still warmed by the heat of her slim, squirming body. That'd be more like trading for the horse, Joe thought, and when his cigar stub tasted bitter he flung it away. That was a pretty high price to pay for a whore, but *ladies* figured they were worth more than a crib girl. Look what one of them cost Joe Langston—blood running down his back while he choked on his pride.

Yessirree, gentry women came high; he'd wear the marks of Miz Susanna to his grave. And now this other one had somehow hung her sharp little claws deep inside his belly and wouldn't let go. Snorting, Joe put his horse into a long lope, pushing the animal until it was blowing hard before dropping it into a walk. That wouldn't do, either, so he stepped off and led it through a marsh where redbirds were like splashes of fire against knobbed cypress trees, where a water lily floated on a pond, its petals unfolded like white arms. He walked faster, skirting oaks graybearded with moss, sweating as he made for higher ground where pines grew and maypop vines hung their little false melons along any dry limb.

When he stopped at a freshet to water his horse and himself, Joe remembered he'd left his short shovel back there at Timmy Santee's grave and sat back on his heels to grin through water dripping over his face. He'd made a better swap on her than the Yank she'd skinned out of the horse and tack; all she got out of it was a little old shovel —less than a New Orleans crib girl would take. Thought she was better than anybody else, did she? She was a heap cheaper than most.

Hell, down there in New Orleans there were fancy women who shook it and humped it and could make an old man young; perfumed Creole belles and Frenchwomen who knew every trick in the whore's book; high yellows and octoroons who looked almost white, with just enough of that gold touch to their skin, just enough of that black spring curl to their hair.

He'd sweated on the docks and saved what little money he got for breaking his back, sleeping in corners and picking out of garbage cans when he couldn't steal enough fruit and dry beans from the warehouses. After a spell, he quit looking over his shoulder for the law, because it seemed they wouldn't trail him all the way from Alabama just for dropping one mouthy slave and one overseer. It might have been different had he killed old man Paisley and his young wife, Susanna, but niggers and rednecks didn't amount to much.

When he got a few coins saved up and got wise enough to pocket more than food from the ships that tied up at the piers, Joe moved into a room down close to South Rampart Street, where the rich white men kept their quadroon mistresses. He got him some clean clothes and a short gun lifted off a drunk cotton trader, and he took to backdooring some of those rich men who didn't come to town often enough to keep their hotblooded quadroons happy.

They told him things, those girls, maybe because he didn't treat them like niggers and because he appreciated them for women caught in a bind not much different from his own. He was selling his muscle and they were peddling their bodies, and neither of them had much sayso about it. So in the magnolia nights, the jasmine nights when the carriages didn't roll up and a planter all white-suited and full of brandy didn't step out, the girls told him what their men were doing, who was buying goods and who was losing so much at the gaming tables down to Madame Duplessis' that they had to sell short. Of course, Joe never had enough money to take advantage of the knowledge, but he got to some folks who did, and they threw him a crumb now and then.

He learned to gamble some, picking his time and place, saying yessir to redfaced gentlemen who spilled near about as much good liquor as they swallowed down, and acting like it was a pure privilege to be allowed to play cards with them. He got pretty good at it and might have made the tables his life's work, if he hadn't had to shoot that Frenchman. Damned fool tried to draw down on him with a little bitty derringer from clear across the room, just because he found out Joe had been making use of his bed and woman. Now if Joe had been a *gentleman,* there'd have been a challenge and a meeting out under the Dueling Oaks come daylight. But since he was only a redneck and not fit to duel with the gentry, the Frenchman saw fit to pop at him without warning.

Sighing, Joe climbed back on his horse and followed the beaten path Ainsworth's men had left. He guessed Marilee would see things the Frenchman's way, too; there was one set of laws for quality folk and another set for the poor ones, black or white. A woman like Marilee Bradburn, now—she'd have ducked behind her fan and got the vapors because the law was hanging some nameless white trash for killing a gentleman, but down inside she would have approved.

But the wiggly quadroon girl understood, and knew she'd find her another man to keep her, so she passed word to a black roustabout and got Joe aboard a river steamer. The *Natchez Belle* was the first paddlewheeler he rode up and down the big muddy, first toting cargo, then stoking the boilers, and finally buying him a lace shirt and tall hat and broadcloth coat in St. Louis, so he could play cards with the passengers. He might have made a good thing of that, because he was getting better at the tables all the time, picking up little tricks from the oldtime gamblers and limbering his fingers. But then the damned war came along.

Shaking his head, Joe moved his horse into a creek and on through the shallow water, seeing where a passel of horses had plowed out on the other side. It was a good thing the experienced Yanks had mostly gone on home, lucky that so many green troops of cavalry were riding aimlessly yonder and back, else they'd have run down the major already. Quantrill would never have left tracks like that.

Marilee could follow them, too. She knew where her
biscuit was buttered and would come loping along to catch
up with her gentleman officer. She'd be in Ainsworth's
blankets tonight. Oh, they'd be careful about it, so as not
to damage her reputation as a fine lady, but she'd purely
be making the ground shake when she got to him, but
somehow acting like she'd never done it afore.

Joe spat at the gray branch of a holly tree. Could be, if
the major didn't already have him a wife waiting to home,
Marilee would have him make an honest woman of her,
and marry the man down in Mexico. She'd get her a white
parasol and a buggy and have raggedy Mexicans jumping
when she snapped her fingers, just like the old times before the war.

And little Timmy Santee, the boy she'd diddled even
while he was dying, wouldn't ever ride back to Carolina
on a silver saddle with his pockets full of gold for his May.
But to give the devil her due, Joe couldn't fault Marilee
for the youngun's death. It took more luck than Timmy
ever had for him to make it to Mexico and back.

Damn it! He couldn't seem to put the woman out of his
head; she stayed with him like a cocklebur, just like Miz
Susanna had, for all these years. Joe squinted up at the
sun and blinked; funny thing—he couldn't put Miz
Susanna's face all together right now. He could remember
her golden body and the way it wrapped around him, but
when he closed his eyes, her face and eyes kind of
blurred, all running together like molasses.

He could recall other women better now, and that surprised him, since he'd carried Miz Susanna Paisley's image with him for these ten years gone, as if she was in a
locket hung around his neck. The last woman on the *River
Queen:* he could see her face plain as anything, hair swept
up in bronze curls, slim neck, and damp mouth touched
with rouge. But Miz Susanna's. . . .

Circling a stand of sweet gum woven heavily with
blooming briars, Joe unslung his canteen and took a swallow of tepid water, glancing back for any sign of Marilee
coming. She was pouting back yonder, he thought, or
maybe waiting out the Yankee patrol; but she'd be along.
He could just see her riding into camp, head up and looking like a boy in that mixed uniform getup, proud as if
she was going to a ball. She wouldn't look at him, she'd

act like he wasn't alive, and pay all her attention to Major Ainsworth, charming the man, tossing of *la's* and *dear me's* as if she was sitting to home in her mansion. But if their eyes did happen to cross, Joe's and hers, Marilee would redden and jerk her head around. She wouldn't forget how she'd pounded back up at him, how she'd moaned and gasped. And neither would he, damn it.

Joe kept the horse going until midday, then hobbled the gelding and fed him some corn, let him graze the deep spring grass. Back against a hickory tree, he made a smokeless fire from dry twigs and cooked bacon and meal. Marilee Bradburn still hadn't come up on him by the time he finished eating and cleaned his kit. He didn't think she'd swung past him, either—not that he could tell.

Mounted again, he pushed on after the troop. What that woman did or didn't do wasn't his business. It oughtn't bother him any, and he was about convinced of that when he caught up with Ainsworth's bunch just about ready to make camp for the day. The rear guard challenged him and passed him through, and the major limped over to him soon as Joe climbed down.

"You left this command without orders," the major said, leaning on his cane. "But I figured you went back to escort Miss Bradburn. Where is she, Langston?"

Joe loosened the cinch on his horse. "Back yonder somewhere, I reckon."

"Didn't you find her?"

"Found her, all right—buried the Santee boy." Joe lifted off the saddle and dropped it at his feet.

"Damn it, man—then why didn't she ride back with you?"

Shrugging, Joe said, "Didn't want to, I expect."

The major's face was set, his eyes intent. "You mean you left her *alone* in the woods, with Yankee patrols about?"

"Same way I found her. This time she had her pick. I'd say she'll be along about dark."

He could feel Ainsworth studying him as the man said, "But she wouldn't ride with *you,* is that it? What did you do to that lady, Langston? By all that's holy, if you—"

Men were watching, listening as they moved about the campsite, so Joe stepped close to Ainsworth and said slowly, said in almost a whisper, "Major, it won't do to

141

holler out somethin' can't be took back. Now I got a respect for you, even takin' into account all that military foofaraw and the fact you can't see the Confederacy is already laid out stinkin' in the sun. I make you out to be pretty much of a man, anyhow—which means I'd hate to kill you. But if you call me out, I can't do nothin' else, and then there won't *be* no expedition."

Ainsworth's right hand trembled upon his cane handle, his left one gripped the butt of his cross-holstered revolver, and the man's face was ashen beneath a layering of road dust. He said, quietly as he could, "I can order you shot."

"If you get out the words," Joe said, "and if'n some more men want to go down for a man already dead. I hope it don't come to that."

The major struggled visibly to control himself and said through his teeth, "Miss Bradburn?"

"Fine when I left her. I didn't do nothin' to her that she didn't want done."

"Then she just didn't care to ride with one of your kind." The tension was easing in Ainsworth, and Joe relaxed some. "But if anything happens to that lady, I'll still hold you accountable, Langston."

Joe turned away, saying over one shoulder, "You do that, major. My kind just don't much give a damn."

Chapter 15

Her body still felt strange, with odd little ripples of warmth popping through it now and then, and she wanted to slap herself because of them. Everything she did seemed somehow alien, the everyday tasks of picking up her camp, of saddling and bitting Bradburn. She was almost painfully aware of each separate movement of her arms and legs, as if she stood outside herself and watched a painted marionette being jerked clumsily, but not comically, about, controlled by hidden strings she had no hand in manipulating.

Marilee was so mad she ached all over, blindly furious at Joe Langston for using her so casually to slake his own animal lusts, sickeningly angry at herself for—for letting something happen to her body while she was being raped. She couldn't understand it; there had been a whirlpool gathering strength and violence that she could not control, that she didn't even realize was spinning her away until she'd been caught up so completely there was no escape.

Leaning her forehead against Bradburn's heavy neck, her nostrils pulling in the pure, honest scent of him, Marilee told herself she had been betrayed by her body, that her weakened flesh had turned traitor. How *could* it riot that way? How could *she* be so lost in far and flowered places that had no possible right to exist for her?

The horse shifted, and she came erect to listen, catching the clink of an iron shoe against a stone, the muffled echo of a man's deep voice. He might be coming back, and she couldn't look at him again, not with the memory of her shameless reaction showing in her face.

Lifting into the saddle, Marilee realized that it might not be Joe Langston, but the Yankee patrol. Her weapons were jammed in the fork of that tree, and she loped Bradburn across the clearing to get them, feeling a shade better when the carbine was thrust into its boot and the revolver snug in her belt.

Another rattle of equipment sounded through the woods behind her, and she trotted the stallion quickly through the brush, following the trail Major Ainsworth's men had taken, the path Joe Langston had gone along. But not for very far; at the first break in the trees, Marilee swung her horse off the track and pointed him almost due west. If the Yankees were close behind, they'd probably stop to look over the abandoned campsite first, then take up the trail of the troops. She would be a fool to let herself be caught between fleeing Confederates and their pursuers—and a bigger fool yet, if she rejoined the expedition and allowed Joe Langston to make her his whore.

She eyed the sun and worked Bradburn quietly through the brush, pulling him up in the shelter of a wild magnolia and sitting there in blackgreen shade while the rattle of other horsemen passed beyond them. The creamy buds of the tree weren't opened yet, still lumpy and green, but already spreading gentle hints of their perfume. Marilee didn't like it now, and she would probably always hate the smell of crushed spring grass, always detest the odor of a man sweating in passion.

The noise faded, but she waited a while longer before pushing the stallion in the direction she'd chosen. In the worst way, she craved another bath, a real one with hot water and soap and a sponge, so she could scrub away every vestige of Joe Langston from her body. She wished there was a way to wash him from her mind.

Coming out on a wagon road, Marilee followed it for a while, riding in a numbness of her flesh that didn't match the constant turmoil of her racing, often wincing mind.

A decent woman didn't act the way she had, not even with a husband she loved—much less while she was taken by force. Of course, her mama had never said that in so many words, because Mama simply did not discuss physical relationships of any sort. But Marilee had grown up understanding what was proper and what could not be countenanced in polite society.

"Always remember you are a lady," Mama had said, and a hundred years of tradition bore heavily upon the warning.

"Lord forgive me," Marilee said aloud, "but now I'm very glad you're dead, Mama, glad you didn't live to know that *your* daughter—that I—I—"

She resisted the tears and turned Bradburn off the road along a winding path. Her mother had also closed her mind to the yard children appearing yearly upon every plantation, never admitting it was remotely possible that a Bradburn or a Crownover or a Maddox could have sired them. Any white blood was due to overseers or slave merchants, that kind of trash—never to quality folks.

Even as a child, Marilee had known better than that. She'd whispered with other girls about how certain wenches carried on in the slave quarters, especially those who were lighter colored and more desirable. And it was common knowledge that young men gained their knowledge of—you know—doing it, from the experienced Nigras.

But that was totally different from love and marriage and raising children. Flirting with your beaux was not only permissible, but encouraged, yet any decent girl understood that a white bride only did her wifely duty in bed because it was expected of her, and a woman's burden. Except for prostitutes, of course—*oh, lordy, lordy, Marilee! How can they sell themselves to just any man?* But prostitutes were trash, too, or Yankee women come down from the North, or those foreign kind in New Orleans or Mobile.

Good women didn't get any enjoyment from sex. A lady never placed herself in a position where she might possibly be attacked.

Biting her lips until they hurt, Marilee whispered, "But it wasn't my fault, Mama. I swear, I couldn't help it."

Then why had she trembled and surged and gone insane at that final overwhelming crest that bubbled and foamed and swept her away? It hadn't happened with that filthy

Yankee, nor with weakened and gentle Timmy Santee—and despite her upbringing, Marilee refused to feel guilty over giving herself to that boy in his last hours. Once her maidenhead had been broken, there was no bringing it back, so she was no more soiled by two men than by one.

Then the third man; then Joe Langston. . . .

Maybe it happened after a woman got used to doing it, and maybe there was something dark and evil lurking within Marilee Bradburn, some mark of sin she hadn't been aware of. She wished she'd gone to camp meetings more often, or paid more attention when she had, instead of giggling behind fans or under parasols with other thoughtless girls.

Straightening her back, Marilee checked the slant of the sun again, and when Bradburn reached the bank of a shallow meandering creek, she dismounted.

She didn't know exactly where she was going and didn't much care, so long as it was far from Joe Langston. She didn't enjoy being alone again, and away from the gentlemanly protection of Major Ainsworth, but she could never stand the sneers and dirty remarks Joe Langston would make, never accept the knowing look in his sleepily hooded eyes.

Trimming some fatback from her slab of bacon, Marilee put it in the skillet, then stripped the stallion and let him feed. He never wandered far from her; they had an understanding, a need for each other. Before gathering dry sticks for a fire, she thought she should conserve her food supply, and used the penknife to cut willow branches. Her shirt made a net of sorts, and she took off the awkward boots to wade the creek with it, sweeping it through the water low down, stirring the muddy bottom.

Working her way into a dip in the bank, she immersed the net, then scrambled to land so she could pin down the quickbacking crayfish and wriggling young mudcats. Swiftly, she killed the catfish and deftly gutted them, beheading them with sure slashes of her blade. Bagging the crayfish in her shirt, she recrossed the creek and dipped water into her fry pan, built a fire, and got the salted water boiling. Then she dropped in the grayshelled crustaceans and saw them turn pink. Marilee peeled and ate them while she was rinsing her shirt, and while fatback and cornmealed fish simmered together in the skillet.

She hadn't been the perfect little lady; as a tomboy, she'd learned from slaves about fishing and snares, from her father and brothers the secrets of hunting and the wily ways of game. The knowledge was saving her now, and she thought she could live off the land as long as necessary. So her mama had been partly wrong—and too much right.

When she donned the shirt again, it clung damply to her skin, sunwarmed and caressing her breasts, the flatness of her stomach. Shrinking her nipples back from the contact, Marilee saw to her horse and checked her gear, lashing everything firmly into place. She thrust the pistol into her belt, vowing never again to allow any man to get between her and a gun.

Bradburn seemed eager to be gone, to put many leagues of this tropic, brooding land behind him, and pranced some when she was astride him. He'd also come from a different place, from somewhere far to the north where the air was cold and it snowed every year. Marilee had seen snow just twice—little bitty flakes of cold white stuff that came spiraling down to create holidays for everyone, including the field hands. And it hadn't stayed on the ground for long, melting almost soon as it hit, but while it lasted, it spread fairy spiderwebbing of strange loveliness over the land.

A little bit of snow was just fine, she thought, squeezing the stallion forward; a whole lot of it might get you to feeling trapped and keep you cold too long. Probably, that's what made Yankees so poisonous. But what was Joe Langston's excuse?

Never had to rape a woman, he'd said, *and if I do, it won't be in a pack.*

So he had slipped away from his pack and come back alone, a coldeyed wolf intent upon his prey. Marilee frowned; but he hadn't hurt her—not really; there'd been no brutal mauling like the Yankee used, no raking of sharp nails. She felt her face go warm. *She'd* used fingernails, not Joe Langston.

She didn't want to think of that, didn't want to recall anything that made her feel so ashamed and degraded. Resolutely, Marilee pushed on through the woods, forcing herself to pay close attention to her surroundings, to stay alert for any warning of danger.

Major Ainsworth's troops had ridden almost due south, but she had turned more to the west, roughly paralleling the course they were taking, but higher up. When they crossed the border somewhere in Texas, she would be hundreds of miles from them, far from the hateful, smirking presence of Joe Langston. Not ever seeing those broad shoulders and narrow hips, not ever having to watch the lazy, catlike way he had of walking, and especially not seeing his light-colored, penetrating eyes anymore, Marilee would be able to forget him, she was certain. She would wipe him right out of her mind, like using a damp cloth on a school slate.

Once that was done, her body would forget his imprint, too.

When a mockingbird ran up and down his scale of brilliant notes, she already felt good enough to smile. Sun was warm upon her face and Bradburn moved easily, sweating just enough, the clear and unfrothed sweat that showed his prime condition. All of Louisiana to cross, she thought, or a goodly part of it, anyway—so much ancient oak and Spanish moss, land where cattail reeds dipped and swayed their round, long heads and shiny red dragonflies darted on gossamer wings.

Already she was farther from home than she had ever traveled before and she noticed the difference in the land. Many trees were the same, but here and there she saw wildflowers she didn't recognize, and the air was heavier, more cloying than in the red dirt hills around Bradburn Plantation.

Most of the plantation's split-rail fences were gone, torn down by passing troops for firewood, the rest fallen into disrepair. Weeds stood shoulder-high and choked together in what had once been productive cotton and cane fields, and on the edges the forest was sending out fingers to reclaim the land. It would take many laborers to cleanse the land once more and ready it for planting; it would take years to rebuild the big house, to put it back exactly as it had been in the good, warm days of Bradburn's glory.

The weight of it came down on Marilee, and she stopped smiling at a giddy yellow butterfly. Heavy though the task was, there was no one left to share it with, and she had to carry it alone. It was her duty to reclaim the estate, because she was the last of her line. There had been Colonel Wayne Bradburn, tall and handsome, with just a shade of gray at his temples, a fine figure of a man obviously born to lead. *Fallen at Corinth, Mississippi.*

And Lieutenant Elliot Bradburn, who loved nothing better than following the hounds, so gay and dashing, an older brother any girl would admire because he never lorded it over her, because he was kind and gentle. *Died in battle, Vicksburg, Mississippi.*

And Private Darrell Bradburn, who couldn't wait for a commission and rode off to war before he was quite sixteen years old; quiet Darrell, as much a horseman as any of them, but you could often find him in the library. It was worse with Darrell, because he came home to die of the arm wound he'd gotten at the Battle of the Wilderness, to die slowly and painfully before his seventeenth birthday.

And Mama.

And Captain Robbie Dee Crownover.

And so many, many more. Even little Timmy Santee had become a passing part of her family.

"The last Bradburn," Marilee murmured. "It's an awesome responsibility. But, no, I'm *not* the last one. There are two of us now—you and me, Bradburn." She patted the great stallion's neck. "Between us, we'll manage."

If she avoided any more rapists and managed to stay away from Yankee patrols; if rednecks didn't trap her and she could make it to the frontier with the horse. A new land out there, a fierce and unforgiving land, from what she'd heard, but offering a chance to start over.

"Next time," she said, "I'll shoot first. I won't give a Joe Langston the opportunity to hold me down and do what he wants to do with my body. Because next time some animal like him may kill me, too—and the plantation will be forever lost. I can't let that happen. I *won't.*"

The stallion stopped, powerful muscles bunching beneath his hide, and Marilee looked down at the path ahead to see the thick, scaly body of a water moccasin easing slowly across it. She stroked Bradburn's shoulder and told him he was a good boy. When the snake was gone, she moved the horse forward again, knowing they would have to travel until just before dusk, so her cookfire wouldn't be seen. There were others journeying these woods, people she didn't want to meet.

Sighing, Marilee thought how much easier it would have been if she were a man. No slavering male would be out to rape her or try to take advantage of her simply because she was a woman alone. She could pretend to be a discharged soldier and nobody would bother her. It just wasn't *fair*.

A mosquito buzzed her throat, and she brushed it away; another whined over her cheek, and she hurried the horse through a marshy area, letting him out into a fast trot that fanned her face with damp wind. Marilee turned him onto a wider trail, one that looked well traveled, and mosquitoes fell away in new sunlight. She realized she couldn't stay in the woods forever, that she'd have to follow some roads leading west. It would be easy to stumble Bradburn into a bog that could suck them both down into black and slimy depths or get the stallion snakebit. They'd have to take their chances on the highways, pulling off only at night when danger would be greater.

And she would have to keep one hand on a gun, lower the disguise of her eyepatch, see that her straggly hair was tucked well up under the forage cap. She just couldn't let anyone find out she was a woman—not again. It would mean the end of everything—all hope of recovering the past, all hope of making a new future.

Careful—she'd have to be careful as Joe Langston himself, never putting anybody at her back, never trusting, never caring for anyone, and always keeping that tightly coiled clockspring of watchfulness within herself.

She had that much to thank him for but she could have said the same for any cunning wolf, if she'd been that close to another one.

Chapter 16

Lying sprawled upon soft linen sheets, Joe stretched and watched the countess's maid dress redbronze hair in ringlets. Sitting before a triple mirror, slender legs crossed and white thighs peeping from beneath the lacy frill of a corselet she didn't need, the Countess Delphine looked downright delicious.

"You'll study some more while I'm gone, Joe?" Her voice sounded as if it had been dipped in honey, but Joe knew how quickly it could change, going husky and demanding in passion or climbing, scratchy and thinned, when she was displeased.

"Sure," he said, sitting up to prop himself against the bed's scrollwork headboard and catching her violet eyes watching him from the mirror. He grinned and stretched again, top sheet slipping low upon his groin.

"A bother," Delphine said in that lilting accent. *"Mon cher,* I would much rather spend the day with you than attend another of those interminable luncheons at the court. But what can one do?"

When she leaned forward to do things to her cameo face with a brush and paintbox, Joe sneaked a lingering glance at the maid. That one was neatly put together, too, but quiet and dark where Delphine was bubbly and brilliant. Joe suspected that just as much fire lay hidden beneath the rose and ivory skin of the Mexican girl—maybe even more. Fingering a slim, pale brown cigarillo, he reached lazily for a match upon the bedside table, still hunting for that other word, the fancy one, to describe Madame la Comtesse Delphine Delacroix. *Vivacious,* that was it—another way of saying bubbly. He'd have to remember to use it.

"Good thing you speak English," he said around a mouthful of fragrant smoke. "Don't know how we'da got along, otherwise—and I wouldn't have me such a pretty uniform."

Pasting a star-shaped black beauty spot below one corner of her gleaming mouth, Delphine murmured, "In Europe, it is of necessity to speak several languages, *mon amour.* But you—ah—you have a special capacity, a manner of speaking with your so magnificent body that is communication of itself, *oui?* You and I, we need no other, but if you are to rise farther in rank, it is better you continue with the books." Then, sharply, "Luisa! Be careful, girl. You do not tug upon the coarse hair of some mestizo."

Joe caught a flash of black eyes in the mirror, a curling of rich lips as the maid whispered quick apology.

"As for the uniform of *le capitaine,*" Delphine said, her voice gentle again as it reached back to Joe, "that can be but a beginning for one of your obvious talents. Although I must confess, *chéri,* that I prefer you out of uniform, just as you are now."

It was funny, Joe thought, how Delphine could talk right through a servant, as though the girl wasn't there, wasn't really alive, but more like Luisa was a horse or something, not able to understand what was going on. He just couldn't get used to that and figured it came from being born into royalty.

"I do hope Max won't hold us into the evening," she breathed, applying some kind of gold powder to her eyelashes. "Our emperor has a tendency to drag out these court affairs. Tell me you will not be bored, *chéri.*"

"Got my schoolbooks," Joe said. "I'll take me a bath and have a good meal and do some more studyin'—until you come back."

"And I will return as soon as possible," Delphine

promised, rising gracefully to make an imperious gesture to her maid. Joe watched Luisa bring the glittering, ruffled ball gown, and watched her hold it open while Delphine lifted one long leg at a time into it. *"Ma foi,* but it is a bother!"

"To the count, too, I reckon," Joe said, comparing the bodies of the two women, one proud and regal, the other earthy and smoldering.

"Him!" Delphine made a cute face and reached for a jeweled necklace. "That *paon*—how you say—peacock? Louis loves only to strut around palaces and heartily detests having to ride out at the head of his lancers from time to time."

" 'Spect you see to it he does, though," Joe said, eyeing the gray ash built up upon the end of his cigarillo. It didn't take a man long to get used to real good tobacco like this, nor to clean sheets and champagne and foods no redneck ever heard of, much less tasted. But it'd take a man a lifetime to get used to a woman like the countess; Delphine had too many tricks, too many surprises hidden in that fine, practiced body.

"Mais certainment!" Delphine smiled, coming over to stand beside the bed and stare down at him. "How else would I have any time to spend with my *pistolero?"* Sloe eyes twinkling wickedly, she whispered, "And see that you do not discharge that beautiful weapon while I am away, *hein?"*

When she bent to kiss him, careful not to smear the rouge upon her lips, Joe breathed in the spiced musk of her, that Parisian perfume dabbed between her generous breasts and behind her little pink ears. A sniff of that and a man just had to think of bed.

For the hell of it, he reached up to cup her breasts, bearing hard upon them the way she liked, and the laugh caught in Delphine's throat as she pulled herself away. *"Non, non!* You tempt me overmuch, *m'sieu*—but the emperor has commanded, and I am his loyal subject."

"Until tonight, then," he said.

She patted him low upon the belly, swiftly, possessively. "Prepare yourself, *mon amour."*

Luisa held open the door for her mistress, and the countess swept from the room in a flowing of long, rustling skirts, trailing sequined light, and tempting perfume.

Joe said then, "Have breakfast with me, Luisa—a Mexican breakfast."

A torrent of midnight hair gleamed as the girl shook her head. "I would not dare, señor."

"You'd dare anything you had time for, I think," Joe said, and she lifted her eyes to him as a tiny smile twitched the corners of her mouth.

"Me, señor? I am but a poor *indio* servant—"

"You ain't that, either. You can read and write, and even get by some in French. I figure you for one of them Creoles whose family got run out of the north by Juárez, maybe from around Monterrey?"

Again she shook her head, but now Luisa's hands were upon her hips, and he saw the movement of her globular breasts beneath the plain, shapeless dress. "Not so far north—Ciudad Victoria, señor. Very well, then—breakfast."

Joe grinned. "Have 'em send up some of those sweet melons with it, and wine."

"Champagne?" Her dark eyes glinted.

"No, señorita, red *vino*—this is goin' to be a *Mexican* day."

"*Sí,*" she murmured, and gave a little wave of her hips as she went out.

Climbing out of bed, Joe stood naked at the arched window and looked down upon the garden, letting air play over his body. High vaulted ceilings and thick adobe walls kept the house cool, while a springhouse in the corner of the garden did the same for the Delacroix wines. While here in the bedroom, Captain Joe Langston of the Household Guards tried to keep down the countess's temperature, also—or at least share it when it boiled over.

"Pretty good life," he said to a bunch of bright red flowers that hung down just outside the window. "Beats hell out of chasin' Juaristas in the mountains, but who knows how long it's goin' to last?"

Not until the French-Mexican government backed a new Confederacy in the Indian Territories, that was for sure. So much for Major Ainsworth's dream of the Stars and Bars rising again, but the major didn't care now; some *bandido* had nailed him through the head a while back, while it had still looked like Maximilian had a chance. Most of the troops had fallen, too—some in running battles along the dry ravines, others with throats cut in cantinas, and a few had turned around and gone home, realizing they were on the wrong side again. A couple had gone over to the Juaristas, depending on loot to carry them instead of French gold, which was getting in short supply.

Joe pulled on a robe, the first he had ever owned, and rolled his shoulders in its silk. He'd just brushed back his hair when Luisa brought in the big tray smelling of green peppers and onions.

The omelet was excellent, spiced and fluffy, the wine chilled, the coffee hot. Joe ate hungrily, seeing the occasional white flashing of Luisa's even teeth, always conscious of the girl so close across the small table.

"I hear some of the Creoles are changin' their minds and makin' deals with Juárez and his generals."

Luisa sipped coffee. "If one listens to all the rumors—"

"Or all the court gossip—somethin' could be learned and passed on."

"If you say, señor." Her ripe lips were damp when she lowered the cup, and she didn't look at him.

"Look, girl," he said. "Because I'm just now learnin' to read, that don't make me stupid."

Luisa exchanged her coffee cup for two stemmed glasses and poured native ruby wine for them. "I am sure the señor knows what he is about."

Tasting the tart wine, Joe grinned. She'd seen to it that the kitchen sent up the ordinary peon stuff, but that was all right. "Your people don't have much use for us *pistoleros*, I know—unless we're on the right side." She had so much of that black, flowing hair, and a special ripeness about her, although she couldn't be over eighteen. "But us *gringos* make it any way we can. You understand that?"

Her shrug was expressive, more so because he could see that Luisa wore nothing beneath her thin cotton dress. "Each does what he must, señor." This time her darkly lashed eyes lifted and stared directly into his own, cautiously, but with hot lights moving in them.

She was dark and tempting and had a flavor about her that was dangerous; she was small and so lush she was about to bust out of her olive skin. So why did Luisa keep reminding him somehow of Marilee Bradburn? The two women were at opposite ends of the stick, alike only in that they were both halfway pointing toward some damned cause or the other. Marilee had had that same dream about the South rising again, the stubborn, blind dream that finally killed Major Ainsworth and a lot of the other boys. And Joe had a pretty good idea that little Luisa here was only playing at being a lady's maid so she could slip tidbits of information out to the Juaristas. The countess had brought a maid with her from France, of course, but after a time the woman had disappeared, and not by chance, Joe figured.

Now, Delphine Delacroix—that one was far more like Marilee, a *lady* to the bone, with all the traits such gentry were born to. Title or not, Marilee Bradburn would think herself just as royal as the countess, and act just as uppity. Come to think on it, using what he'd learned from the books Delphine insisted on feeding into him, Joe figured that Bradburn Plantation was probably bigger than *le comte*'s estate back in Europe. Even here in Mexico, French royalty was thicker than seed ticks in a mule's ear, and *all* of them couldn't own big chunks of their home country.

"You like the wine?" Luisa's eyes still probed him.

"Sure—better'n popskull whiskey I got used to—beats *pulque*, too."

A faint smile moved her red lips. "The señor has varied tastes."

Draining his glass, Joe stood up. After a moment, Luisa began to gather the dishes. He said, "Leave 'em be. Roberto can take 'em to the kitchen after he brings up water for my bath."

Silently, she obeyed, dropping back into the chair with that straightbacked grace all these women seemed to have, and Joe felt her eyes on him as he walked to the canopied bed and tugged upon a red velvet rope. Down in the belly of the house, a bell would clang, and Roberto would start carrying up buckets of hot water.

Cigarillo in his teeth, Joe kept his back to Luisa, looking down into the garden, making her wait as he was forcing himself to wait. She'd be there when he turned around; he knew that. The girl had probably been eager for the chance. A captain of the Household Guards knew more about military operations than a countess, although that was damned little, because nobody at Maximilian's court knew anything.

Marilee Bradburn, now—if he had turned his back on that fiery gal, she'd have been out of this room like a shot from a Walker Colt—but not before she'd tried to put a melon knife into his back. Damn it, why did he keep bothering about her? It wasn't his fault that she took it on herself to sulk in the Louisiana woods instead of joining back up with the troops. It hadn't been like she was a virgin; that fine plantation lady had had plenty of experience before bedding down with Timmy Santee. The dying boy had been too weak to take her maidenhead, and a woman didn't carry on the way she had when she was codded the first time. Silvery hair and skin you could near about see through, down to the tiny blue veins. . . .

"Señor?" Roberto grinned as he moved in his lopsided way to the big tub standing in a corner of the bedroom. "First the hot, then the cold, *sí?*"

"*Sí*, Roberto—like always." Joe turned around.

Chopped-off black hair, brown skin, and bare feet, floppy pants and hangover shirt, Roberto's round face was innocent as he poured steaming water and said, "The other señor—he likes it different."

Joe looked just as innocent. "Maybe that's why the señora keeps one of us out of town all the time."

Giggling, the man slid out of the room, his wooden buckets thumping. Chewing his cigarillo, Joe looked at the girl sitting motionless in her chair; she was barefoot, too, but her feet were finely shaped, trim in the ankles, her calves nicely rounded and smooth. He waited until the cold water came, until Roberto went again, before taking off his robe and striding to the tub. Still, Luisa didn't move.

When he'd soaped himself down, he said, "Come here."

Fluidly, she moved close, and without a word drew the dress over her head. Light played over her full, small body, dancing across the flat brown belly and over the crisp black hair, the dark nipples.

"Room for two in here," he said, and her eyes got bigger, blacker when Luisa climbed into the tub with him.

She was like a greased eel in the warm water, attacking him fiercely, all over him in a thrashing that scattered water and glistening soapsuds. His hands kept slipping on her skin when he tried to hold her close, but that didn't matter. She was hungry for it, for him, and as her thighs closed strongly about him, Joe had the idea that maybe she was getting back at Delphine for all the times the countess had snapped at her, or worse, talked through her like she wasn't there at all.

Wild—Luisa was wild as a pine woods bobcat and had near about as many teeth and claws. She was direct and eager and tried to eat him up with every wiggling inch of her solid little body, and she didn't settle down for quite a spell. When she finally quieted, it wasn't quiet as other women, not like Delphine, who sort of collapsed after an active, sweaty set-to. Luisa kept making little rhythmic motions with her hips, little rippling movements of her belly.

"Ah," she said against his mouth, tasting of soap and a wet fire nowhere near out, but only banked, "the *condesa* knows what she is about."

"And so do you," Joe said, stroking her slidy back, her wealth of long, dripping hair. It was black hair, not silvered and glowing; the girl was small, not tall and long-legged as a blooded filly. But she wasn't a lady, either; if she had a husband somewhere, Luisa was keeping quiet about him, not shaking him in the faces of fancy friends like some kind of trophy. And right or wrong, this one was working for something she believed in, not flitting between the emperor's court and her husband's fine house to dally with a lover.

"I'm kind of glad you know what you're about," he went on, "but you didn't have to mount me to find out what I know. Happy you did, but I been thinkin' some about which way to jump, anyhow."

Her hips stopped moving, and she lifted her mouth from his as her breath slowed. "Señor?"

Moving her off him, Joe climbed from the tub and picked a towel from the back of a cane-bottomed chair. Drying himself, he said, "You ain't stupid, Luisa, unless you count me that way. Sure, I'm Delphine's prime stud right now, but she could change her mind *mañana*, and I'd be back out in the hills gettin' shot at."

When she got out of the water to stand across from him, Joe handed her a towel, and she said carefully, "And you are not so loyal to the emperor as she is?"

Joe toweled his hair. "Loyal to Joe Langston, mostly. Hell, I can sniff the air good as any hound dog, and what I smell comin' is the French gettin' their tails run clear out of Mexico pretty soon. I'd just as lief be on my way north afore it happens."

Holding the towel to her shining body, the girl said, "Then you do not believe in the revolution, either."

"Your business, not mine. I come down here to hire my gun, that's all. The pay's about to run out."

Softly, she murmured, *"El Presidente has use for gringo pistoleros."*

Joe walked naked to the table, found his cigarillo, and lighted it. "Some of *El Presidente's* men kind of got to know me a while back. I figure my welcome is about wore out in Mexico."

When he turned back to her, he could see something like the beginning of scorn upon her brown face. "You would sell us something, then? We do have little gold, señor—much goes to pay your government for guns."

"I can scrape together money enough to carry me a spell. What I want is a pass, *amiga*—a piece of paper to get me to the border. I'm willin' to trade for it. Don't know much now, but I can nose around and find out, do I start playin' soldier boy more at the court."

Her black eyes searched his. "It will take time."

"Reckoned as much." He put on his robe.

Luisa wrapped the towel about her body. "You did not have to make love with me to arrange this."

"Wanted to," he said.

"And I," she murmured. "We will speak more of this."

"Yeah," Joe said, and watched the curve of her buttocks as she bent to pick up her wet dress, as she walked out of the room stately as any jeweled princess in Maxmilian's court.

Joe started to get dressed. He understood Luisa better than the countess, far better than Marilee Bradburn, and if he could trust her, he might slide on over onto the winning side. It would mean hard riding and lean living for a while, but there could be good pickings when the emperor fell.

Trouble was, Luisa and her friends didn't trust him a lick more than he did them. Mexico was pretty damned tired of foreign soldiers of fortune, whether from north of the border or across the seas. What was left of Maximilian's army was made up of near about as many Belgians, Germans, and ragtag *gringos* as Frenchmen, with even more native "Loyalist" troops. Those Mexican *soldados* were as apt to turn one way as the other, depending which way the wind blew.

Pulling on tight breeches and polished boots with bright spurs that jingled, Joe remembered another word for himself and others like him: mercenary. It meant anybody who fought for pay instead of glory and honor and all the rest of that hogshit. When Delphine said it to him, the word took on another meaning, like getting a stud fee, but the dandies at court curled their lips when they mouthed it —as if the honorable Frenchmen weren't getting ready to ship their soldiers back home any day now. Only the mercenaries would be left when the ax fell. It didn't show yet to the untrained eye, but Joe had been noticing the little things: missing colonels and majors who were supposed to be out "crushing rebels" in the mountains but weren't; some of the black-robed priests moving church goods on donkeys' backs toward Vera Cruz; more mean-eyed peons slipping into the city.

And how come the Empress Carlotta went scooting home to see the high muckymuck Napoleon? Buttoning his tunic, Joe shook his head; something funny about that one—a strange light in the woman's eyes; quick, jerky movements of her hands and head.

"Hell," he said, adjusting the gold braid on his shoulders and clapping the belt around his hips, "there's somethin' wrong with all of 'em. Delphine's about the only one with a speck of sense, and most of that is down there atween her legs."

But she'd been good to him, Joe admitted. From the first time he saw her, sitting there in her carriage high-headed and cool, as if Porfirio Díaz's men hadn't shot down her escort and cut loose the horses, Joe hoped he might have a find. Delphine hadn't disappointed him. After the troops had driven off the raiders, Comtesse Delacroix insisted he tote her right on into Puebla on his saddle, calling him a hero and saying how he had saved her from a worse fate than being kidnapped and held for ransom.

Picking up his hat with the shiny peak, Joe set it on his head and glanced down at the saber Roberto had polished as always. Damned fool weapon, the saber—near about as bad as a lance; but Delphine said gentlemen always wore swords, and Colonel Romaine would pull his goatee and frown if Joe showed up without his.

From the first, Delphine had made the colonel understand he needed a—what was it she called him?—"a valiant, gallant officer" in his command, and who better than this *americain* who had risked his life to save her from brigands? Comte Louis had been properly grateful, of course, especially when Joe claimed no other reward for rescuing his wife than to be allowed to serve the emperor better—and closer. Delacroix was a little tight-fisted, but his wife made up for that; Delphine was tight, too—but only where it counted best, and she kind of spread that around.

Joe latched the damned sword onto his belt and adjusted the good Walker Colt on the other side. Sure, he was beholden to Delphine, expecially for making him learn to read some; he could even write—not all that good, because a pen in his big hand wiggled the letters every which way, but they could be made out. And she'd taught him a few words of French, showed him how to bow and smile and play the gentleman, and while the count was off chasing rebels, Delphine showed him a lot of other things—in bed. Damn, Joe thought, he'd figured that the women he'd met knew it all, but they could take lessons from Delphine. Except maybe one—a tall girl with willowgreen eyes and silvery hair.

He went down the stairs, knowing that Roberto would have his mare ready for him. Another present from the countess, that mare: a fine barb with blood hot as Delphine's, almost. The military saddle wasn't all prettied up with silver conchos, but there was better metal hid out—yellow gold coins. Other silver jingled in his pockets as he swung up on the sidling, anxious mare and rode off toward the palace at Chapultepec. He'd show his face there, buy some wine for his superiors, maybe make a round of cantinas later with them.

He had to make his suspicions more solid, come up with something Luisa could trade off to her machete-toting *amigos* for a pass from Díaz Álvarez, or, better yet, from the big dog himself, Benito Juárez. Anything real official-looking might get him by, long as it was gussied up with seals and ribbons and the like, because not many of the *guerrilleros* could read. Not many of the officers would even try, either, did they get a clear look at blue eyes.

As his mare pranced prettily down the street, peons got out of his way and took off their sombreros when he passed, but Joe caught the looks from some—the flat, hard Indian eyes watching and chalking him up in the doomsday book.

He couldn't fault them for it. The *hidalgos* and Frenchmen, all the imperialist hangers-on, acted like they came special from God almighty, taking what they pleased and stomping the peasants if they didn't bow down while they got robbed and their women were raped before their eyes. Hell, didn't Maximilian himself talk about "divine destiny"?

Just like back home, he thought, and tossed a casual salute at a colonel riding the other way with a cavalry patrol behind him, lances and shined-up helmets glittering in the early fall sun, little flags waving and sabers rattling. Back home, royalty was plantation owners and peons were named sharecroppers or hard dirt farmers—or poor white trash. Wasn't all that much difference, Joe thought, damned glad there were more machetes hidden away under those ragged serapes than long guns.

That didn't mean he was going to get down in the dirt and join up with them. He'd seen some of their generals, and they were no better than the French, dripping gold braid and medals, hollering about liberation and revolution and the republic. But all the time, they were filling their saddlebags with loot and wiping their boots on the little man's back.

Before he reached the compound gates, Joe saw Colonel Romaine and some more officers dismounting before one of the adobe cantinas that gathered around the walls of the old Spanish castle. Naturally, an ordinary soldier had to sit out in the sun and hold the horses. Joe trotted his mare up to the hitching rack and nodded at the man's salute.

"Almonte, ain't it?"

"*Sí*, capitán—you remember me?"

Climbing down, Joe tethered his own horse. "Damned right I remember you. That day we chased off Díaz's *ban-*

didos. Neither of us had pretty uniforms then, but maybe more fun, *amigo*."

"*Es verdad*," Almonte said from under his drooping moustache. "I miss those days in the hills, capitán—the *pulque*, the girls—"

"But not the bullets, eh, *caballero*? A fatter life here, with no danger."

Almonte pushed back his hat with a thumb. "If one does not look too closely."

Joe nodded toward the cantina. "And them inside— they startin' to look, too?"

"*Quién sabe?* Perhaps they have heard of the ships."

Joe pretended he knew. "*Sí*. But no room aboard for the likes of you and me, *compadre*."

"As I have been thinking," Almonte said.

"And I think I'll go have me a drink with the colonel," Joe said. "*Vaya con Dios, amigo*."

"*Con Dios*," the man said, and got down from his horse to loop gathered reins over the hitching rail before losing himself in the crowd.

Joe went into the cantina to find out more about these ships.

Chapter 17

Texas wasn't any different from Louisiana to Marilee, just as hot and muggy, but with more flies clouding the air over the muddy streets of Beaumont. People buzzed like flies, too, hurrying back and forth, more people than Marilee had seen in a long time, or cared to see.

Slouched in the saddle, but with all her senses alert, she moved Bradburn at a slow walk, staying to the far side and away from the board shanty saloons that lined one edge of what looked like the town's main thoroughfare. They had to swing out past a bunch of wagons standing head to tail in the middle of the road, some of them with four-mule teams in harness, others with oaken tongues down in the mud.

Nobody gave her a second look, and for that Marilee was grateful. She saw men in floppy hats and wearing galluses hauling supplies from a general store; bonneted, pinch-faced women in drab, worn dresses, children huddled in mute, suspicious clumps or hoorawing through hoof- and wheel-churned swamp and along a plank walkway.

A man in buckskin smoke-blackened and greasy

sauntered past, long gun casual in the crook of his arm, bearded and grimy. His quick eyes squinted over her horse, but not her. Nostrils flaring, leather eyepatch in place, Marilee drew a deep breath, smelling the stench of what passed for civilization on the frontier—mansweat and mulesweat, both rancid; a maisma rising from the filthy street—urine and excrement of man and beast, a drifting of smoke, a passing eddy redolent of raw whiskey and frying meat.

She'd been months away from townsite pigpens, in clean air; if all Texas were like this, she didn't want any part of it. But she'd taken a long time to get here, and surely there must be something better ahead, some place of promise these wagons were aiming for. Besides, she had nowhere else to go.

A faded sign proclaimed a stable, and she moved her horse toward it, swinging down to lead Bradburn into a shadowed barn. She had eight dollars, and the stallion well deserved a good feed of grain and a helping of clean hay. After that, she'd figure something.

"Hep you, son?" Rheumy-eyed and bent, the man scratched a stubbled cheek as he shuffled to her.

Voice pitched low, Marilee said, "Grain and hay, if the hay ain't moldy."

"Clean as a parson's heart, but near about as dear. Fifty cents hurt you too much? All these folks comin' through, it drives up the price of everything."

"I can stand it," Marilee said. "He'll stand tied."

The old man stroked Bradburn's shoulder. "Heap of horse. Stall him for the night? Four bits more gives him mornin' feed and water, and I wouldn't mind rubbin' down this 'un."

"I'll have to see," Marilee said. "More'n like, I might just move on."

"Folks comin' and goin' both ways," he said, gnarled fingers caressing the stallion's hide. "Was I you, I'd find me a bunch to travel with, if'n you're fixin' to go far, special if'n you can't watch two sides to once."

"Made do since Richmond with just one eye," Marilee said.

"That so? My boy was with Hood, but never come home. I keep watchin' the road, though. Reckon he'd be here, was he acomin', but I watch anyway."

"Yes," Marilee said, her heart going out to him but unable to show it, not daring to show it. Flop hat low over her eyes, she reached up and slid the carbine from its scabbard. "Reckon I better keep this with me."

" 'Spect so, and the other hand on that sixgun. One of them newfangled Walker Colts, ain't it? You don't mind my sayin', boy—might pay you to hook up with some outfit, you goin' on west. Apaches actin' up more'n some, and on past 'em, the Comanch', too. It's how come some is pullin' up stakes and headin' east, instead."

Marilee put a greenback into the callused palm and waited for her change. "Saw troops of Yankees comin' this way—ain't they takin' care of the Indians?"

The old man's whiskery face worked. "Them? *Occupyin'* Texas, they are, but more like rapin', I call it. *They* ain't interested in protectin' no Rebs and couldn't catch up to no Apaches nohow, was they to try."

"I'll be back," Marilee said, "after I get somethin' to eat."

"Me and your horse'll be right here," the old man said.

She walked out of the stable thinking about Indians. They hadn't been included in her plans, and her knowledge of them was sketchy. From her lessons, from tutors, Marilee knew the frontier was peopled by wild tribes of redmen, but she'd somehow thought of them as picturesque —and long tamed. Now they were making big trouble, or the old man was exaggerating. She'd have to find out.

The restaurant was a tent, its long tables rough slabs sided with benches, and she flapped her kerchief at flies before sitting down. They settled right back. The meal was a whole dollar, and she paid it grudgingly, thinking that what she had wouldn't take her all that far anyway. She hadn't tasted beef for months, and even though the steak was whangleather tough and burned, it tasted good. So did the potatoes, because she was so used to beans.

Elbows on the table beside her, an oily man ate noisily, and across from Marilee another man in a long black coat and reasonably white shirt stared at her. She kept her eyes on her plate after that, not even looking up when somebody bumped her back in passing. The carbine was between her knees, and the Colt—that well-balanced and rare handgun found on a bloated body north of Shreveport—rested comfortably upon her hip. "First chance you get," Joe Langston had advised, "get yourself a Colt."

Well, she had, but not because of what *he'd* said—simply because it made sense to have the best weapon possible when travelling the way she was. She wasn't sure what had killed the man she came across on the back road; he was so swollen and flyblown she couldn't tell, but it looked as if he'd just made it to the road afoot before falling. It could have been anything: bad water, snakebite, anything. She'd seen too many dead men by then to be badly shaken by one more, but Marilee remembered the feeding flies.

Some settled upon her tin plate, and she pushed it back, with only a little bit of gristle left around the bone and the gravy wiped clean. They could have it now.

The dressed-up man said, "Which way are you goin', lad?"

She didn't look up, but slid off the bench with carbine in hand. "My way," she said, and pushed out through the crowd to walk the boards and lean boylike against store-fronts, looking and listening. Marilee had learned much about keeping to herself since fleeing her plantation, and more about playing the role of a young man on the road.

She'd found that most tended to walk wide of someone who slung a Walker Colt a little low, that young men who'd been through four years of war had old eyes, and the farther west she got, the fewer questions were asked. Marilee had been lucky since Joe Langston deserted her in that tragic clearing marked by a lonely grave and stained forever by what he'd done to her there upon the grass.

Others she'd met tried to be helpful, and as she got easier in her speech patterns, nobody had questioned she wasn't male. She'd helped a Cajun family dig stumps for a week, getting paid with food and forage and some patched clothes that fit her better. She'd helped a chunky widow woman run set hooks in the Sabine River, and maybe that one suspected Marilee wasn't all that mannish, but she never said, and Marilee left with saddlebags packed with smoked fish. What she remembered most about the taciturn woman was the hairy mole on her cheek.

Sometimes there'd be a wagon pulled up to a cook-fire, and she'd be invited to light down. She always let them do most of the talking and slept beyond the firelight's circle, Bradburn's rope looped about one wrist and the carbine beneath the blanket with her.

Most everyone seemed to be dispossessed Confederates or sympathizers driven from their lands by Northern troops and the carpetbaggers following close upon their heels. All of them were seeking new lives to replace the old, new lands where they would be allowed to live as they wished.

But there were others—hangdog former slaves in drawntight bunches; a few lone Nigras mostly riding mules, arrogant and too ready for trouble; shadowy, quick-passing men holding rifles close and looking over their shoulders; and once, a carriage overflowing with painted women and their luggage.

Bluecoats had thundered past her, crowding her off the roads, cavalry and wagon-riding infantry, artillery and caissons drawn by horses much like the one she rode, but not as good. They sometimes sneered at her, but more often passed silently. One trooper back behind his column had paused to offer her a cigar, which she accepted with mumbled thanks and fed to Bradburn later.

Now she was in Texas, where all kinds seemed to be gathering—the ones buying supplies and loading up wagons looking eager, those plodding east drawn and dispirited. She noticed a man put down a bundle: an ax and hoe, a thin bedroll, a shotgun. He rubbed at the small of his back, and she saw that his shoes were worn out, his eyes deep back in his head.

On impulse, she said to him, "Buy you a drink."

Redrimmed eyes, one of them twitching, searched her face. "How come?"

"Looks like you could use one."

"Sure as God, but I hear a glass costs ten cents—silver."

"I got it," Marilee said, "and I'd 'preciate hearin' what it's like out yonder."

"All right, boy." Gathering his belongings, the man followed her into a saloon, where they found a place at the end of the bar. He took a deep swallow from his glass and said, "My."

Marilee sipped the raw stuff and waited with her face

down, boot on the bar rail, and soon the man said, "Lost it all, everything but what I'm totin'—my wife, too. They took her hair, damn 'em. She had long yeller hair." He set his glass down hard, eyelid jumping up and down. "Been out there nigh three years, and never had nothin' to do with the war—always treated 'em good as we could. But they kept gettin' bolder like, and my wife said we ought to get out, after they burned the Wilson place. But, no, I said, the crop's about ready and it won't do to leave it now. And ain't we always treated 'em good?"

Marilee put another dime on the bar and watched a fat man pour with one hand and run a sausage finger behind his bowtie at the same time. He looked at her nearly full glass and picked up the dime. Down the bar somebody hollered, and against the wall somebody else fell out of a chair.

The farmer said, "Wish I'd listened to her. Oh, God, I wish. Red devils fired the cabin and took her hair while I was out in the field. Would of lost mine, too, but they was gone when I come runnin' to the smoke. I found Catherine with the top of her head peeled off and our rations stirred into the dirt, pissed on. Them damned Injuns didn't want our beans and flour; they just wanted the sacks they was kept in—and my wife's hair."

He went quiet, slower with his second glass of whiskey, and Marilee said, "But the army—"

Eyelid jerking, he said, "Folks losin' all they got—women and little girls gettin' raped and tortured by whole goddamned tribes, and there *ain't* no goddamned army. No farms and no cabins and nothin' alive where them bastards pass." He stared into the redbrown whiskey and said mostly to himself, "I been walkin' ever since, but I got no place to light. Boy, you want to buy my ax, a hoe? Might still need the shotgun."

Pushing him her barely tasted glass, Marilee said, "Ask somebody at the wagon train. I—I'm sorry, mister."

When she left, he was still looking into the glass, but she didn't think he was going to find anything.

Back on the swirling, busy street, Marilee stood uncertainly, remembering that she hadn't asked the man how far he'd come, or exactly where the Indians were causing trouble. Maybe it was happening only in a few isolated places; maybe these vacant-faced refugees had all come from the same general locale. Surely the Yankee army couldn't be ignoring attacks upon settlers.

A man paused beside her, a fairly tall man wearing a black coat, a reasonably white shirt, and a tall hat, carrying a cane. He said, "Lad, your hands are small, but they seem to be strong."

Marilee didn't eye his face, but watched his hands. "And what the hell does that mean?"

As if he were a schoolboy holding them out for a teacher's inspection, the man turned his hands palm up, a big diamond glittering as he did so, changing the cane back and forth. "Mine aren't very hard, not used to manual labor, as you can readily see."

They were a mess, Marilee admitted, blistered and nails broken off; the left hand had bled some. She waited, her back against the saloon wall, holding to the carbine.

He said, "I have a feeling you're heading west, into Indian country."

"Thought this was Texas."

Glancing ruefully at his palms, the man let them sag; light flashed again on his ring. "The noble redman won't admit to it and the United States army doesn't seem to care one way or the other. I *did* detect a certain softness in your speech, lad—Georgia, Alabama? No matter, since we are all one great and loving country once more. What does matter to me is gettin' my wagon all the way to California, and I can use someone with strong hands to help."

There was something funny about the way he talked, Marilee thought; part of it was a pretty good imitation of a gentleman, but there were little slips that told her maybe not. "I'm headin' west," she said, "but I got no money for wagonmasters."

"Bless me, lad," he said heartily, "I can see that. What I'm offering you is a free ride—providin' you know something about mules? I thought you might, seeing you come ridin' in on that fine horse."

Head to one side and the rained-on shapeless hat shielding most of her face, Marilee looked at him now. She didn't have to tilt her head back; he was about of a level with her, but considerably wider. He carried pale blue pouches under light brown eyes, and his nose had been broken, but not badly. He had a bright smile and good teeth, with a dab of gold in them, and his face was florid, but that might have been caused by driving into the wind. He might be thirty years old—or fifty.

"Sounds fair," she said with a calmness she didn't feel. A wagon train! An opportunity to keep moving west until she could find a place to settle, a range where she might build some sort of shelter for herself and Bradburn. There'd have to be good grass and water, and mustangs running wild in the hills—tough, wiry mares Bradburn could cross on. There'd have to be. . . .

"Haven't introduced myself," the man said. "Lad, I am Gilmore Frazier, late of Frazier Manor, south of Baton Rouge, and former colonel, CSA. But the unfortunate results of the war, you know—when the bluecoats gave me parole, all I managed to salvage was a wagon and a span of miserable mules. Now, like most of my comrades in arms, I find I must start over. And you?"

Marilee didn't offer him her hand. "Martin Crownover." How easily that name came to her lips again. "Late of nowhere but goin' somewhere. The wagonmaster got anything to say about me comin' along?"

For a second, she thought he was going to take her elbow, and tucked it closer to the carbine stock, but Frazier only switched hands with his walking stick. "Captain Goodnight is paid for one wagon—no more, no less. We are responsible for our own rations, and I believe I have an ample supply."

"Well," she said, "let's go see your mules, mister."

Down the planking, a painted woman tried to pick her way through places not so muddy, red velvet skirts held high and showing patent leather boots that reached halfway to her calves. Frazier tipped his hat to the lady and she gaped a red mouth at him.

"Behind the livery stable," he said, glancing back to watch the woman. "Not so much temptation there for ruffians."

Marilee resisted an impulse to tip back her hat when she saw the mules. They were a mess—heads hanging, sore-backed, and listless. They were still in harness, and she'd wager their mouths were raw, too. "How long have they been here?"

"Just today," he said.

"And still harnessed? Plain to see you wasn't in the

cavalry, *colonel*. Here—I'll get them unhooked and watered, see to their backs."

Frazier sighed. "Ah—I can see you're goin' to be quite a help to me, Martin, my lad—quite a help. I suppose they also need grain and the like? See to it then, Martin. I—I have some arrangements to make."

Beneath canvas in the back of the wagon, Marilee found a sack of corn and a wooden bucket. Using the livery stable's pump, she carried water to the four mules, giving them one bucket each before graining them. She bought a bale of hay and some salve from the old man for two bits, working the healing ointment into sore spots while the animals munched hay. Then she curried their legs and bellies, discovering that one still had spirit enough to halfheartedly cowkick at her. She slapped him along the head and caught the old man grinning at her.

"Dude don't know much—that knothead would of got him," he said, scratching his cheek. "Good thing the train ain't pullin' out for a spell. Give them mules a chance to heal up."

Marilee tugged her hat farther down. "Goin' clear to California with Captain Goodnight, is it?"

The old man grunted. "Not so's you'd notice. Ain't *nothin'* gettin' through the territories now. Goodnight'll likely fort up in San Antonio, does he make it that far. Might just do it, too—if'n he ties in with some Yankees headin' thataway. Course, with a big enough train and plenty of luck, could be the Apaches won't hit him." He squinted at her. "Don't 'spect that'll change your mind, though. Wouldn't change my boy's. You know, I keep lookin' down the street for him."

"Yes," Marilee said, and went into the stable with the old man to see to her own horse.

To herself, to *him* out there somewhere she said: "See, Joe Langston? There are still good people left, men of charity and honor, proud to have fought for a cause they believed in, proud to have given their sons for the South. But you can't understand that, can you?"

No more than she could understand why she kept thinking about him, why he kept living in her dreams. Because he had been such a shock to her, Marilee insisted, because it was very difficult to erase the searing memories of his cruelty, his domination of her. And because he had somehow, in some terrifying, twisted manner, pulled her down to his own degraded level for that blazing, ugly moment.

"I just don't understand, Bradburn," she whispered to the horse as the old man shuffled one-two, one-two toward the front of the stable where somebody else was bringing in a horse. "I still can't believe I acted like that."

No more than she could make herself believe that the stableman's bent back looked proud or that he would ever quit watching the streets of Beaumont for his son.

Chapter 18

She'd never driven a span of four, but the old coachman at Bradburn never seemed to have trouble handling two spanking trotters, and Marilee guessed she must have absorbed some knowhow over the years. For the five days it took to get the wagon train rolling, she hadn't seen much of Gilmore Frazier, sleeping in the wagon and taking her stallion out for exercise and fresh grass every day. She had also spent another dollar and a half on the mules, and they were looking perky by the time Captain Goodnight got the line of wagons headed up and moved out.

Bradburn stalked tied to the tailgate, saddled and bridled but with his cinch loosened, looking somewhat disgusted with the process and daring the mules behind him to get too close. Marilee kept looking back to check on him, while Frazier swayed on the seat beside her, smelling of whiskey, his eyes pouched and veined. They were fourth wagon from the tail, number nine from the front, and she remembered what the old stableman had said about a big train having a better chance of getting through to San Antonio. A dozen wagons wasn't a big train, and there were no bluecoat troops riding with them.

174

The evening before they left, Goodnight had called everyone together and told them he hoped to meet soldiers on the way, but he thought the train could take care of itself anyway, since some of the men had Spencer repeaters. She'd watched his face in the light of a fire, seeing the man tall and shoulder-hunched, lean and kind of drawn in upon himself. He seemed to know what he was about, Marilee thought; he'd been over the trail plenty of times.

Beside her, Frazier took off his frock coat, and she saw rouge on his shirt collar as he drank again from the mouth of a canteen. When he stoppered it, she said, "You owe me a dollar and a half—spent that on the mules."

Rubbing his eyes and sighing, Frazier tipped his tall hat lower over his forehead. "Money won't do you any good for a while, laddie. Besides, I'm sorry to say that I am carrying only letters of credit on a San Franscisco bank. There was more, but—provisions and all, you understand. I'll settle with you in California."

"Don't figure on goin' that far," Marilee said.

This time his sigh was deeper; Frazier took off his hat and placed it carefully behind him in the wagon. Pouring water from the canteen over a kerchief, he mopped his red face with it. "It's the only place, Martin. The land of golden opportunity: golden sun, golden people, raw gold still bein' found in the hills."

As it was to be found in Mexico, Marilee thought. From gossip picked up in Beaumont, the French emperor wasn't doing too well down there, and she felt sorry for Major Ainsworth. But a man of vision and spirit such as that gallant gentleman could still win through. Would a greedy, callous opportunist like Joe Langston last, too? Maybe he'd find the gold he so eagerly sought, and maybe his survivor's luck had run out. A man who'd ridden with the outlaw Quantrill had already used up more good fortune than he was entitled to. She didn't want to think about him anymore.

She said to Frazier, "California wasn't in the Confederacy."

His kerchief made another swipe across his sweaty face, and he said, "The land was riddled with spies and Union men—everybody else too busy seekin' their fortunes and not assisting the noble cause. Too bad, I say. But it's new out there, fresh. Why, lad, I have heard so many glowing tales about the land and its beauty—fruit growing year around, nuggets stumbled over, rich land goin' cheap. It has timber and mighty rivers, seacoasts and mountains, and the sun shines all the time."

Marilee could smell him sweating out whiskey. "Even at night?"

"You jest, lad." He put a hand upon her knee. "A sense of humor will help us through these months to come."

She pulled her knee away, making the movement a resettling of the holstered Colt upon her right hip, putting the pistol between them. "More guns might do it better," she said. "The captain don't have many outriders."

"You fearful of Indians?" Frazier asked. "Those I've seen have not impressed me."

"Them in Beaumont don't," Marilee agreed, "but I hear tell they're different out on the plains." The man with the twitch in his eye knew that.

"Rumors and gossip for the faint of heart," he said. "To win big, you have to play for high stakes." The sun caught Frazier's ring, and Marilee thought it showed a lot of light but not much color. Saloonkeepers and painted women in Beaumont hadn't gotten that, anyway. Frazier put his hat back on and opened his shirt collar more. "If more of these frontiersmen had fought for the cause—"

Marilee said, "My—I had kin fightin', too. Maybe you heard of— But no—you weren't in the cavalry."

"More's the pity," he said, propping his head back against the wagon stay and wincing at a bump in the trail. "But Frazier Manor contributed all its blooded stock to the CSA early in the war, and when it came to raising a regiment—well, I had to be content with an infantry commission."

She glanced at the man from the corner of her eye. If Gilmore Frazier didn't know anything about mules, he didn't know about horses, either; blooded stock at Frazier Manor?

"Fourth Alabama Rifles," he said, reaching for the canteen again.

Alabama, Marilee thought; Joe Langston. She said quickly, "Weren't they at Corinth?"

"Were *you*? No, I expect you were too young then— one of the early battles, you know. That storekeeper Grant was lucky at Corinth, and certain members of our staff wouldn't heed my advice—ah, well, over and done. Lad, I'm not feelin' up to snuff—some tainted meat last night, I suppose. Think I'll lie back in the wagon until I recover."

"Sure," Marilee said, and looked around to see how Bradburn was faring. The big horse didn't care for the dust, and blew it from his wide nostrils every once in a while, and she wished she were riding him instead of bumping along on a wagon seat. "Hup, mules!" she called, and settled back.

She was on her way to San Antonio, anyway. Off toward the sun, the village of Houston lay across the trail —last really safe stop of the journey until they were beyond Indian country, according to Captain Goodnight. Maybe that's why the outriders weren't fanned farther ahead now; this stretch of the road wasn't all that dangerous.

To keep from thinking of other things, Marilee concentrated on the wagon train's population, what she'd seen of it. Bascom Goodnight didn't talk much, beyond occasional pronouncements—only to his hunters and scouts, whelped in the same litter as the wagonmaster. They were quiet men in big hats or skin hats, with squint wrinkles at the corners of their eyes from looking far off. Joe Langston was no frontiersman; she didn't know why the riders should remind her of him.

Wagon drivers had the hulking stoop of farmers, although there was a scattering of watch-chained businessmen among them. Their wives were unsmiling and big-knuckled, down-home freckled or up-north twangy; two single girls just as plain but closely watched, soughtafter sparrows in grays and browns. All the women wore their hair pulled back into tight buns upon their necks, as if that style were law—except for the storekeeper's wife you could hear several wagons away, the one who was about twenty years too old for the butterfly of bright ribbon in her dyed hair.

Four or five towhead boys had been turned solemn by labor and the responsibility of their turns at the reins; there were a couple of ginghamed little girls who didn't often giggle together, and then there was "Martin Crownover" and Colonel Gilmore Frazier, CSA. Marilee glanced back at her horse, then into the wagon bed where the man sprawled uneasily beneath canvas bowed and billowed.

He'd no more worn the gold braid of a senior officer than she had, and she wondered why he troubled to tell the story. It might be his way to act the impoverished gentleman for reasons of his own, but he really should do it better. He had an inclination for strong drink and weak women, and she thought he wouldn't be nearly so red in the face once his indoors skin was toughened by the sun.

Like her own? Marilee eased a thumb up from the reins to touch her cheek. Weeks in the open had oven-browned her, good for her disguise but not her spirit. She'd soon have to whack off more hair, too; it grew altogether too quickly. Would she ever be able to wear it long and pendulant down her back once again, or up in the tricky ringleting of pale curls; were there hairdressers in California?

A golden land, Frazier had said, but she wasn't accepting that until she heard it from others. It could be a tale solid as his colonelcy. Keeping to herself as she was forced to, lest some sharp eye penetrate her façade and see her for what she was, Marilee hadn't talked with anyone else. But she planned to do a lot of listening. If there was gold in California, and cheap land, she might get an entrance through a horse herd sired by Bradburn.

Clucking to lagging mules, Marilee smiled sadly at her daydreams. First there had to be mares, and time for them to produce; she would have to find range for the stallion, build corrals, some kind of shelter from the weather. But if it was always warm and sunny in California. . . .

She saw a gull wheeling overhead, a seagull far from the gulf, perhaps drifted there by vagrant winds over which it had no control. Marilee watched the white bird turning and saw it slide out of sight behind a cottonboll cloud. Would it get back to the sea or be lost forever inland?

Timmy Santee had been lost in a grassy dale, and another part of Marilee Bradburn was left there, too. The first piece of her had been destroyed in a slave cabin, the next close by a newly covered grave. She had to hang on desperately to the rest.

How far was it to Houston—more than a hundred miles? Forever at this creaking pace, and nearly twice that much ground to cover before the train would reach San Antonio. Marilee couldn't extend her thoughts beyond that place, although beyond there were the Apaches.

178

Not like them fish-eaters around Beaumont, the old stableman had said. *'Cordin' to everybody limpin' back through here, them Apache is meaner'n snakes and don't give half as much warnin'. Hammered-down, ugly little buggers that pull out a man's guts slow, just to hear him holler—and what they do to the women, well.*

Not again, Marilee swore—not ever again. Even if her body had somehow turned traitor, even though Joe Langston had tapped some dark wellspring of evil within her core, she would not allow another man to rut upon her, to wallow between her thighs and spurt his sticky juices into her depths.

An odd thought struck her: how many of the Nigra wenches were actually raped? Oh, not by force, because when so much force was implied, it didn't actually have to be used, only threatened. Did some of those women, even the high yellows, resent having their bodies used because they couldn't resist? That was odd, too, thinking of them as *women;* Nigra females were wenches and the men bucks—just as horses were divided into mares and stallions. Both breeds had been stock on Bradburn Plantation, no more.

But mares came in season, into heat obvious to the eager stud. It was possible that wenches didn't. Marilee braced her carbine with one knee and reached across the seat for the canteen. Its lip tasted faintly of residual whiskey for just a moment.

Of course, no Nigra buck had been allowed to rape a wench, or even choose one for himself. Breeding was strictly controlled, trying first one cross, then another, until the get was strong and sturdy. That pair was considered married, and the ceremony of jumping over a broom was performed. Bradburn Nigras had been bred for stamina and hard work, for resistance to disease, and—and intelligence?

The yard children had to be intelligent, for some of them were three-quarters white or even more. Her father usually sold off the golden-skinned wenches, since they brought good prices; the lighter bucks didn't. Too much white blood was considered bad in a buck. For the first time in her life, Marilee faced up to the fact that if mulattos and quadroons were *people,* Wayne Bradburn had been selling her half-brothers and sisters.

Gnawing on her lip, she fought that idea. Nobody considered Nigras as people; everyone said that a single drop of jungle blood dominated any white infusion, and that was why mustees—those slaves who could just about pass for white—were still *Nigras*. To get a mule, a jack had to be crossed upon a mare, and the result was neither donkey nor horse, but something entirely different and something not fertile.

But Nigras bred; light skinned or dark, Nigras bred.

Back of her, Frazier snorted, and Marilee sat up straight. "God, it's hot back there," he mumbled, crawling out upon the wagon seat. "Makes a man's bones feel like they're meltin'. You wouldn't have a bottle of redeye in your gear, would you?"

"Never took to it," she said. "No money to buy it anyhow."

Tilting the open canteen over his head, he splashed water and snorted again. Dust settled upon his wet white shirt. "Ah, yes, your dollar and four bits. When we reach California, I'll give you a gold nugget, and you can keep the change." He narrowed his eyes up at the sky and blinked. "Where are we, lad?"

"San Antonio, you figure?"

Frazier rubbed his face, which was showing light brown stubble. "Do we stop for dinner?"

"Your belly must be feelin' better. You ought to know, mister. You been drivin' this wagon yourself."

"But not in a train," he said. "Came up from New Orleans by myself, but the train was makin' up, and I thought—"

"How much to join it?" Marilee asked.

"Two hundred dollars," Frazier said bitterly. "In greenbacks, too. Took just about every damned dime I could scrape—" He stopped talking and stared at her. His voice changed. "All that was left of Frazier Manor—a bit of silver buried, family plate that the moneychangers paid little for."

"But you got some letters of credit."

His kerchief came out and he mopped his face. "Ah, yes—another transaction. Can you cook, Martin?"

"Learned to in the field with the army," she said.

Frazier looked away from her at the trailside brush, green and insect-ridden. "I had two orderlies, of course.

It doesn't matter—rough fare for rough times. In California we'll dine from golden plates, drink from jeweled goblets, fine grape wine like liquid rubies."

"Aged scuppernong wine," Marilee said, "or Madeira."

"Madeira?" Frazier shook the empty canteen. "Must fill this from the cask, when we stop for dinner."

"And use a whole lot less when we reach the plains," she said.

They didn't stop to make a noon meal, only to water the stock, and Marilee saw that that was how it was going to be—make enough in the morning to eat cold during the day, build another cookfire at night. Captain Goodnight meant to keep pushing on, and that was sure all right with her. But Frazier complained awhile, and slept some more, and looked somewhat better when the wagons were drawn up in a loose circle just before dusk. It was a good campsite, close to a creek, with plenty of good grass for mules and horses.

Marilee untied Bradburn and was leading him off when Frazier said, "Bring back some wood."

She stopped the horse, her shoulder against his. "Mister, I'm beholden to you for takin' me along, but I would have made it farther than this by myself. I'll drive the wagon and do my—tote my part of the load, but I ain't goin' to tote yours, too. First off, I have to see to my horse, so if you want a cookfire real quick, I guess you better get it going."

When she had the stallion rubbed and watered and grained, when he was picketed to graze at some distance from the other stock, Marilee came back, carbine in hand. The fire was too big and too smoky; Frazier was rattling a pan and muttering. She kicked dirt on the edge of the fire and said, "Green wood smokes, dry don't."

"Damn," he said, "if I could have stayed on in New Orleans—there's bacon here, and flour. Beans are hard as minié balls."

"Dried onions and herbs in my saddlebags," she said. "Beans have to soak overnight. I have some dried fish, too, but reckon we'll save that. Don't your deal with Goodnight include meat from the hunters?"

He fanned away the smoke and coughed. "I guess so."

"We'll make do tonight, and get our share next time.

181

Plenty of deer in these thickets, so we ought to eat pretty good—for a spell."

When she had the hoecake done and the bacon cooked, Marilee remembered to make more for the next day and poured water over a pot of beans, thinking it was a good thing that Frazier's wagon was well supplied with cooking gear and such.

Murderin' savages stirred our rations into the dirt and pissed on 'em, the widower had said. *Didn't want our rations, just the sacks they was kept in.*

She looked into the night, past other campfires and beyond the wagons. Apaches might want pots and pans; they would surely hunger for a horse like Bradburn. She ate quickly and carried her tin plate and the fry pan to the creek. A cotton-headed boy there said a quick howdy and darted away.

Shaking water from the washed utensils, she found Frazier kneeling beside her to dip his own plate. He said, "There *is* is a gallon of whiskey in the wagon. I been saving it."

"Best you keep on savin' it," Marilee answered.

"Thought you'd take a small drink with me in the wagon."

She threw him a swift look, but his face was shadowed. "Long as the weather's good, I'll sleep by my horse."

Frazier followed her as she moved off. "Laddie, you're right about treasuring the whiskey. There'll come a time when it's handy, a better time."

Puzzling at him, Marilee said, "I reckon," and stooped to hike the saddle to her shoulder. "Be back for my bedroll."

Softly, his voice trailed her: "Ah, yes, Martin, and I'll be here."

Chapter 19

He rode the good barb mare the way a peon straddles a donkey, feet hanging free of the stirrups and slouched beneath a ragged serape, big sombrero shading his face. Keeping mare and saddle was a gamble for Joe Langston, but he cut the odds by wearing ammunition belts crossed over his chest in the manner of guerrillas or freelance *bandidos,* since there wasn't much difference.

A donkey-riding peasant wouldn't be sporting a Spencer and a Colt, either; some kind of *soldado* would. And he'd play billy hell outrunning a cavalry patrol on anything but this fast mare. So his best bet was to be a peon Juarista traveling on some lonely mission. That way, only loyalist patrols would be apt to get after his hide, and Joe thought he'd left that bunch a long way behind. Any French or native followers of the emperor this far north had to be either flatout lost or hammer-headed as Maximilian himself.

Breathing deeply, Joe could taste the desert dryness he liked better than the humidity of Chapultepec and the Mexico plain. Humidity—that was another of his new words that meant air down there was so soggy it lay heavy in a man's lungs. But up here he had to be careful with his water supply; one gourd for him, one for the horse, and try for another water hole or abandoned *rancho* before they both ran dry.

He pulled up the mare on a sand mound and looked all the way around before digging out a cigarillo and lighting it with the flick of his thumbnail on a sulphur match. He wasn't bad off, and damned lucky to be far from the ring of steel that was fast closing around what was left of the Imperial army. The damned fools who stayed with Maximilian could expect firing squads and hangman's ropes. If the emperor had had any sense, he'd have gone after his wife when she left, seeing as how Carlotta was acting crazy as a half-squashed bedbug.

Drawing on his little cigar, Joe scanned the horizon again, especially the low range of brown hills to his right. Max wasn't a bad sort, just kind of fluttery-like, listening to folks that didn't give a hoot and a holler about his "honor of the Hapsburgs," but were only interested in grabbing something off for themselves. Anybody could see the scribbling on the outhouse when General Bazaine started withdrawing the French troops, but Max kept insisting the master of Europe would send more help, and if not Napoleon, then the Holy Father in Rome, the Pope himself.

Joe blew out smoke and flicked ash off the tip of his cigarillo. The way he had it figured, the black robes were about the biggest troublemakers Max had around him, especially since the emperor didn't give them back all the church property Juárez took away in the first place. He eased the mare down off the mount and kept her moving at a brisk walk, not the first deserter from the Imperial army, but a lucky one. He'd made it this far with no trouble, even though he'd been stopped three different times by ranging groups of Juaristas. His fancy pass from General Porfirio Díaz had gotten him through, once with an apology for detaining him.

Luisa was a woman whose word was good as her body, and that was saying something. No fool, Luisa Valero; she wouldn't accept information that ships in Vera Cruz were there to haul off the French, because anybody with good sense could figure that out. But bargaining with her had been fun, there in her tiny bedroom, or out in the garden, and sometimes in Delphine's scented bed. She didn't know as many tricks as the countess, but Luisa learned quick, being passionate to start with and hot as a mountaingrown chili pepper.

Joe tried to hold out for some gold pieces, but she'd promise only the safe conduct pass, and because time was running out, he gave her the information about General Miguel Lopez. Pretty as new syrup and just as slick, Lopez would sell out if the emperor and his troops pulled back to the Hill of Bells and got in a bind.

"Escobedo will be glad to hear this," Luisa said. "A bargain then, *querido*. But one which means you must leave soon."

"Sooner'n the countess," Joe said, "and she's got her trunks about packed."

"Then let us make this night one to remember." Luisa sighed and ran her tongue into his ear as she squirmed against him. "Tomorrow, you will have your pass, but to-night—ah, tonight—"

And the next day, with the document in his saddlebag, he took leave of the Comtesse Delphine Delacroix there in the perfumed bedroom he'd gotten so used to. Her good-bye was every bit as fiery as the Mexican girl's *adiós*, as she ran through her experienced, well-practiced moves with a hungry and breathless savagery that left him spent.

When he sat up on the bed and reached for what could be his last taste of champagne, Delphine went to her dressing table and brought back something. Standing sweetly sweated and glowingly naked before him, she turned up her palms.

Joe stared down at the ring in each as she said quietly, "My *bon voyage* gift, *chéri*. I wish there was more, but *le comte* has taken the rest of my jewelry to use as bribes and for passage home. One diamond, one ruby; they are worth a few thousand, perhaps enough to save your life. Oh, *mon cher, mon amour*— I weep at the thought of such a body being destroyed."

Kissing her small hands, Joe took the rings. "*Merci*, Delphine. I thank you for everything, not only this, but all you did for me."

Tears fringed her bronze lashes. "It was *magnifique* for us both, was it not?"

"Yes," Joe said, and meant it.

Now the rings nestled in the bottom of a little sack of beans; about four hundred dollars in gold pieces traveled hidden in a similar sack of cornmeal, and he had silver in his pockets. Bacon, salt, and chili peppers, a change of clothes and extra Colt ammunition in the other saddlebag; a bottle of tequila and cigars; blankets and a sack of corn tied behind his saddle—hell, he was well off. This time white trash was coming out on top of the pile, with a whole skin and a rich stake to boot. He could peddle the rings across the border, sell them to some Texas cowman or a Yankee general, and Joe Langston might just turn into somebody to call mister. And why not? He could read and write and get by pretty good in Spanish now, besides speaking a little bit of French.

And to add a little fluffy hair to the nooky, he wasn't all that far from the river. According to the military map in his pocket, he'd been in the province of Coahuila for two, three days now, and ought to be coming up on the village of Carranza by nightfall.

He'd bed down there, and get a shave, scrub the sand and alkali dust out of his ears, eat a pile of tortillas washed down by *vino rojo,* and maybe find a warm *chica* to share his blankets. When he was ready to ride again, he wouldn't be but about two hundred miles from the Rio Grande and the town on the right side of the border, Del Rio.

Feeling good in the sun, grinning at a roadrunner that scooted away from his horse, Joe rocked in the mare's easy motion, moving toward a speck of green that grew slowly larger. Sunlight flashed to his right, and he came awake all over to slide the Spencer out of its scabbard. The trouble with desert country was getting caught so far out in the open with no place to hide.

But the glare hadn't come from a rifle barrel; keeping the horse at a slow jog until he was certain, Joe picked out a flat rock that bounced back the sun's rays as silver winks. That made him think of silvery hair and eyes that burned with a green fire or glazed over in passion.

Texas—hadn't she once said something about going to Texas? But Ainsworth had invited her to come along to Mexico. Chewing his cold cigar, Joe thought that Marilee Bradburn would have been drawn right into the court down there, sashaying around in silks and ribbons, mistress to counts or dukes or even a prince. She sure as hell had all the qualities, a fine-diddling *lady* to start out, prettier than all the French noblewomen he'd seen, and the Spanish Creoles, too.

He could see a haze of smoke ahead, make out a cluster of adobe shacks, and put the mare into a long lope, to feel wind in his face. Marilee had missed her chance; she could have been set up in France right now, fancy as any royal whore.

Before he got to Carranza, Joe dropped his horse into a walk and took a good long look at the village. It seemed like a hundred others, church in the middle, town square, a couple of stores and cantinas, little houses; he didn't see any sign of troops.

Lamps were going on and candles being lighted as he walked the mare to a water trough and let her drink. A bigeyed boy took off a shabby straw hat to tell him *sí, sí,* the *caballo* could be well cared for at Señor Peralta's blacksmith shop.

Saddlebags over his shoulder, Spencer in one hand, Joe gave the boy a coin with the mare's reins. "See to her comfort, *hijo*."

Delighted, the boy walked the mare across the plaza, and Joe turned for the cantina where he could smell something good cooking. The owner's black eyes widened in folds of fat when he saw Joe, and they went immediately to the Spencer, to the Colt slung low and businesslike.

He brushed a quick hand over a few strands of hair combed over a balding scalp. "Welcome, señor. You honor my poor establishment."

"If your establishment will honor my stomach," Joe said, and smiled at the young woman who came from the kitchen—cook, barmaid, the owner's daughter, whatever; in a few years she'd be pudgy as the man himself, but just now she was just ripe enough.

"Of course," the man said. "Salazar himself will serve you. Tequila, *pulque?*"

"Wine," Joe said, and sat at a crude table, saddlebags at his feet, rifle propped against the wall at his back. "Wine to wash away the dust in my throat."

"*Pronto, pronto*—Maria! Stop staring and bring the gentleman wine. You have traveled far, señor?"

"Too far. Whatever you have in the kitchen, Señor Salazar—then a bath, a shave perhaps?"

"Mi casa, su casa," Salazar said, plump cheeks creased in a wide smile. "Whatever you desire. We do not greet many travelers these days."

Joe could see the man trying to figure him, checking the guns, the crossed bandoliers, his *gringo* accent. Joe looked at the girl then, at Maria scurrying back into the kitchen with a flash of shapely brown legs.

Salazar was curious and trying not to show it. "Any news of the south?"

"The south?"

"I thought perhaps you journeyed from—no matter, señor. Is the wine good?"

"Very good—just the right sourness." Joe rolled some around in his mouth and swung back his serape so the butt of his pistol would be free of it.

"Maria!" the fat man called. "Our guest waits. Bring him food and heat water for his bath. I will see to more wood."

The meal was delicious, and Joe wolfed it down, finishing a bottle of wine before Salazar slid back behind his bar. The fat man was sweating. Maria didn't appear to pick up the empty dishes. Salazar kept smiling, his hands nervous upon the bar top, busy at earthen cups. Joe moved dishes aside with one hand and put the Spencer upon the table, finger curled into its trigger guard.

From the front door, a man said softly, "You would gamble your life, señor?"

Joe couldn't see him in the darkness. "And yours."

And from the kitchen, another man growled, "Let him gamble, *jefe.* We have him."

At least two in the kitchen, Joe thought; more in the street; something moving beyond the little window behind the bar; Salazar out of sight beneath the bar. How many he could get didn't matter; just one left alive would get him. Joe slowly and carefully took his hand away from the Spencer.

"The pistol would look well upon the table," the man suggested from the doorway.

Gently, Joe brought out the Colt with two fingers and placed it beside the rifle.

"Lean your chair back against the wall, *pistolero,* and stay in it."

A smart man, Joe thought, his skin prickling and a

cold spot in his belly—one who'd faced quick gunmen before. He said, *"Bueno*—if you will show yourself, *jefe.* I will show you my safe conduct pass, signed by General Porfirio Díaz himself."

They came quickly from all sides, ragged wolves with metal teeth, and only the lieutenant wore part of a uniform. They looked much alike—hoteyed, jaws set, brown eyes tensed—and their guns didn't tremble.

The lieutenant lifted a worn huarache to the seat of the other chair and put his elbow on the bent knee, a pistol dangling from his hand. Two of the fingers had been broken and had healed crooked. "We have your fine mare."

"The mare, yes," Joe said. "She's all I have left—besides my pass. I will bring it out slowly, *jefe.*"

One corner of a scarred mouth lifted. "And wisely, *gringo.*" His free hand reached for the document. "From Díaz himself, you say? Impressive, but Díaz does not command here. I do, and I am Subteniente Torres—himself."

Another man laughed harshly, and Torres said, "The saddlebags, Paco."

Joe watched a chunky man with the heavy face of an *indio* sweep away his saddlebags. He said, "Do you read, *teniente?* That gives me the word of a general, one loyal to *El Presidente,* that I may return unmolested."

"Return from where, *pistolero?* Chapultepec, perhaps? You do not smuggle guns for us—smugglers do not travel so far south, nor do they ride a French saddle."

Shrugging, Joe said, "One acquires things."

Torres pushed back his sombrero with the still-rolled pass. "Such as Spanish with two accents—one *gringo,* and the other Texcoco or Cuernavaca. Emilio, see what else this traveler has acquired."

They were peasants, men of the land, and as such not inclined to destroy food, but they were thorough, also. Joe winced as his gold pieces and Delphine's rings were sorted out and laid before Torres, the cornmeal and beans returned to their sacks. His spare clothing and ammunition was treated as carefully.

"If certain generals were as smart," Joe said, "the French would have been gone long ago. You will not be a *teniente* for long."

"Only long enough," Torres said, turning the glittering

jewels over with the muzzle of his pistol. "Then I will herd cows again."

"Such jewels will buy many cows."

Torres leaned forward, hard eyes snapping. "If I was a Loyalist dog, I would beat an unarmed man. If I was French, I would hack him with a sword, or pin his belly with a lance. Not all Mexicans are greedy for riches, *gringo*—some dream only of a true republic. But even such dreamers know that guns make the reality, that only new, quick-firing guns will keep Apache and Comanche raiders from our fields and drive Yaqui wolves from our homes. Only guns that are not given to us by *gringos*, but sold for such baubles you stole from the people."

"A *condesa* made me a present of them," Joe said.

Several men laughed, but not Torres; he said, "And she gave you the gold, also. What a stud you must be! But I would believe you were paid more for the use of your pistol than that other weapon between your legs, paid for shooting down Juaristas."

Searching for the words, Joe said. "General Díaz paid me with that pass, for valuable service to Juárez. If there is no honor among ordinary *soldados*, how can Mexico expect more of its leaders?"

Torres snatched his foot off the chair with a slap. "Honor? You speak of honor, *gringo?* You who have sold your guns, then sold your *compadres?*"

"I have honor," Joe said. "I will prove it by facing any two of you, any three, if you will return my pistol."

Men muttered and stirred, but Torres said, "A *duelo* —we peasants know nothing of *duelos*, only of hunger and blood. But you are right, *pistolero*—we also know we cannot expect much from our leaders, that we must protect ourselves. *Millares gracias* for bringing us the gold and jewels—they will buy the defenses we need."

Joe waited for a long, stretched-out moment before he said: "And me?"

This time Torres smiled, showing small white teeth beneath a drooping black moustache. "You may go, *gringo* —but only as you came to Mexico, on your horse and carrying your weapons. As for Díaz—" Leaning over the table, he touched the safe conduct pass to the flame of a candle and dropped it upon a plate to burn.

"Without that," Joe said, "it can be a long way to the Rio Grande."

"José, Paco—empty his guns and take them to his horse. Oh—also the saddlebags. A long way to the river, gunman? Longer, if the Apaches are raiding. But you have been fortunate so far. I wish you luck the rest of the way."

Tilting the front legs of his chair back to the dirt floor, Joe stood up and took a last look at Delphine's rings, a last look at his gold pieces. Reaching carefully into his pocket, he placed silver coins on the table. "For the girl Maria, not Salazar."

Torres's laugh was rusty, as if it hadn't been used for a long time. "I believe you could be a stud for a *condesa*. There is a style about you, *pistolero*, perhaps even honor."

Joe walked to the door and looked back. "You wished me luck on my journey, *teniente*. I do the same for you —I wish you luck with your republic. You will need it."

The mare waited for him at a hitching rack, men circling her. Somebody gave him the Spencer, somebody else handed up his pistol. Joe Langston sat weary in the saddle and reined the mare's head to the north.

Chapter 20

That morning, when the train was about four days out of San Antonio, Marilee went out to get the mules. They'd been staked out to graze the night before, but Bradburn had been edgy and ready to fight, so she had kept him close to the wagon.

Marilee found one mule dead, his eyes rolled up and a great, bloody slice of meat sawed out of his flank. The opened flesh was still steaming; the other mules were blowing and staring into the brush with their picket ropes pulled taut.

Bringing out her Colt, Marilee pulled back the hammer and edged away from the slaughtered animal. Indians! But nobody had even seen one yet, not even the scouts. The other mules—could she handle them, spooked as they were by blood smell? And the night guard—what had happened to him?

When she circled the shaking mules and moved farther down the little glade, she found him. Sam Anderson was sitting with his back against a tree trunk, his arms cradled as if he still held his rifle. Horrified, Marilee stared at the awful, loose sagging of his face, the red, raw top of the man's scalped head. A great deal of blood had spilled down the front of his shirt when his throat had been cut.

She lifted the muzzle of her pistol, finger tightening on the trigger before she caught herself. Warning shots could finish the job on the mules, on others jittering farther away as they too caught the unnerving odor of blood. If the animals panicked and tore free of their picket pins, they could scatter for miles before they could be tracked down and brought back.

And somewhere close by, Indians were waiting.

Lowering the Colt, she backed toward the wagons, feeling behind her with one hand, sidling around bushes as her heart threatened to run away. Realizing that the savages could be anywhere, behind her as well as to the front, she lost her nerve and wheeled to crash through a clump of willows whose trailing branches caught at her, tried to hold her back. One of them jerked at her eyepatch, another hooked her hat, but she freed them and stumbled on.

"Hey now, boy! You could shoot somebody, wavin' that gun around." One of the scouts stood before her, the one who looked like an Indian himself, feather stuck in a black felt hat, buckskin shirt and beaded moccasins.

Marilee swallowed hard. "Back—over yonder, Sam Anderson's been scalped, and they—started dressin' out one of our mules!"

"Oh, shit," the man said, bringing up his long gun and loping back the way she pointed. "Tell the others."

She trotted to where Captain Goodnight was just poking up his cookfire. "Indians after the mules—Sam Anderson's dead and that Pecos man took after 'em!"

He came up buckling on a gunbelt, reaching for a rifle. "Billy! Josh! Come a'runnin'!" Then to her: "And you didn't start shootin' blind? How come, boy?"

"Mules was spooked already," she said, ducking her face.

"Good boy," he said, and trotted for the brush as two of his outriders came running to follow. Marilee fell in behind them, running awkwardly in her big boots but with the Colt balanced easily in her hand.

They didn't find anything but the dead mule and the dead night guard, although they ranged the brush close by for a while. When they got back to the clearing, other men from the train were gathering there, staying far back from Sam Anderson, some of them calming the mules, some just standing and holding nervously to their guns.

Goodnight noticed that Marilee was beside him and said, "You come back."

"It's one of *our* mules," she said, and the man nodded.

Then Pecos came gliding out of the trees. "Goddamn Apaches—seen where they hid their horses, but couldn't tell was they Lipans or Jicarillas. For certain, they wasn't Tonks—them Tonkawas would'a got caught still chewin' on that mule. 'Sides, they stay clear of Apache country, and that's just about where we be."

Goodnight said, "You might give this boy—Martin, ain't it?—a hand gettin' the rest of his mules outa' here. Was we farther on, I'd say dress out the mule, too, but we ain't that far from provisions and help."

Pecos scuffed his feet in the grass, and Marilee noticed the gleam of a flat hand ax in the man's belt. She was amazed at how he had been able to tell what tribe they were, without having seen them.

The scout grunted. "Wisht we had us some wolfbane to stuff in that mule. If'n they're hungry, they'll be back to it. Pissin' in there where they cut off some meat won't poison 'em, but it'll make 'em plumb mad. Come on, boy —let's get them mules to your wagon."

When they reached the wagon, women were gathered in tight knots in camp and children hidden in wagons. Gilmore Frazier was just getting out of his blankets and yawning. Blinking at them, he started: "What—"

Pecos didn't even look at him; tethering a pair of mules to a wagonspoke, he pointed a grimy finger at Marilee's horse. "How come you tied him up last night?"

"He—he was spooky, like he smelled somethin' that bothered him." Her hands were shaking and she tried not to show it as she tied the other mule.

Frazier climbed out of the wagon. "What's going on?"

Pecos said, "Hoss like that 'un is worth more'n his keep, do he smell Apache thataway. Some kin, you know, better'n a dog."

"What the *hell* is goin' on?" Frazier said loudly.

The scout walked away, and Marilee said, "A man was killed and scalped—one of our mules is dead. I—I found them." She squatted to push dry wood into ashed-over coals left from last night's fire, but the idea of cooking made her want to throw up.

"One of *our* mules? What—how did it happen? How

can we keep on, with just three mules? There was supposed to be a night guard with the stock."

Watching new flame lick at the sticks, Marilee said softly, "There was—Sam Anderson was scalped."

"Oh, my God," Frazier said. "Indians, and we're not even out into the plains yet. Three mules—they ought to get us to San Antonio, shouldn't they?"

"We can manage," Marilee said. "Think maybe I could use a drink of that whiskey you got in the wagon. I never saw a man with the top of his head gone before."

When he brought her the jug, Frazier kept looking off at the brush. She took a big swallow of fiery stuff and found it was a mistake. She had to fight to hold it down. "Y—you have to cook for yourself."

His hand was gentle upon her shoulder. "It must have been a shock, seein' a man like that. But you saw it before, in the war."

Tears stung her eyes, from the whiskey. "This wasn't war—it was murder. They cut—cut his throat from behind. I—" Marilee pulled from beneath his hand. It would be too easy to rise and bury her face into Frazier's shoulder, to cry like hell and not be ashamed of her tears.

"See to your horse," he said. "You'll feel better, and maybe you can eat later. I ought to pay my respects to Mrs. Anderson."

Still crouched at the fire, she watched him walk away, then got up to tend Bradburn. Frazier had changed some in the weeks they'd been on the trail; for one thing, he hadn't touched the whiskey jug. And he'd eased up on the tall tales of Frazier Manor's lost glories. But he watched her a lot of late—just sat quietly and kept his eyes on her until she got uncomfortable and moved off.

Feeding Bradburn corn from the wooden bucket, she leaned her head against the stallion's shoulder. She kept seeing the top of a raw head, where the scalp had been jerked loose. Oh, good Lord, and she'd meant to make it through this wild country by herself. If Gilmore Frazier hadn't taken her on with the wagon train, her own hair might be dripping from some Apache warrior's spear.

Stiffening her back, she let the horse feed in peace and went back to the fire to stand shivering there, even though the sun was climbing and dew fading from the wagon tops. She'd have to keep Bradburn right at the wagon from here on, have to sleep by the fire herself, not away from it in the dark, as she'd been doing.

Not in the wagon with Frazier so close; not until winter caught them out on the bitter, blowing plains and there was no other shelter. And she would keep her carbine between them. It wouldn't do for him to discover she wasn't a boy. Marilee had known more of her share of trouble, just because she was a woman. Let word get out in this wagon train, and she'd be in for more than she could handle; it would come from the women as much as men, all those pinch-faced women with their own unbendable code of right and wrong. First, there'd be flinty outrage because she wasn't married to the man she was traveling with; then would come the inevitable reaction of "good" women to a "bad" one, the threat they would feel because of her presence. And not only would they feel danger to their men, but also jealousy for their marriageable daughters. It would do Marilee no good to protest her innocence: branded with the scarlet letter, she would be damned and propositioned and probably chased out of the train.

And lurking out there were Apaches, savages who could ease up on a guard and cut his throat, slinking brutes who mutilated a corpse by taking its hair. They were vicious animals who would slaughter a mule for a dripping chunk of its flesh.

She went to the harnesses hanging along the wagon and began to take one set loose. The big mule, Buck, could and would pull in the lead by himself, but a lot of rearranging had to be done, and she might have her hands full until all the mules settled down to the new way. They could really make do with only two animals, Marilee thought; Frazier's wagon wasn't carrying more than food and water, a few blankets and utensils. It wasn't laden with furniture and other people, like most of the other wagons, wasn't toting plowshares and farming tools. But then, Gilmore Frazier didn't plan to farm in California.

She really didn't know *what* he meant to do. He bubbled with vague ideas of riches, grandiose schemes for somehow—without details—acquiring a great store of gold. Fingers busy at the harness, then struggling to convert a doubletree into a singletree, Marilee had to admit that Frazier knew a lot about California, even if most of it was hearsay. When he got onto one of his talking streaks, he could make that far place sound like Eden, where everything was blue and gold and green.

Marliee was more interested in the green of tall grass and the silver of water that could in the long run be as precious as the gold that miners were still taking out of the rich Western hills. She knew it was almost twenty years since the first big strikes out there, knew that California ports were thick with foreign ships bringing goods to sell and taking away things in return—logs and grain and salted-down beef.

It took grass and water to grow beef, and good horses to herd the cattle, which brought her back to her own stallion and the possibility of crossing him on wild mares. California seemed a good place to go, so long as she was with the wagons now. She'd been thinking of it more lately, probably because Frazier was always singing its praises.

When she got the harness rigged and onto the mules, the lead one sulked and sidled until she hit him a good lick to get his attention. Backing them one at a time into place at the wagon tongue, Marilee glanced over at the edge of the clearing where they'd just finished burying Sam Anderson. A woman keened her sorrow, and others gathered to her, while men stood uncertain and uneasy, looking often at the brush.

"Get 'em headed up," Captain Goodnight called, and Marilee watched the scouts move out, fanning this time to the flanks and ahead. Pecos lingered to nod approval at the way she'd rigged the mules, then drifted toward the end of the train as rear guard.

When Gilmore Frazier climbed up on the seat beside her, he looked down in the mouth, and stayed quiet long after their wagon dropped into line. When they were strung out creaking and rattling, and the brush had thinned, he said, "It's a long way to the ocean, and there's probably a man buried for every mile along the way."

"And a woman," Marilee said, clucking to the lead mule.

She could feel his quick look at her as he said, "Yes— harder on women, I reckon. Best way to travel is clear around the Horn, but it costs so damned much by ship that only Yankees can afford to go that way."

"Mules and a wagon cost a heap, too," she said, "and what with the price of flour and staples after the war—"

He placed his walking stick on the floor at his feet, then reached back into the wagon to bring out a rifle. It was a breech loader, nowhere good as her Spencer repeater, and he saw her glance at it. "Came with the wagon," he muttered. "I guess it'll do."

"Good as most of the men have," she agreed. "I just hope those Apaches don't carry any better guns."

Lying the weapon across his knees, Frazier said, "Flatout terrible, that was, poor old Sam. Good thing his wife has a boy and girl to help drive. I ain't—I'm not—much with a long gun, but I can be respectable with this."

Marilee saw the flash of a derringer on his upturned palm, short and two-barreled and deadly-looking. She said, "If the Apaches let you get up real close."

"Might not get to choose," he said slowly, and the little pistol disappeared into his vest pocket. "You know, Goodnight didn't expect trouble this far east, but we're to all watch for it from here on. Damn it, if the Yankee army wasn't so busy lootin' New Orleans, maybe they could get out here and take care of these Indians."

"Texans fought on the wrong side," Marilee said. "Seems the bluecoats don't much care what happens to them now, to us. How many Confederates would you say are on this train?"

"Most of 'em," Frazier answered. "Folks totin' all they own and lookin' for a new start. Reckon most won't make it."

He was depressed by death, by the Apaches, and Marilee said, "We will—all the way to California, before the gold nuggets run out."

Frazier brightened. "Sure we will. A new shuffle and a new deal." He patted her knee and didn't seem to notice when she pulled it from beneath his hand.

As the land opened itself more and thick brush fell behind the wagons, he relaxed and talked more, embroidering his dreams of California, telling her about the Spanish dons out there, the huge land grants that were being usurped by Americans. He was still chattering when she brought out cold johnnycake and jerky for their dinner.

Chewing, she looked back at Bradburn, and then took time out to water the stallion and mules before catching up with the rest of the train. Frazier slept awhile, jerking awake from time to time to stare around at the terrain, hands gone white on the stock of his rifle.

An hour or so before the wagons were circled for the night, he offered her the jug of whiskey. Staring hard at him, Marilee shook her head; he couldn't be that scared. They were more in the open now, and everyone was alert; they'd seen no sign of Indians all day, and even Goodnight must be figuring the attack back by the creek was an isolated incident. A small group of Apaches had picked off a lone, careless man and butchered one mule; they hadn't even tried to run off any other stock, and they might be afraid to attempt a full-scale raid on a train this size, where everyone was armed and turned watchful now.

She made stew for supper, but Frazier didn't eat much. He continued to tap the jug, and his speech thickened a little, exposing more of the redneck than the gentleman he was supposed to be. Marilee wondered where the man was really from, what his true story was, if he'd ever seen a single day's service in the Confederate army.

When she had the stock fed and watered, she tied Bradburn to the wagon again, although the big stud wanted to graze. He was much safer here than out where nervous men walked sentry around mules. In the morning, she would see to grass for him, but every night from here on he'd have to make do with grain and meal.

Fires flickered lower, and she thought none of them would actually go out; people were too jumpy. Gathering her bedroll, she started to spread it beneath the wagon.

Frazier said, "Easier sleepin' inside."

"This is fine," she said. "I'm closer to my horse."

Their own cookfire guttered, turning to red coals. A child complained off in another wagon, and a woman hushed it. Bradburn stamped the ground restlessly as night closed in.

Lying awhile beneath the wagon, trying not to remember the way Sam Anderson had looked when she found him, Marilee turned and stretched, turned and curled under her blanket. Her carbine was there with her, the Walker Colt under her coat wadded as a pillow. It took a spell for her to get to sleep.

She snapped awake when he kneeled beside her, reaching for her pistol and half-rising from the blankets.

"Sh," Frazier whispered. "It's just me."

Groggy, she hissed back: "What's wrong?"

"Nothin'—it's warmer for two sleepin' than one."

Marilee stared at his shadowed face. "You better climb back in the wagon, mister."

"And you better keep your voice down," he murmured, the odor of whiskey strong around him. "Less'n you want to let out a sure-enough woman holler for help."

"W-what do you mean? Look, Gilmore—"

"I been lookin'," he said, "for a long time. I been lookin' ever since I seen you on the boardwalk back yonder in Beaumont. You got the rest of 'em hoodwinked, but not ol' Gil."

Marilee swallowed and clenched the butt of her Colt. "You must be some kind of crazy man."

"Uh-uh—smart as a whip, honey. Ain't one of them as likes boys, neither—just good-lookin' women. But if there ain't no pretty ones to be had, I can make do with plain gals. Only you ain't plain."

Pushing the muzzle of the pistol up against his belly, she said, "Get out of here. Get away from me."

"Or you'll shoot me? Try explainin' that to the rest of the train, honey." His hand pushed away the gun.

She was trembling, and not from the negligible night chill. Sitting hunched, she felt the insidious body heat of him, smelled the whiskey he'd nerved himself with. Her mind darted here and there, not able to find a way out; she felt like a bewildered, panicked mouse seeking escape where there was none.

"Nowhere to run," he said, lifting her blanket. "No place to hide, neither. You got me, or you got every horny pecker on the train after you. Ride on out by your lonesome, and the Apaches'll lift your hair, soon's the whole bunch of 'em get through puttin' it to you."

Marilee sank back, palm sweaty around the grip of her useless pistol. Pulse throbbing in her throat, she knew he was right, that she was cornered. All this time, Gilmore

Frazier had known; somehow, he'd penetrated her disguise and waited until now to make his move.

As his naked body slid in beside her, as his hands started to roam her flesh and loosen her clothing, Marilee whispered in anguish, "I can't. Oh, my God—*I can't.*"

Practiced fingers stripped her, caressed her skin, cupped her secret places. "Don't you worry, honey, you don't have to do a damned thing—ol' Gil will take care of everything. Oh, my—don't you feel all slick and warm— got them hard little tits that just fit a man's hand—"

Closing her eyes, she lay stiff and still, trying to hurl her mind far from what was about to happen to her body. But when Frazier covered her and his manhood pushed insistently at her mound, Marilee's eyes popped open. As he entered her, she turned her head and stared numbly at the dying embers of the fire.

Chapter 21

Herds of longhorn cows and freight wagons milled around the outskirts of San Antonio, so Captain Goodnight pulled his train up on a flat piece of ground nearby. Marilee followed the wagon ahead, guiding her three mules into position and wondering where they'd find graze. Leaving them harnessed, she climbed down and saw to Bradburn first, watering him from the bucket, rubbing down his legs, and lifting off the saddle.

Behind her Frazier said, "Didn't think this would be such a busy place. Yankee soldiers here, all right— plenty of 'em."

She said, "You take care of the mules best you can. I'm goin' in to look around."

He touched her shoulder. "You'll come right back? It looks wild and dangerous."

"Everything's dangerous," she said, "and everybody."

Standing very close, he said, "Marilee, I wish it'd been different between us from the start. I really wish that."

Wish in one hand and pour peas in the other, Lucinda had said, *See which gets full quickest.* "Can't be changed," Marilee said, and turned to watch a squad of bluecoat infantry tramp by; what possible good could infantry do out here on the plains?

"Stay awhile," Frazier said softly. "Help me with supper and we can talk some more. I—I'll find some way to make it all up to you. I swear it."

"On what?" she said. "On your honor as a gentleman?"

Flushing, he stepped back. "I didn't *have* to tell you all I did. I was just tryin' to make things clearer between us, make 'em better."

She stroked Bradburn's neck. "That's right, you didn't have to tell me that you're a complete sham. I knew it from the beginning. You might fool people who've never been around gentry, but you can never fool gentry itself."

Frazier shifted uncomfortably. The wagon train people were stirring among themselves, excited as bees swarming around a new queen. Down the road toward town a cowboy hooted, and farther on somebody let off a pistol. He said, "How was I to know? I mean, nobody could figure you out to be a lady, decked out like that. I saw you were a woman right off, because I have an eye for females. But I didn't know, couldn't know you were a lady."

Marilee stared at him. "It wouldn't have made any difference to you, Gilmore. Clothes and money don't make a gentleman—there are instincts you don't have."

"It hasn't been that bad," he said, fist clenched on the handle of his walking stick. "Damn it, you can't tell me it's been so bad."

He was right about that. She looked at a dust cloud raised by a milling herd and listened to confused animal bawling, to cowhands yipping as they moved the cows along. Gilmore Frazier had been gentle with her, tender with her; there had been none of the brutal rutting, no clawing fingers or bruised breasts. But even though he had done it with worded threats instead of overpowering strength, he'd still forced himself upon her, and rape was rape, no two ways about it.

"See to the mules," she said. "Grain 'em until we can find some hay somewhere. I'll start supper."

One hand lifted as if to stroke her cheek, but Frazier dropped it quickly. "Good, that's good."

He was clumsy with the harness, awkward at feeding and watering, and she glanced sometimes at his fumbling efforts as she gathered enough twigs for a fire. She'd had beans soaking in a crock all day, and brought them out to dump them into a pan now, slicing up chunks of bacon into them. Water and salt added, she squatted on her heels and watched them cook.

Four nights she had bedded down with Gilmore Frazier; the first evening under the wagon, the rest in the wagonbed with him. Each of those nights, her body had belonged to him, not to her; her flesh and juices his to do with as he pleased, the shapings and smoothness his to fondle and clutch. Marilee had nothing to say about what happened, no choice in the matter.

It had not been terrifying; his lovemaking hadn't been painful, but neither had it been anything else. For a while, she had expected something else, lain trembling and fearful upon that brink another man had tumbled her over. But there'd been no whirling away of her mind, no shattering of her control; she hadn't been thrust into a cresting wave, and there had been no sinfully delicious drifting among lotus blossoms.

So she had accepted him, relieved that she wasn't truly corrupt, that she wouldn't always react the shameless way she had with Joe Langston. But she had been just a bit disappointed, too, then guilty about even desiring such an unladylike release again.

Frazier was feeling guilty. Headachy from the liquor he'd consumed, edgy about her daytime reaction to him, he'd kept quiet for a long time after the train moved out. But silence didn't work for him, so he began to talk—about everything except what he'd forced her to do. And his nervousness made him truthful—as much as he could ever be. Marilee sensed that as his disjointed story poured out.

Of course, there was no Frazier Manor; he'd made that up, trying to give himself a background of respectability, one that fit in with that of so many impoverished Southern gentlemen ruined by the war. He'd tried to copy genteel speech, to dress like a planter, and it hadn't been easy for a man from an out-at-the-elbows family that did odd jobs around the city.

"I ran errands, I stole when I had to, and I worked alongside freed blacks for the same miserable wages," Frazier had said. "And after a while, there were the gaming tables on Rue Royale. From sweepin' out the places, I moved up to playin' for the house, and when I got a stake, I went out on my own. But to gamble with gentlemen, you got to act like one yourself."

She'd kept quiet, keeping an eye on the mules, so accustomed to wearing her eyepatch now that it seemed normal to tilt her head. Marilee didn't really want to know any more about the man, didn't want him rounded out and familiar. Oh, Lord, she thought, how much more familiar could a man get than one who had intimately known her body? But she listened to him because she had to, unable to drown out his words in the rattle of harness and the creaking of wagons; they kept coming through the sometime cries of other drivers or the pop of a whip, kept falling upon her like the mantle of fine dust that always hung around the moving train.

And once, in an effort to stem Frazier's confessions, she'd cut at him with: "And you probably never wore the gray, much less the epaulettes of an officer."

It hadn't worked, because Gilmore Frazier seemed glad to accept the lash, to take some kind of punishment. "Bought my way out," he admitted, "until things got so bad the provosts were roundin' up everybody they could lay hands to. Then I cut and run—holed up with some niggers 'til General Butler took New Orleans."

"*Beast* Butler," she'd said, remembering the stories, the insults forced upon Southern women.

"Some called him that, but he didn't come down hard on folks that didn't fight, and I got by all right for a spell. Then my luck went bad—that and Yankee soldiers raisin' hell because they lost at cards, takin' back their money."

With debts piling up and no way to pay them, Gilmore Frazier had been desperate enough to steal a wagon and team of mules, to raid a Union army storehouse for food and blankets. His luck held then, getting him out of the city and on his way west, his last money buying him room with Captain Goodnight's train. When they reached California, he said, the sale of mules and wagon would give him another start.

Stirring the pot of beans, Marilee remembered that he'd said a lot of things, all of them pointing toward an excuse for doing it to her. But it hadn't stopped him from doing it again that night and every night thereafter. So she had no pity to give him, no absolution. He was still a rapist, though a different breed from the Yankee trooper, and different from Joe Langston.

Marilee tasted the beans; Joe Langston wouldn't blame bad luck or circumstances for his own acts. He hadn't even gone into any detail about his whip-scarred body, that powerful, driving body with no tenderness, no gentleness bred into it. Angrily, she stood up and poked at the fire with her boot tip, as if she could push his memory into the flames and crisp it.

Behind her, Frazier said, "I'm awful glad you waited." She didn't look at him. "It's suppertime."

"Marilee—"

Whirling on him, she said sharply: *"Martin!* If you just have to name me something, call me that. Do you want the whole damned train to know what I am, who I am? I should never have told you my real name."

"I—I'm sorry," he murmured. "From now on, I'll remember."

"You won't have to, for long." She kneeled to scoop a helping of beans onto her tin plate; she didn't serve him any. Frazier used the big wooden spoon to help himself and sat on a box near her.

He said, "That town's wild—just listen to it. What can you do there? Somebody else will see through that boy look, and you could wind up in one of them houses."

Blowing on a piece of fatback, she said, "I don't mean to stay in San Antone—there's no land to be settled here, no wild horses."

He frowned. "Folks are sayin' it's real bad out on the plains; Goodnight is even wonderin' if the train can keep on by itself, or if we should wait and tie in with some more wagons, get some troops to ride along. How can you make it out there all by yourself?"

"Somehow," she said. "What do you expect me to do, stay and be your whore?"

Frazier looked down into his plate, and firelight couldn't reach his eyes as he said softly, "I don't think of you like that. I've known whores—they're about *all* I knew, and you're not like any of 'em. You—well, I reckon you're somebody special."

He glanced up at her then, his eyes steady. "I'm not sorry I made you sleep with me. I wish it might of been different, that you were willin', but a man like me and a lady like you—hell, I'd never had a chance that way,

206

never got to know what it was like to hold you up close and feel how smooth, how soft you are. If you was back where you used to be, there on your big plantation, and I was back shufflin' cards, you wouldn't even say howdy to me. So I ain't sorry I got drunk and—and made you do it with me. It's something I'll remember all my life."

Cleaning her plate, Marilee held it on her lap, not moving for a while. Another gunshot popped in town, and a celebrating cowboy echoed it with a whoop. Faintly, she heard glass breaking somewhere, and saw the glare of oil lamps at the near end of the street. She thought she could just make out the offkey rattle of a piano. It seemed strange to be near a town, any town, and when she looked beyond Gilmore Frazier and their own wagon, she could see other wagon train members, still in their protective clusters. Only the scouts, lone and lonely men, had immediately headed for San Antonio's fleshpots; the rest clung to the identity of the train, bound by how far they'd traveled together and a changed sense of what was important.

"I'll probably remember it, too," Marilee said, "but not in the same way."

Putting down his plate and picking up a tin cup to fill from the blackened coffee pot, Frazier said, "Been tryin' to explain to you, but you don't understand. I guess I'm beggin' you to stay on with the train, stay with me, and if my luck holds, I mean to make it all up to you in California."

"Pay me for my services with a gold nugget, maybe?"

"No, damn it! That's not what I mean and you know it. I—" He looked away from her again and cradled the cup in both hands. Softly, abjectly, he said then: "I love you —first time in my life I loved anybody more'n myself, and if you can bring yourself to marryin' me, I'd be right proud."

Someone was approaching their fire, and Marilee was glad. She saw the scout Pecos, Indian-looking, slouched; light winked dully on the butt of his Colt, on the bearclaw necklace around his neck.

"Light," she said, "and help yourself to coffee."

Grunting, he squatted and found a cup, sipped at the dark brew. Droplets of it hung in his droopy moustache and glistened against a nondescript brown beard shot with gray. He said, "San Antone's changed some. On top it looks about the same, but they're all runnin' scared. Cows still acomin' in, but not near as many. Used to be more folks headin' out—not now."

Voice lowered, face half turned away, Marilee asked, "Indians?"

"Lipan Apache mostly, but farther out yonder—" Pecos gestured with his shaggy head—"it gits worse —them damned Comanche."

Edgily, Frazier said, "But Goodnight's keepin' on?"

Pecos sipped coffee, hunkered on his moccasins like any tribesman. "Reckon. Hear tell he got eight more wagons to join up—they been waitin' a spell here."

"Any soldiers?"

Bobbing his head, Pecos said, "Whole six of 'em, but only the loo-tenant's white."

Frazier winced. *"Nigger* troopers?"

"Buffler soldiers, Apaches calls 'em. 'Spect they do look sommat like a buff—kinky wool and all—but don't know as I'd say much for their horns."

Marilee kept quiet, watching Frazier's agitation, absorbing the feel of something behind the scout's casual, news-bringing visit to their fire.

"Just six men," Frazier said. "Not near enough."

"All we'll git," Pecos said, and Marilee poured him more coffee. She said, "Hear anything about the Mexican war?"

Peering at her, Pecos said, "Still afightin', and that's how come more Yanks ain't travelin' around—they're stickin' close to the border."

He was probably dead by now, Marilee thought—all that arrogance and strength, all the animal quickness run out of him through a bullet hole. "Knowed some Rebs went down there after Appomattox," she said. "Supposed to join up with the Frenchmen and get rich." Belatedly, knowing a nip of guilt, she recalled Major Ainsworth, whose goal wasn't loot but a rebuilding of the Confederacy.

"Ain't heard," Pecos said. "But they ain't liable to have it rough as us; rather face Mexicans anytime, than Apache and them damned Comanch'."

"If'n it's all that bad," Marilee said, "how come you're goin' on?"

"Said I would—got me a woman out yonder, too.

Leastwise, I did when I left. Mean to see if'n she's still there."

"We're keepin' on for California," Frazier said, and looked at Marilee.

Pecos wiped a brown hand across his moustache. "You, too—boy?"

He knew, Marilee realized. Somehow, this sharp-eyed old scout *knew* and was subtly warning her of the danger ahead. He waited, and she said, " 'Spect so."

Sighing, Pecos stood up. "Goodnight'll be glad to hear. Boy—you keep a close watch on that there horse. 'Preciate the coffee."

When he was gone, Frazier said, "Thank you, Mari— Martin. I'll make it up to you, I swear."

"You can do that by treating me as if I'm a young man, both *in* and out of the wagon. That Pecos—couldn't you tell he knows about me?"

Stubbornly, Frazier shook his head. "It don't matter. I won't let him bother you, or anybody else. But I can't keep my hands off you, either. Look, there's probably a preacher in town there, somebody to marry us. We don't have to wait until California."

"We," Marilee said, "we! You mean yourself, Gilmore. What do you expect me to do, hug your neck and be grateful because you said you'd marry me? Damn it, you haven't even *asked* me."

"I'm askin' you, then."

"No," she said. "When we get to California, I'm goin' my own way."

Hesitating, he said, "It's a far piece—could be you'll change your mind. I mean to keep tryin'."

"Go ahead," she said, "go ahead," because she knew there was no alternative, that San Antonio held no hope for her and her stallion. She would just have to put up with Gilmore Frazier.

She was restless in the wagon that night, and he had the decency to stay away from her, although she could tell he remained awake a long time, turning in his blankets. He wasn't much, but now he was showing a mulish streak that might turn him into a man, if allowed to flourish. Never a gentleman, but enough of an independent male to make it on his own without trying to be something he wasn't.

And he was the first man she'd refused to marry; Robbie Dee Crownover had refused to marry *her*, until the war was over. Well, the damned war was over, and four men had taken her body, each in his own way, and where was Robbie Dee? She had such a hard time bringing back his face; it kept rippling as if it were a reflection in a pond, and something dark kept stirring the water.

But she could see Joe Langston sharp and clear, and that made her so mad she couldn't sleep either. Listening to San Antonio carousing in the night, hearing in the town's gaiety something of panic held at arm's length, Marilee wondered. Was he celebrating in Mexico, too—a dusky girl on his arm, hot-eyeing her willing body and getting smiled at in return, beckoned on?

No, she thought; he was lying in a gully somewhere, dead as he had every right to be, melting back into the poor dirt he'd sprung from, and so be it.

In the morning, she awoke tired and feeling gritty. The only place she could bathe in private was inside the wagon with blankets hung, dipping a rag in the bucket. At least she had soap now, and Gilmore Frazier was kind enough to hand her in fresh water. When she stood down, reasonably clean, he'd already cared for the mules and Bradburn and had made breakfast.

She wouldn't go into the town; there were too many ragged people around, drifting aimlessly around the wagons, gaunt and worried folks who might never have stolen before. They'd do it now to get away, to go back somewhere the Apaches weren't raiding. And Bradburn wasn't only too precious to lose, he was a part of her; she meant to keep him, even if it killed her.

Nobody tried for him because she was always there with the Colt hung low and the Spencer ready across her arms. She didn't fret about the cowboys; they had their own horses, shaggy and wiry as the men themselves, and they had the look of men who wouldn't steal; they'd be more likely to take what they needed at the muzzle of a pistol. But they had a certain swagger to them, a don't-give-a-damn attitude that kept reminding her of Joe Langston.

Since she couldn't watch all day and all night, too, and because she couldn't walk him out and back to graze and care for the mules properly, Marilee gave in to Gilmore

Frazier the next night. It was more like making a trade, letting him use her body so he'd stand guard over the stallion and their stock. She thought he was going to cry, and that made her feel strange, not exactly sorry for the man, but not exactly wanting to kick him, either.

There were two more days and nights like that before the troopers came, before the other eight wagons joined Captain Goodnight's train, and on the third dawning, they rolled out West. She saw the white lieutenant signal his black cavalrymen right and left of the wagons, watched them bouncing stiffly in new saddles atop half-broke horses that were nothing like Bradburn. It would take her longer to get used to seeing Nigras in uniform than for those greenhorns to get used to their mounts and the horses to their riders.

"Headin' for Fort Inge, then Fort Clark," Frazier said. "Then Goodnight aims to turn north to Fort Lancaster—one military post to the other, like jumpin' from one square to the other on a checkerboard."

"Only these squares are a long way apart," Marilee said.

"Twenty wagons," he reminded her, "and the bluecoats. We'll make it."

Six days, with the sun getting hotter, the air almost dry as dust itself; desert growth she'd only seen as pictures in books—needled cactus, a many-pointed bush that Pecos called Spanish bayonet. The old scout pointed out sagebrush and cholla, and showed her the saguaro prized by Apaches for sweet syrup they made from its pulp, and the *tizwin* they brewed from the syrup—"Stuff that'll get you drunk, kin you hold enough of it down," he said.

Six nights of being drawn close to Gilmore Frazier when one or the other of them wasn't posted as guard, and she tried very hard not to compare his lovemaking with Joe Langston's. If only Joe had been gentle, if he had shown a tenderness. . . .

It wouldn't happen again, she was certain. She'd lain with Frazier so many times and felt only his urgency, his warmth, and perhaps a closeness that was better than being lonely. But never that onrush of madness that melted her backbone and exploded her heart. That had been some crazy kind of accident, a thing that never should have happened the first time.

Thinking back, Marilee was to know that God had

certainly rested on the seventh day, that He had been asleep that pink and falsely soft dawn.

For on the seventh day out of San Antonio, the Apaches hit.

Chapter 22

Del Rio, Texas, had three cantinas and two general stores, a blacksmith, and a feed store. It also had too damned many bluebellies to suit Joe Langston, even if some of them were galvanized Yankees—ex-Rebs who enlisted for the frontier because soldiering was just about all they knew. And because they had nowhere else to get their bacon and beans, they changed uniforms and went west to deliver arms to Juárez and fight Indians. Damned little Indian fighting got done, but a whole lot of riding or marching out and coming back tail-dragging and empty-handed.

Hide-bottomed chair propped on its hind legs and leaned back against the adobe wall of Garcia's cantina, Joe looked lazily up and down the single dusty street, then out to where the soldiers were camped. They were scuffling around again, making a confused hooraw as they got ready for another fruitless patrol.

Chewing on the end of an unlighted cigarillo, he thought that outfit was damned lucky the Comanches hadn't swung in here on their last raid, lucky those fast-moving horsemen had instead run across a prowling band

of their traditional enemy, the Apaches. Good fortune
was about to grin on the Yanks in another way, too; word
was out that the troops were pulling out before long,
headed back to San Antonio.

Not so good for the citizens of Del Rio, that move; it
would lay them wide open for massacre, but the U.S.
army didn't give a doodly damn about that. The folks here
had to protect themselves, or lose their hair, or follow the
soldiers east. A few were talking about packing up and
wagoning north to join up with trains pointed to California,
where there wasn't any Indian trouble.

Thing was, getting there through Comancheria. But they
were atwixt a rock and a hard place, and Joe figured some
were bound to try. For himself, he'd wait around and see;
poker table pickings wouldn't be much good when the
bluebellies left, anyhow. It wasn't every night you got to
trim the tail feathers of a couple of silver-heavy Mexican
bandidos.

Joe checked the street again, but saw nothing beyond
some hitchrack horses flapping tails at flies, and a wagon
getting new wheelspokes there at the smithy, another
wagon being loaded at a general store. It was going to hurt
the *bandidos* when Del Rio was just about abandoned;
they wouldn't have a handy place to dispose of cows stolen
the other side of the border.

She came to the door and stood hipshot near him, rich
body hollering through a simple dress, the top half of her
near about spilling over. Wavy hair blueblack as his own
plunged curling over her shoulders and snuggled to an
ivory throat. Hoop earrings glittered in the late sun as she
smiled down at him. Joe smiled back; he had a lot to thank
Ampora Garcia for, not the least of which was herself.

"He has not come," she said in liquid Spanish. "Perhaps
El Cuchillo will not—perhaps his men were ashamed to
admit the *gringo* gambler won all their money."

"Quién sabe?" Joe answered. "Do I smell tortillas?"

She leaned over him, brushing his shoulder with a firm
ripe breast. "Sniff again, and you might find a better
scent."

"Of woman and roses," he agreed, and dropped the
legs of the chair to slide an arm around her indented
waist. "Tortillas can always wait."

Her smile faded. "If El Cuchillo will."

Standing up, feeling her rounded hip against him, Joe said, "The Knife's edge may be dulled—Apache and Comanche keep Lopez from stealing many cows."

Ampora made a face as they walked into the shade of the cantina itself. "That one—he deals with them both, trades them guns. And what does the *gringo* sheriff of Del Rio do about it?"

"Nothing he can do, *querida*. He's just one man." And again Joe wondered what brought the man this far south, so far from the original German-settled colony in a safer part of Texas. But what led most men anywhere?

Old Hernando bobbed his white mousey head at them as they passed behind the bar and into the little corridor that led to Ampora's room, his near-toothless grin envious. With the door closed, she turned to press her yielding body to Joe. "You are just one man, *mi cariño*, but what a man."

Much-laundered cactus-fiber blankets were soft against his skin as he lay back. Ampora enjoyed undressing him, teasing his flesh with deftly skipping fingers as she did so, bending to caress him with the scented fall of her thick hair. A hungry woman, this widow; a giving, taking woman whose flavor lingered like chili peppers, the searing heat of her remaining for a long time after the sweat of their lovemaking had dried.

Now she was kneeling over him, passing the points of her melon breasts back and forth across his chest, making him quiver and delighting in his reaction. But she was arousing herself as much, and flung herself upon him with a throaty gasp, redsoft lips crushed into his mouth, quick, hungry tongue thrusting and curling.

She was a strong-bodied woman, honest and demanding; her legs curled about him as she lifted and swung her hips, as her belly struck at him, captured him. Rose-ivory skin was smooth in his hands, and the taste of her was good. Joe met her need with his own fierceness, driving into her writhing flesh, hammering back at her with his power, his throbbing strength, in just the way she liked.

But even when the surging caught itself and trembled, even at that special, quivering moment when all the rest of the world should have been closed out, Joe felt another body squirming with him, a body shaped of pale quicksilver, all slim and fiery. He tried to fight the image out of his head, out of his blood, but she clung inside him. She dug into him with sharp nails, bit into his mind and his belly, even as he clutched Ampora's heaving buttocks and exploded himself within her velvet cupping.

"Ah," she whispered. "Ah, *hombre*. We are a match, you and I."

"A match," he breathed, knowing the truth of that. *This* was Joe Langston's kind of woman, always hot and willing, never ashamed to admit the thing she wanted. No goddamned lady, Ampora—only a full-blooded *woman*.

When he'd shown up, gaunt as his bony mare, mean as a rattler poked with a sharp stick, she'd accepted his little bit of silver and put him up in back of the cantina in a storeroom. All that long, dangerous way across north Mexico after the smartass Juarista lieutenant had stripped him of gold and jewels didn't make Joe easy to get along with.

But Ampora got him cleaned up and calmed down, and even took care of his good barb mare. She fed him and made fierce love with him, then staked him to the poker games when he told her he couldn't just stay around like a penned-up stud horse. What more could a man ask of any woman than that? Nobody but a man with his brains knocked out would keep right on thinking of silver hair and a thin, angry face set with willowgreen eyes that slanted a little.

Lifting her lush body from him, Ampora kissed the base of his throat and murmured, "Tonight, my lover—after food and tequila and the poker. Tonight, when there will be much time."

Joe reached for a cigarillo and watched her cover all that moist, glowing body with the plain dress. He saw the little frown, the way she caught her full lip between sharp, white teeth.

"Don't worry," he said, thumbnailing a sulphur match and holding it to his little cigar. "*Los indios* are worse than a single *bandido*."

Ampora brushed at her hair, her back to him. "I think he *is indio*, and he will not come alone."

Joe said, "Do you expect me to run?"

"No," she said, "never that—but a woman worries. A woman who has already lost one man worries."

When she was gone, Joe dressed, and then spun the cylinder of the Walker with the heel of his hand. Ampora hadn't said it out loud, but she knew the restlessness in him and never tried to brand him, to tie him to her through a priest. She knew that by holding him too tight, she might make him want to break away. Maybe she even knew he would break away sometime, but she didn't talk about that.

He had a stake now; the wrinkles were out of his belly and the mare was sleek again. He was one hell of a long way from rich, but his pockets knew the feel of gold once more, and a rabbit-hide sack beneath the pillow was fat with silver coins. When Del Rio was left to the desert, like it would be soon, when the army pulled out and the Apaches and Comanches took turns butchering up folks who were muley-headed enough to stay, Joe Langston would be a far piece away. California was starting to sound pretty good, and this time there'd be some killing before anybody else got his money.

Hernando made gummy, obscene jokes about lovers who had to do a turn in the blankets before supper, and Ampora brought steaming platters of tortillas, frijoles, and chicken soaked with spices that made it celebrate against the tongue. From the street, a sombreroed head reached in and as quickly pulled back.

As Joe lighted his smoke and spilled salt into the veeing of thumb and forefinger of his right hand, a sloe-eyed boy peeped inside the cantina, then was gone. Joe drank a tumbler of tequila with his left hand, licked the salt, then popped a slice of lemon into his mouth—again, with the left hand.

Ampora said quietly, "I will get the shotgun."

"No," he said. "Stay in the kitchen." When she hesitated, he said more strongly, "The kitchen."

Cigarillo between his teeth, he crossed to the bar old Hernando had left and put his back to it. There were no windows, only the door to the street, and the one in the kitchen. Ampora was there, watching.

A man clumped along the packed dirt outside, and Joe flexed his fingers.

"Comin' in," a voice called, and Joe waited. Redfaced, heavy black cigar in his mouth, the sheriff walked in. He walked light for a big man, and Joe thought T. R.

Fehrenbach had to be pretty good. He was the only law for a hundred miles or more, and past his prime. You didn't see many middle-aged lawmen.

Fehrenbach moved to the bar and took off his hat. Wiping a freckled hand over thinning hair, he squinted at Joe from blue eyes heavily lined at the corners. "Was times normal, I'd wait out yonder with my old Greener loaded with buckshot, and hope you all knocked holes in each other, so I wouldn't have to do no more'n clean up the mess."

"See your point, T. R.," Joe said, eyes on the door.

Strong lips worrying his handrolled cigar, the sheriff said, "You ain't caused trouble, but seems like trouble runs after a *pistolero*. Lopez and them two others ain't exactly runnin' from the Los Gatos cantina, but they'll be acomin'. Here to tell you I'd just as soon you kept it in here—other folks could get hurt out on the street."

"Like you say, T. R.," Joe said.

" 'Preciate it," the sheriff said, and put his hat on to walk easy to the door. He stopped there and looked around, then moved out of sight.

From the kitchen, Ampora said, "The back door is barred, but I will open it for you."

"And leave my *cojones* behind? *Gracias, querida,* but I will stay."

They came rattling big concho spurs, walking biggity and spitting, joking with each other in tequila-roughened voices, sure of themselves. Joe waited.

As befitting his rank of *jefe*, El Cuchillo swaggered in the lead, both his men swinging out to each side and a step behind their leader as they came into the cantina.

"Hola, gringo," Lopez said, resting one black-furred hand on the butt of his pistol. "So you are still here, after robbing my poor *soldados* with the cards. I would think—"

Joe never learned what El Cuchillo Lopez would think, because he didn't give the man time to say it. Walker Colt filling his hand, he shot the bandit in the belly, just below the crossed cartridge belts.

Rolling left and going to one knee, he slammed the next bullet through a man's chest. Gunsmoke rolled and thunder roared inside the cantina as Joe went to his belly and spun to his right. He steadied the pistol with both hands and let off another shot that caught the third man too high, only smashing his shoulder and spinning him around. It was the wrong shoulder, because a big splinter of raw wood jumped out of the bar over Joe's head.

Joe fired again. The *bandido* dropped his gun and stumbled backward into the street to fall flat. Blinking against acrid clouds of smoke, Joe came to his knees again, eyes narrowed to watch the two downed men. One was finished. Lopez held to his stained belly with one hand, also swaying upon his knees, his other hand fumbling behind his body, as if to ease the pain there, too.

"You—you did not give me the—chance," he mumbled, mouth pulling hard for air and pockmarked face twisted.

Thumbing back the Colt's hammer, Joe shot him low in the throat. Lopez jerked over onto one side, pumping blood. His right hand flopped out from behind him. Light winked off a two-edged blade.

"That's right," Joe said to the dead man. "Didn't give you time to chunk that goddamned knife you was named for, either."

She came running from the kitchen, dark eyes wide and hair flying. "Joe, Joe!"

Moving her to one side with his elbow, he jacked empty casings from the cylinder and thumbed new rounds into their places before lettting her come to him. Even then, he watched the door over her shoulder, Colt hanging loosely in his hand.

Ampora's face was smeared with her tears. *"Dios, Dios* —three of them, and El Cuchillo himself! You are a *muy grande pistolero."*

"Talked hisself to death," Joe said. "Expected me to listen to his mouth while they all got set. Seems like the world don't never run out of damned fools."

Setting her gently back with his left hand, Joe stepped over Lopez on his way to the door. He looked at the bandit outside, lying on his back with dust settling upon open black eyes, then looked up and down the street. Out past the army tents, a slow feather of dust followed the troops as they plodded out into the open country there, where Apaches could see them coming for miles.

Walking like his boots were too tight, the sheriff came out from behind the smithy, a short, double-barreled shotgun over one arm. Joe waited for him, slowly and carefully putting up his Colt as Fehrenbach approached.

Up close, the sheriff said, "Wasn't but them three. Don't reckon any more of 'em will come in, now."

Joe said. "I made the mess inside—I'll clean it up."

"Fair enough," Fehrenbach said. "You know much about them dry hills out yonder?"

"Some," Joe said. "Rode up clear from Chapultepec, and learned to stay hid—'cept for one time."

The sheriff said, "Out yonder, one time's too much, but a horny toad like you just might get by."

"Doin' what?"

"Spookin' them Apache some. Few folks here mean to stay put and fort up, but it'd be better to have somebody out liftin' a few scalps and keepin' them damned Injuns worried."

Joe looked over the street again. A Mexican poked his head out of a store and came outside to sit down. "You stayin', T. R.?" Joe asked.

Fehrenbach sighed. "For a spell, but I'm gettin' long in the tooth, and goin' back to my own is startin' to look good to me. Folks here got cow money and nothin' to spend it on, since the freight wagons ain't movin' now. Figure they'd pay twenty dollars a scalp."

Nodding toward the wagons being readied, Joe said, "How about that train makin' up?"

The sheriff shook his head. "Won't get out for a long time, if'n atall. Be easier, was the Apache jumpy about gettin' done to them like they do unto others. Then the train could use a good scout, like as not."

Joe said, "You hired yourself a bounty hunter."

Fehrenbach drew out a cigar. "Soon's you clean up that mess inside."

Chapter 23

They came yelping out of the dry, harsh land, quick and wily as gray coyotes, running low to the ground. When a woman screamed terror in echo and guns went off, Marilee sat up groggy in the wagon as Frazier stirred and muttered beside her.

Flinging off blankets, snatching desperately at clothing, she saw a black trooper just beyond the end of the wagon, saw him lurch in the saddle of a plunging horse. His carbine fired into the earth as he pitched forward, an arrow driven through his throat.

Bradburn! He was tied to a wagon spoke, out there in all the firing.

"W-what the hell?—" Frazier said.

Spencer in one hand and Colt thrust into her belt, Marilee bounded over the tailgate and hit the ground barefoot. Eyes rolling and nostrils spread wide, the stallion trembled against the rope, but didn't fight it.

Squealing, a mule reared and went down to kick in spasms. A shotgun went off, its roar deeper than rifles. An arrow *whicked* by Marilee's head to gash the canvas wagontop. She dropped to one knee and levered a shell into the carbine. There was so much yelling, so much dust and blurred confusion.

She added to it: "Gilmore! Come out of there!"

Something almost naked, something animal and dark and squat came darting past the downed trooper. Marilee caught a glimpse of greasy black hair, a mouth snarling in a twisted face grotesqued by red slashes, black slashes.

Point-blank, she fired at him, and jacked another shell into the carbine as the Apache fell. Frazier jumped down beside her, rifle uncertain in his hands. "How'd they—how'd they get in among the wagons so quick? The guards—"

"Get down, you damned fool!" She saw another scuttling figure and shot at it, but couldn't be sure if she'd hit. Marilee was surprised at her calmness, at how steady she was with the Spencer. There just wasn't time to be afraid, except for her horse.

Smoke—too thick and yellow to be gunsmoke, it came rolling over them, and Pecos came loping with its rolling cloud.

"Damned wagon's got to be pushed out—come on!"

Dazed, Frazier clambered up, but Marilee snapped, "I'm not leavin' my horse."

Staccato thunder of gunfire; a mule in braying agony, a man dying hard, too; the same woman screaming again and again. Dust and smoke, and two dead men lying close to her. Squinting, Marilee peered through the smoke, carbine muzzle searching, searching. Had fighting in the war been like this, nobody knowing which way to look, what to fire at, everything so mixed up?

The quiet came down so suddenly it was a shock, but when the guns stopped, the woman began screaming again, softer this time, hopelessly.

Marilee stood up, backing to the horse and reaching behind to calm him with her hand. "Good boy, good boy." She kept looking beyond the wagons, watching through lifting smoke, her finger still on the trigger. After a while, she turned quickly to feel over Bradburn, praying she wouldn't find an arrow in him, a bullet hole with all his beautiful life running out through it.

He was whole, and she gave thanks for it, trembling with the horse now, weaker than he was and more frightened. When Marilee could lift her flushed face from his mane, she turned again to see the burning wagon manhandled out of the circle and pitched onto its side. One wheel was spinning slowly.

Frazier came back to climb into the wagon and bring out the whiskey jug. Marilee said sharply, "No time for that. Get the trunk and boxes out—put them under the wagon in a line."

He stared at her before obeying, and she put aside her own carbine to collect the dead trooper's weapons and ammunition. The man's face looked more gray than black now, but the dirt under his head was black with his blood. Steeling herself, Marilee turned the Indian over, but all he had was a knife.

"My boots, too," she said to Frazier. "My hat."

Pecos came to squat on his heels, rifle across his knees. "Horse make out?"

"So far," she answered. "Did we whip them?"

Pecos grunted. "Injuns don't keep acomin', 'til the end of it. They hit and back off, hit and back off."

"How bad is it—the wagon train, I mean?"

The man looked without surprise at her silvery hair, grown too long now, at her eye without the patch over it. "They got ever' damned one of the soldiers and three scouts, far's I kin tell. Smart bunch of bastards—went for the mules and horses, too. You get that 'un?"

When she nodded, Pecos said, "I make him to be San Carlos, maybe Mescalero. Hard to tell, when they're skinned down for war."

Frazier shoved the last box beneath the wagon and stood up, redfaced. "Are we goin' to run for it? What's Captain Goodnight mean to do?"

Pecos looked at the dead trooper, at the dead Apache. "Hang and rattle, I 'spect. Get strung out runnin' and they'll bite off a piece ever' mile. 'Sides, there ain't that many mules left."

"But—what will we *do*? Can't somebody ride for help?" Frazier's voice was higher than usual, thinner.

Cradling his rifle, Pecos stood up. "You want the job? Won't last long enough fer a payday—them Apache are hid out yonder waitin' for somebody to try. Leastwise, 'til they come hellin' in here agin."

Marilee reloaded both carbines and the trooper's pistol. The wagon to their left was drawn up close, its people under it. The family on the right was doing it differently, all crouched in the wagonbed with the canvas rolled up a little and rifle barrels poking out. She wished she could put Bradburn somewhere.

Frazier said, "I don't think the Indians will come back. They didn't overrun the train, so they won't try it again. You better put on your hat and eyepatch, so nobody'll know what you are."

"I need both eyes to shoot," she said, "and it doesn't matter now. Pecos knew anyway."

"It ain't that bad—I know it ain't."

Marilee put the blanket on Bradburn and swung up the saddle. She bitted the horse and looped reins around the wagonspoke when she took off his rope. Watching her fill saddlebags and canteen, Frazier said, "You figure the Indians to win. They do, you can't ride out anyhow."

"I aim to try," Marilee said, and gathered blankets to drape them over the stallion; they weren't much protection, but it was all she could do for him. Then she looked at Frazier, at the trembling weakness of him. "I won't run off and leave you. Maybe nobody will be able to run off."

He had the whiskey jug, and tilted it for a long swallow. "I won't leave you, either—Marilee. It sounds good to say your name out loud like that—*Marilee*."

A rifle cracked down the line, and someone yelled hoarsely, "Yonder they come!"

Under the wagon, Frazier was with her as they rested carbine barrels on top of ration boxes. She could feel him sweating, but he was there.

A little rise in the ground was topped by a mesquite bush, and she thought it moved. Putting her sights on it, she waited. Beside her, Frazier fired at something, and she carefully squeezed off a shot at an Apache who burst raging from the bush. He kept running straight at them until his legs flopped out and he dug his face into the ground. Marilee flicked a glance at the arrow embedded in the trunk close by.

It was noisy again, all kinds of sounds stirred together, some of them sounds she never wanted to hear again— the wild dog-yipping of the Apaches, a child crying rawthroated, startled death whinny of an impaled horse, and guns, guns.

"Got him!" Frazier yelled. "Damned if I didn't get him!"

Leveling her carbine, Marilee picked up the racing form of a dark warrior wearing only a piece of rag twisted through his crotch. Maybe she hit him; maybe somebody else did. He went down and kicked in a slow, crazy circle.

She fired and reloaded, fired and reloaded, tasting powder acrid upon her mouth, tasting the sweat of fear. Next to her, Frazier grunted and sank back, but he wasn't wounded. When she stared at him in the shadow of the wagonbed, behind the barricade of their supplies, she saw him taking a drink of water. His face was grimed, and he was shaking.

Backing from beneath the wagon, Marilee looked over her horse. Somehow, the big stallion seemed to know to stay close to protection. In the silence of the broken-off attack, she talked to him, her voice far away in her deafened ears.

Another wagon was burning now, but there weren't enough men to wrestle it out of line. She saw a body hanging over its side, turning black, and folks in the next wagon beating off flames that reached for their own. Two Apaches had gotten through the circle to die there, but only after they'd cut a woman's throat and blown a hole through her man.

Such ugly, bandy-legged little men, she thought, dipping water from the barrel to cool her baked throat. Dark, sun-blackened men in fringed leggings and moccasins and little else; no—more like hungry, blind-mean animals than men. Swallowing more water, she peered around the battered, broken circle. It was a mess—animals down, people dead and dying, fire licking hot tongues in the hot sun, a great dusty frying pan.

Slowly, Pecos came across to her, carrying his long gun as if it were a great weight. There was a gash across his leathery cheek, and he walked tired. His feathered hat was gone.

Propping one shoulder against the water barrel, he said, "You 'mind me a heap of my woman. Held our own agin 'em a time or two, we did. Course, she's Comanch' herself."

Marilee said, "You're hurt."

The man's drooping moustache lifted on one side.

"Hell," Pecos said, "I'm kilt. Some goddamn Apache put one in my back—dropped Goodnight, too. Fixed him, though—sawed off his whangdoodle and chunked it in the fire. Son of a bitch can't never diddle a squaw in his heaven."

"Can't—can't I help? We have some whiskey—"

"Beholden," Pecos said as he slid down the water barrel and sat on the ground, his back against a wheel.

When she brought him the jug, he took a long swallow and shuddered, then took another one. Voice a little stronger, he said, "Best you don't let 'em take you, missy. They're goin' to be crazier'n hell, and it ain't purty, what all they'll do to you."

"I won't let them take me," she said.

Sighing, Pecos got out his pistol and laid it on his lap, the hammer back. "Chief hisself'll come ridin' up and set back whilst the next jump wipes us out. Might make 'em some bad medicine, could I put one into the bossman hisself, but they might not back off anyways. 'Member, missy—don't let 'em get aholt of you. My woman wouldn't, neither."

"I won't," Marilee promised again, and jerked around at a movement behind her.

Puzzled, she stared at Gilmore Frazier. He had on his frock coat and high hat and had wiped dirt from his face. He looked almost the way he had when she'd seen him the first time, on the street in Beaumont.

Making a half-bow to her, he twirled his walking cane and she saw the big false diamond flash on his hand. "Might I bother you for a drink, young lady?"

"What the—Gilmore, have you lost your mind?"

Stooping for the jug, he upended it and poured whiskey down his throat. "There," he said, "that's better. If you look out yonder, you'll see that Pecos is right. The chief is sittin' a horse, and the rest are gatherin' like buzzards, ready to pick our bones clean."

She threw a glance at the Indians, then looked back at him. "So you're givin' up, waitin' for them to come in and get us?"

Frazier drank some more, his hand shaking just a little, then passed down the jug to Pecos. The scout had trouble lifting it to his lips. "No ma'am," Frazier said, "I don't intend to wait for 'em—I mean to walk out and meet 'em."

"You—you're insane!"

226

"Ah," he said, and stepped close to her. The touch of his lips was brief against her mouth. "Ah—perhaps I am, but I suggest you get on your horse, Miss Bradburn, and be ready." Hesitating then, reaching up to tilt his hat rakishly over one eye, he said, "You'll give my regards to California, of course."

He was stepping over the wagon tongue and striding over the sandy ground before she could even reach to stop him. "Gilmore—"

"Let him go, missy," Pecos said, reed thin and whispery. "Fella got some sand to him, after all. He's abuyin' you some time. It ain't much of a chance, but better'n you had. Looka there—they think he's plumb outa his head, tetched by the spirit. Injuns mostly walk wide of a crazy man."

Sleepwalking, Marilee untied Bradburn and put the reins over his head. In the saddle, she turned to watch Frazier walk nonchalantly toward the gathered Apaches, swinging his cane and whistling. She knew he was frightened, knew he was trembling, but he might have been strolling down a street in New Orleans, on his way to a card game.

"Move acrost the camp," Pecos whispered, "and when you go, don't stop for nothin'."

"I—I can't leave you all," Marilee said. "I just can't run away like this."

Pecos coughed. "Missy, you're the only one of us alive. My woman'd understand that, and you better."

Low over his neck, she walked Bradburn around the broken circle, keeping close to the wagons and stepping him over sprawled bodies. His ears snapped forward and his head lifted eagerly, but she stopped him and looked back, pulled by a horrible fascination.

Frazier was near them now, closing on the chief who sat horseback and held a feathered lance. They were watching him, rifles at the ready and bows lifted, unmoving. A wisp of the tune he was whistling floated back to her; it was "Dixie." "I wish I was in the land of cotton. . . ."

An Apache backed out of his path, and another slid away, then he was looking up at the chief, slowly raising his left hand to tip his tall hat to the savage. Staring, heart jumping in her chest and her mouth gone dusty, Marilee caught the quick wink of sunlight on Frazier's right hand.

The derringer, she thought, the hideout weapon of a gambler. The little belly gun popped twice, emptying both its barrels. The chief tried to bring up the point of his lance as he rocked backward and tumbled off his horse. Yelping, the pack raved over Frazier, chopping and hacking at him, tearing at him like wolves even after he went down.

Putting her heels into the stallion's flank, Marilee felt a sob rip from her throat as Bradburn cannoned himself over a wagon tongue and broke out of the circle at a dead run. Harsh wind slapped at her face as she urged on the pounding horse, and he gave unselfishly of his great strength, his great speed.

They thundered over ground that blurred beneath them, and she lay almost flat in the lunging rhythm of him, carbine swinging in her right hand, reins loose in her left, her cheek lashed by his flying mane. A squat man rose before them, to be smashed down by striking hooves. A gun went off behind her, and another to the left.

Bradburn chested sagebrush and crashed through it, and suddenly they were slamming through small, wiry horses scared crazy by the big stud shouldering them aside, knocking them down. Marilee fired wildly at the Apache herd guard, then it was all scattered behind her, and Bradburn flashed around the foot of a low hill, stretching out on the flat beyond, running, running.

Frazier, she thought, a liar and sneak thief, a man without much core to him, who'd misspent most of his life trying to imitate plantation gentry. Shabby lord of a manor that didn't exist, cheap gambler and a draft dodger who'd refused to serve his country, he was also someone who'd raped her by threat and made a certain kind of not untender love to her.

He had said he loved her. He had wanted to marry her.

In the end, the gambler played his last weak card, betting his life for Marilee's chance to get away.

All the stinging in her eyes wasn't caused by desert wind as she thought that, with all his faults, Gilmore Frazier had gone to meet death with his head held as high as the finest gentleman's.

Chapter 24

The mountains did it to her, confusing her by rocky heights she'd never known in Mississippi or the rest of the country crossed to get this far. They were jumbled together with hard-to-climb twists and weird, blind ravines that threw off her sense of direction. When Marilee at last came down out of them, she had a queasy feeling that she was too far north, although for days—or had it been weeks?—she'd done her best to keep Bradburn's nose pointed just about due west. Fort Clark was supposed to be that way, next stop on a journey the wagon train never reached.

She had no idea how far they'd traveled, because some of it had been in mad flight, and some creeping along in hiding; endless hours had been spent holed up in secret canyons where sparse brown grass struggled, so the stallion could work at filling his belly. Other things were behind them—the train curling its funeral high into a copper sky, the four Apaches who had raced after them.

Lowering from the saddle, Marilee loosened the cinch and removed Bradburn's bridle. Quiltings of wiry grass grew here in the foothills, and he needed their strength.

Sinking to the ground in the shade of a rock spire, she took bitter water from the canteen and held it in her tilted mouth. It was easier to choke down cornmeal when it was damp.

She watched the horse graze and thought of the strange forage he'd lived on since they'd left the wagons—cactus leaves carefully stripped of spines by her new knife so he could munch the fiber and get a little moisture, too; brush and leaves and whatever else they could come across. She'd shared her store of meal with him, and soaked beans. On the subsistence diet and rough travel, the stallion had lost only a few pounds, and he'd taken to this dry, harsh country as if born to it. She'd learned to depend upon his nose, his instincts to search out widely spaced water holes that meant life to them both.

Leaning back with cornmeal swallowed and chewing on a raw piece of bacon rind, Marilee squinted at the plains below, a tabletop dotted with clumps of mesquite and chaparral that dwindled themselves into graygreen specks off in the distance. It was too open, exposed to any pair of black marble eyes watching from the hills. And it looked seared, baked waterless. But the going would be so much rougher, if she tried to circle that vast flatness, if she kept Bradburn to the low hills; it might take forever.

Northwest, she thought, if she'd missed Fort Clark, then the next outpost would be Fort Lancaster, so very far away, and God only knew if any troops were still stationed there. It was all Comanche country, where she was now, she remembered—and, somehow she had to cross that tremendous stretch of hostile land. Pecos had told her that, called it Comancheria, the crusty, weathered man who'd left an Indian woman to scout for a wagon train. Even though she was one of them, Pecos had still called them goddamned Comanch'.

Carrying no surname and with a bullet in his back, Pecos was sitting propped against a wagon wheel with a pistol on his lap, whispering that his woman would understand when to leave the dead.

Marilee didn't; she couldn't understand Captain Goodnight butchered, and ripped-away scalps of towheaded children, and arrows through black troopers' throats. She would never be able to sort out the sense of Gilmore

Frazier. Only strong through threats, he hadn't possessed the power and cold cunning of a Joe Langston, nor that kind of weapon skill. Where a man such as Joe survived by an animal shrewdness and savagery, Gilmore kept alive by sham and retreat, until that final moment. Marilee was certain Joe Langston would never have sacrificed himself that way; he'd gamble his precious hide for gold, but not for another human being.

Licking her fingers for traces of bacon grease, she knew she wouldn't have pulled up his horse when he was outdistancing that vicious Apache rider. But a goddamned *lady* had, and even though it made a strained kind of sense to give Bradburn a few minutes of needed rest, it was more logical to keep going and hope the stallion held out.

Even now, her jaw tightened as she remembered that run. Four riders had come after her, whooping and flailing their mustangs, wolf-men, hunting dog-men panting hotly after prey. But the great stallion kept pulling away from them, lengthening the distance so they couldn't even get within rifle shot.

They'd slammed on across a mesa, and dipped around a low hill, and for a while she thought they'd lost the Apaches, left them far behind on their straining little horses. But when she topped another rise, *he* was still hanging on stubbornly, although his mount was laboring —one rider on a struggling horse, determined to run her down. Surprised, she stared back at him, and saw the flash of sun upon steel, lifting and falling. No, she thought, oh, no! He couldn't be reaching back and stabbing that horse in the hip; not even an Apache could be so cruel, killing the wiry little beast just to get a little more speed out of him.

But he was. The vicious, mindless savage was doing just that, and horrified, she watched the blade rise and drop, over and over in a steady, merciless plunging. Then she whirled Bradburn and galloped on, the stark image of a gut-wrenching brutality staying with her, making her ill —and angry.

Another crest, and she held the stallion there on the skyline with his sweated flanks heaving. There was only the single Apache and his staggering horse; the others had dropped from her trail or been left beyond her seeing. Marilee walked Bradburn down the slope and found the tangle of brush around a nest of rocks. Pulling him behind them, she dismounted and crawled into the bushes to kneel with her carbine. Waiting, she could smell leaves bent by her passing, leaves whose aroma reminded her of kitchen spices at home.

She heard the broken beat of a weary horse and sighted along the Spencer's barrel, its butt tucked firmly into her shoulder. The mustang wobbled downhill, and she saw the Indian, saw his dripping knife blade. Rifle in the same hand as his twisted rope reins, he was leaning over, peering at the ground.

He sat up just as she began to squeeze the trigger, and his snake eyes widened when he realized his quarry had circled the rocks, as a rabbit will when it seeks refuge from the hounds, when it has run until it can run no more.

Marilee fired. The heavy bullet speared the Apache through his brown chest and jerked him from his horse. Head drooping, the mustang stood blowing upon spread legs when she came out of the brush and stood over the man to shoot him again. She felt no more pity than when she'd killed a poisonous water moccasin in Mississippi, and less of a chill up her back.

She beat his rifle against a rock and threw it away. She wiped his knife through his stiff, greasy hair and thrust it into her own belt, the hair-tufted hilt still damp with the sweat of his hand. The bloody horse didn't lift its head, but rolled bulged-out eyes at her when she slipped the bridle and threw it away, too.

"Go on," Marilee said to the mustang, "go on," and when it didn't move, she left it there and went around to get Bradburn. They walked for quite a while, resting him, because she knew that savage had been the last of those chasing her. She wished all of them were dead.

Now, wishing wouldn't help her get across that plain. She squinted at the sun and inched along to follow the rock's shade. Night would be better, if she could wait. There was always a chance they'd be seen here against the hillside, but not as much as if they were moving. Could she fix her direction in the dark? She would have to, or wind up wandering until her food ran out or until her luck dribbled away and she met up with a roving band of Comanche raiders, whichever came first.

Sparing a little water, she poured it over a double handful of beans in the hollow of a rock where the sun couldn't reach. That would be supper for her and Bradburn, salted to replace their sweat, but not so much it would make them more thirsty. More water might be a long way off.

Tired to the bone, Marilee napped, coming awake with a start to look first at the horse, then out at the plain. She did that through the afternoon and into twilight, at last getting stiffly up to share supper with the stallion. Night sky was clear out here, stars countless and hanging close as tiny oil lamps; night air was cool upon her, almost chill with the sun gone.

"That way," she murmured. "And let's hope you can find us some water tomorrow. What we have won't last long."

Slowly, they traveled, the horse feeling his way, far blinder than she in the dark, but using his sharper ears and nostrils to move confidently in his trust of her. Marilee knew nothing of astronomy—only that the North Star hung off the end of the Little Dipper: her father had shown her that, pointed it out to her in the soft skies over Bradburn Plantation.

"Daddy," she whispered, "oh, Daddy—you couldn't know it might help me save my life, and I wish—how I wish—I could have shown you something to save yours."

She cried awhile then, softly and without sound, weeping for all of them gone, for her family and a man named Robbie Dee Crownover whose face she couldn't remember. She cried for Goodnight and Pecos and Gilmore Frazier, whose faces she could never forget. And perhaps some of Marilee's tears were for herself, the happy girl she had once been and the hard woman she had been forced to become.

But a breeze touched her cheek and she begrudged the water lost to tears, however small the amount, so she stopped crying and tried to keep the big horse on course, aiming northwest, always northwest. When false dawn gray-fingered a cloudless sky, she got down so Bradburn could drink from her cupped hand, and almost wept again because the water wasn't enough for him.

He could lick dew from leaves, another touch of moisture from chewing young brush, so she let him pick awhile for something to eat. Cover wasn't enough for them here, too thin and scattered, but there was another, thicker patch of almost-green farther on, so she mounted the stallion again. Another mile or two, and they could rest there, eat a little bit and stay hidden. Maybe the next morning would see them off the great plain.

The patch of brush was farther than it seemed, and new sunlight was bright upon them when Marilee sat taller in the saddle and peered right, toward a low rim of hills whose base was rimmed in hazy blue. Something was moving there. She narrowed her eyes trying to make it out more clearly—a deer, antelope?

No—horse and rider!

Putting Bradburn into an easy lope, she headed for cover, glancing often at the figure angling just so across the flat, moving to intercept her. It might be a white man, even a lone soldier out on a scout, but she was taking no chances; she stretched out the horse a little more.

There! Up ahead and on her left was another one, and when she swung her head, Marilee saw two more. Skin going tight, she pivoted on the galloping horse to stare behind her. Oh, Lord—several others!

Not soldiers; they wouldn't be circling like this to cut her off, and she could catch no gleam of equipment, no flashes of blue uniform. These were Indians, and coming fast, riding hard.

Crouching over Bradburn's flowing shoulders, she pushed him on, praying he wouldn't stumble over a rock, that he wouldn't step into a hole. He reached hard, throwing himself powerfully on. A jumble of cactus flashed by, and a sage hen flew startled as they hammered past her nest. She kept looking right and left, seeing them more clearly now, men hunkered low upon their charging horses, blending with them as only fine riders could.

And up ahead—Marilee felt the pulse in her throat as her wind-blurred eyes made out two more horsemen trying to close the circle tight, wheeling in like pincers. She couldn't turn, would not turn, and there was a chance of beating them.

"Go, go, *go!*" she cried along Bradburn's stretched neck, and tried to make herself smaller against the wind, lighter upon the saddle.

Earth and bush were quick smears, and she felt the stallion respond, felt the lengthened thrusting of him as he flung his great heart ahead and raced to catch it. Making it—they were making it—surprised dark face whipping past on her left, a frustrated shriek left behind—snapping of sagebrush, a stone ricocheting from Bradburn's hoof. . . .

Then the other rider loomed ahead, too close, too close! In reflex, she tried to swerve the stallion, but his shoulder crashed into the smaller horse and hurled it aside, spun the lean rider high with his arms and legs flailing.

Bradburn staggered, tripped and caught himself. She was jolted off balance, almost going over his head, but she hung on desperately, and he picked up his stride. There was the tall clump of graygreen, no hiding place now, and they thundered through it as she heard yipping behind them. Branches caught at them, and Bradburn stumbled again, righted himself again. They were through the twisted trees then, through the treacherous bushes and needled cactus.

The ground rose, lifting beneath them, and she risked a glance over her shoulder. They were coming fast, not closing on Bradburn, but holding their own. When the stallion seemed to falter once more, Marilee knew she had to pull him up, knew he'd been bruised when they slammed aside the horse and rider.

Slowing him with a touch of the bit, she drew the Spencer from its scabbard as Bradburn rocked along in an easier lope. A yelling Indian pulled alongside on her left, grinning mouth stretched wide and shaking a rifle at her. She snapped a quick shot at him and blinked when the man disappeared, only to bay at her from beneath the neck of his running horse.

Marilee twisted in the saddle and ducked away from a fluttering lance that had already passed over her head. That rider flashed aside, swinging over his horse's withers, clinging by one hooked leg, laughing back at her over one

235

shoulder. She fired high at that one, because she couldn't bear to hit the horse.

They were playing with her, taunting her. That lance could have easily been driven through her back, and they might have shot Bradburn from under her by now. But she was the frantic, running mouse and they were cruelly playful cats. Would they shoot her lamed horse when they tired of their savage sport, drive a spearhead through Bradburn's body?

Sickened at the thought, chilled by it, with reins in her teeth she turned and jacked round after round into the carbine, firing blindly, furiously until the Spencer clicked empty. Marilee held to it, and when a heap of red and yellow rocks climbed out of the ground ahead, she brought her laboring horse to a stop.

She left him with reins trailing, hoping they wouldn't kill him, that they'd capture him for the prize he was. Among the rocks, she dropped the carbine and brought out her pistol, watching them circle like so many diving, wheeling hawks. Bradburn backed to the rocks, facing them with his head high and ears laid back, daring the horses to come in at him.

Oh, God, she thought, please don't let him fight so hard they'll shoot him down. Please make them understand what a great and beautiful stallion he is.

They pulled around him in a loose circle, the horses blowing and dripping sweat, riders watching Bradburn and calling out to each other in a guttural language. She remembered what the Apache had done to his own mount, and thumbed back the hammer of the Colt. If they tried to torture the stallion, she would shoot him herself. Please don't make me, she prayed.

Ammunition for the carbine was in her saddlebags, and all Marilee had was the six bullets in her pistol. One for Bradburn if they speared him, four for that many red devils, if she had to run up so close she could not miss—and the last for herself.

Don't let 'em take aholt of you, Pecos had said. *What they do ain't purty.*

One Indian was walking his horse closer, and she braced the Colt against a rock to center its muzzle upon his buck-skinned chest. He certainly knew where she was, but didn't seem to care. Marilee waited, not wanting to waste a shot, needing to be certain. The man didn't lift his rifle, but just kept coming slowly, eyes upon Bradburn.

His horse was a rangy bay, not starved down but leaned and hard-muscled by travel; a clump of feathers hung in its mane, and another bunch bobbed color at the base of its tail. Eyes and nostrils distended, the horse snorted and jittered as it neared Bradburn.

The stallion didn't hesitate. Bradburn struck in squealing fury, punching his good shoulder into the other horse, big teeth flashing as he caught the neck and jerked savagely. The Indian flew off, his gun bouncing. Another fierce shake, and Bradburn's teeth slipped free of the bay's neck. Going down in a heap and leaping up, the horse fled, back hoofs throwing sand.

Now they'd kill him, Marilee thought, her finger tightening upon the Colt's trigger. The man on the ground shook his head and wobbled to his feet, just in time to throw himself away from deadly back feet as Bradburn whirled and kicked at him.

"*Aiyee!*" Yells broke from the other Indians, and she saw them laughing, applauding, doubling up in glee as they pointed at the scuttling warrior.

Bradburn backed against the rock again and blew at them, challenging. Marilee's heart lifted at his courage, and she wanted to cheer.

But her breath hissed out when the weight struck her violently from behind, ramming her chest into stone. Sparks bursting behind her eyes, she tried to bring the pistol around, but a blow numbed her entire arm and the side of her head rang against a rock slab. She went down, rolling on her back and trying to kick up at him, fumbling for the knife in her belt.

Hooked fingers clawed down at her, ripping her shirt, a stamping moccasin barely missed her head, and Marilee cried out in terror, in shock and pain. Knife slapped out of her hand, she was yanked to her feet, the fingers clamped around her wrist brutally strong.

Eyes clearing as she sucked for air, she stared into his face. Unwinking black eyes stared back, polished stone eyes set behind high cheekbones, a fiercely beaked nose, slashed mouth of hard lips, long hair flowing behind wide shoulders, a bronzed and corded throat.

His eyes flickered as he looked at her pale breasts

237

peeping from the torn shirt, and the knifeblade mouth twitched. He said something, short gritty words from deep in his throat that she couldn't understand.

Bracing her feet, Marilee tried to pull free of his grip, but it was like tugging at a mountain. The man towered over her, lips curling. She said, "I—I don't know what you're saying. You—my horse—let me—"

Again the breath wheezed out of her as her belly came down across his shoulder, as he swept her high and dropped her easily as he might have tossed a leaf. Head flopping, she felt him stoop, then flow erect again, and she squirmed when he trotted her from the rockpile, calling out something to the others.

High-pitched shouts answered him, and Marilee's face burned as he dropped her to earth, sent her sprawling awkwardly. Dazed, she heard the yells change, and got to one knee to see Bradburn coming.

She put out a shaking hand. "N-no, Bradburn—*no!* Stay, boy—stay!"

The stallion hesitated, broke his charge, and walked slowly to her, dropping his head to nuzzle her. Warriors murmured, and the big man said something else. She couldn't hold back the tears any longer, and they streamed her cheeks, as she got up weak-kneed to prop against her horse.

Tall and commanding, the one who'd captured her dropped her weapons, but displayed the knife she'd taken from the dead Apache. Twisting his mouth, he said, "Apache," and pointed at Marilee.

Shaking her head, she licked at dry lips and said, "N-no—not me." She pantomimed firing a rifle, and some of the Indians laughed. The big one only stared, and she pulled her shirt together with one hand.

They were so different from the Apache, taller men more finely made; some of them held buffalo-hide shields, feathered and brightly painted; all of them wore clothing of fringed animal skins; a few had feathers thrust into their long hair.

"No you," the big one said in harsh English. "You no Apache—you *tahbay-boh*, white one. *Tejana*, you? *Tessan?*"

"T-texan? No, I was just—I'm goin' to—"

Comanche! They were Comanche, the fiercest, deadliest Indians of the West, such unrelenting warriors that even the brutal Apache trembled at their name.

And she'd let them take her alive, let them discover she was a young white woman.

Chapter 25

Three weeks out of what had been Del Rio, Joe Langston felt better; not a whole lot safer, just better, because with any luck the Apaches had missed them so far.

He was ranging ahead of a ragtag train made up of lost pilgrims from other places and Del Rio citizens finally spooked out of their forted-up town. Some citizens, he amended; a good bunch of them had cut out the other way with Sheriff Fehrenbach riding herd, driving them back toward the German folks' settlements.

Mare hidden in mesquite, Joe lay on his belly and peered over a fold in the ground to rake slow and careful eyes all around. Could be the smart ones had gone east with old T. R., like Ampora. When that band of Mescaleros lit out of Mexico, she'd lost everything, including her spirit.

Sadly, she'd said, "No more. The *gringo* army will not guard us, and we are too few to protect ourselves. So I will go. Come with me, *mi amor*—come to an older town where I can begin a new cantina—somehow."

He'd been east, and he'd ridden south; he'd never gone to California. And although Ampora hollered some about his wanting to go, and tried to make him change his mind, she understood. But she said, "I cannot take *all* your money, *querido*—all those months hunting them in the hills, the danger—"

Seed money, he told her—so she could grow another cantina in San Antone or somewhere. Besides, he was ahead, and she wasn't getting all his gambling stake, all his bounty money. So Ampora laughed through her tears and kissed him hard before she joined the bunch heading away from a frontier set on fire.

Joe grinned ruefully as he scanned the ground ahead, looking closely at every patch of brush, at each rock that might be big enough to hide a patient Apache. Sure, he was ahead; he had given Ampora nigh onto eight hundred dollars, which left him a dollar and a half and a long-barreled Sharps rifle bought off a buffalo hunter. For a man who'd set out to make his fortune, he still had a far piece to go.

Scraping bottom, the train folks had promised him a hundred dollars if they got to California. That broke down to maybe twenty a month, the price of one Apache scalp, and no guarantee of collecting. All Joe had to do to earn that big pot of gold was fend Indians off the wagons, find water and bring in meat, while keeping his own hide whole.

It seemed clear ahead, and there was a hint of green to the northwest that might mean water and a campsite for the night. Coming slowly to his feet, but with the Sharps ready, he backed down to get his barb mare. That buffalo rifle was purely something, and had earned him plenty of bounty while the town of Del Rio was still able to pay. The lever-action Spencer was fine for up-close work where a man had to put out a lot of lead in a hurry, but it wasn't all that accurate over a hundred yards. But the Sharps, with its heavy .52 caliber ball, could reach out a thousand yards or more and turn an Apache ass over headband. It surprised warriors who thought they were sitting safe and easy out of range, and woke them up in hell.

In his saddle, Joe moved out across the land he'd scouted, pausing once to squint and be sure it was a small herd of buffalo raising dust yonder to the left. Riding with the train wasn't all bad; there was Elizabeth, so anxious to teach him things, hauling out her books and making him read aloud by the fire at night. It came nat-

ural to Miss Elizabeth Hartley, her being a schoolteacher
to start with, but Joe had the feeling she was wanting to
learn something herself, or maybe continue her education
along more practical lines.

Long rifle balanced across his saddle, carbine in its
boot under his right leg, Joe kept the mare going while
he watched the far-off buffalo. Apaches might be tagging
after that meat—or worse, Comanches. Hunting each
other like they had for the past few months, Joe and the
Apaches got to know each other pretty well, but Comanches were something else. He'd just gotten one look at
them, while he'd been lying in ambush for a band of Mescaleros, only the Comanches got to them first.

Ruined hell out of Joe's ambush and there'd been no
scalps left for him when the tall horsemen were gone, almost quick as they'd struck. In fact, they hadn't left much
of anything, except for gutted bodies; they'd driven off the
Apache horses and killed their women, too. It seemed to
Joe those tribes didn't care a whole lot for each other,
and he remembered thinking that if General Lee had had
cavalry like the Comanches, Grant would have chewed
through more than a few boxes of cigars.

Here he was now, with a wagon train depending on
him and two more outriders to get folks through Comancheria. This was still supposed to be Apache country, but
Joe figured the Comanches rode just about where they
wanted to, any time they wanted. He hoped they'd keep
feuding with the Mescaleros and San Carlos and Chiricahua, instead of coming down on the wagons.

Course, this train was a mite different than most, because plenty of Spencer carbines and Henry rifles rode
with it, and two more buffalo guns, all toted by muley-
headed *tejanos* or Mexicans from this side of the river who
were tired of being pushed, shot at, and run over. That
bunch could stand off just about anything but a full-scale
attack by a good-sized tribe. They could shore up weak-
nesses of the folks who were just coming out from back
east.

Elizabeth Hartley didn't know doodly squat about Indians or the land, like most of the new people; books
hadn't taught her those things. But the kind of uncertain,
kind of slidy look in her blue eyes whispered she was interested in learning more than feathers and cactus. Oh, she

242

was all prim and proper and dressed like she was supposed to, like her body was something to hide, but Joe could tell it was waiting to be stroked and handled. And she was traveling alone, with only an old Mexican to drive her mules.

Marking which way the buffalo rambled, Joe angled his mare toward the place he'd spotted a while back. It still looked good and green, but not the color of young willows dipping over a still pond.

Where was Miss Marilee Bradburn now—turned tail for Mississippi, where she could use her wiles on some high-ranking Yankee officer, some rich tax collector down from the North with a satchel full of claims on plantation lands? She ought to be able to wiggle and shake her way right back into being gentry, to use that unforgettable hot velvet of her slim body in trade for just about anything she wanted.

Maybe she was dead. Joe knew a quick chill at the thought, and shook it off. She didn't *have* to keep to herself; she could have followed along to Mexico and made out real well in the French court. Acting like she hadn't given away her body before him, but carrying on like the hottest wench when he put it to her; Marilee didn't *have* to sulk about it and go off on her own. If being all that stubborn got her carried off by some prowling scalawag or snatched up by bluebellies, it wasn't Joe Langston's fault.

She probably wasn't dead; only an Apache would waste that kind of diddling, once he got to know it. *Lady* Bradburn was no doubt safe away somewhere, starting her climb back to riches, and only a damned fool would keep on remembering the color of her eyes and the touch of her skin, the blazing heat and flower smell of her.

Dismounting at the little spring, Joe checked the ground for hoof marks and found none. Buffalo and deer had watered here, and one big old bear that had lost a front toe, but no Indians, at least not for a spell. Looking out at the land, he liked this place for a camp. There was dry wood and some grass for the stock; wagons could circle here with a pile of high rock in the middle just to suit a long-range sniper, and a man up there could see for miles around. He'd wait here for the train. Charley Longstreet would cut his trail and bring on the wagons as usual; Joe would tell Rosario Lopez about the buffalo, and there'd be fresh meat tomorrow.

Watering his horse, then hobbling her so she'd get first crack at the grass, he unloaded saddle, bridle, and the Spencer before taking a cool drink for himself. Could be that Marilee hooked up with some wagons coming west a long time back; she might be clear to California by now. For a painful second, he saw silvery blond hair hanging from a warrior's lance and spat. Not much chance of that; ladies like her always landed on their dainty little feet. Only white trash got skin cut away by a blacksnake whip. Ladies watched.

He watched the wagons come in hours later, creaking slow over patchy sand while he sat blended with mottled stone atop the rockpile. While he and Apaches hunted each other, Joe had learned from them how to be rock or earth or bush; some of it he'd known through riding with Quantrill, by war in Confederate gray and Maximilian blue, but most of it came from stalking and being stalked by desert fighters cunning and merciless as the land itself.

Being alive was proof of his skill, better than the hated legend he'd created among the Apaches. Sheriff Fehrenbach's idea about spooking them had been good, a maneuver that kept vengeful braves hunting the white-eye who ranged over their home grounds like a mountain lion, instead of harrying the settlement at Del Rio. They stayed after him, and wanted his hair so bad they lost their own forgetting that hunted animals—at least those with teeth—circled back after the hunters.

Charley Longstreet came in ahead of the wagons, slouched as a Mescalero atop his wiry mustang, looking as if he was asleep. Joe knew the old scout was watching every blade of grass, and had seen Joe's mare early on. Joe lifted slowly from his nest in the rocks.

"Good campsite, Charley."

"Yeah. Any sign?"

"Just four-legged."

"Good enough, then." Charley climbed up to take Joe's place while the light lasted.

Making up a cookfire for Elizabeth and her driver, Mendez, Joe watched the teacher move and wondered how she could keep looking starchy on the trail, neat as if she was in a schoolroom. She could cook some, too, changing the everyday taste of buffalo or deer meat with pinches of sage and other herbs.

Old Mendez always nodded off right after supper, so Joe didn't mind her pecking at him like he was sitting in her class, giving him new words every night, and going over ones from the night before. Elizabeth was always telling him what a good student he was and how quick he learned; he didn't mind that, either.

She was from Chicago, and come west because—and here Elizabeth had looked away and firmed her chin—because she wasn't getting any younger and the spirit of adventure wasn't dead in her yet, and—and. . . .

"You might find you a man to appreciate you out here," Joe said. "Ought to, I 'spect—*ex*-pect. Must be a heap of blind men in Chicago."

Dimpling at that and going pink, Elizabeth had found something else to talk about, but from then on she'd had that slidy gleam in her eye.

This night, after a meal of buffalo hump and pan bread, and after she'd poked old Mendez so that he snorted and crawled off to his blankets, she unpinned her hair. It was nice hair, holding the firelight in brown waves and silky-looking, clean as the rest of her.

Closing the spelling book, Joe sat still and watched her move in crisp, unwasted motions around the fire as she scrubbed things and put them back in their proper places. Proper was a word that fit Elizabeth Hartley, he thought, a proper, educated woman who said the spirit of adventure wasn't dead in her. Pulling up roots and putting a musty school behind her was the biggest thing she'd ever done in her whole life.

"How old are you?" he asked.

Her quick hands stopped moving around and she squared her shoulders in the plain gray dress before turning around to him. "I'm thirty-two—a spinster." Her eyes were wary, defensive.

"Spinster? That mean an old maid? Well, you ain't old, but you might be a maid, if'n—*if*—that means you're still a virgin."

Elizabeth put down a tin plate and lifted her hands to her face. They trembled there for a moment before she snatched them down and looked straight at him. "Not—

not because I want to be. And thirty-two *is* old, Joe. You're many years younger than—"

He rose from beside the fire and stretched. "Man I knowed, man I *knew*—he told me it don't matter when a horse was foaled, but how hard he's been rode and how many miles he's covered. I've been a long way under heavy loads and had the spurs put to me more'n once. So I reckon I'm a lot older than you, Elizabeth."

She was standing motionless except for the quickened rise and fall of breasts flattened too much by a severe dress front.

Taking up his guns, Joe walked past her to the wagon and put them over the tailgate. Then he put his bedroll inside, too. "Fire's goin' out," he said.

She pushed sand onto ashing-over embers with her toe and put up the tin plate before she came to the wagon. But she came inside quickly, dropping the canvas tie-down behind her and cutting off what little light the stars gave.

In blackness, he lay listening to the rustle of her clothes and the ragged catch of her breath, to bare legs whispering shyly against each other as she kneeled beside the bedding. Joe smelled her hair then, and the freshness of her skin. He reached up and pulled her down to him, easy as he knew how.

Littlegirl soft, she murmured, "I am a maiden, Joe. Be gentle with me, please—teach me."

When he found her mouth, it was damp and trembling, a child's mouth hungry for forbidden sweets, trusting. Naked, her flesh also shuddered against him, and Joe felt the small, coned firmness of her breasts, the smooth length of her flanks, everything tidy as could be.

"Don't be scared," he said into the satin netting of her hair, into the sweet hollow of her shoulders, "don't be scared of anything, especially yourself."

It was teaching the teacher; it was Susanna turned around, only not with her desperate greed; it was almost like being with Marilee, as it could have been, should have been—and what the hell was he doing, thinking of another woman when he had this fineboned one in his arms, against his flesh?

"Here," he said, putting himself into her thin hand. "It's not meant to hurt you with."

"I—I've seen drawings—medical books—I—"

"Hush, now," he said, stroking her, "hush, now."

There was tenseness in her, a tightening-up of muscle and skin even when she didn't mean it, like a young filly new to the halter and spooked of the bit. So he gentled her the same way, talking just so she could feel the sound of his voice, caressing so she might learn the touch of his hands. It was better for her in the dark, so she didn't feel shame herself nor shyness at the look of him. Joe talked easy and stroked easy, until she went soft and the shaking left her.

Trim woman, neat woman, locked into herself all her life and sorry for it now, but with the key still unturned, and it was good for him to use it. Opening her softness, he went slowly into her, reaching blindly to the barred door. Then he had to force it some, to press hard against that ungiving panel as she tried to close herself again.

Not allowing that, Joe held her in place and used the kinder quick pain, the sudden thrusting that freed her and trapped him. Gasping, twisting upon him, Elizabeth struggled to get away, but only for a moment. Then she held him, lifted him and fell back, raised him and dropped back, as shivers wracked her body, quiverings that were strange to her.

"Oh!" she said. "Oh, oh! This is what it is—*this!* Oh —Joe, Joe—I love you, love you!" And when he didn't answer, Elizabeth clutched at his shoulders while her body kept moving, moving, and begged him to say he loved her, too.

"You're beautiful," he said, "and young and a whole lot of woman."

And he wondered why he just didn't say the rest of it.

Chapter 26

They didn't tie her, knowing that ropes on Bradburn were enough to hold her as well, knowing she wouldn't be afoot in that unforgiving land. Unhurried, they rode through the foothills, Comanches boxing her in, the tall leader beside her, flicking her now and then with those impenetrable black eyes. Marilee appreciated their concern for her horse and the bruise that slowed him, but she couldn't stop terror that used coldsharp teeth on her, a fear for them both. Feeling strangely naked without her guns, she sat erect and tried not to show the emotion that pulsed through her, now searing, now numbing.

The Comanches chattered among themselves, relaxed and joking, but she'd noticed the chief sent a rider far ahead and had another drop behind them. After giving his orders, he said nothing else, and somehow that silence frightened her more—that, and the way he kept glancing at her ripped shirtfront, at her hair. Her hands tightened upon the reins as she wondered what he was planning, what monstrous, degrading kind of tortures awaited her when the band reached wherever they were going.

Mounting pressure made her think it would have been

better if she'd been killed back there in the rocks, so it might happen quickly and without pain. Maybe she would be praying for death soon; she lightly touched her right breeches pocket, where the small penknife still nestled.

Through all the long, steady hours they rode without stopping; as talk fell off and horses plodded through heat waves thick as water, she struggled against panic, against vivid nightmare pictures that rose too often inside her head. The Comanches were exceptional horsemen, the finest she'd seen; they hadn't hurt Bradburn and seemed to respect him for his courage, his strength and speed.

No matter what happened to her, they'd care for him, keep him alive, for any horseman with an eye in his head could see how he'd improve almost any mare he was crossed on. Marilee felt better, knowing one of them was safe. He'd journeyed even farther than she had, all the way down from New England, the cold north country where he had been foaled, to end here with Indians. The stallion had survived war and those long, dangerous miles; he'd outrun shot and shell and arrows, taken by fate and Marilee Bradburn to this moment, this place in a vast nowhere. He deserved a herd of mares for his own, and she wished him a long life; she wished him well. Oh, Lord, how she hoped for a special blessing upon him.

Up ahead, a man called back, and the Comanches turned noisy again, faces brightening as they yelled at each other and shook lances, rifles, shields. Marilee's belly went tense in sick anticipation; they were coming into the Indian camp, and fear crawled feathering up into her throat to choke her.

When they crossed the brow of a hill and the straggling column dipped into a green valley below, the Comanches raced their horses, shouting and waving their weapons— except for their chief and the men who held to the ropes on Bradburn. Marilee saw a group of conical tents, smoke rising from cookfires, a rope pen for more horses. She saw peeled-stick racks where hides were stretched, brown strips of meat drying upon flat rocks, water jars, and an old man squatted to chip at stone that sparkled like black glass.

Then she saw the women, the roundfaced children,

249

skinny dogs. Some of the women were gray and stooped, some straight and willowy as reeds, a few squat and wide; they moved toward her as the chief stopped her beside him. Their eyes were frightening, flat and hard, dark and eager.

Chopping his words, the chief said something to them, and they stopped to ring Marilee and her horse in a sullen, menacing circle. Boys drifted up then, the youngsters eyeing Bradburn more than her, sucking air between their teeth in sounds of admiration. One of them lifted a fist in salute. *"Piava, Piava!"*

A quick smile changed her captor's stern face for an instant as he dropped lithely off his horse and gave the boy his reins. Then the man barked an order, and Marilee found herself being dragged violently from the saddle by two women. She started to fight against their clawing hands, but thought better of it and was yanked along by them. She had a moment to look back at Bradburn and see him being led to one side.

Then her clothes were being snatched off. She was rolled upon the ground, her boots torn away, her breeches jerked down limp legs. Eyes shut, she felt vicious fingers pinching her flesh, sharp nails digging her skin, and she wanted to scream. But something warned her not to cry out, not to give these clawing bitches that satisfaction, and she was hauled roughly to her feet again, flung stumbling forward to fall on hands and knees at the bank of a little stream.

One of the women pulled at her hair, the other kicked her buttocks, and Marilee rolled into the water. They were after her immediately, shoving her head under until she choked and kicked, dragging her up to scrub painfully at her flesh with leaves that felt slick, with handfuls of sand that burned and cut.

Through a roaring in her ears, she heard men laughing and other women yipping like dogs, anxious to be in at the death of a hare. Her torturers pushed her down and snatched her erect, bruising her breasts and mocking her pale body, even tearing at the hair between her thighs.

Dimly, her blurred eyes made out the figure of the chief as he stood gesturing upon the bank, and the cruel hands fell away from her.

"*Hu, Piava,*" one of the women grunted, and she was pushed toward him to stand dripping and trembling, to sway naked and exposed to all the staring eyes, especially his.

Marilee half lifted her hands when women came at her again, but this time they only forced a soft skin dress over her head, crammed it over her arms, and someone could not resist a final twisting of skin at the back of her neck.

This chief, this man called Piava, made an imperious jerk of his hand and stalked toward one of the tall buffalo-hide tents. A foot in the small of her back shoved Marilee after him, and squaws tittered behind her. But she only followed him so far, until she saw Bradburn tethered to a little tree, his saddle and bridle gone. Turning aside then, she went to the horse, pushing her way through a crowd of young Comanches. They buzzed at her, rattled guttural words at her, but let her reach the horse.

Rubbing the bruised shoulder, Marilee talked softly to him, crooned lies that everything would be all right, and felt tension leave the big stallion. A boy prodded her elbow and held out a split gourd heavy with some oily, pungent mixture. She dipped fingers into the sticky stuff, then worked it into Bradburn's flesh, massaging in smooth, deep circles.

A squaw came plunging toward her, a woman with creases folded into her face and eyes like a snapping turtle, hissing angrily. Marilee braced at her horse's shoulder and drew back a fist, but she didn't have to fight. Piava barked words that struck the woman like flung stones, and she stopped still. Water dripping down her back from hair plastered against her head, Marilee went back to caring for Bradburn, kneading the muscled flesh, gentle but firm at the point of his shoulder. The Indians only watched, muttering among themselves.

And when she couldn't put it off any longer, she wiped her hands upon the horse's mane and pushed through the crowd, trying to hold her head high and eyes steady, trying to control the tremor of her fingers.

Piava motioned her to a tent of stretched hides, its walls splashed with bright symbols. He lifted a flap back; the jerk of his head told her to duck inside. There was an odor of smoke, of grease and hides, and sunlight sifting through an opening up high showed her a heap of furry buffalo skins, a ring of fire-blackened stones, a few clay jars piled to one side.

When he came to stand before her, she couldn't control her shaking. There was something hawklike and fierce about him, a sense of tremendous strength and a savage pride flaring in his opaque eyes.

Lifting one strong hand, he touched his chest. "Piava."

She copied the movement and said, "Marilee." Her knees were a little weak, and she couldn't lie to herself about what was coming. But this chief of the Comanches hadn't hurt her yet, and she could go on hoping he wouldn't; it was something to cling to while vivid images of torture and unspeakable horrors raced sharply through her mind. Maybe he would just take her; maybe he wouldn't use his knife on her or make her scream insanely with a firebrand—maybe.

It took all her inner strength not to flinch when he touched her cheek with his fingertips, then roamed his hand gently over her hair. *"Plata.* Ma-ri-lee, you *habla español?"*

"N-no." His hand stroked her hair, and up this close she could scent him, mansweat and animal hide and smoke odors.

"No hablo tejano, me." There was a curious quality to his deep voice, a timbre at once resonant and gritty. "You one good—*caballera."*

Marilee could not stare up into his eyes. They were too direct and piercing, telling her something she already knew, that this savage wanted her and would take her very soon. He surprised her by whirling away, then striding across the tent to a piling of furs. She stood very still, hands at her sides, breathing fast as he eeled from his buckskin shirt, stripped away moccasins and breeches. There was something misshapen and alien about his. . . . Marilee swallowed hard as Piava removed a little pouch that had been hanging between his thighs, a soft leather pouch attached by a thin strip of sinew. He placed it carefully at his head when he lay back upon the buffalo robes and crooked one imperative finger at her.

Step by slow step, she approached the naked Comanche, her mind racing wildly, afraid but wondering if she could somehow turn his lust for her to advantage. If she pleased him greatly, if she tried very hard to make him care for her even more, it was possible he wouldn't use her brutally, then turn her over to the entire band of warriors. Could she pretend, might she delude him, or was he different from other men who had known and reveled in the reluctant pleasures of her body?

Before Piava commanded her, Marilee reached down to catch the hem of the dress and draw it over her head. Skin prickling, feeling as if she were looking down upon her shameless body from some faraway vantage point, she watched her naked self stand straight and tall, so the reclining savage could feast his black, hot eyes upon her exposed flesh.

Stiffly, forcing herself to her knees, she made herself lie down beside him, turn to fit her body to the length of his darkly bronzed one. He was scarred and muscled and hairless upon the chest, and the shaft of his manhood was hard; it was large and throbbing, held against her. Piava's hands ranged her body, cupping her haunches, stroking her flanks and back as he might calm a skittish mare.

She expected him to kiss her, but he kept touching her hair as if its color awed him, murmuring some gentle word in his own language. But Piava's unexpected tenderness was soon past, and he suddenly rolled over on top of her, one knee spreading her limp, unresisting thighs.

As Joe Langston had spread them, a thousand years ago.

He set himself firmly against her softness, and thrust strongly, entering her body with a shock that traveled throughout her being, burying himself deep and thick. Eyes shut, teeth locked into her lower lip, Marilee endured the powerful stroking, the heavy rhythm that moved her body up and down against the soft fur robes.

Piava was heavy, but his weight didn't crush her. He was strong, but his hands didn't bruise her. He didn't speak, didn't call her names or gasp words of endearment, but his body communicated with hers, lancing to impossible depths, withdrawing only to plunge again and again. Panting, holding to her hips, Piava rutted upon her, his belly oiled, his chest smooth, and his thighs hard, surging, lifting and falling.

Breath gushed out of him as his fingers clamped into her opened thighs, and Piava sagged upon her body, his long, black hair spreading itself across his own shoulders and hers, his cheekbone pressed into her throat. Marilee stared up at the crosspatch of narrowed, peeled poles that formed the tent's top, at the woven design they made against the opening around them. The sky was coppery blue beyond, and she could see the skirt of a cottonboll cloud.

Once she had been a virgin, saving herself for the man she meant to marry, would have wed, if there had been no war between the states. Gentleman, gentle lover bound by his upbringing and tradition, Robbie Dee Crownover had never lain upon her like this, had gone to his unmarked grave without claiming what was rightfully his, preserved by mutual promises and sacred vows.

Now she was no better than rouged and perfumed women who flaunted their wares on the dusty street of Beaumont, no more than the yellow wenches whose beckoning eyes and sensuous hips promised easy seduction. Three times raped, Marilee Bradburn had also given herself freely, without benefit of bell and book, she had accepted men without even struggling. Was life so sweet that she could betray the Bradburn honor with any man who might hold some kind of dominance over her?

She could, and she had.

The Comanche chief lifted his weight from her, and she sighed in relief, but he kept her impaled. Piava rolled to one side and lifted one of her slim legs over him. Softened a little, but still unreadable dark marble, his eyes stared into hers, and his pelvis began to move again— the slower, more lingering reach of him started all over again. Now her breasts were against his chest, now an arm was across his shoulders.

"No," he said quietly, "no Ma-ri-lee. You Nadevah— Nadevah—"

He was still powerful, his strength and his lust undiminished. But Piava wasn't hurried now, and Marilee was conscious of a small heat growing deep within her body as the long, steady rhythm continued, as it seemed to match the beating of her own heart. Caressing fur beneath her did strange, tingling things to her bare skin, and

254

she breathed faster; her arm tightened across the man's shoulder and her hand learned the feel of his back, discovered the sleek muscling there, the fine sheen of his sweat. Of their own will, her fingers traced sinewy outlines, and Marilee could not tear her eyes away from the hypnotic power of Piava's gaze as her hips began a spasmed, ticktock movement.

This wasn't her; the only daughter of Colonel Wayne Bradburn couldn't lower herself this way; the young mistress of Bradburn Plantation would never twist and shudder uncontrollably while a man held her close—a strange man, a primitive man whose skin was almost dark as a slave's.

Something had gone wrong inside her, that murky wellspring of forbidden passion had been tapped once more, that seething core whose geysering had always been so carefully capped, until released by Joe Langston.

Then she had thought it was only a weird accident, and she'd felt safer because it had not happened with Timmy Santee, not ever with Gilmore Frazier and his shammed brand of tenderness. But now, now—Marilee gritted her teeth and valiantly tried to keep her body still, but her flesh was rioting, and nerve ends were quivering, going raw.

No, no, no—but her body would not obey, refused to stop its reaching, its lascivious grindings, and, so she would not hate herself so much, she turned it upon this savage instead, raking that broad, hard back with her fingers and taking the flesh of his shoulder between her teeth. She struck back at him with all the concentrated power of her hips, the pistoning of her belly, and tried to throttle him within the gripping of her thighs.

For a blurred passing of gasping and contorted time, Marilee was as fierce as he was, just as strong, attacking him for what he was and what he was causing within her body. Straining with her, to her, inside her, Piava thrust and recoiled, hammered and retreated, but she would not allow him to get away, refused to accept his domination.

She cried out when the couch rocked violently beneath them, when the tepee whirled and somehow the sun came thundering down the lodgepole to explode searingly inside her writhing body and send its whitehot tendrils rocketing to the farthest corners of her stunned mind.

There was stillness then.

Breath stirring against her ear, he murmured, "Na-devah," over and over, and she realized this was his name for her. It was better, for she had been changed so much she could probably never be Marilee Bradburn again.

Chapter 27

Closing the book, Joe propped it on his chest and turned his head upon his saddle. "I can hear him holding prayer meetin' clear over yonder," he said. "If that preacher is what comes from book learnin', I don't know if I want to keep on."

Sitting hugging her knees near the fire, Elizabeth said, "I wouldn't call Reverend Samples educated—his Bible is probably the only book he ever read."

"Reads it like it suits him," Joe said, "and he figures gettin' elected leader makes him special anointed. Only the *tejanos* don't think so, and it's like we're two camps now. Won't be good, if we run into trouble."

Bringing out a comb, Elizabeth ran it through her hair. "It was the democratic way, and there happened to be more Easterners. He's not interfering too much with your scouts, is he?"

Joe grunted. "We don't let him. Left to hisself—himself—he'd get us lost as Israelites, and we don't have forty years to wander around this desert." As she continued to slowly comb her shining hair, Joe glanced at her. "That old peckerwood been at you again?"

257

She kept looking down into the fire. "It isn't only him, Joe. I—well, it's common knowledge that you and I are—that we're—"

"Livin' in sin? Hell, living' any way but how *he* says is a sin. Crossing the noble redman's ground is a sin, and if he could take hold of some Apache, he'd tell that Injun all his whelps are bastards because they wasn't born in holy wedlock with the key turned by a white-eyed preacher. I halfway hope he gets the chance, so I can see how much brimstone he'll holler with his hair lifted."

"He means well," Elizabeth said. "It's a social order, Joe—civilization. The West is wild and careless now, but soon it won't be—more people will come, bringing stricter rules with them."

Sitting up, Joe placed the book on his saddle and picked up the Sharps to run a rag through its barrel. "Rules that work back East get folks killed out here."

"They will work," Elizabeth said, and he thought she sounded sad. "In time, they will. Joe—you don't already have a wife, do you?"

There it was, and although he'd known it was coming, Joe kept hoping it wouldn't. "No," he said, wondering at the change in himself. Two years ago, he'd have lied to her because it was the easy way out.

"Am I too old for you?"

He concentrated upon cleaning the rifle. "No, Elizabeth—I told you that."

"You told me I'm beautiful, and I'm not."

"You are to me."

Abruptly, she stood up, jerking the comb at her hair. "Then *why?* Together, we can do so much in California, build a good life for ourselves, maybe—maybe have children."

Joe didn't say anything.

Elizabeth took a step toward him and stopped. "It's the idea that you're low born, not good enough to be more than a gambler, a soldier of fortune, a—a gunman? You are, Joe—oh, you *are*. I've heard you speaking fluent Spanish with Mendez and the other Mexicans, and you're certainly not illiterate anymore. Why, I've never seen anyone learn as quickly, and so eagerly, and you just don't forget anything. In a few months, a year at most, you'll be able to move at any level of society and be accepted. Joe, Joe—you can be anything you want to be."

Looking up at her then, he said, "And what do I want to be?"

Her eyes were shining. "A big rancher, a banker, a successful businessman—anything. You're a *leader*, Joe Langston, with something in you that makes other men look up to you."

"Or down on me," he said, "if I didn't pack this Colt."

"Oh!" Elizabeth said. "Can't you think of more than guns and horses?"

"Not out here."

She hesitated, pulling the comb from her hair and holding it tightly in both hands. "Or other women? That Mexican woman in Del Rio—"

"I don't think about Ampora much," he said. "She's a good woman—maybe not like you and the preacher would class her, but a good woman, and she's gone now."

"You're in love with her," Elizabeth accused.

Joe got up and leaned the rifle against a wagon wheel. "Never thought so."

"But you—you slept with her!"

"She wasn't my first woman."

Pressing the back of a thin hand against her mouth, Elizabeth said, "Does that mean I only *think* I love you because—because you're the only man who ever touched me?"

It could be that way, Joe knew; it could be all mixed up with sunshine on creek water and a woman haloed by golden hair, a beautiful lady who knew it all, a boy who didn't. About a thousand years back, he'd been in love with Susanna, and hated her for only a few hundred. Now he couldn't put all the pieces of her face together, and even when he tried hard to recapture the sound of her voice, all he could hear was bells that rang a little tinny.

"Might be, Elizabeth—maybe the first means more to a woman, or it could wear off after a spell, same as with a man."

Twisting the comb in her hands, she said, "Love is more than just *that*—much more than simply joining flesh."

"I reckon. Your books and poems tell it different, but I just never felt pretty about the moon or petted a flower. All I know is that you and me are good together. In Cali-

fornia, we might not be, if I didn't turn out a big cattleman or a good storekeeper."

Hurt slipped into her voice, fuzzing the neat, always-
right words she put together. "Joe, I don't want to—to
beg you."

"Woman like you don't have to beg," he said, and was
glad for the shout of an outrider, the beat of running
hoofs. He reached around for the carbine. "Charley's in
a hurry. Climb in the wagon."

Across the camp, Preacher Samples was amening so
hard nobody over there knew Indians were straggling up,
standing out dark against a sun that would go down before long. The time of day favored the train; Apaches
didn't cotton to fighting at night, if they could get out of
it. They might send in old men and squaws with their
hands out, to smell around a white-eyes camp and tell its
strength.

Samples and the eastern bunch caught on when Joe and
Rosario Lopez loped through them with guns, when *tejanos*
started to fort up. Humped over and skinny, flapping like a
turkey buzzard in a black coat too short for his skinny
arms, the preacher hollered not to shoot, to let their red
brothers come on in.

Down on one knee, Henry barrel resting across a wheel
rim, Rosario watched the slow, dragging Apaches and said,
"Muy loco, no? Those red brothers have been killing their
brown brothers ever since this one can remember, since
my grandfather can remember."

"They are not coming to raid," Joe said. "Not today,
that is. *Mañana—quién sabe?"*

Rosario kept his sights on them. "Perhaps *el padre loco*
will show them the error of their ways."

"Or beat them to death with words?"

Rosario laughed grimly as Charley Longstreet came
trotting up to join them. The Apaches came on, three men
on potbellied horses, as many women plodding behind.
They drew up to let one man ride ahead.

"Wore-down dog soldier," Charley grunted. "Got him a
U.S. cavalry hat and coat he's goin' to claim was give him
by his good friend, the white chief."

"Got the only rifle, too," Joe said.

Charley wet a grubby forefinger and touched it to the
front sight of his carbine. "Onliest 'un in sight."

Reverend Samples walked to meet the Apaches, tipping his stovepipe hat and grinning widely, Adam's apple bobbing as he talked, as he held out empty hands.

"Damned Injun don't know a word he's sayin'," Charley commented, "but watch him turn big dog, account of our chief went to meet *him*, 'stead of waitin' for t'other way around."

Straightening on his horse, the Apache said something gruff, and bumped the breech of his rifle against his belly. Samples kept grinning and chattering.

"Oh, hell," Charley said, "you or me?"

"I'll make talk for 'em," Joe said, and walked out with his Spencer in the crook of his left arm. The Apache was past his prime, he saw, a wizened brave with ribs showing where the army coat hung open, some dead trooper's blue hat jammed down on greasy hair. His horse was gaunted, too.

"There you are," Samples gobbled. "Tell our brother he's welcome, welcome."

Joe made the hand-talk sign of warning, and said in the border Spanish most Apaches spoke well, "It is wise you left the others back there."

Black lizard eyes flicked at him. "I am Nantan of the Chiricahua. This is our land, and you'll pay tribute to cross it. Meat, salt, tobacco, tequila."

Shifting his eyes to the others, then back to the leader, Joe said, "The Chiricahua have fallen on hard times, if you are chief to such a tribe."

The Apache's face tightened. "Be careful, white-eyes."

Samples jerked at his coat, moved his tall hat around, bobbed his head. "What's he saying? Tell him we're his brothers."

Ignoring the preacher, Joe said, "You call me *pindalik-oyi* in your own tongue, and that is good. I am the white-eye who hunted beside the big river and grew fat on game I found there."

Hissing through thinned lips, the Apache leaned over his horse's shoulder to peer closely. *"Es verdad.* Women without husbands have cursed you as they cut off fingers in mourning—shamed warriors have said your eyes are pale as the underbelly of a rattlesnake."

"The fortunate ones," Joe said, "for I do not warn like *la cascabela.* How many Apaches have looked into the serpent's eyes and lived to tell of it?"

The Apache's chin rested on his chest, the arrogance gone out of him. "I have guided white soldiers—this hat and coat—"

"Taken with the scalp. No lies, Nantan. I see your flat belly and the hunger of your women and will give you food, three blankets, but no tequila and no ammunition for your empty rifles."

Tugging at Joe's sleeve, Samples said, "What are you saying? Why haven't you invited them to join our services? As rightful leader of this wagon train, I demand you tell me—"

"Buffalo are far north," the Apache said, "and the Comanche closer. We go to find other Chiricahua if any are left. The Comanche rode by moonlight and struck hard. A few rounds of ammunition only, hunter of men. I do not demand—I ask."

Over his shoulder, Joe called, "Charley, Rosario! Give 'em meat and meal, a handful of salt. Three old blankets, too. And Charley, since he's totin' a Henry, spare him a handful of brass."

Samples flailed his arms. "You're not following my orders, Langston. These poor people can be shown the light, given our friendship and love, and you—"

"Preacher," Joe said, "it's best you get the hell out of my sight. By yourself, you folks would be just that damned close to havin' red ants stuffed up your nose, especially if there's more of 'em out yonder. *Back off.*"

When Samples went muttering away, the Apache and Joe kept looking at each other. Beyond their leader, the others waited without movement, very still in slowly waning light. Charley Longstreet brought the provisions tied in blankets and handed them up. The Apache took the bundle and held out one dark hand, palm turned.

Charley passed over some shells, and said, "Damned if'n I don't feel like he's markin' our names on 'em."

"Might be a Comanche name or two," Joe said, "and that'd be some help."

"I will not thank you," the Apache said. "It is our land."

"Tell the Comanches," Joe said, and watched the man turn his horse.

Charley Longstreet said, "Reckon that's all of 'em?"

"If it's not, they'll have to come down on us with bows. They been runnin' so long they haven't hunted much."

"Means them damned Comanch' could cut our sign any time."

Joe stared after the departing Apaches, saw them fading as sunset touched its red to the low hills. "They'd give their medicine sacks for a chance at our horses—theirs are done in."

At the wagons, Samples shrilled, "Langston—I want to talk to you!"

Charley said, "I don't see all that good at night. Gittin' older'n I ever figured to be."

"I'll trail 'em," Joe said. "You and Rosario move out the wagons as usual in the mornin', and I'll catch up time you make camp for supper."

Grinning as he walked beside Joe, Charley said, "Could be, the preacher'll make medicine for you."

Joe brushed right on by Samples and went to Elizabeth's wagon, where he put blanket and saddle on his mare. The canteen was full; one saddlebag always held jerky, meal, and beans to carry him a few days, the other ammunition for rifle and carbine. Seeing Elizabeth looking out of the wagon at him, he said, "Mind handin' down my blankets?"

"You don't have to go out there at night," she said.

"Better somebody does, and Rosario covered a heap of ground today. Charley's more than half horse, and don't—doesn't—see good at night."

Elizabeth climbed down, blankets in her arms. "You're angry."

"Only at the preacher. He wanted those Apaches sleepin' in with us, and come morning, when throats were cut and horses gone, he'da said, 'Oh, mercy me.'"

"But you gave the Indians food. You're angry with him because of me, because he insists we be married in the eyes of God."

"I'm mad at him account of he's so damned stupid," Joe said. "And you reckon God don't have more to watch out for than you and me?" He lashed the bedroll behind his saddle.

Elizabeth's mouth was tight. "You don't have to be sacrilegious. If you don't know that word, it means—"

"Look," he said, "I'm a man grown and I can't set easy in a schoolhouse corner."

She softened. "Joe, I didn't mean to play teacher like that. It's just—oh, I don't *know*. I don't know myself anymore—what to think, how to act. I'm only certain of how I feel."

Lifting himself to the mare's back, he said, "That ought to be enough, but if it's not, you can tell me about it at supper tomorrow."

"You'll come back?" she asked, her voice high and stretched thin. "You won't just go riding off and leave me—us?"

"Said I'd stay with the wagons, and my word's about all I got to give."

"Just your word," Elizabeth said. "Not your name."

He wheeled the horse and walked it across the camp, pulling up for a moment where wagon tongues had been lifted to make room for him to get out of the circle. Looking back, he saw Elizabeth standing neat and trim, standing straight and pulled-in, like she was holding onto herself. Firelight danced over her slim body, across her white face, and something tugged at him.

Urging the mare into gathering night, Joe told himself it was nothing like that other time. Elizabeth was a different kind of woman—smart not just because she'd been born to it. She was kind of short and her hair was brown, and she wasn't spitting hate at him, calling him white trash.

Still, it felt a little bit like when he rode off and left another woman behind. He grunted; Marilee Bradburn wouldn't have asked him to come back. She'd have dared him.

Chapter 28

All her body ached, and even though her hands had been toughened by menial labor, they were sore, too. But Marilee's biggest hurt was coiled deep inside, festering where she couldn't reach it.

Putting down her load of wood, she kneeled for a moment to rub at the small of her back, knowing now why a few slaves back in Mississippi had suddenly, inexplicably gone crazy, exploding into blind violence that could only bring them the lash and irons, or death.

It wasn't just the weight of being owned, of being enslaved and not able to call any hour in your life your own; it wasn't even that your body belonged to someone else. After a while, that was accepted as a cruel and inescapable fact. What nibbled and gnawed and burrowed so deeply were little things—sly pinches, spit clinging to your face, being tripped so the fall was hard and unexpected, hair jerked so hard the scalp bled.

It was never being allowed to forget you were lower than a cringing dog, despised and reviled and commanded —always, *always* commanded. It was being slapped because your skin was different, kicked for your hair color,

265

twisted and gouged and fisted because they were so damned superior in every way.

Being born to slavery might make it a little easier to take, but to have once been free, like the miserable blacks bought at auction straight off slave ships—Marilee could understand now; she could fit all the wrongs together and see the whole for what it was—monstrous.

No slave on Bradburn Plantation had ever been mistreated—but no, that wasn't true. The wenches—the *women* had no say-so about who used their bodies and had to smile their appreciation when they were bedded by white men. And wasn't it cruel to pat another human being as you might stroke a pet animal, to make them less than human by that sort of patronizing kindness?

For Marilee knew both torture and kindness with the Comanches, these *Nermernuh*, who so arrogantly called themselves *"The* People." Piava was gentle with her, loving to her in his savage fashion, and the warriors respected her knowledge of horses, for having owned the great stallion. Even old Mookwar-ruh, the Spirit Talker, was turning more and more friendly of late. That puzzled her, because she would catch him staring at her and surprise a quickly gone expression of something like awe in his shifting eyes.

But nothing the women did could puzzle Marilee, especially the viciousness of Piava's other wives. Those two —sadistic, wrinkling Topsannah—oh God, how could she ever have been named Flower?—and younger Mowkona, the Spring Rabbit—immediately made her life hell whenever Piava rode away on a hunt. They were bad enough when he was just out of sight, but they saved their most delicious humiliations for times when all the other women could gather to cackle at their mastery.

Marilee was just climbing to her feet when the kick landed. The force of it drove her down across the wood she'd piled, slamming one breast into a sharp stick and scattering the rest.

"Bitch dog." Flower laughed. "You cannot even stack wood properly. Crawl up and do it again."

Spring Rabbit clapped brown hands in delight. "Why, Flower—that name is better than what our husband calls her. Nadevah? What would a Moon Woman be doing crawling on her belly like that? Come, Nadevah—"

Spring Rabbit snapped her fingers. "Carry a stick in your mouth and bark!"

When Marilee came shakily to her knees, she saw the gloating faces, the ring of women eager to enjoy her helplessness, like a pack of coyotes gathered to worry at a crippled deer. Beyond them, children paused in their play to watch, and warriors called jokes about the game to each other.

Piava—where was Little Buffalo? Close by in the tepee, she thought, but he was paying no attention to the commotion he could surely hear. Had he deserted her? Was he tiring of her?

Flower reached down to twist hard fingers into Marilee's hair. "Obey my sister and bark, dog woman!"

So blind with pain she couldn't even see the grimy wrist her teeth sank into, Marilee heard herself growling like a maddened animal. Flower yelped and pulled her hand free, to stagger back from a sharp blow by a stick of wood. Marilee hadn't realized she was swinging it.

Hurling herself up and out, she chopped at Spring Rabbit and knocked the woman sprawling. Flower clawed at her, and Marilee flung the length of wood into another startled face in the crowd, slamming her body savagely into Flower's chunky flesh, fiercely exultant in the pure release of frustration. A knee driven into the other woman's belly, a balled fist smashed into a pendulous breast, and Marilee stood over Flower writhing on the ground. But only for a split second; lips curled back from her teeth, she went for Spring Rabbit like a lunging puma, tearing and snarling.

She was sitting on the woman's back with both hands wound into long, black hair, pounding Spring Rabbit's head against the earth when someone caught at her. Spitting, Marlilee rolled off Spring Rabbit and blazed up fighting. She ripped at them, punched and clawed and kicked. Hands struck back at her, but she didn't feel them; moccasins thumped her ribs, but she didn't pause in her fury. They'd have to kill her to stop her, because she would rather die this way, in respect for herself, than to live any longer as a slave. The berserk rage behind her fists and feet burned cleansing throughout her mistreated body and purified her mind, giving her an insane strength.

Abruptly, Marilee stood panting alone, her feet spread

wide apart and her chest heaving. Two women were crawling off like snakes with broken backs; two more lay still and bloodied; others had run away, looking back at her with wide and frightened eyes.

Now there were only warriors, stern-faced and watchful, a quiet circling of silent men, and foremost among them was the Spirit Talker, Mookwar-ruh. Cheeks lined by many winters, sharp eyes boring at her from beneath his buffalo-horn bonnet, he held out his medicine stick.

Marilee braced herself, conscious of blood seeping down her cheek, knowing that Piava had lifted the tepee flap and was standing before it. The Spirit Talker's medicine stick was like a lance point aimed at her.

Through bruised lips she said, "You call yourselves The People, boast of being The Humans. Are the *Nermernuh* only a pack of dogs, then? Give me a knife and let us see which one of you has the courage to count coup on me."

There was a stillness, and over the crest of the mountain the moon rose. Its rays touched her hair, grown long now and spread about her shoulders.

The Spirit Talker said, "I have seen this in my dreams, and now the tribe sees it also. Look how the Comanche moon comes to give his daughter strength, how his silver hand is placed upon her silver head. It is a sign. The spirits have told me this time would come, for how else could a mere woman ride such a great stallion and speak with horses? How else could any *tahbay-boh*, a white one, destroy so many Human women in battle? Our chief knew a vision when he gave her the name, for she is truly Nadevah—the Moon Woman."

They shouted then, a great, rolling shout which broke around the tepees and echoed off among the horse herd. Warriors beat the ground with the shafts of their lances, laughing and capering, for such a sign was good medicine, powerful medicine.

Swaying, Marilee might have allowed her knees to give way, but there was a warm, strong hand at her elbow, and she leaned gratefully against Piava.

"A feast!" he said. "A feast to honor this best of all wives the moon has sent to me! No more is Nadevah a captive; she is my wife and full sister to all the *Nermernuh*. Hear me!"

"We hear you, Little Buffalo!" they yelled, and Marilee

thought that Mookwar-ruh shouted loudest of all, dancing and shaking his buffalo horns, pointing his medicine stick to the sky, to her.

Unmarried women came to bathe her face and tend her wounds, as they might have done for a warrior returning from battle. They whispered excitedly as they led her into the tepee and brought out a ceremonial dress of soft buckskin, beaded and feathered with bright designs. She waved them off then, and sank down to the fur bed she shared with Piava.

Drums were going outside, skin-topped gourds filled part way with water, so each spoke with a different voice; Marilee could see fires leaping high and flinging their shining shadows across the sides of Piava's tepee.

She'd thought she understood the Comanches after so long, but there was always something new to learn. This year and more, she had been so afraid to stand up to her tormentors, fearful that some quick-tempered brave would kill her for rebelling. Or worse—she might have been staked out for slow death by indescribable torture. The tribe hadn't brought in any captives, hadn't been at war, for hunting was good and life had been easy, but she'd heard them recounting bloody, stomach-turning tales of earlier raids. They'd delighted in outdoing each other to perpetrate the most horrible agonies upon defeated enemies; fire and slow peeling of skin, red ants pushed into every orifice of the human body, burial to the neck in sand, hapless victims whose eyelids had been cut away so they would stare into blinding sun until death released them.

And their strange code demanded respect for the enemy who died well, despite all they could do to him; if he did not scream, somehow they were shamed. The *Nermernuh* were paradoxes no white would ever be able to fully understand, gentle with their own children and heartless to others; dedicated to their horses and scorning the hated Apache for mistreating his, but yipping happily beside a staggering buffalo feathered with arrows and slowly bleeding to death, for to kill him would put an end to their joy.

Now this—suddenly elevating her to the status of a tribe member and wife to their chief, after degrading her for so many long and wearying hurtful months.

Of course, they were superstitious; every male carried a medicine sack between his legs, safely protected behind his loin cloth. She'd seen Piava's the first night he had had her and remembered thinking he was malformed until he took it off. Nobody else knew what magic articles were secret in any man's medicine bag, what bits of bone and feather or dung or flower leaves.

Each band had a Spirit Talker and relied heavily upon the omens read in the sky and earth or the steaming entrails of animals. Mookwar-ruh had been watching her, weighing her, perhaps because Little Buffalo named her Moon Woman, simply because of her hair. Or maybe it had not been so simple; the Comanches were also mystical about their names and the origin of them.

Now that hers had been accepted and read as a good sign, she might do something about escaping. There had been no chance before, and every time Piava rode Bradburn to the hunt—*his* horse now, and grudgingly borne by the big stallion—Marilee fretted and prayed until they returned safely. It would be worse from here on, for the Comanche moon was rising full and the warriors made restless by it. Big and bright, it was their fall beacon. They rode to war by moonlight, galloped far and fast to strike terror into Apaches and whites and Mexicans, for all men were their enemies.

She didn't want Piava riding Bradburn into battle. She didn't know how she could stop it, but there had to be some way.

Marilee rose from the couch of furs and smoothed her ceremonial dress over her hips. Nadevah went from the tepee to join the celebration.

Late that night, when the drums were silent and fires guttered low, she came to Piava before he beckoned her, slipping out of the dress and standing naked in moonlight that puddled down through the tepee's smoke hole.

And she was the aggressor, startling him by the urgency of her demands, the softsweet fury of her thighs. She tried to use him as he had so often used her, but Piava was strong, and in the gasped, rhythmic twining, they met as equals. Marilee attacked as a Comanche, striking hard and retreating before he could follow, battering him with her breasts and coiling him within her legs. He knew the method well, and pursued with cunning, letting her break free only to trap her again. The moon was gone before they slept wrapped in furs and each other's arms, sweated and sated.

In the morning, she prepared his food, for the fire had been already started by Flower and Spring Rabbit, fresh water drawn, and everything put to her hand, as befitted the favorite wife. They were bruised, cut, and sullen, but moved quickly for her, defeated giving way to victor in the way of the Comanche.

Going with him to look over the horses, she stood at the rope that fenced Bradburn and his mares from the rest of the herd. The stallion nibbled grain from her hand, and she said, "My husband, I wish to ride with you to war."

Piava stroked a pregnant mare's flanks, then scratched her neck. "Already you bargain as a Human. You wish to ride the stallion. But he is mine, as you are mine."

"Yes," she said quietly. "I do not ask to take him— only a chief such as you should ride so fine a horse. I ask only to stay close to both of you. And Spirit Talker said I am a good omen."

"It is sometimes done, women riding behind a war party, but this happens on very long journeys, or long retreats. Spirit Talker is not always right. Did I not know you for Moon Woman long before him?"

"*Hu*, Piava," she said. "Yes, Little Buffalo—therefore you will be wise and take me along, for will not the Comanche moon smile upon his own daughter?"

Piava laughed, throwing back his head and shaking his mane of hair. "*Aiyee*, but you are a prize equal to the stallion. I was watching through the flap when you attacked my other wives."

"And you did nothing?"

"Why should I? It was a war between women, and I knew you would not lose, that all The People would see you are strong and full of courage, like the stallion you rode when the spirits sent you both to me." Turned serious, his eyes searching hers, Piava said then, "What if we ride against the whites, if we go to kill *tahbay-boh* or tejanos?"

Marilee didn't hesitate. "I am Comanche. The People's enemies are my enemies."

He touched her shoulder. "You speak well, and I know

how you ride, how you shoot. Perhaps Mookwar-ruh is correct—all right, then." Pointing across the corral, Piava said: "You see the spotted mare?"

"The one with fine legs—yes, I have been watching her."

"Good—she is yours. I have named her *Tabay-neeka*— Hears the Sunrise. The stallion has bred her, but she is many moons from giving birth, and she is fast, with a good heart. Become familiar with her, so she may carry you well."

"Thank you," Marilee said, and the Nadevah in her knew this was not the time to ask him about her guns. If he fully trusted her, that would come later. Possibly, he'd never arm her; certainly, he'd never return the Walker pistol. She moved through the other horses, so Hears the Sunrise could get to know her scent.

In days to come she worked the mare, but always close to the camp, always with Piava's eyes upon her, cueing the horse with her knees and getting used to the flat hide saddle and its crude stirrups. She even practiced hooking one leg through the strong band of rawhide that looped around the mare's chest just behind the shoulders. Comanches used that trick to swing off the back of a running horse, to present no target as they fired beneath the outstretched neck.

She watched preparations for war, guns being cleaned, knives sharpened, new stone teeth driven into clubs, short, powerful bows tested, and flinthead arrows made by older men. Marilee wondered what would happen if they went raiding against whites, if they were to swoop down on a wagon train like the one she'd been with. Gilmore Frazier, she thought; Pecos and Goodnight and so many others, all the others.

Could she get away in the confusion? She might be shot down by Piava or any of his warriors, if she tried; or she could be killed by her own kind, mistaken for a Comanche. And how was she going to get Bradburn away from Little Buffalo? He would sooner give up his hair, that long, cared-for hair of The People; no man could get into heaven without it, for the spirits would scorn him.

At night she slept with Piava, not meekly, but with as much passion as she could muster, wise enough so she didn't ask which enemy they would ride against or where that enemy was. And when all preparations were done, new black and red face paint made, when quivers were full and food packed, when the horses were fed so they were eager to run, Spirit Talker made prayers to the full moon and burned offerings in the fire. That night the men danced and the women watched; that night Piava did not touch her, but saved his strength. In the very early morning, when all the camp was stirring with excitement and the children running around like so many rabbits, he told her.

They were going to strike the Apaches.

The lift Marilee felt was real, her relief mingled with a touch of disappointment, for there'd be less opportunity for her to find her own kind. Still, there might be a chance.

She would never leave Bradburn behind. Leading him from the rope corral and presenting him to her husband, she told the stallion that, through the lingering of her hands, pouring her love and promise into him through her fingertips.

Swinging up onto her mare, she waited until Piava gave her a knife, and waited again. He handed her the Spencer carbine, but not the pistol. She smiled at him and held Hears the Sunrise in place while the warriors fell in behind their chief, taking her position at the end of the column, as was proper for a woman, even one who was wife to a great chief and called Moon Woman.

Handsome and magnificent in fringed buckskin and horned war bonnet, carrying the new shield blessed by Spirit Talker, Piava raised his rifle and yelled, leader of chorusing wolf cries, and his band galloped after him to take the sacred warpath. Close into their dust, Marilee ran the mare after them, and it was only when the others slowed to a steady pace that she realized she had also been screaming and shaking her carbine high overhead.

Chapter 29

Piava sat the stallion beside her, his sharp eyes following the three hunters fanned out to look for sign. Marilee held the mare in check, feeling the cool wind of early dawn upon her face, wind with a hint of sharpness in it.

He said, "In my father's time, this valley was covered with buffalo as far as the eye could reach. Now we must search for them." Making a spitting sound, he said then, "White men—they kill only for hides, for the tongue, and leave the meat to vultures. Someday, The People will be starved from our hunting grounds—unless we can kill all whites."

"They are many as the buffalo once were," Marilee said, hunching her shoulders a little against the wind. "They will cover the land."

Looking left, looking right, Piava said, "I see this also. The *Kuhtsoo-ehkuh*, *Kwehar-renuh*, and other Comanche tribes speak of peace—war chiefs accept gifts and trade away their lands. This cannot be. White men and The People do not live the same or think the same. We must fight."

"They are many," Marilee repeated. "Each sunrise there are more of them and less of us."

Piava shook his head. "Still we must fight, we must hunt in the old ways. When we accept the white man's beef, we are no longer hunters. If we take his hand in peace, we are no longer warriors. If the Comanche cannot hunt, our eyes will dim. If we do not make war, there can be no honor and our hearts will grow weak. You understand this, Moon Woman."

"I understand," Marilee said, "and know sorrow."

Shrugging as if he could throw off foreboding, Piava pointed his rifle. "Look there—Shaking Hand is gone from sight beyond the mountain. Nawkohnee moves slowly and without success, and Antelope Leg has found no sign. *Hu*—we may be reduced to eating fish and birds when the snows come."

"There will be buffalo," she said, "this winter and the next."

He glanced quickly at her. "You have been given a sign?"

"No, my husband. I feel this in my heart."

Piava smiled at her. "As you felt when we fought the Apache together? *Aiyee*—the great chiefs and medicine men still speak at council fires of Piava's wife. It was a mighty victory, and you have done me much honor."

Shifting uncomfortably on her mare, Marilee looked down at the carbine he still trusted her to carry and said nothing. There was no way to explain, no way Little Buffalo could understand *why* she'd gone insane that stark and moonlit night. Her emotion had been a woman's hurt. It would make no sense to a Comanche, for none of them had even blinked when they saw the captive child being tortured at an Apache campfire.

All they'd seen was bad medicine, far too many of their traditional enemies gathered in one camp. The spirits had not told them the Apaches were gathered there for a war council of their own, that several bands had come together.

No fools, The People; finest horsemen on the plains, they knew well the best attack was one that struck swiftly and against lesser numbers of unprepared foes. No Indian liked prolonged combat, drawn-out and bloody confrontations that might cause great losses on both sides. So the Comanche war party was disappointed when they discovered they were outnumbered two to one, that the Apaches were alert and well armed. They were ready to slip back north and wait for a better time.

But all Marilee could see was the child at the center fire. His ankles lashed together, the boy couldn't run. Each time the grinning Apache touched the point of the knife to him, he cried out and tried to inch along the ground. Marilee had clenched her hand so hard around the stock of her carbine that her fingers ached; because of her tension, the mare stirred uneasily beneath her.

She might have backed off with the rest, keeping silent and resisting the angry sickness within her, if the Apache hadn't taken a burning stick from the fire. Staring over the ridgetop behind which their horses were hidden, she saw the leering savage wave the brand around the boy's head and knew with a turning of her belly that he was about to set fire to the child's hair.

The mare leaped when Marilee's heels dug her flanks, and they went up over the ridge to race downslope into the camp. Dirt flew from the pounding hoofs of Hears the Sunrise, and a full-throated scream of rage burst from the throat of Nadevah, Moon Woman of the Comanches.

Apaches scattered, but they were only blurs to her. She fixed upon the single brave with a terrible intensity, low over her horse's shoulder and firing as she came thundering. He rolled through the campfire and flung aside his brand, dark face twisted up at the apparition almost upon him.

Chopping at his bobbing head with the barrel of her carbine, Marilee reined up the plunging mare and pivoted her, spun her striking forefeet. Guns exploded around her; men shouted and women screamed. The Apache stooped quickly and cut his captive's throat. When he swung the bloody knife up at her mare's belly, Marilee shot him through the chest just before he was smashed down by the horse's flailing hoofs.

For a bleak, static moment, she looked down upon the small corpse of a young Mexican boy, knowing that Comanche horses were whipping past her, that Comanche warriors were shooting and slashing into panicked Apaches, but she saw only a boy's blood.

There were leaping fires then, wickiups torched and hurling sparks skyward into the moonlight; there were bodies and ringing, triumphant cries. She was sick; her eyes smeared and she couldn't see, didn't want to hear.

"Come," Piava said to her. "A few dogs have run away, but no more live, and we are driving off their horses. *Aiyee!* It is a great night, Nadevah, one all tribes will speak of—The People, those cowardly Apache, Kiowa, Cheyenne—all will know of the Moon Woman who led the Comanche to a mighty victory."

"A mighty victory," she repeated numbly, and followed him into the silver path of the moon. Piava didn't mention the murdered child; none of them did. It was a captor's right to do what he wished to a prisoner; it was law.

So now, as Marilee followed Piava slowly down into the valley, her need to escape was stronger, more vital. She'd come to know the Comanches well, to speak their language and communicate deftly with hand talk, for The People were best at that. She'd learned to find game where a white hunter would see nothing, to smell out water, to close off her body against cold and heat.

There were times when she was Comanche through and through, reveling in the respect paid her when other tribes of The Humans gathered to celebrate the great defeat of the Chiricahua. Rarely had a woman sat at the council fire, but Moon Woman did, honored by fabled war chief Set-Tainte, and by the renowned leader Ten Bears. Even the feared medicine man Coyote Droppings stood in awe of her, Eeshatai declaring that because of her, Piava and his tribe were favored by the moon. And she was proud of Piava, of his courage and handsomeness other women envied her for.

But often during the nights, warmed beneath furs and by Little Buffalo's body, she lay awake and became Marilee Bradburn again. One day more captives would be brought into camp; one day there would be fresh scalps upon Piava's lance, hair blond or gray or childish red. She had to get away. She couldn't sit by and see anyone tortured at some warrior's whim. *She had to get away.*

"Shaking Hand is coming fast," Piava said. "He has found the buffalo."

Marilee saw the horse running full out, Shaking Hand a perfect blending in its rhythm. Her mare stood at the lip of a water hole, drinking daintily, Bradburn very close; she looked down at the Walker Colt thrust into Piava's fringed breeches, at the rifle across his lap.

Pulling up in a cloud of dust, Shaking Hand called out: "Whites! Far away beyond the red mountain there, but I have seen the tepees-that-roll!"

"The hawk has given you his eyes," Piava said. "How many, Shaking Hand?"

"I could not count—they are too far away. But there will be much treasure, and long-eared horses, and women to carry off."

"We will gather the other warriors," Piava said, lifting in his stirrups to wave a signal at his other two hunters.

The end of the mare's rein wrapped around her right hand, holding to the carbine with both hands, Marilee leaned and hit him in the ribs. Up from Bradburn's back and off balance, Piava spun out of the stirrups and fell to the ground as she lunged frantically to clutch at the butt of the pistol.

Walker jammed into one legging, Bradburn's reins now in her teeth, she clung to the mare's lead and to the carbine as the big horse bolted. Piava's outraged yell broke behind her.

Wind sang in her ears and her hair flagged behind. Although her body tensed for the blow of a bullet and her mouth was suddenly dry, Marilee's heart sang with the wind. She was on Bradburn again, one with the stallion again, and he was responding to the urgent grip of her legs, to her cries for speed, as he'd never run for Piava.

A gun went off, but nothing touched them, and the valley floor flowed beneath Bradburn's racing hoofs. A slight tugging at her right hand told Marilee that the mare was having a difficult time keeping up, but Hears the Sunrise had heart, too, and would run herself to death before quitting.

Pointing Bradburn's outreaching head at the hilltop Shaking Hand had ridden over, in the general direction of a faraway wagon train, Marilee knew she'd done the right thing by taking the mare. It left Piava afoot, if he didn't jerk another warrior off a horse. And the mare could hang on for a while; all Comanche horses were good for a hard, short burst of speed. Bradburn's unmatchable stamina would begin to tell as the straining minutes blurred by.

They topped the hill, but she couldn't see wagons, only a red sandstone mountain, and down below a twisting of canyons offshooting each other, doubling back one upon the other. She glanced back and saw three horses coming, Shaking Hand straight behind her, the other hunters angling in from the left, but farther back. She couldn't see Piava. Had she hurt him, the fall broken an arm, a leg?

Dipping into the canyon, she slowed the horses and tried to find tracks left by Shaking Hand's horse. Nothing —he must have come in from a different direction. She let Bradburn out again. Comanche horses were trained to be led, and the gallant mare kept her head at the stallion's shoulder.

They were down the hill now, and turning into a twisted gorge with a sandy bottom. She let the horses trot awhile, looking back often, glad for the comfort of the Spencer and the Walker Colt in her legging. When the canyon widened and looped, Marilee hesitated; it might be leading her the wrong way. When she heard the rocks echo a yell, she put the horses into another gallop, for there was no turning back now.

Piava would be furious at her betrayal, maddened because she'd struck him and taken the horse from under him, and in the presence of his braves. To be bested by a woman, his wife, even though she was the Moon Woman, was an insult to his fierce pride he could never forgive. But somehow, Marilee didn't think he was the one who had fired at her.

Narrowing, the gully forced her to drop the horses to a trot, then walk them around a clump of Spanish bayonet that partially blocked the way. The gully spread itself again beyond the needled growth and turned around a spire of rock. The right way, she thought in relief, and the ground was rising gently beneath Bradburn's galloping feet. But high walls still towered on both sides, and she flicked uneasy looks at their rims, hoping not to see riders skylined up there. She would have to shoot, and she didn't want to.

Would Antelope Leg and the others fire down on her? Had Piava shouted orders for her death, or did he want her dragged back so he could humble her and so erase the stain upon his chief's honor? Marilee shuddered; she might be turned over to the Spirit Talker for punishment—or worse, to the women.

The beat of her heart quickened when the canyon floor changed again, dropping treacherously and putting the red mountain's crest farther beyond reach. The wagon train, she thought; she had to reach it, had to pray that sunlight on her pale hair would stay trigger fingers, pray even harder that it would be a strong train with experienced and well-armed outriders. For if it was small and weak, and The People came down on it in all their swift, hawk-striking fury, the best she could hope for would be that all might die quickly, herself among them.

Bradburn stopped so suddenly that she almost went over his shoulder, and the mare's weight yanked at her arm. She lifted the carbine when she saw him—Piava stripped to only breechclout and moccasins; Piava with his chest heaving and glistened by sweat.

Her blood chilled at the sight of him, even though he had no rifle. Good Lord, she thought—he'd run so far, driven his body beyond its great strength, up and over the steep ridges he knew so well, along their rims, running, running the ancient Comanche trails to find her and put himself before her.

Piava's mouth was pulling wide for air, and his hair was wet; blood ran down his legs from cactus clawings, from ignored rock scrapings. Welts marred his ribs. His eyes were wide, too, bulging and strained and fastened upon her.

The Spencer shook in her hand, even as its sights centered upon his pumping chest. She had lain too many times against that chest and known the drumming of his heart. She could only stare at him as he stared at her. Then he took a slow, trembling step toward her, and another.

Marilee couldn't shoot him, and she could not ride him down. There was a branching of the canyon to her left, and she threw Bradburn at its mouth, leaning away from Piava, dragging the mare as they went into the turn at breakneck speed. He might have shouted after her, but what she heard could have been the clatter of stones, or the roaring in her own ears.

Pounding on, leaving Piava behind, she raced the horses uphill, thankful for the climb of the land, for the top of the mountain they would soon reach. Blood on his legs; cruel rips along his sides; those black eyes staring—oh, God—how *could* he have run like that?

The ravine ended. Just like that, it stopped itself against a sheer rock wall. She had swung into a blind canyon and was trapped!

Marilee turned the horses, her eyes darting along the wall, searching for a path they might climb, for any way out. There! A little break masked by a growth of sagebrush, and daylight beyond. She urged Bradburn toward it, not knowing where the trail might lead, making the horses walk over a shifting spread of rocks that had tumbled from higher ground.

She felt him coming, felt his eyes upon her back, and when she turned in the saddle, saw him following at a dogged trot. He was stumbling, catching himself, but coming on as if every step weren't jarring his spine, as if he meant to chase her to the end of the land, all the way to where the spirits said the moon swallowed the sun.

Sobbing now, Marilee urged Bradburn across smoother going; up ahead, canyon walls began to lower, and more sky showed itself close to the ground. Hears the Sunrise was beginning to lag and was breathing in windy, nostril-flared gulps. The mare was tiring; a horse was tiring and back there a man was pushing himself beyond human endurance.

But she'd be free of him. In a little while, Bradburn would carry her over the lip of the pass and she could run away from that impossible determination of Little Buffalo, proud chief of a proud tribe.

Antelope Leg brought his horse in first, sliding it down loose shale—then Nawkohnee, and after him, Shaking Hand. Spacing themselves across the narrow pass before her, they drew up and waited. Behind her was Piava; before her three warriors who were not just Comanches, but men whose faces she knew.

She could turn and ride over Piava. She could try to fight her way past the *Nermernuh* ahead.

Or wait and let them take her.

Chapter 30

He had holed up beyond their nearly hidden campfire that night, tying the barb mare in mesquite and eeling forward on his belly to make certain the Apaches hadn't shown flame just for his benefit. But they'd been there, eating and huddled close, so he had to wait a long time to be certain of his count. Joe Langston stayed where he was for hours after he checked out all of them, but no other Chiricahua came slipping down from the hills to join Nantan's little band of ragged survivors.

Evidently the Apache chief had been telling the truth, and his tribe had been wiped out by Comanches. Working his way silently back to his horse, Joe decided to lead her to high ground, where he could look down on the camp come morning, in case. He hadn't kept his hair safe this long by trusting to appearances or to luck.

With the mare hobbled in a vee of rock that he would have had trouble finding in the dark, if it weren't for the bright moon that showed it, Joe bedded down to wait out the night. He wasn't only being certain the Apaches kept moving in the right direction and didn't collect allies; it was a kind of relief for him to be alone for a change.

It was something Elizabeth wouldn't understand, and he wasn't about to try explaining. She was a solid, giving woman, a fine woman for the right kind of man. He was grateful to her for being good to him, for feeding the hunger of his mind as well as that of his body. But she had those Chicago schoolteacher ideas, egged on by Preacher Samples and the other Easterners, and Joe was feeling boxed in.

Turning beneath his blanket, he listened to the night, to the slow breathing of his mare. Damn it—could be he'd read too many books and listened to too much poetry and such. He could have told Elizabeth he'd left a wife in Mexico, or one clear back in Alabama, and she'd have still snuck out to meet him. It wasn't like he was taking anything from Elizabeth that she didn't want to give, and even if he didn't get to bed down in the wagon every blessed night, one little bitty old lie would have turned it better all around.

Another thing—he could let that arm-flapping, neck-jerking preacher say the words over them, and walk away just as easy when they got to California as he meant to anyhow. He could shake loose and make it to the gold fields, or deal poker awhile and get a stake together, and what the hell could Elizabeth Hartley Langston do about it?

Joe didn't know why he just didn't go the way the wind blew, but it riled him to be pushed on. Through the rest of the night, he slept listening, one part of his mind alert as a napping bobcat and the rest of it fretting. When the sun peeped up, he was already sitting humped under his blanket, chewing on cold jerky. He halfway wished some more damned Apaches *would* show up, so he could bust them and hightail back to the train, where that kind of news would keep her and the ameners off his back for a spell.

No such luck—the Chiricahuas ate and went straggling on to the east. Joe let the mare graze on bunch grass awhile, then fed her some meal, and went hunting for a water hole so she could drink. From a taller hilltop, he stared down at the train lining itself out, little toy wagons that could tote so much trouble. To the north, a redbrown mountain looked better, and his far-ranging eyes picked out a suggestion of green halfway up that meant water.

He could spy out the ground for a long way around from up there anyhow, and seeing as how he'd already come this far, it was the thing to do. So after he'd climbed the mare to a little puddle of clear water that drained itself out of a trough in the mountain, Joe rested her some before taking her on up to the crest. It was a long climb, and she picked her way slowly, making sure of footing in loose shale he was sorry they'd come across.

Patting her sweaty neck, he told her she was a good horse—near about good as that big, muscled stud with a Yankee brand on its hip. Marilee Bradburn never said where she got that stud, but it was easier on the mind to think about something besides women, and so he put his head to it. Up here, the air was fresh as a man ought to keep on his face, air perfumed by sagebrush and freedom, not all bottled up dusty in a store, not air come secondhand from other men who'd breathed it.

Just ahead and a little higher was a saddleback cut into the mountain by wind and time; eroded, that was the word. Joe headed up for it, peering over its spine before he showed the mare and himself targeted on the skyline.

Joe came off the mare in a hurry then, backing her from the high ground so he could loop her reins around a limb of red sandstone and scoop a handful of Sharps brass from the saddlebag. He found a low place on the rim where his head would look like just another rock, and braced the buffalo gun to sight along its barrel. Down below, where a canyon opened its mouth into a tongue reaching up for the top where he lay, he could see three of them fanned out to block off another one.

The one off by himself straddled a big red horse and had a spotted one on a lead. All of them wore buckskins; not Apaches, then—so they had to be Comanches. Joe put the front sight square on the back of the middle Indian, but eased off on the trigger. They had no idea he was up here, and if three of them wanted to gang up on another damned Comanche and do him in, who was Joe Langston to stop it? Besides, if he dropped one, the other two might make it to cover in the rocks and try to circle up on him. The Sharps was a single-shot and it took time to reload; the carbine could jack out quick fire, but it would never reach out that far. Hell, Joe thought, he'd just lie back and watch.

Lifting over his side of the mountain, sunlight went spearing down to settle around the Comanche, to light up silvery long hair on the one facing off the rest.

"*White*, by God!" he said, and dropped his sights to squeeze off a shot that knocked an Indian's horse out from under him, the boom of the Sharps rolling down the slope and jerking heads around.

He got another horse before its rider could run it to cover, and the third one just as it started around a pile of rock. Calmly, reloading with practiced deftness, Joe centered upon a stunned Comanche getting to his feet and put him down for keeps.

The second one rolled behind his dead horse, not knowing how hard a .52 caliber ball could hit, until it had punched clear through his pony and knocked him kicking.

The third man made a mistake, too. The white rider had thrown himself and both horses straight up the mountainside, jumping off quick in the echo of Joe's first shot, but the last Comanche wanted him so bad he stood out in the open and shot fast at the fleeing man. The carbine flew spinning out of the Comanche's hands when a heavy ball took him in the belly.

White hair flapping out long behind him, the rider came on, fixing where Joe was by the smoke puffs lifting there, riding like hell but still hanging on to that other horse. Pretty good riding for a grizzled-up trapper, Joe thought, but the ornery old man ought to turn loose the spotted horse; it was dragging back more than some. The red horse was a lot stronger. . . .

"*Damn!*" The word jolted out of Joe's mouth, because he knew that horse, or one just like him. Nostrils blowing wide and pink, foam flecking his mouth, and a deep, powerful chest, that stallion climbed like a goat. That *stallion!*

Rolling aside when the big horse plunged over the ridgetop, Joe lay on his back and stared up as it slid to a stop. He stared at the US brand burned into its hip, at the long-legged, slim figure in buckskins who sat trembling atop the heaving horse. She had hair the color of polished silver, all wind-tangled and hanging longer than Joe had ever seen it before. There was no mistaking that hair, and he knew before she turned a thinned, browned face to him that her eyes would be willow green.

A Spencer hung heavy in her left hand, and he saw

the butt of a Colt sticking from her right leggings, the stallion's reins clenched hard in bared teeth.

All he could say, lying there on his back like a turned-over turtle, was, "Why didn't you turn loose that spotted horse?"

Big, growing bigger with each second, her green eyes reached down to him and held. Joe watched a pulse jumping in her tanned throat, watched her lips move without making sounds.

Then she said, "B-because he would have caught her and come after me on her." The words sounded rusty, as if she hadn't used them for a long time.

Joe got to one knee and shook his head at the world, at himself, but most of all at Marilee Bradburn sitting her Morgan horse like she hadn't been left a thousand miles and two years behind. "I got all three of 'em," he said.

She swayed, and he raised up to catch her when she slipped off the strange saddle, but she held to herself and climbed down stiffly. "There's one more."

"Didn't see him."

"He's afoot."

Moving back to his position in the rocks, Joe looked downhill. "Don't make him out yet. Must really be after your hair to be afoot out yonder. What'd you do to 'em, besides steal a horse?"

Marilee sat down, holding to the mare's lead, holding to her Spencer. If it wasn't for her hair and eyes, she looked pure Indian, he thought; beaded headband across her forehead, buckskin shirt and breeches, geegawed up with more beads and paint, fancy moccasins that turned into leggings reaching clear up to her knees. She toted a good-sized scalping knife, too, a heavy-bladed thing with a horn handle all carved pretty. Joe glanced back into the valley.

She said, "Shaking Hand saw a wagon train; they were going back to camp for the other warriors. I—I just couldn't let that happen."

"Called that Indian like you know him," Joe said.

"I knew them all," she said. "They caught me a long time ago—I don't know just how long. It was somewhere out of San Antone when Apaches hit the train I was with."

He saw something moving far below. "Those ain't—aren't—Apaches."

"No, they're The People, Comanches. I—I got away from the massacre, and they picked me up later. Can we go now?"

"Where?" he asked, eyeing the figure down there, seeing it growing slowly into the shape of a man.

"Anywhere—that wagon train. They should be warned —other hunting parties are out, and they'll see it, too."

Earing back the hammer on the Sharps, Joe said, "Scoutin' for that bunch myself. Get you to 'em before long. How come they had you along on a hunt? Comanches must be some different, takin' their women."

He felt her move closer, thinking she not only looked like an Indian, but smelled like one, kind of smoky. "I was sort of—of special to the tribe. Please, Joe—let's go."

"About to get him in my sights," he answered. "He's a big one, but he don't even have a gun."

Her hair brushed the side of his neck, and he flinched. Marilee said quietly, "That's Piava, war chief of the *Pehnahterkuh*—I was his wife."

Joe had known that, somehow, but still her admission dug at him. Trust her to land on her feet, to snare herself another man to take care of her. She might have made out all right with the Apaches, just as well. Even if every other woman on a wagon train got passed from one horny brave to another before one of them ripped up her belly, Miss Marilee Bradburn would get by. Her kind always did; they'd had so damned much practice on their plantations, studying all the soft, beguiling tricks that could trap a man so easy. A lace-sleeved gentleman or starry-eyed boy or a grinning black buck, even a bloodthirsty Comanche.

"Married legal, were you? Or did some medicine man shake a painted stick over you and the big chief? I wonder how come he liked you better'n the rest of the braves that wallowed you around."

When she answered him, her voice was flat and tired. "I don't expect you to understand. You don't know how it was, don't know anything about the Comanches, or even about me."

"Yeah," he said, "I'm just a dumb ol' redneck boy— white trash, remember? How the hell could I know anything?"

Her tone changing, going thin, dry, Marilee said, "He's

been running for so long his feet must be raw. I didn't think any human being could follow horses so far."

Joe caught the man's naked chest in his sights. "He ain't *human*—he's a damned Indian." He was about to make the staggering Comanche a good damned Indian, just ready to squeeze the trigger of the Sharps, when she stood up and pulled the spotted mare with her, to stand on the ridge in plain sight.

"What the *hell?*" Joe said.

Halfway up the slope, wobbling at the knees and blowing like a spent horse, sweat running off him in streams, the big Comanche stopped to stare up at Marilee. Joe watched the man spread his feet so he wouldn't fall over and saw blood on his legs, across his heaving ribs.

She called out something to him, throaty, guttural words that Joe hadn't heard the like of, but the Comanche caught on quick. Face set and not showing a sign of pain, he answered Marilee, and when she talked back again, there was a catch in her voice.

Trying to catch his breath, the Indian hollered in Spanish, then: *"Hombre!* You in the rocks—*Inde,* Apache?"

Joe kept the Sharps steady and said, "No—only the man who is about to kill you."

Marilee said, "Piava!" sharply, but the Comanche didn't look at her. He called to Joe, "The woman is worth many horses to me—a hundred fine *caballos.*"

"Which you will take back with my hair?"

"You have my word, *hombre*—not the lie of an Apache, but the honor of a Comanche chief. A hundred horses, and the white-eyes may go in peace, all those who ride the wagons."

Joe said, "The Comanche will need another to lead them, and the wagons will pass anyhow. There are many *tejanos,* many long guns, and they will be warned. Have the Comanche so few women that this one is worth so much?"

Cutting in on their talk, Marilee spoke quickly, throwing words at the Indian, and Joe watched the man's big shoulders drop. Then she let go the spotted mare's lead and spanked the horse on a flank; it trotted down the hill. Beaten by her words, the man crawled painfully up on the horse and began to walk it away; he didn't look back. "What'd you say to him?"

She was also slumped, tired. "Probably the worst thing I could. I told Piava he owed his life to me, that a woman stopped you from killing him. And I swore if the tribe attacked the wagons, he would find me dead. Then I said I was making him a present of Hears the Sunrise— that's the mare—so the others wouldn't laugh at him."

Horse and man were diminishing into the valley. Joe let the hammer down easy on the Sharps. "Tried to swap a whole herd of ponies for you. He must have wanted you bad."

"He did," Marilee said. "I never realized how much."

Joe grunted. "Three of your friends, his braves, down out yonder and you had him on foot, forty miles from nowhere. He wanted you, all right—wanted to stretch you over a cookfire and baste you 'til you got done to a crisp."

Turning from the ridge, she walked past him, lithe and graceful as ever in her squaw dress, keeping that same kind of eye-holding wiggle to her—more even, since all that polished hair swung back and forth to call attention to her hips.

Marilee lifted onto the waiting stallion and said, "If you won't take me to the wagons, I'll find them myself."

He stalked to get his mare, to scabbard the carbine, and hold to the long rifle. "You're welcome, Miss Marilee, ma'am—I don't mean for you to go out of your way, just to thank me for savin' your life." Harsher then, he said, "What did you *expect* me to do—leave you out here by yourself?"

Green as willows but steady, her eyes locked into his. "You did once before."

Joe winced. "Damn it, that was different. I—"

"Yes, it was different. You had time for rape then."

Feeling kicked in the belly but more mad than hurt about it, he shoved his mare past and pointed down the red mountain.

Chapter 31

He was so wary, animal-aware of his surroundings that Joe Langston might almost be a Comanche, she thought, jogging not quite beside his horse but a step behind. Though he seemed to ride relaxed, she could tell he was watching everything—the skyline, the ground, each clump of brush and jutting of stone. His blueblack hair, the lithe and broad-shouldered shape of him, the strong planings of his tanned face, his assurance were all marks of The People.

But there was his individual stamp: the thin scarline at the corner of his mouth that made Joe Langston always seem to be smiling cynically at the world, his pale and disturbing eyes. It puzzled Marilee to discover how well she remembered their color, and in that first shock of recognition on the ridgetop all of him came sweeping back, the man himself and the use he'd made of her.

When she rode at the puff of gunsmoke, she knew she might be running straight into an ambush by blood enemies of the Comanches. But when no bullets reached for her, when other warriors fell to join Shaking Hand in death, she began to think she had a chance.

Then, to see Joe Langston rolled onto his back, big,

vital and deadly as ever, sprung from Texas earth like an avenging—no, not angel; there was nothing heaven-sent about *him*. Luck, fortune, whatever brought him to that place and that time—Marilee owed her life to it.

Maybe not; she watched him rise in the stirrups to scan a line of hills. Fate had a way of canceling debts, and certainly this man owed her something since that long-ago scene upon a patch of crushed grass.

She'd hated him for that, almost as much for what he did to her, as for the thing he'd awakened within her. Southerner, white man, he should have known a set of ethics different from the Comanche. Piava was a conqueror and saw bedding a captive woman as his right; Joe Langston was supposed to be civilized.

Her escape must have stunned Piava, bewildered him, for he couldn't conceive of anyone not wanting to be a Comanche. And she knew he'd loved her in his way, been tender in his way. She didn't know if Piava would have killed her for running; he might have severely punished her, no more. That also was his choice, his right.

She moved Bradburn closer to the mare, not wanting to dwell upon the memory of a dejected figure riding slowly away, alone. "Will we reach the wagons today?"

Turning his head as if he were surprised to see her beside him, Joe said, "Before night. Don't worry about being caught alone with me."

"I'm not."

He uncapped a canteen, drank a swallow from it, and passed it to her. Wetting her lips, she thought how strange water tasted trapped in metal.

"Wouldn't think you'd fret after livin' with Indians so long, but I've seen squaws who didn't want much to do with white men. They'd fight, even."

"Any woman can understand that, but not you. And I'm not an Indian—get that through your head. There was a time—but I'm still Marilee Bradburn."

Taking back the canteen, he said, "Yeah, from the big white house in Mississippi, still lookin' around for your slaves."

"Not slaves," she said. "Not slaves ever again."

"Well, you learned something anyway."

She flared at him. "And what have *you* learned? To

speak Spanish in Mexico—I heard it pass between you and Little Buffalo, but I don't see any sacks of gold, and didn't that mean most to you? Gold would make you a gentleman, you thought."

Joe shook his head. "Never said that; I don't even know what your kind of gentleman is. What happened to 'em when they ran out of lace cuffs and blacks to do their work—any left around?"

"They'll be rebuilding," Marilee said. "The old families will start over and rise to their places again. *Blood*, Joe Langston—bloodlines will always tell, in men as well as horses."

Pushing his mare into a longer trot, he said over one shoulder, "Be catching up to the wagons, so it's best you stay behind me, but close. In that getup, somebody might take you outa the saddle."

Yes, there was something else new about him, Marilee saw; he had developed an infuriating way of ignoring some point she'd scored and going on to something else. She didn't know why she bothered, except there was something about him, an animosity that struck immediate sparks. Joe Langston would never be anything more than what he was, never—and that wasn't much.

A horse was pulled off the trail ahead, shadowed in a spire of rock, and the man sitting it returned Joe's signal with a waved rifle. They approached him, and Marilee saw a Mexican under a big sombrero, a small man with a drooping moustache and bright eyes in a pockmarked face.

"*Hola*, Joe! What you got there, *compañero?*"

Marilee saw him taking in every detail of her dress, the Indian rig on her horse.

"Comanches had her," Joe answered.

"*Comanches*," the man said as if it was a curse, and crossed himself. Jogging his horse beside Marilee he said, "And a *gringa*. I am Rosario Lopez." He started to lift his sombrero, but didn't.

She introduced herself, wondering how the man would react if given her Comanche name. Already, she could sense uneasiness in him, a kind of drawing back, and in a moment he withdrew physically, drifting his mustang around to close in on Joe. Gesturing, he said something in rapid Spanish and Joe answered brusquely.

She saw the wagons ahead, lumbering themselves into a protective circle for the evening, creaking and rattling, raising dust. Mules and horses and people, voices calling, a dog barking; Marilee felt her skin tighten. It was so familiar, yet somehow strange; she had once been part of a wagon train like this, among these people whose skin matched hers, who talked of homes that had been and a life that would be. Now it all seemed busy and alien, and she felt a little knot of something close to fear; she knew herself to be a stranger.

People climbed down from wagons to stare at them as they rode in, and Marilee saw the shock on women's faces, surprise quickly followed by a closing off and sly whisperings. Men stood looking, holding reins, carrying rifles or buckets or frozen in the act of removing cookpots from wagons. As Rosario Lopez and Joe swung from their horses, she continued to sit on Bradburn, watching a spare, gangling man hurry toward them, a man in a black coat and round stained hat.

"What's this, what's this?" he gobbled.

"Preacher Samples," Joe said to Marilee. "Elected train boss. Preacher, this is Miss Marilee Bradburn. Took her back from the Comanches."

"An Indian captive?" Samples's small eyes licked up at her. "How long did you stay with them? Where were you taken?"

Faces—so many watchful faces, shaggy men, gaunt women, a few children—all of them staring. One woman came walking, straightbacked and tidy, brown hair drawn back and gleaming, to stand at Joe's elbow. Marilee said, "I was with a train wiped out by Apaches. I got away and Comanches caught me. I don't know where it was—somewhere back there. And I don't know how long they held me—the Comanches don't keep calendars."

The slim, erect woman said, "She looks like a squaw."

Back in the crowd, a stooped, grizzled man grunted, "*Is* a squaw. Know how come them Injuns didn't kill her?"

Samples coughed over a rising buzz of voices. "Now, now—we must show this lost sheep Christian charity. Get down, child, get down. You are back in the fold. We will get some decent clothing for you and pray that you be absolved for your sins."

293

Joe Langston thumbed back his hat. "Whatever happened to all that brotherly love, preacher? Don't it count when red skin gets rubbed off on white?"

"Joe," the neat woman said, "Joe," but he reached to help Marilee down, and she was grateful for the support of his warm hand.

What was the matter with them? Did they think she'd voluntarily gone to the Comanches, that she'd chosen to stay in a tepee? Marilee held her chin high, despite the hissing of women and the way children were being edged back from her, hidden behind skirts or herded into wagons. Disjointed words fluttered about her like black and biting moths: ". . . fallen woman . . . sinner . . . didn't have the decency to kill herself . . . squaw woman to all those men . . . hussy . . . keep the children away from her . . . shameless . . . sinful. . . ."

She said clearly, "If it was a sin to want to live, then I'm guilty."

Raising a bony hand in benediction, Samples intoned, "Repent, and ye shall be saved."

"I'm *not* sorry I'm alive."

Joe moved her away from the open-mouthed preacher, leading the horses so the crowd had to move aside from them. Only Rosario and the woman followed. Tying Bradburn and his mare to a wagon tailgate, Joe said, "Kind of expected something like that."

Rosario said, "Not from my people—too many of our women have been taken by Apaches."

Then the woman: "And did you always accept them back, soiled as they were?"

Rosario stroked his moustache. "Some men did. I would have, *señorita*, and gladly. But when we found my wife, they had built a fire upon her belly."

Joe said, "Damn it, Elizabeth, unless it's happened to you, don't go passin' judgment."

"I-I'm sorry," she said. "It's just that—I was so worried about you being gone so long, and you were angry when you left. Miss—Bradburn, is it?—please accept my apologies. I'm Elizabeth Hartley, Joe's fiancée."

Joe looked up at her, surprised, but said nothing.

Shifting his feet, Rosario muttered that he should see to posting of night guards, and his rowel spurs clinked as he walked away. Marilee and Elizabeth looked at each other as Joe said, "I'll find some firewood," and left them alone.

"You must really want a bath," Elizabeth said. "The water's cold, but you can wash inside the wagon, and I'm sure I can find a spare dress. You're taller, but otherwise we're about the same size."

"Thank you," Marilee said, "but I bathed this morning, and I like this dress."

"I suppose it is—practical, but wearing it will only draw more attention to you."

"I'm already wearing a brand on my forehead," Marilee said, "a scarlet letter. Changing clothes won't erase it."

"No, I guess not. Has Joe told you about me? I don't know why he should, but you must have talked about something after he rescued you. Other than your travails, I mean."

The woman was too bright-faced, changing too quickly from open dislike to a shallow acceptance, and Marilee said, "No, he didn't mention you. Tell me, does he know the meaning of 'fiancée'?"

Elizabeth had reached into the wagon for pans. Now she glanced sharply over one shoulder. "Of course—he's a literate man, eager to read, to learn. Why do you ask?"

Shrugging, Marilee went to slip the Comanche saddle off her horse, to lift his feet and check them, to run her hands lightly over his legs. She found two little cactus spines embedded in the skin and removed them. Joe Langston a literate man and engaged to be married to this attractive but prissy Yankee woman? Two years had made a few alterations in him, but still only patches and stitches.

Deliberately silent, she looked over her carbine and the Walker Colt, peeping at Elizabeth bustling efficiently to ready supper, catching the woman peeping back at her. Across the camp she could see other women gathering in intimate knots, heads bobbing like so many sage hens. Cookfires blazed up and a child cried; a mule brayed as it was being led to pasture.

Off across the red mountain and up on a grassy mesa, The People were eating, too; Flower and Spring Rabbit would be standing back, waiting until Piava was done, not questioning him. Later there would be a council, and Spirit Talker would chant medicine for the tribe's losses —and perhaps Little Buffalo would lose stature because his wife was gone with the great stallion. It would take a great war victory to restore him, but Piava would not attack this train; Marilee was certain of that.

"Food's not much different, I expect," Joe said, "but we still got—have—coffee and sweetening."

Sitting cross-legged on the ground, Marilee accepted the tin plate and cup. "Beans," she said. "They smell wonderful."

An older, sort of shriveled Mexican joined them and said something about *frijoles* and Joe interpreted. "Mendez claims anybody who thinks beans smell good has lost his nose. Reckon the Comanches don't grow beans, though."

Poised upon an upended box, Elizabeth said, "What *do* Indians eat?"

"Anything, when they have to," Marilee answered, twisting her mouth at the flavor of coffee. "Comanches won't touch birds or fish unless they're starving, but everything else goes in the pot—grasshoppers, certain roots, and herbs, sometimes a rattlesnake."

Elizabeth made a face and coughed, then put aside her plate. "My! And you seem to have adapted so well—to everything."

Joe sipped from his cup. "She had to. When you get hungry enough, you'll give anything first bite and swallow him before he stops kickin'."

Steadily, Marilee ate until the plate was clean and licked the spoon. Elizabeth watched her. Marilee said, "Major Ainsworth—is he still in Mexico?"

"Buried there," Joe said, "like about all the troops."

Elizabeth stood up. "Did you know her *before*, Joe? Did you meet her in Mexico?"

"She was with us for a spell—that Confederate troop I told you about. She didn't get to Mexico."

"You never mentioned her," Elizabeth said, "and she never said—" Moving stiffly, she began gathering plates, snatching Marilee's, holding her back very straight. Tin rattled in a bucket as Elizabeth splashed water and stooped to thrust her hands into it. "Where is she going to sleep? Reverend Samples is willing to put her up."

Marilee said, "I'll stay with my horse."

"When it's close to men, night guards, *anybody?*"

Rising, Joe said, "There's blankets, Marilee. You can stay by the wagon or at the corral."

Slamming a tin plate, Elizabeth said, "I'll have you remember this is *my* wagon, Mr. Langston."

"I ain't forgetting that," Joe said, unlashing his bedroll, and to Marilee: "Show you where to bunk down, where to put the stallion."

"And come right back," Elizabeth said. "I'm sure she can find plenty of friends without you."

"Elizabeth," Joe said slowly, "just shut the hell up."

At the temporary rope corral, he helped Marilee stake Bradburn out to graze and spread his blankets for her beneath a mesquite bush, all in silence.

Marilee said, "I'm sorry."

"Don't be. Woman acts like she's got me branded and ear-cropped, and it's not like that—never was."

"She acts as if she's in love with you."

"Or with the idea of getting married. She ought to be married, but not to me. Well, looks like you and me will eat here in the mornin'. Right now, I'm going back for more blankets, then bed down with Rosario. Marilee—"

"Yes?"

"Oh, hell—nothing, I guess."

She rolled in blankets after he was gone, blankets smelling of him, of tobacco and dust, too. Head pillowed on her hide saddle, she listened to Bradburn grazing, to other horses moving, softly snorting. A hint of paleness against far stars told that the moon would soon rise, a Comanche moon, big and glowing to give its light for fierce, proud men to ride by. It took Marilee a long time to find sleep.

Up before full dawn, she collected twigs and was given fire by a Mexican woman to start them blazing. Joe brought a pot soon after, and they breakfasted upon buffalo stew as several men found excuses to wander by and look sideways at them.

"You can ride with Rosario," he said. "I'm due to hunt some today. There's another scout—"

Another man slouched up, a man stooped and worn as his buckskins. "Yeah, that'd be me, Charley Longstreet."

"How do you do," Marilee said.

"Howdy. Joe, that preacher man's callin' hisself a meetin' got to do with you and this woman here."

"And Elizabeth Hartley," Joe said.

"Reckon so. You want to walk over yonder?"

Voice quiet, Joe said, "You standin' with me, Charley?"

The man scratched at his beard. "Anywheres else, but these is white folks we signed on to take care of."

"She's white, too."

"Hard to tell, after years with them damned Comanch'."

Marilee started to say something, but Joe quieted her with a motion of his hand as he came to his feet. "Then don't stand against me, Charley."

Shaking his head, Longstreet said, "Got my own notions, but that don't make me a fool."

Watching him adjust the holster on his hip, Marilee said to Joe, "Don't you be foolish, either. They don't want a squaw woman corrupting their children and seducing their men, so I'll just go. If those fine, upstanding church people will be charitable with blankets and water and a few provisions, I'll leave."

Harshly, he said, "And go where? That's big, mean country out there. You wait right here, and I'll settle this."

"No," she said. "I'm coming with you."

He walked swiftly, long legs scissoring so that she almost had to trot to keep up. Stopping in front of Samples, before the half-circle of men and women, Marilee felt the tension aimed at Joe, the hate directed at her. Carbine cradled in her arms, Colt thrust into her leggings, she waited.

Joe said, "Well?"

Lifting a bony forefinger, Samples jabbed it at air. "We have taken a vote and arrived at a compromise. Most of these good people desire—" the finger made a circle and pointed at Marilee—"this unrepentant woman, this Jezebel of the plains, to be abandoned by the wagon train and left to her deserved fate. The decision is just, for surely she can rejoin her Comanche friends."

There was a mutter of approval from the crowd, smirks upon women's faces, shame on one or two men's, and the Mexicans stood off to the side, separating themselves, or perhaps always apart.

Wagging his head, clasping his hands before him now, Samples went on. "The Texans among us brought up a practical point, one quite apart from morals—and that is, the Comanches may attack in order to get their concubine back. Therefore, her presence among decent, God-fearing folk puts us all in danger."

Marilee saw Elizabeth standing erect and still, her face pale, her hair brushed and drawn back.

"But—" Samples raised both hands to the sky—"we have been shown the way of charity, the path of mercy by our sister, one who has been led astray, but who still finds it in her heart to forgive."

Marilee noticed that Joe slid one foot forward, that his hands hung at his sides. She looked over at Elizabeth again, and the woman's brown eyes were knife points.

Gathering breath, Samples loosed his ultimatum at Joe. "Seducer, betrayer of maidens, you have been given a golden chance to set things aright. When you have been joined in holy wedlock with Sister Hartley, that slut of savages will be allowed to remain until we reach the next army outpost."

Hands tight upon her carbine, Marilee went taut inside, too. Before Joe could answer, she took a stride toward the preacher, and saw men shift rifles, put their hands upon pistol butts. She said, "You mealy-mouthed hypocrite— you whining, bluebelly trash. Who the hell are *you* to pass judgment on your betters? Little factory slaves, little dirt grubbers, you call the Comanches savages? They were kings when your miserable ancestors were cracking lice in debtors' prisons. And if my husband—yes, I said my *husband*—Little Buffalo, didn't respect me, you'd all be dead right now, your hair hanging bloody on the lances of better men."

Marilee spat at the ground in The People's gesture of contempt. "Slut, am I? A fallen woman, a concubine? I am Nadevah, the Moon Woman, respected and honored by all Comanches, feared by the Apaches. Stay with this wagon train, crawl to vermin like you—no! I will ride away, and perhaps see you turning slowly upon a spit as you beg for death!"

Whirling blindly, she heard a man snarl. "Threatenin' us, bigod! Means to call down the Comanch' on us."

And Joe's voice, cold and even: "Hold right still, Norton."

Marilee kept herself from running, held back tears of anger and sickness as she found Bradburn and put her saddle on him. Cinching the rawhide fighting strip behind his shoulders, she snapped around when someone came close.

"Señorita," Rosario Lopez said, "here is food and water, ammunition for your guns. The blankets are thin, but no thinner than my courage, or I would ride with you. *Magnifico*, señorita—go with God."

"T-thank you," she murmured, and lashed the sacks behind her saddle, the water canteen around her waist by a thong. Her hands were shaking and she didn't want him to see that.

Legging Bradburn, she loped him away from the corral, pounding past the wagons without glancing at them, putting her face away from the sun. Damn them, *damn* them! Making her out a whore, but absolving Elizabeth of any blame, any sin that couldn't be righted when Joe Langston married the woman. So smug and righteous, certain of their purity, every tight-faced woman among them positive she would protect her white Christian honor by suicide before allowing any savage to touch her.

As if they would; as if they *could* before lusting braves spread them for ravishing. Liars, liars!

Wind whipped at her tears, the fresh wind of morning cool in her hair and singing lonely in her ears. Why had she run from Piava—for this? Were these her own kind— Samples and his posturing, Elizabeth and her desperate, frightened jealousy? The Comanches named her Moon Woman, the whites named her bitch, and now she belonged with neither race.

Stretching out, eager for the running, Bradburn moved strongly beneath her, Marilee's only friend and her only hope. Back there, even though he'd acted as if he meant to protect her, to stand up for his rights, too, Joe Langston had been—just Joe Langston. As always, he had taken the easy way out, making the decision better for himself. Nothing else, no one else in the whole damned world meant more to him than his own precious neck, his own narrow, unimaginative dreams of the tomorrow he couldn't see beyond.

She rode fast, angrily brushing away tears and gauging her direction. Rosario had brought her supplies, but not

Joe. Right this minute he was standing humbled back there, saying "I do" to an imitation marriage ceremony, with his neat, tidy bride holding to his hand. The seducer would be washed clean, and Elizabeth would somehow have her virtue restored.

Slowing Bradburn, Marilee fought to clear her mind. She was going to need all her senses sharp and alert, if she meant to get through this unforgiving land. There were still Apaches about, and maybe she would now be a prime target for any raiding band of Comanches, a happy surprise for lawless *comancheros,* those bandits who traded guns and whiskey to The People.

And there was the land itself, waterless for long, wearying miles, then lying in wait with alkali-poisoned springs for unwary thirsts. Heat and dust storms; puma and bear sniffing for Bradburn's blood, and if the buffalo were gone north or hunted to near extinction. . . .

"We can do it, Bradburn," she said, "find game where *they'd* starve, uncover water when *their* tongues are swollen black. We've learned from the best, so all we have to do is be very careful. It doesn't matter to us that w-we're alone, because that's how we started, and now we'll find our place, by ourselves. We don't need *them*—thankfully we don't need them."

Roughly paralleling the wagon route but moving much faster than plodding mules, she rode west. They didn't own the land. Pulling up in a protective dip in the ground to adjust sacks behind the saddle, she took a sip of what could be precious water. Bradburn sucked some from her cupped hands and lifted his head, signaled with his ears.

Something was near. She whispered to him to stand, *stand,* and bellied down to snake up a little slope, Spencer steady in her hands. If one of those holy Yankees, one of those bitter *tejanos* was following her, he'd soon wish he hadn't.

A horse and rider showed black against the sand, loping easily, growing larger in her sights as Marilee curled a finger delicately upon the trigger. She was no coldly logical Joe Langston, to shoot a horse from under a man: there'd be time to cut down the man before he could reach shelter. She would rather shoot the man and let the horse run free.

The man stopped his horse. He took off his hat and waved it; sunlight probed hair black and shiny as a crow's wing.

"Marilee!" Joe called. "I know you're playin' possum out there—I can see where you started walking your horse. *Marilee!*"

She stood up so he could see her, and her knees were trembling.

Chapter 32

She would have chosen the place herself—an L-shaped gully where a small fire could be built without being seen for any distance. It had a tiny spring and bunch grass for the horses and would be difficult for Indians to come at, except from the front. When Joe stretched his lariat across the narrow mouth, boxing the horses in, they were snug as anyone could reasonably be in this hostile country.

Twilight was drawing a misted cloak across the hills when Marilee sizzled bacon and made fragrant cornbread. Joe cared for the horses and pushed a little blackened pot into the coals, so bubbling coffee odors mingled with the rest. She glanced at him as he sat back with his plate and spoon, firelight flickering across his face and hair.

When he had ridden up to her that morning, Joe hadn't said much, except that it had taken him a while to get together supplies. "The preacher was put out when I quit," he said, walking his mare next to Bradburn, "and for a spell I thought I'd have to drop somebody or other. But Charley Longstreet made 'em see they at least owed me provisions for taking the train far as it got."

"So you didn't marry her?" Marilee asked.

"You expect me to? *If* this old boy ever gets wedded,

it's going to be my own choosin', not because somebody else says so." Joe had jogged his mare then, and said, "Come on, I'd just as soon make those foothills before dark."

Now they were here, and there was so much hanging unspoken between them. She was glad not to be alone, glad for his presence in the night. But Marilee also felt tension building and tried to ignore it. When they were done eating, she scoured the tinware with sand and put it aside to sit and drink the last of bitter coffee. Bradburn snorted the mare and she warned him off with a fretful whinny.

"Joe, where do you mean to head, California still?"

"Good as any," he said. "Can't tell, though—I might come across something along the way."

She emptied her cup and looked into it. "I'm sorry you had to leave the wagons because of me. I never thought they'd hate me so, for something I couldn't help."

Lifting his cup, he said, "Maybe you was remindin' them what could happen to them, when they was all the time pretending it wouldn't. You looking so damned Indian didn't make it any better."

"But I *couldn't* beg their forgiveness for a sin I didn't commit."

"I can see that. But folks look at you and see Comanche crawlin' over your body."

"*One* Comanche," she said sharply, "just one."

"Then you're luckier'n most women they take, and just one Indian is too many—like one black buck is more than a bellyful. Funny thing—half that bunch are Yankees, but they tote just as much spite against blacks and browns as Rebs do. Listen to 'em during the war, and you'd think all they had in mind was everlasting good for all poor colored folks."

The fire was burning low and a suggestion of desert chill began to creep into the gully. Marilee said, "I was a slave, beaten and despised and used any way they wanted; if I hadn't been the chief's wife, I'd be dead. I know what slavery is now, and I'm beginning to see what it's like for other freed slaves. Nobody's going to give us anything or take us to their bosoms. Things got better for me, because I went crazy one day and fought the people torturing me. Since they were Comanches, and Comanches respect courage more than anything else, I became one with them, on the same level as my masters. Blacks could never rebel like that and be accepted by whites, and maybe they never will."

Joe put his hands behind his head and stretched long legs. "You have your own troubles, Marilee. Blacks and Comanches don't count in 'em."

She looked steadily at him. "Didn't Piava count with you? You wanted to kill him, even though he was unarmed and afoot, but why? Because he was an Indian, or because you sensed he was my lover, a white woman's lover?"

Sitting forward, he felt in his pocket for a thin cigar, lighted it from a glowing ember that threw the angularities of his face into sharp relief and pointed up the permanent cynicism of his thinly scarred mouth. "You said there was one more comin', so you must have wanted him shot. Else we could have ridden on off without ever seeing the big chief. You ever think *why* you told on him? Maybe Miss Bradburn needed to get even but lost her nerve."

"It wasn't like that," she said. "If I hadn't put Little Buffalo into a position where he understood I didn't—didn't love him, and give him back some shred of dignity with the spotted mare, he would have kept following me until he dropped—or he *had* to be killed. I just didn't want that. In his way, Piava was good to me."

Joe's even teeth glinted around his cigar. "That so? Like you were good to the Santee boy, and any others you could get to?"

"That's a—a hell of a thing to say! Timmy was the only man I ever gave myself to freely and of my own accord, and you know damned well *why*, but you're just too muley-headed to admit it. Yes, I guess I could have fought Piava when he brought me into his tepee, but it wouldn't have accomplished anything. I'd only have gotten hurt, and he would have taken me anyway. It was my *life*—can't you see that?"

Taking the cigar from his mouth and staring thoughtfully at its red tip, Joe said, "Reckon you couldn't lose what you didn't have, so it didn't count all that much. You wasn't—weren't—a virgin with the Santee boy."

Marilee came to her feet, drawn tight as a bowstring. "No, I wasn't a virgin, but that didn't make me fair game for a rapist, either. How dare you judge me? You're as bad as—as those hypocrites with the wagons. Tell me, Saint Joseph, were *you* a virgin when you held me down and forced me? I'd say I was only one of the women you raped."

Joe bit down on the cigar again. "You liked it."

"So did you, but *I* had no choice. All that counted was what *you* wanted. Is that how it was with Miss Neat-and-Tidy Elizabeth? Did you throw her down and pin her arms over her head because you're bigger and stronger?"

Hunching forward and looking into the guttering fire, he said, "No, and she never had a man afore."

"That's *before*—your new education is slipping. So if she was all that pure and virginal, and just what a man demands in a woman, why didn't you go ahead and marry her?"

Joe threw his cigar into the fire. "Because I never asked her nor any woman, because I can't be a storekeeper or run a bank or strut like a goddamned plantation owner the way you women want. And because I just ain't about to be pushed. *Ain't,* damn it! Elizabeth had to keep peckin' at how I talk and I took it because there's so much to know in books and she could show me. And you might as well admit that a man bein' a virgin and a woman bein' one—well, that's two different things. *Everybody* knows that. And hell, no, I never raped a woman afore—never had to. You were naked and shiny and just fresh from lyin' with that boy—"

As his voice trailed off, Marilee said, "So you thought that gave you a right to my body, too."

"I told you how it was. I didn't ride back that day just for you. I got to feelin' bad about the boy."

"Big, hard, all-for-himself Joe Langston showing human mercy and kindness? I find that difficult to believe."

Swinging up to one knee, he glared at her across the dying fire. Off across the hills an owl hooted. "I could have let the Comanche chew you up and spit you out—wasn't no skin off *my* backside."

"You didn't know it was me."

"Saw that hair and knew it wasn't a damned Indian. And when you got close—I never could forget your hair. I never—hell, woman! How come you always twist me around and make me mad? They teach you tricks like that back on your fancy plantation, like you learned how to tempt and devil a man—or is that born into your kind of woman?"

"My kind of woman? What's that—the same thing the preacher and your—your *fiancée* meant?"

Joe's hand fisted. "A man just can't talk to you decent."

"A gentleman can," she said.

Cat-graceful, cat-quick, he was around the fire with his hands on her shoulders, his dark eyes furious and close, so very close. "All right, then," he breathed. "Maybe a gentleman wouldn't claim his debt, but I never pretended to be more than I am. So I'm tellin' you that you owe me, Marilee Bradburn. Like you told that Comanche, you owe me your life."

She didn't resist when his hands slipped down to her waist, when she was lifted so that her breasts came against his broad chest, so her lips came against his mouth. Joe's breath fanned the embers of her feelings into leaping flame, shot sparks throughout her flesh and sent them spiraling inside her head.

Stars were swinging dizzily overhead when he laid her back upon the blankets, when his hands roamed her flesh, insistent but strangely gentle. Marilee closed her eyes as he stripped away her dress and held them shut as she felt his throbbing hardness pressed against her belly. She was limp and flexible for him, holding the core of herself from him until he kissed her again, until his tongue went dancing across her own, all honeyed and man-strong, man-demanding.

Then her teeth clashed his, and her hands came up, her arms twined around his neck, holding him to her as her body arched to greet him, welcome him exultantly into its seething depths. She couldn't hold back the wind or bring down the sun, and she couldn't keep any of herself from him. Coiling and meeting his thrusts, she was *powerful* as he could be, *hungry* as he could be; reaching and finding, retreating slowly only to attack once more with fierceness, she rocked Joe Langston and rocked herself. She shook the very mountains, and the world quivered in echo.

A rainbow swelled brilliantly within her body, curve after ecstatic curving of geysering colors; music trilled over her straining flesh and sank into her pores to crescendo in her brain. A great white flower unfolded satin petals and trembled proudly in its exquisite beauty.

Marilee cried out, and the ringing call dropped to a whimper, then to a very soft sob that caught in her throat because its roots were still held fast in her heart.

Ticking eons matched the slowing of her breath, and eternity paused to admire the rising of a special silvered moon. But time gathered itself and rushed on, the moment his weight was no longer upon her, and Marilee locked her teeth against a final moan. When she could lift to an elbow, she saw him wrapped in a blanket, his back to her.

"Joe," she whispered. "Joe?"

Without looking around he said, "I've been learning from books, while you were gettin' educated by a Comanche. No wonder he didn't want to turn you loose."

Through the sudden pain, the deep and unfair hurt, she said, "You bastard," and rolled into her blankets. She heard him move a little way into the rocks, the faint clink of his rifle. She tried to will sleep, to beg blackness, but it didn't work for a long time.

In the morning there was silence and chores awkward for her, another small fire, and food eaten because she had learned never to waste it. Only Bradburn was real and not brittle, his hide warming against chill that only clean, hot sun could burn away. She curried him, looked at his feet, dressed out his mane and tail with a fishbone comb.

"If you're through messing with that stallion, we best be movin'," Joe said.

She saddled the horse and bridled him, reluctant to speak. "Yes—I saw the smoke, too."

"Something burnin' pretty good, but I don't figure it's the train—too far south."

"It wouldn't be the wagons—he gave his word."

Joe moved out his mare. "Maybe the others didn't hear him. You can trust the Comanches, but I sure as hell don't."

Marilee shut up. He didn't trust anyone or anything, probably not even himself, but she refused to feel sorry for him. Joe Langston's walled-in kind of loneliness was something he brought upon himself, a voluntary condition. And he was welcome to it, to all the bitterness of suspicion and doubt.

When the sun was high, he found a water sinkhole and dismounted to test it with a fingertip before allowing the horses to drink. She sat in the lacy shade of a stunted bush and chewed buffalo jerky, feeling sun on her skin and drawing in air spiced with sage. Heat waves rippled upon sand, wavering and uncertain as her own future.

Back against a rock, long gun across his knees, Joe said, "You still mean to get together a horse herd? Way the army's fritterin' away mounts and never catching up to Indians, it might not be a bad idea. Trouble is, it'll take some time to round up mustang mares, breed 'em, and get the foals weaned. Then, not many folks will buy them until they're ridin' size."

Marilee drank a little water, then got up to use her skinning knife on cactus, carefully stripping away spines and outer covering so the horses could munch soft fiber. She felt his eyes upon her and said, "You don't have to make conversation—I don't care what you think. Go ahead and practice your reading—I saw the books she stuffed into your saddlebags."

"Gave 'em to me before," he said. "And there's only a few words in them I don't know—what I'm after is the ideas."

Biting her lips against a mocking answer, Marilee continued to work so Bradburn and the mare could hold their strength. When they'd had enough, she kicked sand over fire embers and climbed on her horse. When he'd left the wagon train to join her, she'd formed an image of Joe helping her, of them working together to gather mustangs and corral them. She knew how to make a tepee that would shield them against winter, if he brought her buffalo skins, and in the summer Bradburn's foals would be on the ground, showing his bloodlines. They could have gathered brush and smoked meat and searched out a salt lick; they might have started a ranch in some grassy, protected valley.

And someday, when others had seen Bradburn's colts and fillies, a house and barns could be built, seed put in, hay harvested. After that, however long it might take, Bradburn Plantation—a triumphal return to the heritage of that rich and dignified land.

Last night had killed most of that dream, for Joe Langston wasn't part of it now. It would take her longer to accomplish her purpose without his help and the protection of his guns, but she would reach her goal anyhow. Marilee Bradburn hadn't come this far and suffered so much to let one man's stupidity put her off.

She rode behind him the rest of the day, alert because the habits of The People were strong within her, knowing they could be open targets for any skulking Apache. Grudgingly, she gave Joe credit for knowing what he was about, for taking advantage of cover and scanning the land thoroughly. But what should she expect of a cunning animal whose only thought was survival, who never reached beyond a full belly and a warm female? Wolves were sly, too; so were coyotes.

Before dusk, they made camp on a little hilltop, waiting until dark so smoke from their rock-shielded fire wouldn't be seen. The water hole was small and muddy, and there had been horse sign around it, so after watering their own horses, they'd moved them up to the mesa and staked them out.

Over cornmeal mush and bacon, Joe said, "We're closin' up on Fort Stockton, I reckon—maybe a week more, without trouble. Have to get some fresh meat before then, and I don't like the Apache sign around here."

She said, "For a while I was glad you came after me —I thought it was *because* of me. Now I know it was just an excuse to get away from the wagons and that woman. So don't worry about me—you can leave me at Fort Stockton and I'll go on by myself."

"If you want," he said, and moved off, placing his guns at hand and lying blanketed next to the fire.

She spent more time hating him and the pull he had upon her, fretting under chilled stars as she listened to the horses grazing, listened for other warning sounds that might mean Apaches. It was late when she saw Joe stir awake and prowl noiselessly around the small mesa. Marilee went to sleep then.

Right after breakfast, Bradburn pulled his picket rope and mounted the barb mare. "Damn," Joe said. "She came in heat that quick, and he didn't waste any time. If I hadn't brought her up from Mexico, I'd swear that mare came off a Southern plantation."

"Not a hard dirt farm," Marilee said, "or she'd be in season *all* the time."

"Fits 'em both, I expect. Us, too."

"No," Marilee said, "no, no," but she was denying the racing of her blood brought on by the stallion's powerful thrusting, the way he held the mare's neck firmly in his teeth while his muscled hindquarters bunched and drove upward. And when Joe Langston touched her, she turned on him violently, fighting him and herself.

He didn't let her go, and her struggles changed to a frenzied attack, for she would not remain passive and simply allow him to use her body. Hard and furious, their coupling was done with in minutes, without tenderness or kisses, and she despised him for feeling so proud of himself.

As he climbed back to his feet, she cut at him, "Comanches do it better."

Chapter 33

Blood will tell, Joe remembered her saying; bloodlines always come out, either in men or horses. So what the hell did that make Marilee Bradburn, because she was sure a mess that her own daddy wouldn't claim now.

Gentry, she was—acting like a princess who mislaid her castle and so damned sure she'd find it again. But being a squaw so long had done something to her, too; she could outsnake an Indian when she had to. Look what she'd done to those two *comancheros* who tried to slip up on the horses. Didn't squall and throw fainting fits like a *lady*—just shot one and hightailed it after the other until he left his horse and took to the rocks.

"What are we going to do with two more horses?" he'd asked, and she had said, "They're mares for Bradburn to cross on, and that *comanchero* can just shank's-mare it back to wherever he came from."

She'd have lifted the man's hair, if Joe hadn't called her off. Went yelling after the breed with a Colt in one hand and skinning knife in the other; scared hell out of the *comanchero*, who figured he'd stumbled onto some poison-mean brave, instead of a helpless woman.

312

That wasn't the way gentry acted. Maybe she was a good part siren, one of those women who lay back on the rocks and sang to drive men crazy, like in that book about Ulysses. There was a kind of music to her, all right, something you didn't have to listen for to hear; you just *felt* it. She moved like singing, except when he got hold of her in the blankets; then she turned into wild Indian drums. And he always had the feeling that if she didn't need him to help her, Marilee Comanche Bradburn would just as soon put that knife into him as not.

Lady of the big white house, hip-swaying siren trying to keep a man from the golden fleece, hard-riding Comanche, she was even more—she was about half mule, stubborn and ornery and waiting any chance to kick. She'd put a hoof into his belly with that thing about Comanches doing it better, kicked him so damned hard and low down it took him a spell to get over it.

But he could no more stay away from her than he could stop breathing. She had some kind of spell on him, something that got deep in his blood and wouldn't wash out. So after they had passed on through Fort Clark—what was left of it—he had bedded her again, taking a long time about it, holding her when she fought, turning her loose to bite and claw him when she got in her short rows. He showed her he was as much stud as any damned Comanche, as much stallion as that horse she cared for more than a man.

Marilee was a woman on fire at those moments, even though she laid her groin into him as if she were trying to tear him off at the roots, hating him while she was doing it back to him.

But when there was Apache trouble, when they had to hole up all day long beneath a sun that baked the juice from their bones and near about fried the tops of their heads, she had as much iron in her as any man—more than some. Never a whimper out of her.

A lot of men would have been real down at the mouth when they rode up to Fort Stockton and saw the gates standing open, when no sentry challenged them. It was spooky inside those old walls, so quiet Joe could hear the beat of his pulse, and his nose flared at burned stink still clinging to the corners.

"Apaches," she said. "Nobody's left."

He'd nodded and got down to make sure, stepping over bodies flattened out and dried inside their uniforms, prowling barracks and storerooms where the fire hadn't reached. Stalking carefully, Spencer in hand, all he found was more bodies, so butchered up and burned he could just barely tell they had been white.

Marilee didn't get sick or go pale. When he was certain no Apache was lurking in the fort, she went with him to see what they could salvage. There wasn't much left, for the Apaches had torn up whatever they didn't carry off. But she found breeches to fit her, and a couple of shirts, an officer's coat with dried blood and a hole in it, a battered cavalry hat.

He was the one who came upon the payroll. Some smart officer had dropped it down an outhouse hole tied to a string, and if Joe hadn't had to go right then, he'd never have found it. But there it was in a canvas bag—two thousand dollars in shiny U.S. gold pieces, pretty as anything in the world, prettier than a French countess and her jewels.

Out in the quadrangle, he found her shaking off dried peas and pouring them into a sack. She said, "There's rice, too. The Apaches didn't know what it was. And they left some rope in the stables."

"Threw bodies down the well," he said, "so the water's no good. But they missed this—look."

She didn't jump up and hug him, didn't seem to know what the gold meant. Marilee kept blowing off peas and adding them to the sack. She said, "So you got lucky at last."

And he said, "It's as much yours as mine," but she didn't get excited about that either. The woman had the damnedest way of making him feel like nothing he did counted for much. So he put the gold in his saddlebag and when she was done filling her own sacks, they rode out of the fort and kept going west.

It didn't really get dry for another two weeks, but Marilee could smell out water better than most horses, and found feed to keep the stock going. She fed him roots he'd never seen cooked up and a kind of paste made from cactus, to go with the deer and antelope he dropped. Her snares produced rabbits and quail; she knew which berries were good and which could cramp a belly. He was

314

hard put to show his own skills, but figured he kept about even.

Some nights when she was so quiet and sulky, he kept to his own blankets, even though it was a lot colder out, with mornings bringing frost. Some nights, he just had to go to her, the sap in him was so strong, the juices she raised by the tilt of her head or the swing of her slim legs. Marilee quit fighting him outright, but did another kind of battle under the blankets, never letting him master her and leaving her marks on his hide. It was like bedding down with a she-bobcat, but he kept going back for more.

They talked some when she wasn't pulled into a hard shell like a terrapin or didn't have her quills out like a porcupine. Then he tried to make her see the South wouldn't *ever* be rebuilt; if it got out from under the Yankees and rose from its ashes, nothing could be like it was before.

It would, she insisted, it most surely would. The land couldn't be killed, and Southern aristocracy would come again into its own. Bradburn Plantation would be hers again.

"Aristocracy," he said. "Hell, I knew some royal folks in Mexico, people with sure-enough titles, and they weren't better than anybody else. Maximilian didn't know which end was up, and in his court everybody was out for all they could get. Except for one, maybe."

"A woman," she said.

"A *comtesse*," he said. "You're so ready to think ladies and gentlemen have some kind of special right, you'd have kissed her hand."

"And you did," she said, "among other places."

"Hell," he said, realizing he couldn't talk sense to her.

They talked to each other, though, because there wasn't anybody else. There wasn't much chance in the daytime, what with keeping a sharp eye out for Indians and *comancheros*, and the time taken up with hunting, so they had to keep talking at night. Sometimes they talked about the books he had read and about others he'd never heard of. And he wanted to know how she knew so much.

"Because my father and brothers raised me like one of them," she said. "They figured a woman had the same rights as a man to ride and hunt and read. Mama—my mother was always puzzled by us."

"My folks weren't puzzled by anything," Joe said. "They knew their place and stayed in it, never wonderin' how it was some had so much and them so little. We were slaves just as much as any black, slaves to that sour, hard land the Paisleys didn't want."

"Paisleys?" she asked, and Joe found himself telling her about the crabbed old man and his squint-eyed overseer, and somehow Susanna got into it.

Marilee said then, "So that's the reason you hate planters so much—because of one woman. She hurt you worse than the whipping did. But Joe, Susanna was only *one*—"

He'd said too damned much and knew it. "Was she? How many other fine ladies used black studs for their pleasure, how many more Susannas made promises to redneck boys they knew wouldn't be kept?"

"Did she actually make you any promises, Joe?"

"She—she—" He turned his face from Marilee and rummaged in a pocket for a cigar stub he'd been saving. He wasn't looking for pity, and he hadn't meant to run off at the mouth about his whip scars. It was like opening the scars again, and he resented Marilee for probing his wounds. It was the last he said about it.

It was better when he talked about Mexico, telling her of the bewildered emperor so proud he wouldn't shave his beard and get away, so stupid that he stayed to die.

"Max depended on that other emperor to save him," he said, "that Napoleon. Bein' one himself, he didn't know that *no* aristocrat could be trusted. Why, his wife was wild-eyed as a turpentined cat, and all his generals ready to sell him out."

"And you got out safely," Marilee said. "Did your royal countess help?"

"Some," he admitted, and because she looked so good there by the little fire, her hair shining and her slanty eyes so green and deep, Joe kept talking so he wouldn't start something by reaching for her.

Frowning, he wondered why she laughed so hard about him losing the jewels and gold to that bunch of Juaristas so close to home. No matter what he said, it seemed as if Marilee took delight in poking holes in it. He couldn't make her see that today was good enough, that nobody got a safe conduct pass for tomorrow, so there wasn't much use laying plans for a long time off. A bullet, an arrow, a horse stumbling in a gopher hole—and it was all over.

"You've lived too long in wars," she said. "You've been fighting all your life, and you don't know there's anything else. There's peace and goodness and the rich life."

"For some," he grunted. "For some that picked out the right mama and papa."

They had one running brush with a mangy band of Apaches on the flatlands this side of El Paso del Norte, but the Indians peeled off when they saw their carbines couldn't reach out like Joe's buffalo gun. They just about ran out of water once and the horses suffered until they lucked up on a wet hole in a rocky creek bed. They fought the land and the long, grinding trail, and fought each other until Joe could have hollered out loud when he saw the adobe houses bunched up beside the Rio Grande.

"Here's where that Fort Stockton payroll comes in handy," he said. "We'll put up awhile here, fatten the horses, buy some mules and a wagon, whatever else we need. Rations and plenty of water barrels, some white man's food—beef, maybe even potatoes."

By then Marilee was out of her squaw dress and into a dusty getup that made her look like a skinny discharged soldier, all that fine hair rolled up under her campaign hat. If he didn't know better, Joe would have had trouble telling she wasn't a boy, and it was better like that. El Paso del Norte was no place for a woman by herself; he could see that right off.

The town was all spread out, squatting on the bank of the muddy river, which was not much more than a trickle. Across it Joe could make out Mexican lancers in polished helmets and fancy uniforms, which went to show the Juaristas hadn't learned a thing after they whipped the French. Mud houses over there were about the same as on this side of the border, maybe poorer, but there were as many sombreros here as flop hats, as many Mexicans as *tejanos*, and it was hard telling them apart.

Feeling strange riding into a town after so long in the open, Joe got edgy and kept his stirrup close to Marilee's. Ornery as she was, she still ought to be glad he was with her going down this swirling, noisy, and sun-baked street. Buffalo hunters, greasy and whiskey-eyed, stared at her horse and the pair of mustangs she led; swaggering Mexican *pistoleros* with low-tied guns and big silver spurs looked after and whispered to each other; a bedraggled and toothless Apache with whiskey-shaken hands drew a ragged blanket about himself and peered at Bradburn with dull eyes, remembering better days.

Smoke wafted over the town, and rank smells reached out of alleys; men whooped in a saloon, and a buckboard clattered slowly through a crowd gathered to watch a fist fight. Wagons were everywhere, some yoked behind lumbering oxen, some drivers cursing cantankerous mules and cracking long whips.

Joe saw a livery stable and a cantina close by. He said, "Good enough place, I reckon. Cantina's got rooms over it, and we can get bath water there after we eat. Put up the horses and then—look out, El Paso. Ol' Joe Langston's got gold in his pocket, a flat belly, and a mighty thirst."

Marilee was strangely quiet, he thought, either overwhelmed by the bustle and noise of the town or going into one of her sulks again. But he felt too good to care much, and he whistled as he unsaddled the mare and hung saddlebags over one shoulder—bags heavy with gold. Marilee went about caring for the stallion, seeing him stabled and rubbed down and grained while Joe fidgeted. Then the mustang mares had to be seen to. At last, she came traipsing after him, with her baggy breeches and dusty coat, old blue hat hiding her hair.

A gold piece got them a bottle of tequila, a steaming meal, and a tub of hot water waiting in a room upstairs. He was feeling pretty good and he told her to use the water first, as he lay back on a civilized bed and kicked off his boots. The tequila was fiery enough to match his mood, and he watched her slim body glistening with soap bubbles, eyed the shapings of it so well known to him and yet always such a mystery.

One hell of a woman, he thought; slick and beautiful, with heat to her. All she was missing was good sense, and in time he might be able to get that into her head. By the time they got clear to California, Marilee Bradburn ought to be tamed down and easier to get along with.

When he swung off the bed, she was drying herself, and Joe went over to put his hands on that trim little waist.

She said, "The water will get cold, and you look better with that beard scraped off."

He laughed and patted her bottom. "Guess I can wait a spell. Tell you what, missy. Take half that gold out of the saddlebags and go see about buyin' us a wagon and mules and all that goes with 'em."

Shining hair damp and long down her naked back, hips swinging in that special, beckoning motion, Marilee went to the saddlebags on the table. He was undressing when she said without turning, "You're presuming I'll go on to California with you."

Taking a long, burning swallow of tequila, Joe grinned and said, "Sure. What the hell else *can* you do? Hang around El Paso and get put to work in a crib house? Make you a lot of money that way, I reckon—the Mexicans ought to go crazy about your hair. But you wouldn't ever get any farther—no big horse herd, no goin' back to Mississippi and starting another big white house. Women that make a livin' on their backs find it's easy work, and even though they talk a lot about doing somethin' else, they never do."

"You'd know about them," she said, beating dust from her clothes before putting them on.

Joe eased into the tub of water, folding himself nearly double to fit. "Get yourself some new clothes, too. You look like a skinny boy in those things. Get some dresses, fancy ones, so I can show off my woman."

"Oh," she said quietly, "am I your woman now?"

Splashing water, soaping himself, and reaching now and then for the bottle, Joe said, "Hell, yes, and I don't mind claimin' you, once you're cleaned up and *look* like a woman. Go on, now, and line up that wagon and stock —best take your guns, too. Wouldn't do for some *bandido* to know you're carrying gold."

Marilee hesitated, and for a second he thought she was going to get stubborn and give him an argument, but she just counted out gold coins and put them into her sack.

"If you take too long, you won't get any loving," he said, "because I'm liable to be in a poker game downstairs." Pouring rinse water over his head from a bucket, he was snorting and only halfway saw her pause in the doorway. When he blinked again, she was gone.

Whistling, he lathered his face and used a straight razor

on it. The cracked mirror over the washstand told him Marilee was right; he looked a whole lot better without the beard, but kind of pale below his cheekbones. Leaving the Sharps and carbine beneath the feather mattress, he shouldered the saddlebags again and checked the Colt's cylinder.

The cheerful Mexican who sold him new clothes was glad to get rid of the old ones for him. Heeled and curlicued boots were worth all of ten dollars, and the big hat was a good one with conchos on its band; expansively, Joe bought two more shirts and some extra breeches —even some underwear. A fringed leather jacket and bandanna, and Joe thought he looked pretty much like a dude; only the age-softened gunbelt and the worn butt of the Colt might make other men think differently.

She wasn't in their room when he put his purchases on the bed, but he hadn't really expected Marilee back so soon. It took time to find decent mules and a good wagon; if she paid attention to what he'd said, she was also laying claim to provisions enough to last them clear to the ocean.

Only two men were fiddling with cards at a table in the far corner of the cantina—one of them a grinning little Mexican, the other a somber *gringo* with a fishbelly face and watery eyes.

The Mexican was polite and careful with his guarded silver pesos; the sick-looking man played as if he didn't mind losing, and that one Joe kept an eye on. He bought cigarillos and another bottle, the tequila taste mingling nicely with salt and tobacco smoke, and passed a pleasant hour or two. Joe was about four dollars behind when he got to wondering about Marilee and what she was doing.

He said to the Mexican, "How long does it take a woman to buy pretty clothes?"

Teeth flashed as the man answered. "To speak of women and clocks in the same breath is to make a puzzle, señor. It is one no man has yet been able to unravel."

The other man said, "I don't *sabe* much Spanish, but I heard you both say woman. You mean that gaunted youngun' that came in with you, mister?"

"Wait'll you see her in a dress." Joe said. "Come to think on it, I never have either." That was pretty funny, and he laughed while pouring drinks around. But when she didn't come into the cantina after a while longer,

Joe got up and left the table to go looking for her. He stopped at the bar to drop a bit of silver down the ample bosom of the serving girl, a pretty, round little *chica* with sparkling black eyes and a promising wiggle to her. Her *gracias, caballero* followed him out into the street.

Joe looked into a shop where a woman with eyeglasses and a sagging neck told him no, she hadn't seen any girl dressed like a man. Two storekeepers didn't remember her, either, so Joe went on down to the livery stable. She must be in there, he thought, still messing around with that stud horse.

The stableman had a twisted leg and a disposition to match. "Yeah, I recall the young fella—trooper one time, by the look of him."

"Well," Joe said, "did she—he—come back here? I don't see that big stud in the stall."

The man grunted. "Reckon you see pretty good. Stud's gone, all right, and the mustangs with him. Your mare's still here, though. See her, too?"

"Damn it," Joe said, "when? How long ago, and where'd they go?"

"Ain't got a pocket watch," the man said, dragging his leg over to the empty stall. "And I don't never ask where a fella's headin'—ain't none of my business."

Joe said softly, slowly, "Mister, it wouldn't take much for me to bust up your other leg. Suppose you make a real good guess at which way she went."

Straightening, the stableman rubbed at a whiskery cheek. "Swear I didn't pay no never mind. He—or she—paid and saddled that stud horse and loaded them mustangs down with sacks and water jugs and lit on out of here. That road yonder's full of folks agoin' six ways to Sunday."

"How long ago?" Joe asked, his mouth gone stale and his throat turned gritty.

"Two hours, maybe three—too long to track less'n you knowed where she was headin'." Scratching his cheek again, the man said, "Got this here leg busted by a ornery ol' mule; swear he looked around and grinned at me when I was laid flat out on the ground. Seems that fella rode outa here with them horses had the same look to him—like he got him in a real good lick."

321

Chapter 34

Flat and marshy, the valley spread itself green and vast as she pulled up at the base of the last rolling hills. Hard-won experience made her sweep her eyes slowly and carefully across the entire area before she moved Bradburn ahead, with the tied mustangs following.

It looked clear to her, no skulker waiting to get off a shot, no lone brave ready with taut bowstring. Marilee feasted her eyes upon greenness and breathed deeply the air that carried the welcome smell and beautiful flavor of water. It was wondrous, after endless miles of parched desert and seared mountains, an elixir that lifted her spirits and perked up the horses.

They went cautiously into the flats, and she had to jerk the lead rope to keep the mares from dipping their heads at the first grasses. Marilee knew how the horses felt, because the same excitement was rippling through her own thinned body, an anticipation of richness and rest.

A grove of fragrant trees clustered around a spring ahead, and she brought the horses to it. Slipping Bradburn's saddle and bridle, she let the stallion run, but hobbled the mares. As she kneeled to drink sweet water,

Marilee knew she'd have to allow the horses to graze for only a short time, then tie them up, or they would founder. But for now, it was so good to watch them drink and cavort, to see them tear at high, strength-giving grass.

This could be the place, she thought; surely other wild mares could be trapped in the low hills over there, and corrals built to hold them. A lean-to here beside the spring, and later on a cabin, a barn and fences. . . .

Marilee smiled to herself and went about gathering dry wood for a fire, started setting up a camp. The mares had been handy as pack horses, and some of the money she'd spent back in El Paso had bought enough provisions and ammunition to take her through all that harsh, sere country without having to do too much hunting. The horses had suffered more than she had, because the corn ran out after the first weeks, and they'd had to make do on stripped cactus and what browned, wiry grass they could find. But it was all right now; they'd come this far safely, and this just might be the place she'd been searching for.

Putting a sulphur match to piled twigs, Marilee drove green forked sticks into the soft earth and hung a sturdier one across them for the pot of water. This day she'd have a stew, and her mouth was already moist at the thought of it. Pulling her neck a little deeper into her heavy man's jacket, she squatted to warm her hands at the growing fire. Winter was coming on fast, and she would have to work hard to get shelter for herself and the horses, but that task seemed small now.

What else could she do but go with him, Joe Langston had said in that arrogant way. Well, she'd done what he might not be able to; she'd come alone through half of Comancheria and deep into Apache country, where he'd have lost his hair. And it hadn't been all luck; it was because she was Nadevah and could speak fluent Comanche, because even the Apaches had a superstitious fear of the Moon Woman and she could hand-talk with them.

She'd come upon the hunting party of Comanches before they knew she was anywhere near, so she'd let them know of her presence in the time-honored way, by standing her horses on the skyline and keeping still until they noticed her. Surprised and cautious, they'd approached her slowly, half a dozen riders spacing themselves into a half circle.

Giving the hand sign for peace, she waited until the lead man was nearer before whipping off her hat and allowing her silvery hair to blow free in the wind. She saw beadwork and trappings that told her the tribe was *Kuhtsoo-ehkuh,* and was glad this band wasn't a far-ranging one of her old tribe.

"I am Nadevah," she called out. "I would pass in peace."

The lead rider pulled up his horse sharply. "Moon Woman!"

Other horsemen stopped, muttering, staring at her hair, at the great stallion she rode and the mares behind. Marilee sensed their unease, a nervousness alien to The People and said, "Yes, Moon Woman—and you?"

"Pahayuca," the warrior answered, a long scar disfiguring his bronzed face. "Ten Antelopes. The Moon Woman is dead—she fell with warriors of Little Buffalo."

Now she knew why they were afraid. Piava had returned to camp alone and said nothing. She could picture him going into mourning, fasting on the mountain and praying to his gods. He would search for some way to overcome the great defeat, the loss of his hunting party, his wife and medicine woman, his powerful stallion. It was better the tribe thought both horse and the Moon Woman dead.

Pahayuca shifted uncomfortably in his saddle, carbine across his lap. All the Comanches wore their winter buckskins, so familiar to her. He said, "Only the Spirit Talkers can understand. What—what do you wish of us, Moon Woman?"

"Only to ride through Comancheria to where I must travel. I make no bad *puha* for The People, nor for Piava, who was my husband."

Silently, the others watched her, sitting their shaggy mustangs and barely able to hold themselves from whirling away from this medicine woman who had risen from the dead upon a chief's dead stallion.

"None would touch you," Pahayuca murmured, "not even the Apache—they remember Nadevah's attack too well, and feasted when news of your death reached them. Now they will also hear of your rising. Spirit of the Moon Woman, may we go?"

Happy to get away from her, the hunting party galloped from sight and Marilee looked after with—what? Surely not a feeling of nostalgia—maybe a sense of once having belonged, possibly a small sorrow over Piava, who had been good to her in his fashion.

Now, whittling strips of buffalo meat into bubbling water, she remembered how she'd steeled herself against that kind of softness, for Piava had *owned* her. Marilee Bradburn would be no man's property, no chattel for him to use or rid himself of when he pleased. It was why she had left Joe Langston, because he could not get it through his thick head that she belonged only to herself. The chains he'd put on her through dependency, his smug superiority, his decision-making—they were nearly as strong as the institution of slavery itself.

Damn the man; he knew she was capable and strong, that she was about as good with guns as he, and maybe better on a horse. But would Joe Langston admit any of that? Had he even asked if she might not *want* to travel on to California with him? Of course not; he'd simply assumed she would follow meekly along, doing whatever he ordered. She would have enjoyed seeing his face when he found she was gone from El Paso with half the money found in that overrun army fort. It wasn't as if she'd stolen the gold, either; he'd offered her the share before. If, as he said, she'd just wind up as a crib girl, she'd shown Joe being *his* whore was expensive.

She poured flour into the stew and salted it, added a pinch of dried chili peppers and two wild onions she'd dug out of the foothills. He had some odd hold upon her, she admitted, some dark alchemy of flesh that weakened her body and made it respond any way *he* wanted. There was something in Joe Langston that brought forth a shameless abandon from her; the feel of that hard, magnificent body touching hers released an almost frightening wildness that could be both greedy and soft.

With Piava, she had almost had that, too, so there had to be other men like them, perhaps one more man somewhere in this sprawling land who might also know how to be gentle and understanding, a very special man who might ask to know *her* needs and not just have her submit to his own.

Stirring the pot, she glanced over at Bradburn grazing close to the hobbled mares. It was early afternoon and there was plenty of light left; the sun wouldn't dip for hours yet, and she could put together some kind of shelter after she ate. Except for Joe Langston nagging at the tail end of her mind, Marilee felt good, happy about finding grass and water that had the smell of home about them.

A temporary home, she thought, a beginning place for however long it might take to build up a ranch here, make it big and productive enough, safe enough that someone else would buy it. Then Marilee could really go home—to Bradburn Plantation—and take her rightful place upon that true, rich land that had been in the family for so many generations. It would be Bradburn soil again, for that many more generations to come, for regal ladies and handsome gentlemen, for brighteyed children and blooded horses. As it used to be; as it was meant to be.

When she finished wolfing down the stew, Marilee sighed and propped her head back against the saddle. "All right, Bradburn," she said, "that's enough for now —come here."

Cocking his finely modeled head at her, the stallion trotted over to accept his rope halter. She tied him on a short lead to a tree, then went to gather the less tractable mares. When she'd brought them back to the stand of trees, her senses, sharpened by years of alertness, warned her of something.

Immediately, she swept up the buffalo gun she'd bought in El Paso, and put the Spencer close by, knowing the pistol riding her hip was always at hand and always ready. Bradburn's ears pointed and his nostrils flared.

They came from the south at a slow canter, careful but not overly so; an Apache in the grove could have dropped them both before they knew he was there. Marilee watched them draw near, dressed alike in wide, blown-back sombreros and batwing chaps; she could see the glinting of sunlight on rowel spurs and thought what fools they were.

When they made out the shape of her horses against greenery, both stopped short and slid carbines from saddle scabbards. The hard mountains behind her and the even more hostile desert, all the Comanche lore that she had been steeped in, almost caused her finger to tighten upon the long rifle's trigger. These men could easily be *comancheros,* gun runners and whiskey dealers greedier than Indians and more cruel.

But she hesitated and called out strongly, "That's far enough!"

Their heads lifted, then swung back and forth at each other. One man shouted something in Spanish, and she yelled back, *"Hablo un poco!* Just keep your distance—I can drop you easy from here!"

One man made a slow performance of handing his carbine and pistol to the other, of showing her uplifted and empty hands before kneeing his horse into a walk toward the spring. Marilee watched both of them closely, centering the front sight of the Sharps on the closer chest.

When he got near enough for her to make out the black, drooping moustache and tanned face, she said: "Right there, *señor.*"

"A *gringo? Hola*—you trespass on Hacienda Carboca."

"And you'll be trespassing in hell, if you reach for that hat, mister." She glanced beyond the man to where the other sat quietly, then back at this one.

"A woman!" His black eyes widened. "A *gringa* out here—it is impossible. Where is your man?"

"I don't need one," she said. "Don't make me prove that, *vaquero.*"

"A man should not keep his hat before a lady," he said. "There is no small pistol in my sombrero, señorita. *Con su permiso?*"

Marilee allowed him his bow, finger brushing the trigger of her buffalo gun, because this one didn't talk or act like a rum-soaked *comanchero* or swaggering *bandido.*

"I am Manuel Venegas, señorita—*y usted?*"

"Marilee Bradburn."

"Might one ask how you come to be here on Hacienda Carboca, alone and unprotected?"

Smiling grimly, she kept the rifle on him. "I'm not unprotected, and I thought all this territory was open."

Venegas put his sombrero back on and shrugged, holding his palms up to show their emptiness. "I know nothing of politics or *tejanos*—only cows and Apaches and horses —and that is one *muy magnifico caballo* there. Oh, yes, and I also understand the orders of my master that no one is to be on his land without his permission. Perhaps it is as you say, señorita—you can protect yourself. That or *Dios* himself has ridden at your side through Apache country. But I must ask you to come with us to speak with the *patrón*."

Marilee shook her head. "You seem like an honest man, Manuel Venegas, but who knows what others are in these hills? No—if your *patrón* wants to speak with me, he'll have to do it here."

Sighing, Venegas said, "It is unheard of, and I dislike telling him this request. Señorita, there are few Apaches here because Don Carboca has many *vaqueros*—surely, he will bring more with him."

She said, "I have been forced to kill Apaches and *comancheros*. I have also ridden with the Comanches as an equal. If this is really some man's private land and he asks me to move on, I'll do it. But I won't be *driven* off by anyone. It's a long way from El Paso, and my horses are tired."

The man whistled softly. "El Paso del Norte? A long way, indeed. Do you know you are now in what the *gringos* call the territory of Nueva Mexico?"

"I know my horses are tired," Marilee repeated.

Lifting his sombrero by the crown, Venegas made a half-bow in his saddle. "Very well—I will face the *patrón* myself, although this may not be my lucky day. *Adiós, señorita*."

"*Con Dios*," she said after him, lowering the rifle only when both men had trotted beyond the range of their carbines. Even then she watched to see that they didn't try to circle her before gathering brush and spreading part of a wagon trap for cover.

Moving the horses into the trees, she allowed her cook-fire to flicker out and took up a position away from the makeshift tepee, a place from where she could watch all sides. She'd reached New Mexico Territory, found this green Eden only to be told it already belonged to someone else. And she wasn't waiting here out of pure stubbornness; it was true the horses were drawn and needed rest, needed this grass to fill them out again. Maybe this *patrón* of many *vaqueros* would let her stay awhile, tell her which way to go, so she might find another spot like this—if there was another.

And if Venegas had been lying, if the don was only chief of just another gang of *bandidos*, there wasn't much Marilee could do about that at the moment either. The valley was broad, and she could easily be caught out in the open. Better to fight from cover, if she had to, and try to escape by night.

He came alone, straight across the meadowland with his black horse at a long, flowing lope. Tall in the saddle, riding easy and erect, he loomed nearer, and Marilee kept looking beyond him for other riders, at the hills for signs of an encircling movement. But he was alone and cantering swiftly into range of her long rifle.

Silver conchos glittered in the late sun, shone around the band of his sombrero, down his long legs, upon the saddle horn—everywhere. This man wasn't afraid of being seen from a distance—he *wanted* to be, announcing his presence with more rich trappings than ordinary riders ever thought about, daring others with them.

Coming out of the brush, Marilee stood the long rifle against a sapling and walked to meet him in the open. Reining up in a sliding stop that showed the special training of his horse, the man dismounted and swept off his big hat with a graceful flourish, with a flashing of bright and even teeth, a glitter of eyes black as any Comanche's, but deeper, deeper and penetrating.

"Ah," he said in cadenced English, "my men did not lie, although I could not believe a *norteamericana* lady was out here alone. Allow me, señorita—I am Don Alfonso de Carboca, and most delighted to be of service."

Marilee was a little stunned, gone suddenly awkward and remembering how she looked, the rough man's clothing she wore. This Don Alfonso was handsome as a rising hawk, little silver featherings slim and winglike above his ears, a trim moustache above a full, rich mouth and a prideful chin. He was as tall as Joe Langston, with the same kind of animal litheness to him, but a wiser man, ripe and polished.

She hated herself for stammering. "I—maybe they already told you my name—but I'm Marilee Bradburn, from Mississippi."

"Marilee," he said, her name musical upon his tongue as he strode to her, and she hated herself again for feeling peculiar when he lifted her roughened hand to press his lips against her fingers. It had been so long since a gentleman kissed her hand, so long since she had *seen* a gentleman. "Welcome to Hacienda Carboca. Ah, that fool

329

Manuel—he did not say how beautiful you are, nor that your hair is the color of the moon. You have traveled from the Confederacy, then—at least, my *vaquero* was intelligent enough to recognize a lady when he saw one."

"Th-thank you," Marilee murmured, "but I don't look much like a lady now."

He still held her hand, but lightly, his long, agile fingers gentle upon hers, not trapping them, but seeming reluctant to let go. A silver mounted quirt dangled from his left wrist. "A man of discernment sees where others do not. *Por favor*, Señorita Marilee, do me the honor of being my guest at my poor hacienda." Before she could answer, he threw back his head and laughed. "A *pistolera,* they said, but I find a jewel of great price."

Marilee swallowed. "My horses—"

"If you will allow me to call my *vaqueros? Mil gracias.*" Smoothly, deftly, he turned and blurred a pistol from his side, firing into the air with the same fluid movement, firing three times. As gunsmoke swirled and ringing echoes reached out into the green foothills, he smiled down at her again.

She said, "They're out there, yet you rode in alone. I *am* a *pistolera* of sorts, Don Alfonso. I was prepared to fight if I had to, and I might have killed you."

This time, his laugh rang loudly, edged with some secret excitement. "*Sí, sí,* and I do not doubt that you would have tried—a small, slim *torera* facing the bull with much courage. Yet would I wear the *banderillas* and face the sword a thousand times for the delight of meeting such a woman, a woman whose hair is bathed in moonlight, yet one whose eyes of springtime warn of steel close to the skin, and of flame waiting only a little deeper."

Reaching all the way back to a time of violined ballrooms, to crinoline and wine-colored satin and hoops, Marilee murmured, "You embarrass me with compliments, sir. I am not deserving of them."

Swiftly, the hawkish face changed, the lips narrowing for a fleeting second, the jetblack eyes peering into her own. "I have heard the same recitation in Atlanta and New Orleans, from so many others. You are different from all those identically pretty girls, and apart from the more fiery, lovely women of my own country. I see this with my heart and know it in my blood. And my other eyes inform

330

me that no woman I have ever known could have ridden from El Paso del Norte alone, through Comancheria and the Apaches. There is also a great beauty to strength, señorita."

"All right," she said, because the fan-fluttering, lowered-lashed phrases did sound silly out here, "all right, I'll admit to being strong, Don Alfonso, and to being grateful for your invitation. I'll go with you—gladly."

Vaqueros were racing across the flatlands, ten, a dozen of them. Once more he brushed her hand with his lips and released it. "And I will escort you to my home— exultantly."

Chapter 35

Tossing his head and very much alert to the dark, prancing mare beside him, Bradburn was no more aware of that nearness than Marilee was of the mare's rider. She wished she were under as much control, that she didn't feel clumsy and shabby riding beside Don Alfonso in all his silvered finery. Behind them, and at a discreet distance, his vaqueros led her mares with their packloads. The crimson sun was just sliding beyond a range of rolling hills to the south when they topped a low ridge and she saw the hacienda.

She hadn't expected anything like it—the huge house a red-tiled quadrangle and walled as some ancient fortress, barns and sheds and small workers' homes clustered around it for protection. It was set off by so much greenery —lacy trees and exotic flowering shrubs and neatly hedged gardens; her soothed eyes even caught the glimmer of a reflection pool. The thought came that this was a Western Bradburn Plantation, styled differently but with the same sort of quiet grandeur and aura of pride and antiquity.

Don Alfonso drew up his mare, and she touched Bradburn's bit as the man's knee touched her own. He said quietly, "For centuries, this area was called Cienegas, a Hundred Springs. There to the west—if you look closely you may see its tip—is Lake Aguirre, mother or wife to all those springs—possibly both. And to the south, the border villages of Sa Sabe—a few miserable huts upon each side of the river."

"And the ranch itself?" Marilee asked. "How long has it been in your family?"

"For centuries also," he answered, "and I was beginning to wonder if it would continue in the Carboca name."

The slight frown upon his face puzzled her. "Trouble with Apaches, thieves from both sides of the border? With your ranch so close to the river, I'd imagine—"

"Nothing like that," he said. "The Carbocas have always maintained their own army—small, but well trained and equipped. We have also continued arrangements with whatever politicos are in power on both sides of the Rio Grande, for Hacienda Carboca lies partly in Mexico, partly in the Territory of New Mexico. We have survived." Just before he nudged his mare forward, Marilee caught a hard setting of determination upon the maturely handsome face, and Don Alfonso said, "We *will* survive."

It was only after they'd ridden through a portico and into a courtyard, only after stableboys had scurried to take their horses' reins, that it occurred to Marilee that surely this man must be married. With a quiver in her stomach as she dismounted, she looked up at the balconies for a señora, an olive-skinned beauty to match the husband. She saw nobody and wondered at her sensation of relief, because the wife could be anywhere in this vast home, and children didn't always run to greet their father.

Others gathered, though, as Don Alfonso held her arm and guided her into a candlelit vestibule. Brown and barefoot girls in simple loose dresses, blackhaired girls who didn't look up glided to take the don's sombrero and pistol belt like so many silently wheeling dark moths.

"Rosa, Elena—care for the señorita," he snapped. "See to her bath, her every need, *comprehendene?*"

"*Sí, patrón,*" they whispered, hesitant brown hands reaching for her saddlebags and battered cavalry hat. Marilee gave them up, and her long guns, but kept the Colt belted around her waist.

Eyes twinkling, Don Alfonso bent over her hand. *"La pistolera poquita,* always so very careful. You are secure now, for *mi casa, su casa*—my home is your home, and tonight my kitchen will outdo itself in your honor, and the cellar's best wines will applaud your lips."

Nodding her thanks, Marilee followed the straight-backed girls across a long room with many curved archways. The heavy, dark furniture was highlighted with brightspun Indian blankets and quiet gleamings of brass and silver. Formal portraits hung on mellowed adobe walls. There were fur rugs and a polished tile floor; a great fireplace dominated the far end of the room, crossed rapiers above its mantel.

The stairway was curved, its handrail smoothed by ages of touching hands, and candles sparkled everywhere along the hallway lined with heavy, ironbound oaken doors. A girl opened one, and Marilee walked into a sitting room; to the left was a tiled and mirrored room with a dry sink and a high copper tub; to her right she could see a curtained bedroom.

One of the maids hurried to light lamps, to crack a window so the slight musty odor was wafted away. The other carried Marilee's things into the bedroom, and she felt their liquid black eyes assessing her, flicking at her from beneath lowered lashes.

Softly, one of them said, "I am Rosa, señorita. I go now to see to your bath water." And before Marilee could ask anything, the girl was gone. She stopped the other one. "You're Elena, then? Well, Elena, tell me—is there a Señora Carboca, any children?"

"I—I cannot say, señorita—you must ask the *patrón.* Everything must be asked of the *patrón.*"

"You can't answer such a simple—" Marilee stopped; Elena was suddenly someone she could recognize—any house servant in any Southern mansion talking to a visitor, submissive and ill at ease. Naturally she would be reluctant to discuss her employer. "All right, Elena—what do I do next?"

"The water will be but a moment, señorita—then I will help you undress and bathe you. There are perfumes in—in the bedroom, and perhaps the don will—" The girl still didn't look up, and her voice was soft, the braids of her hair raven black.

Unbuckling her gunbelt, Marilee placed it upon a sofa, and sat down to take off her boots, but Elena went swiftly to her knees and did the task. It had been so long since Marilee had been waited on that it now felt uncomfortable to her, but she thought she'd soon get over that. She looked up to see Rosa and two more almost identical girls bearing water buckets that steamed. She got up to shed her clothing, every inch of her skin anticipating the luxury of a hot, soapy bath.

As she sank into sinfully delicious water, whispers eddied around her in such quick Spanish that she could catch only that it had to do with the color of her hair and her skin where desert sun hadn't tanned it. Elena and Rosa's hands were agile, soothing, and Marilee felt no embarrassment at their touching her; she was too grateful for the scrubbing, the marvelous hot water, the thorough washing of her hair. And when they were done, she leaned back in the big copper tub to soak drowsily, to smile contentedly, to smell perfume.

And when she at last lifted herself languidly from the tub, Rosa and Elena were there to dry her with great, fluffy towels, wrapping her in them and leading her into the big room with its canopied bed and a dressing table stocked with cutglass enchantments. But the great surprises lay across the silken coverlet—gown after gown in a dazzling array of colors, wondrous dresses daringly cut, marvelous dresses lacy and frilly and clinging.

No hoopskirts here; pirouetting, Marilee held a gown up to her body. These were designed in the Spanish fashion, low necklines and made to snug the length of a woman's body in disarming simplicity to just above the knees. They flared there in cascades of needlepoint roses or spread themselves into sequined trains. So many *real* gowns, and this one—the shade of a pale claret wine.

"It—it's beautiful," she whispered to a mirror filigreed in gold, to the silently watching maids. "Once I had one something like this, but not so—so scandalous. Why, my mama would have had the vapors, if she saw me coming down the staircase in something like this—"

Breaking off, she saw they didn't understand enough English, and her Spanish couldn't express what she felt, could not convey the sudden onrush of emotion and nostalgia. For a dizzying moment, she had been in her own

335

room at Bradburn, with her own dear maid fussing over her; then her mind whirled, sickened, to that slave cabin and a cracked, peeling mirror, to a stubblefaced Yankee trooper leering at her.

The sound of guitars floated up from the patio, and Marilee came gladly from her haunted reverie to try on the dress, smoothing it down over her hips and finding it a lovely fit. She sat before the dressing table and stared at a new woman while Rosa brushed out her hair, a woman with older eyes and sun-darkened skin that shamed the snowy whiteness below her collarbone.

"El patrón sent these for you also," Elena breathed, and Marilee's eyes went wide at the necklace of emeralds crusted with small diamonds, the matching earrings. She realized she held not only a fortune in her hands, but also something of the Carboca history, a thing very precious. They brought out the color of her eyes.

"A mantilla and comb," Rosa suggested. "This white one, perhaps?"

They brought her heeled slippers to try on, slippers of many sizes, and Marilee's teeth tugged gently at her lip as she wondered why Don Alfonso would have such variety on hand. A white doeskin pair fit well, and she moved about the room to practice her balance in them, the gown caressing her body and swirling gaily about her feet, a high ivory comb making her seem even taller, the lace mantilla adding a demure touch. The Spanish women knew what they were about, she thought; almost any man would be smitten by such a costume.

Perhaps not Joe Langston, because he rebelled at any sign of superiority, any reminders that different castes still existed in his world. Leaning to dab a subtle, musky fragrance at her throat, Marilee corrected herself, because that wasn't completely true. There'd been that French countess in Mexico, who surely must have paraded herself superbly gowned and jeweled at the emperor's court; and he'd accepted a kind of superiority in the knowledge of that schoolteacher on the wagon train, that Elizabeth woman.

But why should she be thinking of a man like Joe, when a Latin aristocrat waited downstairs for her? *"Gracias,"* she said to the maids, dismissing them so she could stand alone in the sumptuous bedroom and adjust herself. Smiling, she realized that even though she'd eaten only hours before, she was hungry again—for civilized food, for the company of a charming gentleman, for music like the strumming of guitars from the patio.

How old was Don Alfonso? Forty—perhaps even older? No matter; he was intriguing and handsome, with those silver wings in his glossy black hair. And the lines about that almost girlish mouth were marks of character, the tiny wrinkles at the corners of piercing eyes tracks of wisdom and time. Older men could be so much more appealing, and Marilee wondered why she had not discovered this before.

She left the apartment and walked slowly down the corridor to hesitate at the top of the stairs. Majestically, that proud old room awaited her, and she tried to descend into it with the dignity required. He must have heard the click of her heels upon the stairs, for he came quickly from another hall to look up at her, his smile brilliant and pleased.

Don Alfonso wore black velvet, a short coat and frilled white shirt above a scarlet satin sash; his breeches were tight over slim, hard thighs, tapered over his calves and flared at the ankles. His boots gleamed, and he wore a large diamond on his right hand, a many-faceted gem that threw back tiny rainbows of candlelight. A short, flowing tie of black lay against the base of his tanned throat, and on the midnight waves of his hair rode those silver feathers she found so attractive.

This time, his lips burned lightly against her hand, and he kept her hand in his as he steered her toward a dining room whose carved table might have seated the statehouse of Mississippi. There were only two places laid, hers at his right hand, beside the tall-backed chair engraved with eagles and entwined serpents. Silent, shuffling men brought wines, keeping to the shadows as they served, only their hands easing unobtrusively into golden light from a candelabrum.

"*Salud,*" Don Alfonso said, his voice a caress, "*y pesetas y tiempo para disfrutarlos . . .* your health, and wealth, and the time to enjoy them."

"I feel so—so inadequate," Marilee said, lifting her goblet to his. "I must learn more Spanish."

"You cannot be inadequate at anything," he answered, and the intimacy of his eyes was so unsettling that she hid her confusion behind the wine glass. The wine was cold, brought quickly from some deep cellar, and its flavor exotically heady upon her tongue.

"You wear the emeralds perfectly," he said. "They should have been designed solely for you."

"Th-they're gorgeous. And this dress, the shoes—I never thought to feel so civilized again. I don't know how to thank you for everything."

"Por nada—the jewels thank you for making them beautiful, and I am grateful you sit at my table and once more make wine celebrate within my mouth. When first I saw you, I knew you were lovely, but I could have no idea just *how* lovely. The small *pistolera* is gone, and here is a magnificent young daughter of the Confederacy, but with a touch of Mexico. The combination is exquisite."

Yes, she thought, the food was perfect; she adored the guitar music, his house, and everything about it. And she found him easy to talk with, despite the tension between them, the sort of carefully balanced woman–man pull she acknowledged for what it was. Marilee learned of twenty thousand acres, and longhorn cattle uncounted, and horses with more than a dash of barb blood to them.

But Don Alfonso de Carboca never said a word about the lack of women and children in his house, and Marilee didn't ask. Instead, she talked of her own home in Mississippi, what it had been and must be again.

"Bueno," he said, "you have also a pride of family. It is what impressed me most during my travels in your South, this attention to bloodlines. A pity the other side won, as in Mexico—but these times pass, and the true masters rise again."

The table was cleared, but for new goblets and a different, more powerful wine. Don Alfonso placed his hand over hers. "Tell me, Señorita Marilee—how did you manage to reach this place, not merely from El Paso del Norte, but all the way from your own state? How does a lady such as you come to be a *pistolera* who kills Apaches and rides as an equal with the fierce Comanches?"

Quickly, she glanced at him and away. His *vaquero* had reported her every word to this man. Now her silken gown seemed uncomfortable, and with the trailing away of guitar music beyond the dining room, the sharp-edged reality of her life came back.

"I did what I must to survive," she answered. "My father and brothers made me familiar with hunting and guns. I used a Yankee's own pistol to kill him after— after he forced himself upon me. I took his horse and fled—that stallion I ride. He carried me from a burning wagon train Apaches struck—some fell before my carbine, but not enough. We tried to outrun a band of Comanches later, but could not. The chief took me for his wife."

Watching his face, she saw no change, no outward sign of revulsion because she had lain with an Indian; Don Alfonso seemed only interested, so she went on. "To protect my stallion, I rode with the Comanches on a war party against Apaches and went a little crazy when I saw a brave torturing a Mexican boy. After I led that attack upon the camp, my own tribe respected me and called me Moon Woman. I was good medicine for them, for my husband, but I escaped because I had to. Much longer and I would have been forever Comanche."

Candles flickered, and their light moved across the hawk's face, the predatory eyes. Marilee wondered why she hadn't told this listening man about Joe Langston.

"So," Don Alfonso said at last, "you have killed as *el tigre* might, tasting blood. That flavor is special, *querida*, like rare wine, and few know how to savor it properly. Beauty, fire, and steel, I said—now I add blood. Can any man ask more?"

Rising from the great chair, he held out his hand. "Come."

A bit unsteadily, Marilee got up. "So much wonderful food, the fine wine; I—I must ask your indulgence. I'd like to go to bed."

"Of course," he said, his fingers strong upon her elbow. "That is where I am taking you."

Chapter 36

For a while, Joe wasn't interested in much of anything. He holed up in the *posada* half the day, absorbing books and pamphlets bought from traders and wandering preachers. There were more books to be found across the border, and he got so he enjoyed reading Spanish, too.

In late afternoon, he might wander the now chill and dusty streets of El Paso, or take his mare out for a little exercise, since she was growing big with foal. Evenings he spent in one cantina or another, playing cool and conservative poker and slowly adding to his stake. It was only in the still hours before dawn when he thought of her and how she'd abandoned him. He'd drink some decent *vino rojo* then, for he'd found tequila only made him more restless and angry.

The damned little fool, going off alone into country where Indian troubles were getting worse every day, by herself in a trackless wasteland where anything might happen to her. He'd asked trappers and buffalo hunters coming in from the west if they'd seen a towheaded youngun in a castoff Yankee uniform too big for him and maybe wearing a patch over one eye. He asked about the big stud horse, because Bradburn stood a better chance of taking the eye than a skinny rider looking like a hundred others. Nobody remembered seeing the horse, and after a while, Joe stopped inquiring.

There'd been no cause for her to leave him like that, without saying a word about it. He didn't give a damn that she'd taken half the gold; Marilee was entitled to her share. What riled him was not knowing *why*.

Hell, it wasn't like he'd raped her again; she had come to him willingly, sometimes starting things herself and never failing to give back just as good as she got, maybe a little bit more. Of course, it seemed like they were always jawing at each other over her fool ideas. Such as how the old South could be brought back to life by gentry like her, and her not understanding one damned thing about the way poor whites had felt about it, back then and right now; such as her talking about the Comanches like they were real folks instead of vicious, torturing animals best put down wherever they were found.

He'd never even thrown it in her face her being a squaw woman, although there was a time or two he wanted to slap a knot on her for calling that chief her "husband." But Miss Marilee Bradburn never missed the chance to rowel him good about breeding and bloodlines —all those misconceptions that had passed away at Appomattox and died with Maximilian on the Hill of Bells.

Ornery and headstrong, Marilee had taken the chance to pay him back for that first time he had taken her, for leaving her behind in the Louisiana woods, abandoning her as she insisted. She conveniently forgot that she *wouldn't* come with him back to the troops, that he'd have had to rope her and throw her across her saddle. Even then, he'd expected her to get over her pout and join up later—that or go on back home where she belonged.

As months passed, thinking on her got to bothering Joe like a sandbur under a horse's saddle, so he went about forgetting Marilee the best way he knew, by finding another woman just as pretty and just as fierce.

Estrella was a wiggly armful of fiery young woman who clawed at his back and hissed border obscenities into his ear, and he tired of her.

Margarita had a touch more polish, since she was no barmaid, but a respectable widow whose brothers operated the saddle shop bequeathed her by her husband. But making love with her in the same bedroom where a candlelit altar glorified a tintype picture of the departed Señor Rubio soon palled. Besides, Margarita had a certain desperation about her, something he had come to recognize as an overwhelming desire for respectability through marriage. And her brothers had begun to eye Joe with a frowning speculation that would mean trouble he'd rather avoid.

So he turned to a more practical arrangement and changed his lodgings to move in with Becky Taylor, madam of a plush brothel and a woman who knew how to cater to a younger man. Becky was a handsome piece who'd brought girls west from Georgia even before the Confederacy collapsed, losing some along the way and picking up replacements. Near to forty, she took great care to look much younger, and the carrot color of her hair wasn't the same between her legs.

It didn't matter much to Joe, since Becky was easy to be with and had no illusions about marriage or anything else. And even though they were from the same kind of poor dirt stock and could talk about how it had been for them both and how they weren't near about going back to scratching for a bare living, she kind of looked up to Joe because of all he was learning from books.

So winter slid by, and springtime, and he was thinking of throwing in with Becky, buying a share of the saloon and whorehouse, because it seemed as if the border troubles wouldn't amount to much. The settlement was a shade too big to be attacked by Indians, although outlying ranches got worried some, and the army rode here and there without accomplishing anything.

The stud colt was foaled in early summer, a little bit early, far as Joe could figure, and the memory of that big stallion mounting his barb mare brought it all back to him, hurtful and nagging. He and Marilee had mated only moments later, both of them stimulated by what they'd seen, and it had been good. It had been better than being with any other woman, before or after.

"Mighty fine colt," Otto said, "and your mare didn't have a lick of trouble." The stableman limped around the stall and pointed. "See how he holds his head real high-like? And if he don't grow up fine-legged but chunky, I'm a wall-eyed Comanch'. Wouldn't have it in mind to sell him, would you?"

Joe leaned an elbow on the stall rail. "He just might bust your other leg, Otto. The sire of that youngun was a hotblood Morgan that didn't mind takin' on Apaches or anything else, did his rider point him at them."

Otto rubbed his hip and grimaced. "Nothin' muley about this 'un, though. Man could raise him proper and have one hell of a horse, way I see it."

"Suppose you halter-break him and teach him to lead," Joe said. "We might talk about dickerin' for him later. He *is* right pretty, red as his sire and about as snorty."

Becky Taylor didn't give a damn for horses and said so; she didn't even like to drive a buckboard and sat all tightened up when she just had to ride in one.

Pushing her hands nervously at her flaming hair, she'd say, "I just don't want to be hangin' around nothin' that weighs a thousand pounds and got a brain no bigger'n a pecan. Them damned things'll *hurt* a body."

Joe didn't hang around the stables much, because looking at the growing colt always brought Marilee and her plan to cross her stallion on offblood mares. And that thought just naturally led to what she meant to do when she had a herd and a place to keep it—back to Mississippi as a fine, high-toned lady. Only once in a while did he allow himself to admit she might not be going anywhere, that Marilee and the stud horse named after her plantation could easily be just bones by now, anywhere out on that Indian-ravaged desert between here and California. She'd already used up more than her share of gambler's luck, and unless she tied in with a strong wagon train, one heavily guarded by troops, Joe wouldn't give a single white chip for her chances.

That made him fret, and Becky Taylor thought he was just getting saddletramp fever and was about ready to move on, when the truth was he was pretty well content. That is until that damned breed showed up. He'd been down tending to the mare and handling the colt some and didn't see the first set-to between Becky and the breed. But when she told him about it, she was mad enough to take a bite from a beer mug and spit chewed-up glass.

He was stretched on her bed, boots off and smoking a cigarillo, when she came storming in. "The goddamn *nerve* of him! Tellin' me I *got* to give him whiskey and a woman, right in my face, like he was a pure-D white man."

"Who?" Joe asked casually.

"Calls hisself Cherokee Bill," Becky said, pouring herself a shot of straight tequila and tossing it off. "Slapped little Nancy around some, and woulda tore up the bar, hadn't been for George's sawed-off and a couple of the boys backin' it up. Meanest son of a bitch I ever seen. Got eyes like a water moccasin and disposition to match."

"Breeds sometimes got a call to turn poison," Joe said. "If he's Cherokee, he's a long way from home."

Becky made a face. "It ain't only he's half Injun, but the other half's black, and you know damned well I can't let neither one mess with my girls, or I'd be outa' business in a week. Bastard swore he'd be back."

"Firewater talk," Joe said. "He'll forget it when his head starts to hurt."

"Hope so," she said, "because word is that he ain't but twenty-one years old and done killed twelve men."

"Gunfights and gunfighters get exaggerated," Joe said.

"Fella from the Oklahoma Territory said this here breed's been called—lemme see how he put it now—yeah —a wolf in human form."

"A wolf doesn't kill for the hell of it—I'd say that was a misnomer."

Becky grinned at him. "For a ol' piney-woods redneck, you sure know a lot of fancy words. Fancy women, too— but you didn't learn about *them* from no books."

She'd got that look in her eyes. She'd already peeled off the frilled and sparkly dress she wore in the saloon and was reaching back to undo laces on a corset she didn't need, except for fashion, when she hesitated and said seriously, "No need for you to mix into it, Joe. Old George is right handy with that shotgun."

"Sometimes George is a long way from it," he said. "But never mind—just get on with what you started, gettin' off that thing."

Becky's flesh was clean and sweet, and she used her body with abandon, moving from one experienced kind of trick to another, using all the things she'd learned from all her men. Big in the breast and slim in the flank, she was all over him in lusty, grinding passion, but even while he held her writhing in his arms, even as she moaned and bit gently into his throat, Joe's mind was filled with images of another woman.

It was a bad thing to do to Becky Taylor, pretending she was somebody else, because Becky was an honest whore, and Joe had the feeling that even whores could tell when a man wasn't really concentrating on them and nobody else. But he did the best he could, stroking her and whispering nice things, and when it was done, he guessed she was content.

Cherokee Bill came back the next day.

He didn't come inside the saloon, but stood outside in the street and hollered for Joe Langston to come on out. "Hey, you whore man! Hey, you fancy gambler son of a bitch! I been hearin' about you, Joe Langston—"

Three other men were at the table with him; they got quiet and the early drinkers at the bar got quieter. George the barkeep reached beneath the mahogany and lifted his sawed-off into sight.

Out in the street, the breed kept yelling. "Fancy man from the South! Yo' whore's too damn good to lay with the likes of me, but not white trash—that it, fancy man?"

From the top of the stairs, Becky said, "Don't go out, Joe. George, slip out back and around the—"

"No," Joe said, the three men at the table looking at him. He got up and slid back the long coat he'd taken to wearing, clearing the butt of the Walker Colt.

"Joe," Becky said, and shut up.

Inside the door, Joe looked out to see Cherokee Bill. The man was standing spreadlegged in fringed buckskin breeches and moccasins; he wore crossed gunbelts, and from the waist up he dressed like a white man—shirt, kerchief, old cavalry hat. It was like he was flaunting his mixed blood, Joe thought, although there was no disguising it in his dark face.

Calling out, Joe said, "I have no quarrel with you."

The laugh was a high-pitched whinny. "Sho' you ain't, but I got one with *you*. Come on out here and whup me like you whup niggers where you come from. Come on

345

and take my hair like you done to Injuns in Texas. Two for one, whore man—two for one."

Quietly, Becky said from the stairs, "Shoot him where he stands."

Joe said, "If that black and Cherokee mix is botherin' you, take it on back to Oklahoma. I never owned a slave, red or black, and I worked a damned sight harder than either, for a damned sight less. I don't want to kill you, boy."

"Boy—*boy?* I'm a heap more than any whorin' white trash. Killed me a round dozen of you nigger-whuppin' bastards, and if that whore ain't gelded you, come on out here and be number thirteen."

"Oh, hell," Joe said, and looked up at the sky for a moment to adjust his eyes to the outer brightness. Then he walked out through the batwing doors and into the dusty street.

Becky was right; the man had eyes like a snake, but muddier. Long, yellowish teeth gleamed as Bill grinned hugely.

"Now," he hissed, "now, white man—"

He was pretty fast, but Joe had never seen a *pistolero* who could keep his mind on two guns at once, and Cherokee Bill wasn't much different. He got off one shot with his righthand pistol just as it cleared leather, and the bullet kicked dirt a yard wide of Joe's boot. The lefthand gun was just coming up when Joe shot the man in the chest.

Standing firmly, right foot pushed out a little, he sighted down his barrel and shot the breed again as Bill staggered back and dropped one pistol. The third bullet hammered the man onto his back and Joe watched dark fingers uncurl from a notched gunbutt. Only a damned fool would count coup on his gunbutt like that, advertising that he was a gunslick and inviting everybody to take a pop at him.

People began easing out of storefronts and moving along the street. Joe broke open the Walker and jacked out empty shells to thumb refills into the cylinder, then slid the pistol back into its holster. He looked along the street, then up at the sky where a black bird was slowly wheeling.

"No sense to it," he said, to nobody in particular. "Just no damned sense to it."

A shabby man was crouched over the breed. "Tough 'un, weren't he? Took three to put him down, and I kin cover the shots with my hand, they was that close together."

"Keep that hand to yourself, Amos," Joe said. "If he's got any money, it's for his buryin'."

Amos flinched back, ferret face screwed up. "I kin just as well tote him on out yonder where them fleabite Injuns is camped and dump him there. Cain't I even have his guns? Lemme dump him out yonder, Joe—he belongs with them, not buried amongst no white folks."

"That was his trouble," Joe said softly. "I guess he didn't belong anywhere. Some don't—some of us don't."

For some reason, then, he waited for the law and the undertaker, waited so nobody would strip the body of everything, even dignity, and only after he'd seen Cherokee Bill driven off in a buckboard did he turn and walk back into Becky Taylor's saloon.

She cut him off as he headed for the stairs, both soft hands upon his arms, looking earnestly up into his face. "Joe, Joe, you big fool—you didn't have to face him down."

"I did," he said. "I wish I didn't have to, but I couldn't have turned a card anywhere in the West, if I hadn't. And now—"

Becky hurried up the stairs after him. "Now you can forget that breed and come in with me. Hell, you don't even hafta put up a share."

"He called me righter than he knew," Joe said.

"So I'm a whore and you're my man. I'm a good whore and you're a good man. Ain't nothin' wrong with that."

"You're right, too," he said, taking off his long coat and vest, removing his gunbelt. "A while back, I would have said the same thing and meant it. Now, I just don't know, Becky. But one thing I *do* know—and that's every twobit gunman in the country will come lookin' for me—to try and kill the man who killed Cherokee Bill."

She put the back of her hand to her mouth and said around it, "We can stop 'em, Joe—sawed-offs, hired hands, the law. Damn it, Joe—how come you're rollin' up your stuff?"

"I guess you know, Becky. I've been in El Paso too long."

Becky stalked to the dresser and poured whiskey; the bottle rattled against the glass. "You been mopin' after that Marilee too long, you mean, and this here's just an excuse for you to walk out on me."

"Marilee?"

She drank and glared at him. "That damned woman's name you call me sometimes, right when we're doin' it. You think I never heard? You think I ain't heard you mumble in your sleep about plantations and such? Hell, what makes you think *you* got a greenhorn's chance in hell with a high-falutin' lady? You and me's outa the same litter, Joe Langston, poor dirt folks that can never scrub off the stink of the hogpen. Onliest way we goin' to make it is to get together enough hard money so's we can spit in the gentry's faces. And you know what? When we do, they won't even wipe it off, pretendin' it never happened and lookin' right through on us like we ain't here. But goddamn it, I aim to keep on spittin' until they *do* take notice."

Rolling clothes and blankets into a slicker, Joe tied the bundle with a string and reached beneath the bed for his saddlebags. "That sounds like me, a while back, but I don't figure on humbling the gentry any more, because there isn't any. Not like we knew them, Becky."

"Then why the hell are you doin' this? You got it real good here. And it ain't just drawin' gunfighters—you got that Marilee woman in your craw, and she's apt to choke you to death."

"Maybe so," he said. "Look—I'm obliged for everything you've done for me, all you've been to me, and that's been a lot. You're a fine, honest woman, Becky Taylor."

Sharps slung over one shoulder, saddlebags over the other, and the carbine in his left hand, Joe moved close to her, but she moved quickly back, blue eyes wide and hurt, her painted mouth quivering.

"All right, then," he said. "I'll always remember you, Becky."

She followed him halfway down the steps and stopped with one hand on the rail, the other against her belly as if she had a pain there. "Joe—it ain't much good to tell you to come on back, that you'll always be welcome here. It won't do no good to say that, because a man like you—he don't ever go back to anywhere, or to anybody. Remember that, Joe—you can't ever go back to *anybody*."

"I'll remember," he said, walking past the poker table and through the saloon.

Her voice trembled after him: "A man like you totes dreams in his head. Damn you—I toted 'em too, 'til they got so heavy they like to broke my back."

On the boardwalk, he heard her final, plaintive words, "Dreams can kill you, Joe Langston—kill you dead."

Chapter 37

She came awake languorously, slowly arousing to the caress of silken sheets around her body, eyelashes fluttering open to focus hazily upon a white and vaulted ceiling. With a half-smile, Marrilee turned onto her side, facing a window where the spicy odor of a late-blooming fall flower lingered. Gauzy curtains stirred there in a quiet eddy of wind, and Marilee sat up to stretch. It was so very different, being tucked beneath a roof, sleeping undisturbed and deeply because she didn't have to listen for the warning snap of a twig or the alarmed snuffing of a horse.

Then she winced, because parts of her body were tender, even sore, and as the maid Rosa came padding barefoot into the bedroom as if she had been awaiting some signal of awakening, Marilee remembered the night and felt warmth leap into her face.

But if Rosa noticed, the girl was too well trained to show it. She came bearing steaming hot chocolate and a honeyed roll upon a silver tray. *"Buenos días,* señorita. Would you like your bath before breakfast?"

"I—I think so," Marilee answered, accepting the fragile china cup and sipping its dark, faintly sweetened contents. "Has the don—"

"*El patrón* rode out early, but will return soon. I will prepare your bath."

When the girl was gone, Marilee slid out of bed and glanced down the length of her body. There was a light bruise upon her left thigh, and another upon her breast; as she turned to put the empty cup upon the bedside table, she could feel scratches upon her haunches, light marks left there in the fury of Don Alfonso's passion.

She felt something else, a tremble that began in the pit of her stomach and tightened her skin over her breasts. Last night hadn't been rape or even the threat of it. She was certain that if she had resisted, if she'd struck out at him and insisted he let her alone, Don Alfonso de Carboca would have bowed graciously and departed. But she hadn't even tried to put him off, because it seemed so—so ordained, as if it were meant to happen from the first moment he kissed her hand. And she hadn't *wanted* to resist, not even for a moment.

Whispering to the empty room as she found a black and lacy dressing gown draped over a chair back and put it on, Marilee said, "Maybe there's something basically wrong with me, but I don't feel *bad*. I feel sort of wonderful. If it's bad to admit my own lust and enjoy it, then I guess I'm an evil woman."

From the door, Rosa murmured, "*Perdón,* señorita?"

"*Nada,*" Marilee said quickly. "I'm not used to such luxury—not since a long time ago anyway."

Two other girls carried buckets of water, and when they'd emptied them into the tub, Rosa said shyly, "It is said the señorita has crossed Comancheria by herself, fearless and strong as any man."

Helped from her robe, Marilee slipped into the water. "I was lucky and had help from time to time."

Even softer-voiced, the girl said, "From *los comanches* themselves?" And when Marilee looked quickly around, Rosa dropped her black, almond eyes. "I mean no disrespect, señorita. It is just that *mi madre* was taken by them long ago and rescued later. There is talk I may not be my father's daughter."

Impulsively, Marilee touched the brown hand. "There's nothing to be ashamed of, Rosa. Some Comanches are great people."

"*Gracias,*" Rosa whispered. "My mother said there are

351

many kinds of slavery, and perhaps that of the Comanches is not the worst."

Marilee frowned. "What do you mean?"

The girl slipped away. "I talk too much. I will bring more hot water."

Soaping herself, Marilee was glad enough to be alone, so she could taste again the bittersweet flavors of the night past. It had been a nervous moment when Don Alfonso led her into the apartment, his hand strong and warm upon her arm, his thigh brushing against her own. She saw a bottle of wine upon a table and wondered if he'd anticipated her acceptance or if it was the gesture of a host.

A fireplace fanned welcome heat into the room and spread the only light, dancing—inviting golds, mischievous, tempting scarlets. She had had to lift her narrow skirt so she could kneel upon the furs before the fire and was conscious of her white legs flashing long and slim. She covered them with the mantilla, but not before Don Alfonso's eyes gleamed appreciatively.

"Wine?" he asked.

She shook her head. "I've already had too much."

"Merely a taste, then, to answer my toast." He handed down a crystal glass and touched his own to it. "To perhaps the luckiest day Hacienda Carboca has ever known —to this day, graced by you."

"Thank you," she said, and looked away from the compulsion of him, the certain, male nearness of him. Beside her upon the furs, he put aside their glasses and laid his fingertips gently against her cheekbones, staring deeply into her eyes as leaping firelight painted suns and shadows upon his hawk's face.

"I am glad there is no coyness in you," he said, "no false modesty of the simpering girl. For you are fully a woman, *querida,* and even if you were not, time is too precious to me for the playing of little games. So—"

There were dark and swirling depths in his eyes; they made Marilee dizzy—or was it the wine? She repeated, "So?"

And found herself in his arms, not without a certain tenderness, but in a fierce hunger that overwhelmed the gentle part. Their teeth clashed and her tongue met his in startled wildness as his hands cupped her breasts. There was a whipcord strength in him, a demanding power that bore her along in its tidal wave of urgency.

Don Alfonso's hands were adept at removing her dress, and she helped him by lifting herself, by raising her arms so he could slide the gown over her head and away. There was a ravenous kind of delight upon his intent face as he stared hungrily at her exposed flesh, as his fingers stroked and caressed.

He was in her hand then, her own fingers closing convulsively about the veined throbbing of his erect manhood, and she clung to him as he rained hot kisses upon her throat, upon both her breasts, the wet fire of his tongue licking, licking.

"Superb," he muttered hoarsely. "*Magnifico*—such a wondrous body, with delicate roses hidden beneath the snow. Such erect nipples, *mi amor,* the legs sheer artistry, and this silvered fluff—ahh, ahh!"

Her heart leaped crazily as the firelight when he twisted himself from her hand and nipped at the skin of her heaving stomach. Marilee lurched to her elbows as his fingernails dug beneath her trembling haunches and she was spread for the moist gustings of his breath.

"N-no—oh, please—"

So tiny that she could barely hear it herself, her voice fluttered helplessly about his shining hair and broke against its graybright wings. Then she had no voice, only a stunned and throaty gasping that shuddered itself up from somewhere deep within the core of her. She had no eyes, only starbursts that geysered madwhite sparks, whose comet tails burned swiftly out only to be reborn in new savagery.

Was this Marilee Bradburn, squirming and thrusting so violently, this abandoned wanton responding so lasciviously to something that had to be sinful? Could this be the plantation lady, thrumming in every pore of her debauched body, moaning and crying out in a rapture so intense that it would surely, surely kill her?

She did not die. The crest carried her foaming with it, spun her and drew all strength from her limbs, all reason from her mind. The great, bubbling wave smashed her down upon a beach whose silken sands seared her, consumed her.

Quivering, softened and gone boneless, Marilee knew that something else was happening to her, that her lax body was being entered, impaled by him as he reached deeply, so deeply. She flinched at the ring of his teeth around her breast, at the raking of his nails, but her body lifted to meet him, hurried to batter itself into him.

It started all over again, in a different way, a more ful-filling way, a pounding rhythm that blended them and churned them, submerging and surfacing and gasping for air. He was feral, greedy, turning her this way and that, but she could match his fury and did, enveloping this man, locking him within her and swiveling upon him, contracting upon him until he also cried out.

Flames applauded; fur cupped her as she cupped him. The room swayed and shadows played hide and seek across the celling. Softness. Wholeness. Completion.

Rolling from her, he sought the wine bottle. The fur across his chest was crisper than the rug, darker, sprinkled with gray. He was older and younger; he was stronger and weaker. She sat up, her hand unsteady upon the glass, but meeting his eyes without shame.

"Your teeth are sharp, *querida*."

"Did I hurt you?"

"Pain can also be pleasure."

"Then I'm not sorry."

He saluted her with his glass. "Never be sorry for any-thing. That should be emblazoned upon the de Carboca coat of arms. To you, my silver *pistolera*, my *gran caballera*, my proud, fierce lover—and to those luckless de Carbocas who have gone before me—they never knew such a woman."

"To you," Marilee said, and the wine was tart upon her tongue, honeyed down her throat, for she was sud-denly thirsty.

They drank more wine and made more—what? Not quite love; it was too demanding, too greedy for love. But whatever it was, their repeated joinings were sensuously gratifying to her because she could also attack, attack, because she could take as well.

Marilee stirred in the cooling water and opened her eyes to Rosa standing ready with towels. Languidly, she climbed from the tub and allowed herself to be dried, all her body still tingling with memories. Sitting nude before the dressing table, she sniffed at bottled scents and toyed with small containers of rouge as the maid brushed her hair and exclaimed over its color, its softness.

There was a riding habit waiting, soft white shirt and

split skirt, a darling little jacket, and a saucy brimmed hat with a cord for under the chin. Lovingly polished boots were already spurred, and Marilee somehow knew they would fit her feet to perfection.

"*Hola!*" she said to the mirror, to Rosa. "Thus does the Spanish lady go down to breakfast."

"*Madre,*" Rosa whispered, and furtively crossed herself. "If it was not for your coloring—"

"Oh," Marilee laughed, "I know I'll never *be* a grand señora, but it's fun to pretend. Do grand señoras ever admit they're starving?"

Rosa didn't laugh with her. The girl blinked at the finery, and backed up a step when Marilee picked up a little silver-mounted quirt, a smaller copy of the one Don Alfonso carried. Marilee smiled. "To beat off anyone who tries to stop me from eating an entire cow."

"*Sí,*" the girl murmured, "*sí,* mistress. I will—to clean up the bath—I go—"

The house was quiet as Marilee went downstairs, but she could hear bustling in the kitchen, and noises outside in the patio. Belatedly, she thought of Bradburn, but from what she'd glimpsed of the don's stables, her horse was being well cared for. Still, it was something she liked to do for herself, and thought she'd see to the stallion's grooming soon after breakfast.

A round woman turned as Marilee entered the kitchen and stared at her with wide, black eyes. "Oh, no, señorita. If you please, *por favor,* be seated in the dining room, and I will send Luis *pronto* with food. Melons, a chili omelette, browned bread and coffee—if that is to your liking."

"And bacon, too," Marilee suggested. "But I don't see why I can't eat in here. It's much cozier. Sausage, if you don't have bacon. I'm very hungry."

The cook clasped hands together. "Forgive me, but *el patrón*—bacon, *sí,* and sausage—anything, señorita, if only—"

"Very well—I wouldn't want to break any rules of the house," Marilee said, and thought the woman looked very relieved.

She sat at the great table, peering down its glistening length at the lines of chairs like so many dour sentries along it. For some reason, she hadn't dropped into the taller, more ornately carved one Don Alfonso had sat in last evening. She wished he were in it now, talking and smiling, for this morning she could watch his face and know the tempestuous truth that lurked just beneath his olive skin.

He didn't appear until she had worked her way through a steaming platter of delicious food and drunk several little cups of strong, thick coffee. She had just walked out into the courtyard and was starting toward the stables when he rode through the portico and leaped from his black mare. Hands outstretched, he strode to her, and for a moment she thought he was going to take her in his arms, but Don Alfonso only caught her hands briefly before releasing them.

"You look every inch the lady," he said, eyes approving.

"And you seem to know my exact size," she said, "even to the boots."

"Most women could wear those clothes and still appear to be peasants, but not you. You were born to them. But tell me, *amor*, where were you going?"

"To the stables," she said. "I'd forgotten my horses, and the stallion—"

"We go together, then. The stallion, yes—a proud beast which strikes fear into the peons, but my master vaquero already knows him."

Walking beside him, she said, "I don't really like anyone else handling Bradburn. I'd rather groom him myself. Oh, I'm certain he's getting the best of food and care, Don Alfonso, but—"

His hand tightened upon her elbow. "Servants do such tasks here. Please remember that. Ah—here we are, and see how the great stallion tosses his head, now he greets his rider. I can understand his eagerness to have you touch him, to have those fine legs about his body."

Damn it, she thought, why did the blood rush to her face like that? It was a girlish reaction, and she was fully a woman; Don Alfonso had said so, had complimented her upon not being coy and silly.

Vaqueros moved away from the stall, one of them a bent and whitehaired man with a twisted nose and small, uncertain feet.

"José," Don Alfonso said, "the mistress asks after the welfare of this stallion."

Hat in hand, wrinkled lips stretching to show missing teeth, José said, "All is well, *patrón*. A horse such as this one—a king among horses, señor."

"Care for him as such, then," Don Alfonso said. "The mustang mares are on pasture?"

"For a short while only, *patrón*. This stallion will be led out after his *chicas* are taken off the grass."

"*Bueno*." He took Marilee's arm again and moved her firmly from the stables. "You see, *querida*, old José knows his duties. A duty for everyone, a time for every duty."

Glancing at him, she said, "Is that on the de Carboca coat of arms, also?"

He laughed, white teeth flashing. "Perhaps it should be. But no, the motto of the de Carboca family is less personal but more to the point, and in Latin, of course. The Castillians were always very conscious of the church. *Oderint dum metuant*."

"What does it mean, then?"

Don Alfonso stopped in the courtyard and reached a tanned hand for a blossom that grew close to a barred window. He snapped it off between quick fingers and gave it to her. "The de Carboca motto is this: *Let them hate, so long as they fear*."

Holding the flower, she hesitated, and he motioned her into the house.

Chapter 38

Left boot heel propped up on the windowsill, Joe
Langston looked down on the bustling street and beyond
it to the cluttered harbor. It would take him a spell to get
used to the noise, the constant comings and goings, the air
of industry and excitement that filled the city. Freshly
bathed and shaved, his hair trimmed to a reasonable
length, and at last out of blackened buckskins, he felt he'd
reached something he'd been stretching for all his life,
that the pot of gold was down there somewhere and all he
had to do was put his hand on it.

It had been a long, grinding trip from El Paso, and it
still bothered him to think of leaving that good young colt
behind. But Otto the stableman loved the young stallion
more than anything else, and the trail would have been
rough on the horse, if not fatal.

Biting into the end of a new cigarillo, Joe thought that a
lot of things had to be left behind when a man moved on.
Traveling far meant traveling light, and although he'd
fretted some at having to scout for another wagon train,
he knew he'd never make it to California without the
group. They'd been lucky, though—only a few brushes

with Apaches, a couple of snakebite deaths, only three losses from fever.

Now the train was gone, broken up as some wagons were sold and some went on feeling their way north along the coast, a few even heading north to the Oregon country. Joe didn't mean to go anywhere else. He didn't want to look for land so he could dig in the dirt or scratch for gold in the mountains; all the good claims were long taken and well guarded. A miner could still find pockets of nuggets or break his back panning the streams, but Joe had a hunch the big strikes had been made.

The money was right here in San Francisco, brought in miner poke and cattleman saddlebag, gathering itself in banks and saloons and growing stores. It fed upon itself and got ever fatter, sending those tall ships over the seas to carry back precious goods that made still more money. Joe meant to get his share of it and more, the only way he knew.

He slid a knife into his boot before lifting it from the windowsill and made certain his cache was well hidden. Colt belted on, he took just enough gold coins for a good stake. He'd passed a dozen saloons and twice that number of bawdy houses; where whiskey and women flourished, so did poker tables. There'd be no lack of men who thought they could gamble—sailors in port after a year at sea with wages heavy in their pockets, miners celebrating a small strike, small businessmen looking for an easy way to expand their holdings, cowboys eager to buck the tiger and burn it all out in a few furious days before going back to the hard, lonely months of another drive.

And the big cattlemen, Joe thought; mustn't forget them, the large landholders who could scatter gold with both hands and never look back. They were the barons who'd gotten out here early and overrun the Californios, grabbed land and cows, snatched haciendas and women, and been tough enough, bold enough to keep all they took.

As he moved down the stairs and into the multilingual noise of the lobby, for some reason Joe thought of Marilee Bradburn. She had wanted to be queen of a vast cattle and horse empire, too, but only in order to go back and play princess of a great plantation again. What could her dreams mean here in this raw, roaring city that just didn't give a damn? Even if she had managed to stay alive, little Marilee and her piddling three-horse band would be trampled in the dust.

Self-effacing and hurrying Chinese drifted aside to let others pass; Mexicans looked sullenly at the crowd; just-arrived sailors cavorted in the street while others, sick and sorry, stumbled back to their ships. Miners and cowhands and merchants; here a black-robed priest and there a bewildered Indian, both without parishes now and not yet admitting it; a carriage with high wheels and prancing horses carrying tall-hatted gentlemen and their parasoled ladies; black freedmen out at the elbows and down in the mouth, lost. Harried muleskinners, stage drivers, railroad men, everything mixed sweating and swearing into this bubbling pot. A man with an ante to put up, and skill and backbone to back it, could skim off the top of that pot.

Turning into a garish saloon, Joe brushed by some painted ladies and looked for the poker tables. Two were back against the wall, all chairs filled, cigar smoke heavy above them. He could wait awhile and watch a spell, maybe see who was dealing crooked. In the meantime, there was the bar with an ornate chandelier over it, but the prisms were cracked and gapped.

"Your pleasure?" the barkeep asked. He was a jowly man in a stained shirt, beady-eyed and bald as a peeled egg.

"Whiskey," Joe said, and watched the man pour it sloppily, brown liquid spilling over the rim of the glass. The man didn't wipe the bar. He said, "Just in off a wagon train? Fellas off a train generally get all shined up first thing."

"From El Paso," Joe said, and tasted the whiskey. It was raw and bitter. He put the glass back on the bar top and turned to watch the tables. The barman hovered behind him. "Interested in a game? Somebody'll go bust before long."

A frowsy woman sidled up and Joe waved her off. At the far end of the bar, another man poured whiskey for a drunken sailor. A scarecrow in shirt sleeves thumped on an out-of-tune piano.

"Stakes can get pretty high over there," the barkeep said. "Drink up, wagon man—next one's on the house, with a beer chaser. Know that stuff's pretty green, but it gets drunk up fast as they can make it. Goes better with beer."

Joe agreed it washed down better with beer, but the two drinks still lay heavy in his belly. He paid for his round with a double eagle and took his change, moving from the bar to stand near a table, but not so close some gambler might think he was placed to signal the house dealer.

The cigar he was smoking tasted bitter, too; he ground it under his heel and wondered why he was sweating so. The clattering piano seemed overly loud and the high giggle of a whore sounded like the shriek of a diving hawk. The floor dipped and he locked his knees to keep from swaying with it, his stomach churning before it went numb and he couldn't feel it at all.

Bald pate shining dully, the barkeep was suddenly at his elbow. "Poor fella's taken sick. Hang on there, wagon man."

Thickly, fuzzily, Joe said, "That—that damned whiskey—"

"Green as a traveling pilgrim," the man chuckled. "Lemme give you a hand, mister—"

And there was spiderwebbed mustiness, a shadowed room that smelled of the sea, that stank of the sea's putrid leavings. Hands were upon him, pawing, imprisoning him as his head sagged.

"Feel him for a handgun," the voice said. "Them wagon men are liable to carry one."

"Can't—can't reach it," somebody else panted. "He's a big, heavy bastard. If you was to get your hand outa his pocket—"

"What he's carryin' is mine," the barkeep grunted, "and it don't mean you still don't owe me for him. Like you said, he's a big one and strong—be worth a heap on a China-bound ship."

"Damn him—he keeps foldin' at the knees. Still can't get aholt of his gun, but I guess he ain't about to use it, fallin' down like he is."

Joe had one hand that would work. Straining his mind,

he willed it to work, to move and lift slowly, lift fumbling toward his mouth. The rest of him sagged, but he managed to get a finger down his throat.

"Look out!" somebody yelled. "Son of a bitch is pukin'!"

When they dropped him, the jolt of the floor against his cheek was welcome, a blow that jarred his dizzy mind. He retched again and curled onto his right side, fighting to clear his eyes, to make his other hand belong to him.

"Ain't that dory here yet? Open the trap and take a look—*they* can haul him down. Damn—he ruined my shirt."

Wood rattled and slid back, a gust of salt air splashed up at Joe's fevered face. He could feel the butt of the Colt; he could *feel* it.

"Pull off his boots and coat—they're worth somethin'—and kick him over so I can get his gun belt."

The shining, hairless head loomed grotesquely over Joe, wavering and rippling. He battled the pistol from its holster and jerked at the trigger, not able to aim. The explosion shook the room.

"Watch it! Bastard's gun—"

"Don't run over me—look out for the trap door—"

"Get him! Damn it, *get* him!"

Joe triggered the Colt again, its muzzle higher this time, and a hole punched itself through a wall. Fighting for breath, for some kind of stability, he painfully got one bent knee under him before someone hit him beside the head and somebody else got hold of his gun arm.

He didn't know he was feeling for the haft of the skinning knife until it snugged into his hand as if it had pushed itself from his boot top.

"*Aaahh!* I'm stabbed—ohmigod—my leg—"

Two knees then, and still hanging grimly to the handle of the Walker Colt, feeling the blows on his head with a savage kind of joy, because they were driving away the numbness and the pain felt good, good.

Cutting left and right, Joe cleared a space around him. He twisted his head and sank teeth into a grimy wrist, and his gun hand was free. They were rolling about him, obscured by gunsmoke, yelling and cursing, but he got both knees braced and the pistol bucked comfortingly in his hand. A man screamed and cartwheeled through the open trap to splash into bay waters.

Then Joe was up, his legs wobbling and threatening to give way, but braced erect with the bloodied knife in one fist and deadly Colt in the other. They scurried from him, but a flung club hurt his shoulder and he knew they weren't through. Stomach turning over, he forced one boot to follow the other and made it to the door.

Faces swung toward him in the saloon, none of them friendly. Somebody threw a chair, and as it crashed against the wall, Joe let go a shot that shattered the big mirror behind the bar. He kept walking stiff-legged, holding himself together with an effort, trying to edge along sideways, so he could keep them from coming at his back. How many bullets did he have left?

Another chair skidded across the sawdusted floor and he stumbled over it, barely catching himself. He pointed the gun and two men plunged beneath a table, but a hurled bottle missed his head by a whizzing inch, and men yammered behind him like a pack of mountain wolves deprived of their prey. Turning back made him dizzier, but he had to fire a shot to keep them back. A man cursed bitterly, so he must have nicked somebody. If only his eyes would clear, if he could *see*—

The air was cleaner outside, but the boardwalk uneven, and he nearly fell. Somebody else had a gun now, and he staggered to one side as the shotgun jerked a handful of splinters at his feet. Joe fired back, but when he eared the hammer again, it fell upon an empty cartridge with a click loud as a gravedigger's shove on a tombstone.

Back against a wall, he faced them with the useless gun, with the outstretched knife. They came hungrily, lunged greedily from the saloon, yapping for his blood. Other men scattered along the street, taking cover, running from trouble. A carriage pulled up suddenly as the horse reared in its shafts, spooked by the gunfire.

"Come on," Joe grated. "Damn you—come on!"

And they came.

Until the whip began to fall among them, heavy, vicious lashes of the long blacksnake that popped like rifle shots. They fell back, tripped one over another to get away from the petticoated fury that swung the whistling whip with an expert hand, its leaded tip jerking blood from a cheek, making another man whine and clutch his belly, tearing off the shirtsleeve and leaving a scarlet line.

"Get—get! Off with you, you scum, you filthy trash!" Her voice was high but strong and filled with righteous venom, and the woman's face was whitely set in determination.

They eddied and stumbled, cursed and yelped. Now her coachman was with her, a huge black man who snatched two of the pack from their feet and banged their heads together. And another man came loping across the street, a man slim and saturnine in a gambler's coat, a derringer winking in his hand.

Breaking, the pack scuttled for the saloon doors, vanishing into its smoky darkness with squeaks of outrage and hurt. Dumbly, Joe Langston stared after them, conscious now of blood dripping down his face, of pain getting claws into him.

"Come," she said firmly, "I don't think they'll have the courage to show their faces again, but you never know with trash like that. Come, sir—"

He had no choice; massive black hands lifted him into the carriage, and he could hear the woman thanking the gambler who'd come running to help. Head lolling back, Joe allowed her to take the pistol from his tired fist, to remove the skinning knife. The carriage lurched forward and moved along a street filling itself again with the curious, now that danger wasn't immediate.

Thick-lipped, his head still uncertain upon his shoulders, he said, "What were they—why did—they jumped me without cause, ma'am—fed me a poisoned drink and—"

Up on the seat, the black turned his head to answer. "Shanghai folks. Time you woke up, you'da been halfway to China. They gets a hundred dollars a head for men, 'cause won't nobody sign on this end, and most of them as gets here in the first place jumps ship."

She said, "That awful Barbary Coast! It simply has to

be set to the torch someday—it's the only way to drive out vermin. And you, sir—you had no business there."

"Just—just got in off a wagon train," Joe mumbled. "Lady, where are you takin' me? My hotel—"

"Which of these ratnests is it? Oh, that one. Marcus, please go up and get this gentleman's things. What did you say the room was, sir? I do hope you had the good sense to hide your valuables."

Feeling rocky and fighting the impulse to be sick, Joe told the black what he had and where it was secreted. Then he put his head back once more and breathed deeply. He must have slept, because when he knew anything again, he was being carried like a child and placed upon a couch.

Liniment stung his forehead, and he winced. She said, "Just lie still, sir. Ah, there seems to be no permanent damage. You were very lucky."

"No, ma'am," the black said, "them boys just got hold of a bobcat this time. I expect they chunked more'n one dead man into the bay, after they tangled with this 'un. Reckon he was lucky at that, lucky we come along and you lit into 'em."

"Marcus," she said, "you everlastingly rattle on. Why don't you tell Sarah to bring warm milk laced with the good brandy and a raw egg in it. I'll finish cleanin' him up while you put his things in the east room."

Wet cloth cooled his face and the brandied milk settled his stomach, helped to clear his eyes. She sat beside him on the couch, and he was surprised to find her looking so young; she'd sounded much older. "Joe Langston, ma'am —once of Alabama and a lot of places between here and there. I'm indebted to you for saving my life."

"Possibly," she said. "You were at bay, but undefeated; bloodied but still dangerous as a fightin' bull. I could not resist helpin' you. And do stop calling me ma'am. My name is Mrs. Samuel Fitzhugh-Morris— Martha to my intimates. Alabama, you said—did you know General Fitzhugh-Morris?"

Gingerly, Joe touched fingertips to his aching head. "I never even saw a general."

"Perhaps you met him when he was senator?"

"No, ma'am—ah—"

"Martha."

"Then no, Martha. I didn't move in those circles."

Her sudden smile made her face almost girlish. "Just as well—Samuel was an insufferable bore, and I suspect a somewhat confused general. But then, most of them were—bankers and planters and the lot playing at war. My Samuel did have a good head for business, and he was practical about everything else. He had the good foresight to put me aboard ship when the war was about to begin, and I brought the family fortune safely to California. Minus, of course, the money he spent to raise and equip his regiment. It was the only way they'd make him a general, and in that respect he was a little boy."

Joe focused upon her—the fine lines around her stubborn but rich mouth and gray eyes, the no-nonsense set to her head and shoulders. He couldn't tell her age; she was neatly, almost plainly dressed, and her chestnut hair was severely styled. Martha hadn't bothered to disguise its hints of gray. He said, "But he saw ahead of time that the South would lose."

"It was inevitable—we agreed on that. His compatriots scorned Samuel for sending me off, for converting all his property into gold. Poor, practical man—he still felt his duty was with them, and I understand he died well. As if there is a good way to die."

When Joe smiled up at her, the corner of his mouth hurt. "My sentiments exactly, Martha. And I'd say, among other things, that your husband was a fortunate man—he had you."

For just a moment, there was a small movement within her gray eyes, then her mouth tried to hide its richness and she murmured, "I wouldn't know how Mr. Fitzhugh-Morris felt about that. Ah, there's Marcus to tell us your room is prepared, and your bath. He'll look after any wounds beneath your clothing. You might need laudanum in order to rest. Shall I—"

"Some more of that fine brandy might do the trick," he said, smiling again. But when he sat up the house wobbled, and he was glad for Marcus's supporting hand and surprised at the weakness of his legs when he was guided up a set of curving stairs.

A black girl sway-hipped out of the room as they entered, tossing her head and flashing wicked sloe eyes as she passed. Marcus said, "Go 'long, Sissy, ain't nobody got time for you, nor the druthers, neither. Langston, you say your name is—Joe Langston? Get your clothes off without help?"

"I reckon. They got to me pretty good, got my money, too. Good thing I had that cache in the hotel."

Casually, the huge black sat on the side of a satined bed and stretched out treetrunk legs. "Notice you hung on to your handgun and knife. You pretty good with 'em and them long guns I toted?"

"Good enough, when I haven't been poisoned." It was strange that this black wasn't calling him mister and saying sir. Free or not, blacks weren't all that far along in a white world. He looked closer at this one and saw the scarred eyebrows, lumpy lips, and an ear folded over. "Your master used to put you to scratch, Marcus."

"That he did, and I made money for him, too, knockin' them other bucks around some. But he paid me good— give me my freedom papers before the war started."

"You were free, and you stayed with her?"

Big shoulders rolled in a shrug. "She's a good woman. Others stayed, too—that tail-switchin' gal you saw, a cook, and a houseboy. Free don't put no bread in your mouth, and like I said, Miss Martha is a good woman."

Stripping, Joe found a welt along his ribs and a place on his shoulder turning blue. He hadn't missed Marcus calling his employer "Miss," but not putting a handle to Joe's name. He could imagine the big man fighting fiercely against other bucks brought in to test his fists, while white men gambled and shouted encouragement, nobody really caring if one fighter killed the other; like pitting roosters, like making dogs fight.

He said, "Martha made him stop matching you."

Marcus grunted. "You got a conjure eye, man. That she did. But if you can see things, so can I—like them whip marks acrost your back. You never kept no slaves."

"Had trouble enough keepin' myself. Just white trash, Marcus."

"Uh-uh," the black said, getting off the bed to point Joe into a bathroom. "Trash don't care if it's black or white. Trash wouldn't of stood to them shanghai folks like you did. Here—let me help you into the tub. Cold water comes outa that tap there, from a cistern on the roof. Sissy totes up hot water, but she'll devil you. She's right good at it, and Miss Martha plays like she don't know, but it frets her some."

"I'll remember that," Joe said. "Lord, Lord—but this feels *good*. Never knew they hit me so many places— never knew much of anything, to tell the truth. I was near played out when she jumped in with that whip—no time to reload. I owe her for that—I owe you, too."

"Here's the soap," Marcus said.

"Can't stay in this fine house long, though," Joe went on. "Never saw the inside of a plantation house, except when it was burning, but it couldn't beat this. Can't take advantage of her hospitality after I get my legs under me, because your mistress and me—we're not cut out of the same bolt." The hot water was making his head swimmy and his tongue loose.

"I'm only a gambler, Marcus—when I'm not chasin' after Indians and scouting for wagon trains. Martha is a lady, and you don't know it, but I'm putting a different connotation to that term now. I used to spit when I said it—that, or choke on my own bile."

Marcus said slowly, leaning back against the wall with his muscled arms crossed, "She's a lady right enough, and used to be just about the richest one in San Francisco. The senator—he left her real well off. Miss Martha is right smart and comes out with what she means, but a lady is only a woman. Without the right kind of man to look after her, a woman can get robbed."

Joe poured water over his throbbing head and blinked. "She has you."

"I'm big and I can be downright mean, do I have to, but I'm black. Big and mean don't stop no bullets, and black just calls 'em."

"Look," Joe said, "I'm not right in the mind yet. If there's anything I can do for her, I will. I'm beholden to her, and I won't forget it, but you'd better tell me about it tomorrow, after I drink half that bottle of brandy and sleep off whatever they poisoned me with."

Catching Joe's extended hand, Marcus lifted him from the tub and handed him a towel. "You just might be the man, Joe Langston. I hope you don't forget you're beholden to her or pass it off."

Vaguely angry, Joe made it to the bed. "I won't."

"And don't forget what else you said," Marcus almost whispered. "She's a sure-enough lady. You remember that, gamblin' man."

Chapter 39

The *vaqueros* resented her; Marilee could feel that, sense it in their sidelong glances, their muttered replies to her questions. Grudgingly, they acknowledged her horsemanship, and their admiration of Bradburn was obvious, but they avoided her personally whenever they could. It was never out in the open, this smoldering dislike, for in only two days she had seen that Don Alfonso ruled with a hard, swift hand and moved in an aura of respect and awe.

Marilee tried to ignore the ranch hands, to enjoy instead the vastness, the mellowed beauty of the great hacienda. She adored the herd of barb mares and appreciated the careful breeding that had gone into them, and she just knew Bradburn could do a much better job. None of the stallions could anywhere near match him.

She rode him near the hacienda, and noticed that two *vaqueros* always followed, not too near, not too far, heavily armed men who evidently had orders to guard her. She watched patrols of four and five riders come and go and understood that this was how Don Alfonso kept close watch upon his rancho. There were line stations set in strategic places from where sentries could signal the presence of Apaches by mirrors. It was a good system and one that worked; beyond a few stolen cows, the huge spread wasn't bothered.

Seeing all this, she wondered how Comanche warriors would react to such a challenge, for that was how Piava and his kind would see it. Maybe they would strike very hard at some isolated line shack and be gone before enough riders could be gathered to follow them. Then they would swing in a wide, misleading circle, only to hit somewhere else. Marilee gnawed her lip; she'd have to stop thinking like that, but it would take time.

Putting Bradburn into his private run, where good grass was fattening him, she strolled into the courtyard and watched an old man tending the flowers. He swept off a battered straw hat as she passed and ducked his head. Greeting him, she lingered upon the open porch, wishing that Don Alfonso hadn't gone off on business. He hadn't told her where or why, only that he would return before nightfall.

Seated alone at the big table, Marilee had a delightful lunch, and when Rosa brought chilled wine, she asked the girl to stay, to sit with her.

"Oh, no, señorita. I cannot." The dark eyes were frightened.

"Don Alfonso? He's nowhere around, and I'm lonesome. Besides, I'd like to know more about him, about this place."

"*Por favor*, do not ask me. His ears hear everything, his eyes see everything."

"But surely, if I *asked* you? Very well—let's talk in my room, then."

Hesitantly, Rosa followed her upstairs and stood trembling just inside the door. Marilee said, "Oh, sit down. You won't betray any deep, dark secrets. I'm simply curious. He's been married, hasn't he?"

"*Sí*, the first señora died before I was brought here."

"Then there has been more than one wife?"

Rosa fidgeted. "I—I served the young one. Until she—" the girl crossed herself—"until she went mad and took her own life."

"How awful," Marilee said. "And there were no children?"

"No niños, although it is said the first señora died trying to give birth. This house—it is a place of tragedy. And it is not only that death has visited so often, but he—the other things, the sh-shameful things!" Catching herself, hand lifted to her breasts, Rosa's mouth quivered. Then she wheeled around and ran from the room.

Marilee stared after, wondering what had caused the outburst. Superstition, or the fact that Marilee herself was here in the apartment of Don Alfonso's former wives, but as a mistress? She shouldn't have kept after the girl like that; she'd brought something to the surface she hadn't wanted to think about herself. It was so pleasant here, so lush and privileged that she'd kept putting off looking at the facts. It wasn't *her* home, and Don Alfonso wasn't her man—except physically.

He was outside her experience, the prideful don, more an aristocrat than any planter she'd ever known, a handsome, steely man who wore his cloak of power regally, as if it could be no other way. And his lovemaking— Marilee fidgeted upon the couch and glanced at the fireplace, at the soft fur rug before it. The memory of his hard body and strong hands moved over her, and she could almost feel the hunger of his demanding mouth, the raking of his teeth in small, sweet pain, the sharpness of his fingernails. . . .

Abruptly, she got up and moved to the window, tapping the silver-mounted quirt against the side of her boot. Would it be possible for her to work out some arrangement with him? Out there by those springs—he had no cattle grazing there, no band of horses. If she could ask him to accept Bradburn's services in exchange for some acreage there, somehow get a small home built, she might have to search no further.

Lifting the quirt, Marilee tightened both hands upon it. Her own services would go to balance the bargain; she could not deny that. If that made her some kind of prostitute—but she refused to accept that idea. She hadn't *sold* her body like some common woman of the streets; she had enjoyed the incident as much as he had, possibly even more. She'd heard that whores didn't.

A woman moved across the courtyard below, walking smoothly and erectly with a basket upon her head. The wizened stableman—José?—carried a harness around a building. Marilee heard the laughter of a child, quickly silenced, and the clang of an anvil.

She was tired of travel, of hiding and dodging and coming close to starvation, weary of sleeping like an animal upon the ground, of not enough water. She was very tired of having to stay alert and ready to kill. It was wonderful to relax, marvelous to know she was safe and cared for, protected.

And California was far away through unfamiliar country where more Apaches waited, and perhaps her luck had been stretched thin; maybe some cunning brave would get an arrow into her, or worse—into Bradburn. Apaches, a horse laboring, doing its best, that flat-faced warrior sticking his knife point into its sweating, heaving flanks to get more speed from the poor beast, speed it did not have. . . .

Marilee cut her quirt at the curtain with a vicious stroke. She was glad she'd killed the man, and his tribesman who'd cut the throat of a tortured Mexican boy. If she had to pass through Apache land again, if she was forced to continue toward the sea, she would have to be Moon Woman once more, fully and fiercely. They would not take her.

She hadn't heard him climb the stairs, and snapped her head around at the sound of his voice. "So," Don Alfonso said, "the temper of *la pistolera* shows. It is a sign of hot blood and strength. But tell me, *mi amor*—has someone angered you?"

Marilee glanced at her quirt, slipped it over her wrist, and dropped it upon the couch. "No, of course not. I was just thinking of—something in the past."

"Or someone?" he asked, touching her everywhere with his eyes as he leaned indolently against the doorframe. "Surely you have had other loves, but I would brand each of them a fool for allowing you to escape him."

"Not *loves*," she said, "only men I couldn't refuse, who forced themselves upon me."

"The Comanche," Don Alfonso said. "He must have been a savage lover."

Marilee frowned at him. "Does that bother you, señor?"

"No," he said swiftly, "oh, no, *querida*—not in that manner. I wondered if you killed him in the end."

Shaking her head, she said, "No. I saved his life, but I

left him because I had to. Is that understandable, Don Alfonso?"

He came toward her, saying quietly, "I understand more of you than you imagine, Marilee, and I will know more still. Come downstairs now, for I have brought a guest."

Her hands rose to her hair. "Are you certain you want *me* to—"

Laughing, he said, "This one does not matter. *Es verdad*, none of them will matter before long, for I have always walked on my own path, and what man dares tell me to walk his?"

Leading her onto the landing, he whispered, "This one, a *gringo* whose land adjoins mine to the north. He has little water and is always coming to me to use more of mine. There is also trouble with Apaches on his rancho, seldom on mine."

With a flourish, Don Alfonso presented her to the heavy, redfaced man who grunted up clumsily from a chair, his watery eyes bulging at sight of her. "Miss Bradburn, Señor Jesse Flagg—a neighbor."

Flagg was almost as wide as he was tall, with thin strands of sandy hair straggling over a pale scalp, and sunburn below his hatline. He said, "Damned if I ever expected to see a white woman away out—howdy, miss. You're sure a sight for these here old eyes. But how'd you get here? Didn't hear nothin' about wagons passin'."

Don Alfonso cut in before she could answer, "Miss Bradburn is my—guest," and Marilee flinched inwardly at the hesitation, for he was making her position in his household plain. Why? What reason had he to flaunt her before this sweaty, staring man?

"Marilee," he said then, "if you would please see how preparations for dinner are coming along? Señor Flagg and I must talk business, which would bore you."

She was being dismissed, smoothly but definitely, not allowed to carry on a conversation with the neighboring rancher. Marilee tried not to show her resentment as she walked slowly into the kitchen, feeling the man's eyes on her all the way.

The cook fluttered and sidled, but Marilee ignored her and passed right on through, going out a back door and around into the patio. She had just been paraded like a prize mare, and she didn't like it. There was no reason for Don Alfonso to show her off that way, merely to make another man envious.

Circling the main house and ignoring the curious glances of peons, she found a back stairway and climbed it to struggle with a heavy door before it creaked back. Finding her rooms, she flung herself across the bed and stared at the ceiling. There were quirks to Don Alfonso de Carboca she hadn't seen in this brief time, probably many of them, and not all pleasant.

Marilee closed her eyes and rested. Let him wonder where she'd gone; let him search for her. He had told her his house was her house, so she could go where she pleased. The picture of the marshy land kept coming into her head, its green grass and clumps of trees, the knoll farther on where a house could be erected.

She awoke to Rosa softly calling her name, and sat up quickly.

"*El patrón* says it is time for dinner."

Rubbing her eyes, Marilee said, "The other man, that Jesse Flagg—is he still there?"

"No, señorita—the *patrón* never has *him* at his table. They do not like each other, and smile only with their mouths. I am to help you bathe and dress, and—señorita; please, you will not tell him I speak so with you? I would not, but you were a captive of the Comanche, as was *mi madre*, and I feel—"

Marilee touched the girl's hand. "We're friends, Rosa."

Rosa's smile was sunny and genuine. "*Gracias*—one needs a friend here." Her expression changed suddenly, the brown face serious. "I hope you will not change when he— Come, your water is ready, and I have laid out the dress he chose for you."

Bathed and scented, her hair thoroughly brushed, Marilee put on the white dress, all filigree and wide-skirted, but somehow effectively simple for all its furbelows.

"This time a ruby, señorita. He does not always wish the green stones."

It was pigeonblood, its depths pulsing with dark fire, a single great ruby on a golden chain that hung warmly into the upper cleft of her breasts. Marilee caressed it as she descended the stairs and made her way into the dining room ablaze with candles. Two young men waited to serve, and Don Alfonso rose to kiss her hand, to seat her beside him.

She watched him as he talked fluently, wittily about Jesse Flagg and the man's problems, as he spoke of the de Carbocas who had gone before, descendants of *conquistadores*. Marilee was quiet, trying not to be mesmerized by his handsomeness and the grace of him. They had this in common—the respect for family and lineage, the liking for the good things of life. As he pressed wine upon her, as she sampled exotically spiced dishes that either rioted against her palate or insinuated subtle flavors there, Marilee forgot the afternoon and laughed with him, talked with him.

Always conscious of his physical presence, of his flashing eyes and the promise of his fingers as they brushed over her own, she knew a tremulous anticipation. Would it be as enchanting with him this night? Would there be the open fire dancing upon their bare flesh and fur lending its caress?

Looking up, she saw a new serving girl, a young and slender one little more than a child, with soft doe eyes and a dimpled cheek. As the girl removed dishes, Marilee said, "What a pretty child."

"Yes," he answered. "I choose them for beauty and train them well. Here, a final taste of this brandy, and then—" He left the rest unsaid, but a pulse began to throb in Marilee's throat. She barely tasted the fiery brandy and leaned back simply to look at this many-faceted man while the strumming of guitars came in softly from the patio. The young girl never came back from the kitchen.

He said, *"Querida?"*

And she said, "Of course," rising with him and moving to the stairs with her hand in his, her head against his shoulder. At the doorway, he turned her to him and stroked her hair as she tilted her mouth upward for his kiss. Gently, his lips locked to hers, Don Alfonso moved her backward with the pressure of his thighs.

Eyes closed, she heard the click of the door as he shut it with his heel. Abruptly, he let her go and moved away. She saw the fur rugs waiting, the firelight dancing welcome —and gasped. For the reflection of flames played over

Rosa, her face cast down, and over the new serving girl, standing taut as an untried filly.

Both of them were naked.

"*Alfonso!* What does this mean? Why are they—"

His smile was thin, his eyes wicked. "You know Rosa, of course. The other is Juanita. Rosa is experienced, but this is Juanita's first time—with me, anyhow."

Rigid, her hands clenched, Marilee said, "I don't know what you mean to do, but if you expect *me*—"

Like a striking rattler, his hand flashed out and ripped her bodice, tore the filigreed gown to her waist. Marilee staggered and covered her breasts with both hands. Cat-like, he was upon her then, hooked fingers tearing, flinging shreds of white, clawing her skin. Blindly, she drove a fist at him, and white lights exploded inside her head when he slapped her.

"Bind her," he hissed. "Damn you, hurry! If I take the quirt to you both—"

She was too stunned to struggle, turned numb and sick. Marilee felt woman flesh warm against her, sweaty against her as hands fumbled and leather bands were laced around her wrists, her ankles. Through blurred eyes, she stared up at him as he stooped to lift her easily and position her upon the couch.

"A vantage point," he said, "so you may see clearly, *mi amor*. And be very certain that you watch, *comprende?* If I should find your eyes closed, I will not hesitate to apply the quirt."

He wanted to whip her; Marilee could see the blood lust in eyes turned different, glaring wild and hot now. She shuddered, bound upon the couch as he stripped, as he stood arrogant and commanding in that muscular lean body. The hardness of him was like a swollen lance, and he used it mercilessly upon the cringing girl Juanita, plunging it forcefully into her fresh body.

When the girl cried out, it only spurred Don Alfonso to more savage efforts, and he used her brutally, pinned her writhing and sobbing upon the disordered furs. All the while, Rosa sat meekly by, her face shamed but without a hint of rebellion in her sloe eyes. And when he at last rose panting from Juanita, she obeyed his orders silently, moving her body this way and that to accommodate him.

Marilee wanted to scream, needed very much to

squeeze her eyes shut and blot out the scene, but something warned her to do neither. Her wrists ached, and her legs; the ruby—the bloodred ruby—lay between her breasts.

He was standing over her then, smirking at her, and she saw that the silver in his hair wasn't shaped like wings, but horns.

"Your turn, my love. See? I am still capable. Ah, pale one, you will learn to truly appreciate me, and these others. There is much for you to learn, *mi paloma*, my little dove, so many experiments to try. Here—here—"

Somehow, she endured. Somehow, Marilee Bradburn closed off her mind and made it stand apart from her abused body while he took a slow and tedious pleasure with her. She would not look at the others, could not bear to see them watching what he did to her. She winced at the pressure of him, the thrusting weight of him, not deft now, but cruel.

She thought of Mississippi, but its magnolias were creamy skulls and its leaves dark wreaths. She saw the chimney of Bradburn Plantation blackened, and recoiled from blood on the floor of the slave cabin.

Finally it was over, and she lay panting for clean air, the tears flowing salty to her bruised lips. He was moving; they were stirring. She was limp when they untied her and rubbed the marks from her limbs. She was unsteady upon her feet as Rosa and Juanita dressed her in somber black, fitted her unresisting body into a highnecked gown that trailed the floor. A mannequin waiting to be pushed, she stood until he took her elbow. Awkwardly, her feet stumbling upon the stairs, she looked down upon the gathered faces, the blazing chandelier.

Dully, Marilee stared at the man in the hooded brown robe, a man who wore peasant sandals and had black beads about his neck, a man with a withered face and sunken eyes.

"Padre," Don Alfonso said calmly, "we are ready. You may begin the ceremony."

Chapter 40

Delighted that he had an interest in books, Martha kept them piled nearby for Joe—fat historical volumes, slim books of poetry, everything she thought he should be interested in. Since he owed her and didn't really mind the rest, he played invalid for the widow, bothered only by the pert and saucy Sissy, who kept flirting with him.

Normally, Joe would have taken up the girl on her obvious offer, but, playing a gambler's hunch, he didn't. Mrs. Fitzhugh-Morris was friend to her former slaves, but he sensed a certain watchfulness about the woman, a withdrawn quality armored in the old traditions.

And she was charming, seeing to his every need, discussing books with him, talking about the commerce of the city in a way that showed she had a good head for figures and knew as much about what was going on as any man. Martha began taking more pains with her appearance during the few days he recuperated in her home; her dresses became less drab and her chestnut hair was brushed until it shone. Joe took to watching the way she moved, seeing a held-in kind of stiffness that shouldn't be, making out grace and ripeness in the body she kept so well covered.

And one day Marcus said to him, "Reckon you can catch 'em all at the ranch house today. Hear tell they're gatherin' some cows."

Eyeing the huge black, Joe said, "She's smart enough about banks and the like—why not about her ranch?"

Rolling his shoulder, Marcus said, "She's like ladies in all them books. Talks good, thinks good, but when somethin' turns real and ugly, she don't know what to do about it. Except when it's right to hand, like that pack of wharf rats draggin' you down. You want I should hitch up the carriage? Ain't but an hour drive."

Joe grinned. "Never rode a carriage in my life. And what does she think about this, me goin' out to look over her place and the men?"

"Too proud to ask help," Marcus said, "but she knows I done talked to you about it, and Miss Martha will appreciate it."

"Well, then," Joe said, "guess I'll ride out yonder like a sure-enough gentleman, and you can kind of tell me what's going on while we're traveling."

Before they left, he looked around for Martha, but she wasn't in sight. Dressed in his long coat and new hat, wearing a clean white shirt, Joe put the Spencer into the carriage first, on the floor up front, then climbed up beside Marcus and checked the cylinder of the Colt.

"Gentlemen rides in back," Marcus said, moving the horse smartly out through crowded streets.

"Can't do it all at once," Joe said. "Could be too much for this ol' redneck, and I might get to like it. Tell me about her ranch, Marcus."

As the carriage worked along rutted streets and past wagons loading and unloading, through riders and walkers and such coming and going that it seemed half the world had been tossed up here, Marcus told Joe about the ranch. Martha had bought it as an investment, and for a while it had paid off handsomely. But for the past two years, it had been going downhill steadily.

"Seems like there's just as many cows, and Lord knows the price of beef ain't low," he said. "But them men she hired—I figure they're pocketin' what's rightfully Miss Martha's. Trouble is, they're mean, and maybe in cahoots with what law there is, which ain't much. Sure hate to see her lose that place—might mean her losin' the big house later on."

Joe said, "The foreman?"

"Kelso—wears a low gun, he's tight with two more—Sands and Norton. Sands ain't been there long. Rest of the hands are Mexicans and do like they're told. Now Miss Martha, she don't admit to bein' scared, but I see that's how come she ain't told that bunch to light a shuck." The big ebony face turned to Joe. "You might just be the man. I'll help if I can."

"Stay out of it," Joe said. "Seems like it'll be a while before a black man don't get his neck stretched for killing a white man, no matter how lowdown the white is. If it starts, hit the ground, but hang on to those reins—I might need the Spencer and I want it close by."

Trotting smartly, the gelding brought them into a curved road and through green fields. The ranch house was adobe, as were the barns beyond. The gathering pens looked tight and kept up, and Joe could see a cook wagon, and, beyond, longhorns milling in a fenced pasture. At first glance, there were four or five hundred of them, a good tally for a short drive.

Nobody was at the house, but when the carriage swung around it, men looked up from the stables, from fresh horses saddled and ready to move the herd to town.

A man with a flat black hat came toward them. He was gaunt and long-legged, with a full beard. "Kelso," Marcus whispered.

Slowly, Joe got down and brushed dust from his coat; he took off his hat and dusted that, too. He watched vaqueros stay where they'd been working, and saw two other men following their boss. It was familiar, Joe thought: the backup men drifting wide on each side and spacing themselves. As they neared, he made a show of using the kerchief upon his hat and even leaning to wipe it over his boot tips. But beneath his brows, he watched them, the potbellied man chewing tobacco, the grinning youngster who wore his shaggy yellow hair too long.

"Good morning," Joe said, straightening up.

Kelso lifted one corner of a hard mouth, dark eyes taking in every detail of Joe's new clothing before reaching beyond him to the carriage and Marcus. He said, "Nigger —told you I don't want you on this place. Yo' missus wants to send a spy, you let that *white* man come by his-self—even a dude."

Joe put his hat back on. "I said good morning."

Kelso grunted. "And I was talkin' to the big nigger."

Behind him, the potbellied man had stopped suddenly. His stained mouth hung open and small, round eyes peered. He pushed the wad of tobacco out through stained teeth with his tongue and said, "Kelso—"

The yellow-haired stripling turned his head, puzzled.

"Sands," Kelso said, still ignoring Joe and keeping flat eyes on Marcus, "might be this nigger forgets how a black-snake feels. Go get a whip."

"Kelso," the man said hurriedly, as if he were choking on something, "damn it, I seen that fella afore. Seen him in El Paso."

The corner of the foreman's mouth twitched. "This here dude keeps makin' his good mornin'? Now who could have toted him this far?"

He was close enough, so Joe hit him in the mouth with his left hand, a vicious blow that spun Kelso back and dropped him stunned to his knees. Joe's right hand swept back his boat and splayed ready fingers above the worn butt of the Colt.

He said, "And you never answered me. Do it now. Say good mornin', real polite."

Sands's arms went out stiffly, away from his sides. "For godsakes, Kelso—say it! That's the fella gunned down Cherokee Bill."

A trickle of blood seeped from the corner of Kelso's mouth; his eyes were venomous. He was coiling himself. To his right, the blond boy looked uncertain.

"I'd just as soon kill you kneeling," Joe said. "Might help you stay out of hell a minute longer if you die like you're prayin'."

Sands whispered, "Kelso—goddamnit—he's liable to gun us all."

Balanced and eager, Joe saw Kelso hesitate, saw the flat eyes turn muddy and unsure. The foreman's bearded lips trembled. "Good—good mornin'," he mumbled.

"Polite enough, I reckon," Joe said. "Don't move anything but your mouth. Sands—you, boy—drop your gun-belts, easy and careful."

"Three of us," Kelso said, throat strained. "Damn it—there's *three* of us."

"Not me," Sands stuttered. "He put *three* into that breed gunslick you could cover with a playin' card. Norton—do like he says."

Kelso shivered when the other gunbelts hit the ground, and his nostrils flared. A cow bellowed; a horse stamped.

"Hell," Joe said, "you're not going to try it. A man like you, he's real bad when he's pickin' on somebody can't fight back or when he's got a big edge. Just unbuckle your belt, bad man, or go for your gun—but right *now*."

Gunbelt in the dirt, Kelso dug his fingers into his beard, his eyes closed. He stayed that way until Joe took a long step and jerked him to his feet. "I don't want to see any of you again," he said into Kelso's face. "Not here, not in town, because if I see you, I'll just have to figure you mean to ambush me, and I'll kill you."

Letting go the man's shirt, Joe stepped back and raised his voice to call in Spanish, *"Hola, vaqueros!* Bring their horses, but without carbines. These bad men are in a great hurry."

The blond youngster said, "Hey, now, we got stuff in the house—"

And Sands said, "Boy, please shut the hell up."

They rode off quickly, heading north. In the dust that rolled behind them, a vaquero laughed, then another.

Marcus said, "You're the man—couldn't be no righter."

"Hear me," Joe said to the other hands. "Things have changed. The count will be honest. Who among you has served longest on this rancho?"

An older man edged forward, sombrero in hand. "I am Gonzalo Sandoval, señor."

"You are *jefe*, Sandoval. As chief, come into the *casa* with me. The rest of you find work. Your new *jefe* will speak with you later."

Marcus said from the carriage, "What you want me to do?"

"You might bring Miss Martha out here so we can go over the books together. And Marcus—I heard you move that Spencer with your foot."

The black grinned widely. "Must have bumped it accidental. I'll go tell Miss Martha." He began to whistle as he turned the horse and drove away from the yard.

It was afternoon before Joe discovered what he needed to know. The ranch had been systematically plundered of beef and horses, of lowgrade ore and timber. There was something left, but it would take hard work to bring back production.

Sandoval rolled a brownpaper smoke and offered the tobacco sack to Joe. *"Gracias,* but I never learned to roll them. Cigarillos are easier for me."

"I am sorry, señor," the man said. "All of us are sorry, but we feared their guns, and the señora seemed helpless. We made only our wages, no more. It was a pleasure, a wonder, to watch you turn them into cowering puppies—it was also a shame to us because we had not done it ourselves."

"Honest men have little use for handguns," Joe said. "You are not blamed, *compadre.* However, if this hacienda is not brought swiftly back to what it once was, all will share the blame, myself included."

Puffing his rolled cigaret, Sandoval said, "Then we are still employed?"

"The señora will see it as I do," Joe said.

"Our thanks to her, and our apologies—*mil gracias.*"

"Por nada—perhaps you will not thank me when everyone sweats from sunlight until past dark."

Sandoval stood up and put on his sombrero. "It is a way to repay her. We do not know about guns, but we know how to sweat."

With a clatter the carriage rolled into the yard, and Joe went from the small house to greet Martha. She piled down with a rustling of skirts and a breathlessness he had only seen in her when she was swinging that blacksnake whip. Her carefully combed hair was mussed and her eyes shining.

"Joe, oh, Joe! Marcus hitched a fresh horse and we came as quickly as we— You've done it—you actually chased them away!"

Smiling, he led her into the house. "We stopped them before they stole everything, but you've been hurt, Martha."

She held to his hands. "No matter. Now that you're here, everything will be all right. You *will* run the ranch for me, Joe?"

"I know a little about it," he said. "I'll learn the rest, if you want me to."

"I do, oh—I do." She was excited as a schoolgirl, skipping around the room. "Oh, look what they've done to it—how filthy! I wager you haven't eaten since this morning, and if I can find—"

She was different now, excited and bubbly; she was more the fiery woman who'd sailed into the wharf rats with the whip, not the stiff and proper lady moving within the walls of her townhouse. Martha looked younger and more alive.

He said, "I can get one of the *Californio* women to fix—"

"Nonsense! I haven't forgotten how to cook, even if I have to make do with whatever I can find." She looked at him. "And I want to."

Over bacon, eggs, and coffee, Joe watched her shining face, heated by the stove, and saw the wisp of sorrel-silvered hair out of place, the top button of her dress loosened. He told her what she'd lost and what had to be done to make the ranch productive again. Brood stock had to be counted, fences repaired, hay seen to; the firewood and timber operation had to be gone over, the crews set to work properly.

"Somebody knows how to handle the diggings," he said. "Your foreman was runnin' ore wagons out quick as he could, but I reckon I can find who he was selling to and maybe who put Kelso up to cheating you. He wasn't smart enough himself. The miners are still here, but that lowgrade ore is the least profitable part of the whole, and maybe you should just let that slide until the rest gets going again."

Martha tilted her head at him. "Whatever you say. It's in your hands."

Sipping coffee, Joe said, "Never figured I had a head for business but this isn't really like storekeeping. I guess I can handle it for you, Martha."

"You can accomplish anything you want," she said seriously. "You have an innate grasp of ideas, and you don't seem to forget anything. There's another talent I've noticed, Joe—your ability to look beneath the surface and see the depths."

He put aside the cup. "How would you know that?"

"Your restlessness, for one thing." She came around the table to hold a match to his cigarillo. "I sensed how you felt, recuperating in my home—as if you were ashamed, as if you were a—a kept man."

"I've been that before," he said. "I don't mean to be again."

Quickly, she said, "You won't be. And you won't be working *for* a woman, either. I'm offering you a partnership. Now wait, Joe, and just listen. Without a man—a strong man—to manage this place, I'll lose it. A widow is fair game for so many predatory men, but they'll let you alone. And you'll earn your share, every penny of it, working very hard and keeping off the wolves."

Through a drifting of blue smoke, he looked at her. "That's not what they'll say in San Francisco."

Martha stood close, blownout match still in her slender fingers. "I suppose not, but I can ignore the gossip if you can."

Joe said then, "That wasn't really what you meant about me looking below the surface, was it? You've felt me watching *you*, and seeing more than you show."

Dropping the match, she put both hands to her cheeks. "I—I don't know. Yes, I do. What I don't know is myself. I mean, I'm so much older than you, and I've never been—my husband and I weren't very close, I suppose. Oh, I'm talking as if I have no ethics, no shame, no sense of—of propriety—"

Her eyes were very big, her cheeks pink, and her voice sort of ran itself down, like a clock that hadn't been wound or whose spring had been coiled too tightly for too long. It creaked out as a thready whisper: "I don't even know what l-love is. I'm already so old, and I never found out."

Joe put his hands upon her waist and drew her between his spread knees, feeling the stiffness of her body, the material of her dress against his lips as he said, "You're not old, and I'm not young anymore. I stopped being young when I was about fifteen."

She remained tense. "Marcus—"

"Tell him to come back for you tomorrow."

"But he'll know—"

"That it's your own decision—no more."

She was still resisting mentally. "This house, dusty and strange."

"Different, new for you—better than your own home."

"How can I—" she began, and he turned her in his hands, turned her toward the doorway. When she stood puppetlike there to give Marcus orders, Joe cleared one of the bunks and spread a blanket there. Martha remained in the door, even after the carriage drove away, and Joe had to bring her back inside.

When he laid her upon the bed, she covered her eyes with an arm, murmuring about the windows and the light.

"There's no shame to this," he said softly, "and no fear. Only pride, Martha—pride and a need for both of us."

Gently than, as he would soothe a trembling young mare, Joe undressed her, hands stroking and caressing, being slow and easy. Her body was good, firm, the small breasts solidly coned, the whiteness of her thighs silken. He kissed her throat, her ear, his fingertips trailing over her quivering flesh, touching her breasts tenderly, and at last she turned her face to him with half a sob, half a cry, and her mouth was frantic in its giving.

Still, he caressed her, fondled the sleek haunches and petted the tremulous vee of her femininity, easy and careful, teasing and slow. Martha flinched at the initial reaching of his tongue, but her teeth were soon raking his, and her breath gusting, moaning. Only then did he start to enter her resilient softness, intruding cautiously into the humid, clinging depths, holding her closely and keeping his weight from her arching, twisting body.

There was still a part of her he had not reached, some long-hidden secret place withheld from him, so Joe held himself back, probing delicately for that forbidden gateway, ever so slow, ever so gentle. Bit by bit, she opened herself to him, gasping in the newness, and at last calling out in the shuddering crest of total release.

He held her. He murmured to Martha of her sweetness, her loving. He cradled the woman-body tenderly, knowing this was the first time it had known completion and made proud by that knowing. And after a while, she began to move again, to caress him back, a newfound freedom in her actions, an awareness of her own power.

This time, the blending bordered upon fierceness, a

hunger within her that demanded to be assuaged. Joe gave of himself more fully, strongly, but with his lust held in check. The bed creaked with their rolling, and the room echoed with Martha's small, soft cries of delight.

She lay quietly, with her head pillowed upon his chest, one slim leg across his thighs, smelling of a flowery perfume, of aroused womanhood, musky and intriguing. Lips against his skin, she whispered, "All those years wasted."

Hand upon her hair, Joe said, "Not wasted—only waiting."

Martha was silent for a long time, then said, "It was worth it, if it led to now, to you—to this. I will always have this, even after you are gone."

"Martha—"

"Hush," she said. "I know you will be gone someday, and you know that also. Let us accept it, my darling. The tomorrows cannot mean as much as the todays."

Joe simply held her, realizing the truth of it.

Chapter 41

He'd caught up with her half an hour from the house, but Marilee wasn't trying to run away. She'd taken Bradburn to work him, loosen the stallion and keep in condition, riding out alone in the morning to feel clean, fresh wind upon her face. She wanted the taste of Don Alfonso out of her mouth.

But there he was, loping the black mare beside her without talking, his presence in itself a warning, in case she had any idea of escape. At least he hadn't ordered his men to take her guns, certain of his authority and his hold upon her. But she knew that before she might cross half the huge ranch, word would be flashed from mirror to mirror and back to him; he would have her pursued.

Slowing Bradburn to a trot, then to a steady walk, she ignored his presence—her *husband's* presence—and went all tight inside at the thought. Don Alfonso pushed the mare up and reached down for Bradburn's reins.

"You have been riding a long time, señora—time to rest." He was icily polite, evilly handsome in rich riding clothes.

She took back the reins and stopped her horse, then stepped off and stood beside the stallion, her shoulder against his. "That priest—"

"A sop to the peons of my hacienda, this friar who travels from pueblo to pueblo—Father Villano."

"A tame priest, following your orders."

He swung down and brought his mare around so that he faced her. "Of course, but a priest nonetheless. Our holy wedlock is quite legal, I assure you."

"Holy," she said, then, "Why? You have your young girls—Rosa and the other maids who are your slaves—why marry me?"

Taking off his silver-spangled hat, he ran a hand across his hair. "Surely you can reason that out."

"You don't love me," she said. "You can't love anybody."

"I do not recall mentioning *love*," he said, smiling. "The stallion there—must he love his mares in order to breed them? I think not."

Marilee stared at him. "You mean—"

Don Alfonso ground-tied his mare and leaned against a pinnacle of rock, dark and graceful, the stone no harder than the man. "Bloodlines, señora—the name of de Carboca. We hidalgos must continue, we *will* go on, despite misfortunes. Your bloodlines are good—you have the strength and fire that will be necessary for my son. There will be no weakness in him." He swept a black-gloved hand. "To hold this land, to outthink those who would be his enemies, to carry on the name. This is the only importance, so of course my son has to be a legitimate heir. Therefore, our marriage, witnessed and solemnized, the papers gone for registry in El Paso del Norte and in Mexico."

"Making me your prisoner by law," Marilee said.

Don Alfonso adjusted his hat at the proper rakish angle. His white teeth flashed at her. "My *wife*, a thing of pride."

"Your brood mare, you mean," Marilee said, and would have said more, but she saw him stiffen as he looked beyond her to the hills.

"*Bastardos!*" he hissed. "The mirrors signal *indios*—somehow, those *hijos* have slipped through the outposts."

390

"The rocks," Marilee said. "If the Indians are close, no *vaqueros* can reach us in time."

"Hide?" he asked scornfully. "A de Carboca skulking from those animals—"

"They won't allow us to stay hidden long. Too many tracks they can't miss." Already, she was drawing Bradburn behind her, pulling him into a tangle of rocks and sagebrush where he could be protected. Marilee pulled the Spencer from its scabbard and clicked its lever, acting now from reflex, because of hard lessons learned well. Saddlebags here, ammunition within easy reach, canteen there, a narrow cleft from which she could see the flatter ground for a distance. She frowned; she didn't like that arroyo to the right, nor the hill close by. Apaches would tuck their mounts behind that crest and eel through the arroyo on foot; they always fought dismounted when they could. If any of them circled this rockpile. . . .

Grumbling, Don Alfonso came in beside her, and she saw he had only a handgun. He said through his teeth, "If my vaqueros do not come flying, I will have the skin off their backs."

"Better think about saving our own," she said. "Maybe the Apaches will pass by."

"Give me the carbine," he said.

"No." She saw a telltale wisp of dust beyond the opposing hill, and waited. Time enough to fix her sights upon the lip of that arroyo. They'd have to cross open ground to get around her.

"*I* am the man," he said. "Give me that carbine."

"If you weren't so damned sure of your army, you would have carried your own. This is mine, and I can handle it."

"Woman—" he began, but she hissed him into silence. Something flickered in the narrow, twisted canyon, and she could make out no more dust. The Apaches had found hoofprints and figured where they led; they were coming. Marilee focused upon the arroyo opening, Spencer barrel braced upon a slab, her finger taking up slack in the trigger.

Swiftly, low to the ground, the first one whisked from cover, but when her bullet shattered rock inches from his bent head, the Apache wheeled and dived back, out of sight.

"Didn't lead him enough," she murmured.

Close beside her, Don Alfonso parted sagebrush with one hand and peered down. "You fired at a shadow."

Smoke blossomed below and lead whined past them. Marilee said, "The shadow shot back."

Concentrating, very calm, she aimed carefully and kept them to ground, kicking sandy dirt here, ricocheting a bullet from rock there. One man tried it anyhow, breaking from cover like a hungry bobcat, and she knocked a leg from beneath him, fired again and missed as he scuttled back into the narrow ravine, dragging his leg.

It was quiet then, and Don Alfonso said, "My riders—where are my riders?"

Marilee said, "The Apaches will think this out. Some of them can swing around the hill and come at us from behind while the rest hold us here."

"I would not flee," he said, "but there comes a time—"

"Time's past for running. They'll drop the horses before we get going good."

"They speak a bastard Spanish," he said. "I'll offer them gold."

"They want our horses and guns," she said. "They want our blood." But he had given her an idea, and it was best to use it now, before the warriors split their forces.

Marilee stood up and yanked off her hat, letting her long hair blow free in the wind.

"Are you *loco?*" he gasped. "Mad—you have gone mad!"

"*Hola!*" she called. "Hey, *indio!* Look you—see who it is you face!"

The quiet stretched itself taut, and she stood higher to move her hands in sign-talk, making each movement definite and sure in that silent language at which the Comanches were most proficient.

Men lifted from the arroyo, only five of them, holding their weapons loosely and staring, staring.

Her hands sent the message: *I am Nadevah, the Moon Woman of the Comanches. See me, know me. I can be no other.*

Slowly, unwillingly, one man detached himself from the rest and climbed over the rim of the canyon to stand wide-legged. Hoarsely, he shouted in Spanish, "We could not know, spirit woman. We—we are few, driven south by tejanos."

Clear-voiced, she answered: "Where do you go?"

Uncertainly, the leader gestured. "Mexico. There was tejano whiskey—"

Others were climbing out, and one man stumbled as he led horses slowly out of the arroyo. She saw loot upon them, sacks and the bright pattern of a woman's dress, jugs of whiskey hanging. The horse herder stumbled again; he was drunker than the rest.

"Go then," Marilee said sharply. "Ride swiftly before other spirits find you."

"We go," the squatty leader said. "We hear the woman who has risen from the dead." He fumbled himself onto his horse.

She watched others mount clumsily, drunkenly, and saw the last man hesitate. Four started off, but he was slow, his back to her, the white woman's dress flapping in the breeze. Marilee picked up the Spencer, and when he suddenly wheeled his horse, when he shrieked and came pelting at the rocks, she hit him clean. The horse swerved as the rider pitched off backward,' his rifle spinning, swerved and ran in a wide circle to follow the other horses. The Apache lay upon his back, arms outflung.

Head thrown back, carbine over her head, Marilee loosed the triumphant war cry of the Comanches, the fierce battle cry that chilled the blood of all who had heard it and lived. It sounded over the valley floor and across the arroyo, echoing upon itself, rebounding from the rocks like so many flung scalping knives.

The others heeled their horses into a dead run, heads bent over flying manes, riding for more than their lives, fleeing from dark spirits that could lay claim upon their souls. When the dust fell back, they were gone, the drumbeat of hooves fading quickly.

Don Alfonso stood up beside her. *"Magnifico!* I have never seen Apaches so afraid, and of a woman, a single woman. And that offhand shot—a thing of beauty. That one was dead when he struck the earth."

She said, "He was too drunk to be afraid."

"They called you spirit woman, said you were raised from the dead. What does that—"

"There are many kinds of death," she said, moving back from the rocky cleft to see to Bradburn. She wouldn't tell him of Piava, of Little Buffalo's silence that had made her into a legend on these plains.

He was right at her heels, excited, and when she brought out the stallion and ran her hands over him to see that he was all right, Marilee felt he might put his hands on her, that her *husband's* lust was somehow stirred by death and blood. She moved away from him, pushed by him to lead Bradburn into the flat and lift into her saddle as she sheathed the carbine again.

Hurrying after, he would have said something to her, but she put Bradburn into a gallop and never looked back at him, nor at the dead Apache. Marilee heard the drumming of the mare's hooves coming after and let the stallion out some more; Don Alfonso's mare could stay with him only for a short distance, she knew.

Up ahead, coming fast from the direction of the hacienda, a band of *vaqueros* appeared, and she had to slow for them as they spread themselves into a crescent. Don Alfonso came up beside her, sitting tall and arrogant upon his lathered mare, once more the lord of the land.

"*Patrón*—you are all right?"

"No thanks to my *vaqueros*. Who allowed those vermin to trespass upon de Carboca soil?"

Manuel Venegas took to his sombrero. "They came by night, through the outposts, and were not seen until a short while ago. We came quickly as we could, Don Alfonso." The man's eyes slid away from the anger of his master and briefly touched Marilee.

"Is that the excuse, then?" Don Alfonso asked roughly.

Venegas looked uncomfortable. "It is said that—"

"Go on," Don Alfonso said.

"I do not wish—*patrón*, there is talk that *she*, that one, has caused a blood debt with the Apaches, that they will continue to raid, even upon Hacienda de Carboca, so long as she is here."

Viciously, the silvered quirt slashed across the man's brown cheek. A line of blood leaped forth.

"She?" Don Alfonso spat. "*She?* You dare speak of the señora in that manner? That one, you called her. Listen, you *hijos de los putas*, the señora is my wife. Understand this. She is Señora de Carboca, lawful mistress of this hacienda and she who will bring forth my son. If she wants your worthless head for your discourtesy, she shall have it—upon a pole!"

Venegas did not touch his bleeding cheek. He hung his shaggy head and trembled. *"Perdón,* señora—I but repeated what others said. I ask your forgiveness, señora."

"It's all right, Manuel," she said. "But the story is wrong."

"Do not *explain* to them," Don Alfonso snapped. "Command them, as I do. You slugs, you gossiping snails —there is a dead Apache behind us. Go and loot his body, then leave it for the vultures. Oh, yes—and take his hair as warning to others."

Obediently, the rescue band rode off, none of them looking back, and Marilee said then, "You were hard on them."

He spurred the mare and the horse leaped forward, throwing her head. It was something else he didn't have to do, Marilee thought—another way of hurting something because his own pride had been bruised. She noticed Don Alfonso had not made it clear who killed the Apache, letting it be assumed he did.

She followed at a slower lope, glad he had let her keep her guns. If there'd been only his pistol out there, it would have been considerably more difficult to make those warriors believe who she was. Up close, more than one of them might have gambled his life, and probably taken theirs. The long-range shooting gave her a chance to make them think a little, and gained time for the dramatic appearance of the Moon Woman.

But now the *vaqueros* had more reason to resent her; even though Manuel Venegas had accepted the slash of the quirt, it must have bitten deeply into his heart. A blood debt between her and the Apaches? Of course, but not one of those cruel little men would try and collect. The legend of Nadevah was too strong, too much medicine for them to face. Now it would grow with the telling of those who fled to Mexico, for the one who had defied her powers had died.

Don Alfonso was puzzled, and anger seethed within him; she knew that, knew she had somehow caused him to feel inferior by saving them both. Before, he had had only her word—and the familiar way she handled weapons—that she was a *pistolera* of sorts. Now he knew that that was true and wondered how much more he didn't know.

He was waiting when she brought Bradburn to the stables, and by the scurrying of barn hands, Marilee could see he'd worked off some of his fury upon them. His face was still dark, the well-shaped brows knotted, when she swung from the saddle without accepting a hand down. Don Alfonso jerked his head toward the house; she left the Spencer upon the saddle and asked one of the boys to clean it, but she kept the Colt at her hip.

He went directly up the stairs, motioning Rosa aside and ignoring young Juanita's worshipful eyes. Waiting for her in the apartment, he was tapping the quirt against his boot, silver horns prominent in his ebony hair.

"You heard them," he said, "and you heard me silence them. That is the way you will react as my wife—swiftly and without weakness. Now, answer me truthfully—what is this thing with the Apaches? They have not dared my rancho in years."

Marilee placed her hat on a chair and went to the dressing table in the bedroom. She was running a brush through her hair when he said, "Answer me, woman."

"The Apaches fear me," she said, "even more than they fear the Comanches. Once I led a raid upon their camps—now I'm supposed to have risen from the dead. That ragged band was made up of renegades, outlaws to their own kind. Didn't you see the loot they were carrying? They'd hit some isolated ranch, maybe a weak wagon train—somebody chased them this far and they were running for safety in Mexico. We just happened to be in their way. No Apache would come *looking* for Nadevah, the Moon Woman."

He stalked across the room and flung himself across the bed, hands laced behind his head, staring up at the ceiling. Don Alfonso said, "You will not speak of your rides with the Comanches, nor any more of this—this Moon Woman. The peons are superstitious and already whisper about you."

"All right," Marilee said, and sat to continue brushing her hair.

"And," he said, "you will never, *never* turn away from me if I put out my hand to you. Understand that, señora."

It was enough. Marilee whirled up from the stool and braced her feet apart. "And you had better understand something, señor. You remind me that I am your wife, and I will not let you forget that, either. You will not

396

have me bound again, nor shame me before your wenches."

Don Alfonso came up from the bed, his face mottled.

Coolly, she looked him in the eyes and put one hand upon her right hip, just above the butt of the pistol. "I don't care how many servants you make submit to your twisted pleasures, how many girls you bed. But not before *me*—not with me. If I am to bear you a son, I will not be treated as one of your whores. You forced me into marriage, and that can't be changed. So Marilee Bradburn is no more, and the Moon Woman is gone—there is only Señora de Carboca. I bear your name and I *will* have your respect."

He glared at her, his rich mouth working beneath the neatly trimmed moustache, but slowly Don Alfonso's expression changed, grew thoughtful. "And if I refuse this —this ultimatum?"

Marilee didn't give. "You may take my Colt, my Spencer—in time, perhaps. But you also cannot forever be on your guard, forever awake. You'll come to me some night, and I will put steel in your belly. The Comanches are very good with knives, too."

"You would," he breathed. "I believe you would. And this hidalgo line will be no more—the name dies with me."

Suddenly he laughed, a great, pealing sound that rang through the apartment. "*Dios, Dios!* I have chosen better than I knew. This one is already a de Carboca!"

Chapter 42

Between acts in the ornate theater lobby, the crowd milled—men in stiff shirts set with diamond stickpins showing off bejeweled women showing off glittering gowns. Joe led Martha to a quiet corner and paused to light a small cigar before bringing her a glass of sherry from the bar. Men said hello to him and a few women smiled into his face; the banker nodded coldly, as did the mining man; whispers drifted in the wake of his cigar smoke, but he didn't give a damn anymore. They all knew where Joe Langston stood, and where *they* stood, so there would never be anything more than careful whispers, nothing ever said right out loud.

As for the banker, that greasy little man bulging like a stuffed turkey—Mr. Ellsworth Fowler had walked on eggs since that day Joe first bearded him in his office. Handing Martha her sherry, Joe grinned at the memory of Fowler's round face going near purple in indignation.

"Sir! You dare to come into my own office and accuse me of such nefarious—"

Sitting on a corner of the immense desk, coat drawn back to expose the Walker Colt, Joe said, "About now is when you'd better get something straight, banker. I *dare* just about anything, but I know better than to meet you in your home pasture—courts and lawyers and such. That deck is stacked. So I intend to play my own game. I know damned well you were behind Kelso. Too many of Mrs. Fitzhugh-Morris's cows were shipped through your pens, too much of her timber loaded on your ships, and the ore—"

Puffed up and indignant, Fowler had sputtered, "Accusations like those—no proof—wild lies—"

"Hold on," Joe said ominously. "Calling a man a liar can be dangerous, banker. In fact, I've known it to be downright fatal. Thing is, I don't mean to try proving my charges. I just want you to know I'm not a fool, and I figure you're not one either. Which means that if a hired hand takes a pop at me some dark night and misses—and nervous bushwhackers miss a lot, you know—then I'm going to come visiting again. Same thing goes if *anybody* bothers Mrs. Fitzhugh-Morris's interests in any way. And next time, Mr. Fowler, my callin' card is going to be three, four bullets from this Colt. Courts and lawyers can't stop them—nothing can, except maybe a better gunslinger, and I just don't think there is one in San Francisco."

Fowler's color had faded from apoplectic purple to old ashes, and his nearly bald pate shone with tiny beads of sweat. Joe said casually, "So long as we understand each other. And by the by, you might pass word to your silent partner in the mining business. Randall Murdock acts like a man who wants to keep on enjoyin' life."

He'd left the office then, walking lazily, hesitating at the door to scratch a match on dark wood paneling and touch it to the tip of his cigarillo.

Martha brought him back to the present, saying, "You're smiling, but not at me."

"Just thinking," he said. "You've taught me so much, but damned if I can make head nor tail of most of what they're saying on stage. If you hadn't made me read the play first, I couldn't halfway keep up."

She had a good honest laugh now. "Shakespeare is a bit confusing for people unused to the theater."

"All those fancy speeches while they wave swords around. I can tell you sabers were never worth a damn, and when you mean to kill a man you don't keep telling him about it. He's liable to do it first."

Laughing again, she put a hand upon his arm. "To quote the bard, the play's the thing. It's entertainment, Joe, not reality, and you must admit the beauty of the language, the musical flow of the words."

"It's pretty, I reckon, but no more than you." He meant that; Martha looked younger, a straight and graceful woman no longer nervous about being seen in public with him. Her face was thinner, and her skin pale from being sick sometimes, but artful rouge glowed her cheeks. Her eyes always shone, ever since that first day at the ranch house. "You have that kind of elegance, Martha, that sort of muscial flow."

Softly she said, "I wish I could kiss you."

"Kiss away."

"Not here, Joe. I'm not quite that brazen."

"Only where it counts," he said as the crowd began to stream back into seats. "In bed."

"Once I would have blushed at that, sir. Now I want to shout it for all to hear, but of course I will not."

"Of course," Joe said and led her back to their seats. There was only one thing that puzzled him about this lady now. As he'd come to know the city and the men who ran its commerce, Joe understood her reluctance to flaunt their relationship before that society. But she'd adjusted in time, becoming proud of them and what they had together, envied by other widows, gossiping younger wives, and sullenly jealous girls.

"You're so handsome," she'd told him. "And that swashbuckler's air—few women can resist such a combination. Male beauty spiced with danger—a temptation for them all."

"I'm only interested in you, Martha."

"I know." She had said this from a sick bed, hair loose against a white pillow, slim body quiet beneath covers, her hazel eyes bigger in a pale face. "I know, Joe, and wonder at it."

Marcus stood silent in the background, even the flirtatious Sissy was temporarily quiet. Martha looked dimmed by the strange illness, but still so alive. He said, "It's been good. Let's make it better, Martha."

"Better?"

He looked at Marcus and the big black pushed the girl from the room, drew the door shut. Joe said, "I never asked a woman this before. Marry me, Martha."

Visions of another woman, one insisting on marriage, demanding it, so desperate and tensed in her need—Elizabeth, younger than Martha, very neat and tidy. Visions of women whose names he'd forgotten, whose bodies were only warmed-over memories—the glamorous *comtesse;* Becky Taylor, who would have laughed in his face at the mention of marriage.

And Marilee Bradburn? Suddenly bright inside his head, all silver and softened, flaming flesh. Marilee.

"I thank you," Martha said. "I most sincerely thank you for asking me, Joe Langston. But I cannot say yes."

He'd been sitting on the edge of the bed, holding her hand; he leaned closer. "Why not?"

"So you can make an honest woman of me? Because of you, I've grown beyond such farces, darling. Let them talk—I have *you,* and I would not exchange one moment with you for—for all eternity. And the city knows you're your own man, that I'm not keeping you. The way you've made the ranch pay, the deals you've made—"

"You're just giving me reasons why you should marry me," he said, "not why you won't."

She withdrew her slender hand and touched it to her temple where chestnut hair was damp and threaded with gray. "In the beginning, there was the word—and our word was *today*. Neither of us promised tomorrow. Please, let us keep it that way."

"The difference in our ages doesn't mean a thing, Martha."

Sadly, she gave him a tired smile. "I agree, but there is time itself, darling—time. Please—I would like to sleep awhile now."

So he had left her and sought the doctor. A passing weakness, the doctor said, and responding well to treatment. Not to worry.

Now, in the theater with costumed actors cavorting on the stage, Joe was still puzzled by her refusal. She'd been ill a time or two since, but always came back quickly, happily, and this night she looked better than ever. He wasn't hurt by her refusal exactly, but he never asked again, and Martha never mentioned the moment. They were happy at home in her big house or out at the ranch;

she showed him paintings and brought him special books; he spoke to her of Alabama and Mexico and Texas, of wars and a blind sort of searching that had brought him here at last, to her at last. Martha spoke of philosophies and politics, of art and meanings, he of what seemed a good buy in commerce, and what he should sell. They learned from each other.

On stage, somebody rolled out a sonorous speech and waved a sword. The curtain came down to enthusiastic applause, and the actors came back for bows.

Joe leaned close to her ear. "Are you sure you feel up to going to the party?"

"I wouldn't miss it. Don't forget, the senator will be there, and he can do you favors."

He helped her up as the crowd puddled and began to stream in the aisles. "Don't know if I'll ever get used to playing all these games."

"You're doing wonderfully well at them," she said. "Look what you've accomplished in such a short while. You don't have to toady to the senator, Joe. You wouldn't, anyhow, and he doesn't expect it."

"Senator Littlefield wouldn't pass the time of day with me if it weren't for you. He'll talk about Mr. Fitzhugh-Morris half the night, and those good old days in Washington before the war."

"Ah," she said, "but the other half—a word here about what the government's going to do about that new revolution brewing in Mexico, a hint there concerning the railroads—all grist for your mill, Joe."

Shrugging, he knew she was right, and he didn't mind going to the party. Some of the men there liked him, admired him for building his small stake and his share of the ranch proceeds into a thriving little empire. Others resented him for being "sponsored" by a rich widow, and still others feared he might encroach upon their own holdings, given time. Business wasn't all that difficult, Joe thought; it was only a matter of smelling out who needed what and buying low, selling high.

It was easier than dealing stud poker and safer, not as much risk. His gambling days had given him good experience for speculating, though, and saved him from many a trap set by his fellow competitors. Crooked dealing was the same anywhere, and Joe had long ago learned to sense a bluff or when to pull in his horns.

Marcus drew the carriage up before the theater, and Joe helped Martha into it. If the men he'd played cards with could see him now—all those *bandidos* and soldiers of fortune, the drifters and cowhands, scouts in buckskin and wagon drivers chewing great wads of tobacco—they'd turn up their toes. But then, none would recognize Joe Langston in a beaver hat and black broadcloth, a coat with tails to it and a starchy shirt. If they did, they'd sure think him a tinhorn, and think the big stickpin was false. But it wasn't. Diamonds were a handy way to show money and keep it at the same time.

Tucking a robe about Martha's legs and seeing that her shawl was in place, he nodded to Marcus and the horses stepped out. San Francisco had a tendency to be foggy at night, chill even in summer, and he didn't want her taking sick again. The carriage creaked, its lanterns spreading yellow light.

"Joe," she said thoughtfully, "do you ever miss wandering alone on the desert? I've been very lonely in my time, but seldom alone like that, with only the stars and a soft blackness all around."

"Miss it? No, I reckon not. Out there, you never really sleep—your mind is too busy listening for something that might mean an Indian's sneaking up on you, or a *comanchero* who'd cut your throat just for your boots. I'd just as soon be in a soft bed behind walls."

She snuggled close. "I'd be comfortable anywhere, if you were there. I think I'd like it on the desert, by a fire, hearing the night and feeling very safe because you're close."

Martha would try, he thought; she had the courage to do just about anything. But he couldn't picture her out on the windy plains, hair chopped short and jammed up under a shapeless hat—Martha Fitzhugh-Morris with a pistol on her hip and wearing men's breeches, hunkered over a campfire cooking bacon and beans. She had the courage, but what was it big Marcus had said a ways back—*When somethin' is real and dirty, Miss Martha just don't want to face it. She's like one of them folks in a book.* Something like that, anyway.

Joe could smell the sea, salt wind coming in fresh off San Francisco Bay. It would clear the fog if it kept up. If Martha hadn't come driving by just at that moment, when he was out of ammunition and blinded by that poison, Joe Langston would have ridden that sea, off to somewhere, shanghaied aboard some wormy freighter. He'd never have made it home, because if they had put the lash to him, they'd have had to kill him and drop him over the side.

"Your scars, Joe," Martha would breathe in sorrow. "Your poor scarred back."

He would pat her hand and tell her it was all right, that they were marks of ignorance; he had gotten them for doing something stupid he'd never do again. And Martha would say how cruel, how unjust for a boy to suffer because of first love. No, he would say, it wasn't love, just ignorance of how things were, and try as he would, he couldn't remember Susanna's face.

But he never forgot a thin, tanned face with willow-green eyes, framed by hair like molten moonlight. Stubborn damned face, a mouth that could be so ripely soft, then turn hard as a Comanche's heart. Sometimes, when Joe closed his eyes and thought on her, he could make out every detail of Marilee's features, see each sleek line of her body. Then he'd put her image roughly aside, and go on with whatever he was doing, because it was no good remembering all that.

Up ahead on Telegraph Hill, lights flared and the strains of music lifted. Other carriages and buggies clustered around the circular drive, just leaving room to pass. Marcus edged the horses in deftly and pulled them up before the great doors. Senator Littlefield's liveried servants pranced out to open the carriage door, black men of course, and Joe wondered how different it was with them now. They were doing the same things free they'd done as slaves—being field hands and house servants.

But now they could leave, he thought; if they wanted to chance an empty belly or go off in the mountains and dig for gold, nobody would put dogs after them. It was different, and he saw that, saw it mainly in big Marcus and the man's quiet dignity, in pert Sissy being able to pick which man to bed instead of getting herself bred like stock, with no say-so. He grinned, thinking that Sissy was always in heat, and that she wouldn't much care who got under the sheets with her, so long as the man was tireless.

Then they were into the foyer, having hat and shawl taken, moving on into smoky noise and bright lights, music and talk flowing around them like a downhill river. Most of the theater crowd was here, and others—men and women strange to Joe but recognizable because they were so much alike, clean and prettified and shiny, here not so much to enjoy another man's whiskey and cigars as to be seen in the right place by the right people.

A ship's captain in blue carried on about the China trade, and a railroad man kept asking when more yellow laborers were coming in. Joe saw a general with gold epaulets, his aide hovering close; the uniform was fancy, and he frowned. It was much like those of Maximilian's royalists, except for its color.

"What's a Mexican general doing here?" he asked in Martha's ear in the press.

"You remember," she answered. "More trouble down there—they're always changing governments. It's something we should know—how Washington will react."

Thinking of a Juarista lieutenant with hard eyes and a dream far back in them, a ragged officer who'd taken gold and jewels to buy arms for his people, Joe figured a man like that would still be ragged or dead, his dreams with him. But always, somebody made money from revolutions.

"I figure old Juárez will be around for a long time," he said.

"Díaz seems to be powerful," Martha said.

Porfirio Díaz—a safe conduct pass with ribbons and seals and the great general's name on the paper It hadn't meant a damned thing to the peon lieutenant. And now Díaz was rebelling against his former beloved leader. Would *pistoleros* cross the river again in search of easy loot? For gold and glory, Timmy Santee said. Funny— Joe hadn't thought of the boy for a long time, and all those gray uniforms were gone from his mind too.

A servant passed chilled champagne, and Joe took glasses. Martha sipped at hers, bright eyes probing everywhere, speaking graciously to those she knew, acknowledging introductions and presenting Joe to pompous gentlemen and their ladies without a flicker of embarrassment.

"My very dear friend," she said, and he was all that, lover and friend and would-be husband to this woman he admired and respected. He found a clear space on the ballroom floor and moved her about in a swooping waltz, easy on his feet only because Martha had taught him well. "Ball gowns blue, ball gowns green, prettiest gals I ever seen"—better ease up on that squaredance thinking or he'd stumble over her dainty slippers.

"What a striking man," she said, and when he spun her around, Joe saw the one she meant, tall and perfectly tailored in those short jackets worn by early Californios. He had his glossy head close to the Mexican general's, talking, looking more used to command than the officer himself.

And beyond him—Joe made a misstep and caught his balance but went stiff on the dance floor because he couldn't hear the music anymore. He stared at the woman whose bare shoulders rose elegantly from a frothy dress of color of palest wine, seeing the sparkle of emeralds against the creamy stalk of her throat, seeing mostly her eyes like softest springtime budding.

Martha tugged at him. "Come, dear, the senator is joining them and it's time we paid our respects."

Music coming back, but off-key; babble of talk that didn't make sense, Martha pushing determined through the crowd and making a space. Senator Littlefield reaching gladly for her hands, distinguished gray man greeting an old friend; Martha smiling, tossing her head.

"My very good friend, Senator—Joe Langston."

"Ah, yes, good to see you again, young man. I've been hearing much about you."

"Sir," Joe said, staring into Littlefield's eyes because it was folly to look elsewhere, and then not being able to avoid it because he was touching palms with the man from the New Mexico Territory and muttering something in return.

Then the man said, "And may I present my wife?"

She gave him her hand and it was no colder than his own. Joe lifted it to his lips and dropped it immediately. His voice sounded odd in his own ears. "Señora," he said.

"Señor Langston," she replied.

But he was only Joe, and she was Marilee, staring back at him.

Chapter 43

She was still a little numb when they returned to the hotel, but Alfonso didn't notice. Marilee hadn't had much to say to him lately, not after their latest flareup.

In their suite, she took off the emeralds and returned them to the velvet-lined box, her hands unsteady. It had been like coming face to face with the past, a dead past resolutely put behind her, when she looked across that crowded ballroom and saw Joe Langston. For a long, frozen moment, she could not believe he was actually there. The man she'd known was rowdy and so hard that it showed in every plane of his face; the man who'd taken her savagely in a long-ago grassy field was a tattered, self-ish soldier of fortune, an opportunist who sought only the blood money his guns could bring him. Scout, scalp hunter, gambler—the man at Senator Littlefield's home looked none of those things.

Oh, he was still strong and lithe; the years hadn't changed his body, nor lined the set of his face nor soft-ened those autumn-blue and hooded eyes. Even the scar at the corner of his mouth was the same, giving his lips that cynical twist. But the rest of him—raffish, threadbare Joe Langston in formal clothes that fitted so well he might have been born to them, a diamond gleaming from his shirtfront, ravenwing hair neatly trimmed, hands clean and manicured. The hands hadn't gone soft, though; that brief touch of his palm spoke of calluses still there, of hard work, and she would have bet the entire hacienda that Joe had a pistol hidden somewhere.

Joe, waltzing smoothly across the floor with that older woman in his arms, a lady of obvious quality and breeding; Joe, the renegade fast gun, confidante of a senator, known by bankers and wealthy businessmen. The woman—possessor of the proud old Fitzhugh-Morris name—a graceful quietness to her, a calm beauty that belied her years, and Joe was her "very good friend." Indeed. It might be that only Joe's outer skin had been sloughed off in metamorphosis; he was yet the opportunist, and it seemed that this time he'd captured the golden goose.

Marilee undressed slowly, hearing her husband move about the bathroom, and she could not pull her mind from the other man. There'd been only the fleeting fragment of time with him, only that brief touching of their hands, yet it seemed that years had suddenly dissolved between them, that they stood naked before each other, and the impact was brutal, dizzying, tense. With an effort, she'd torn her eyes from those light blue ones and forced herself to turn aside, to place a hand upon Don Alfonso's arm.

And Joe had been as anxious to get away; only a few words with the senator, only quick formalities, and he'd taken the stately woman back into the swirling of party-goers. Later, while her husband was closeted with General Portrero, Marilee heard whispers about Joe Langston, scandalous talk about his aging sponsor, guesses—some of them not too far off about this man's shady background. She drank too much champagne.

Tasting it now flat upon her tongue, she brushed her hair while seated at a mirrored table in her shift. Don Alfonso came from the bathroom and stood behind her. "Tomorrow the doctors," he said. "Rosa will be your duenna. I have other things to discuss with the general."

"Guns," she said. "Alfonso, suppose you're wrong? Half the hacienda below the border, and Mexican soldiers never too careful about crossing the river. If Juárez holds power—"

He wheeled from her and took off his shirt. "You are many things, *querida*, but you know nothing of politics. The *porfiristas* may very well control the north, and Díaz is more of a patrician than that peasant *presidente*. Leave business to me."

Nude then, he stretched upon the bed, watching her. Marilee felt a chill at the back of her neck. Not tonight, not this night. He said, "That *gringo*, the big one escorting the rich old woman—have you known him before?"

Brush slowing in her hand, she lied. "No—why do you ask?"

He bunched a pillow beneath his head. *"Quién sabe?* A certain spark passed between you—even the woman who keeps him noticed it."

Marilee continued to brush her hair. "I didn't."

"Just as well," he purred. "What is mine remains mine. So tomorrow we discover if you are barren."

She didn't want to fight him again. Several months before, when he came to her in one of his black rages, Marilee had stood to him, and it had almost come to blood between them. Closing her eyes, she saw it all ugly and stark as it had been.

"Bitch," he'd said. "It is almost two years, and you are not pregnant. You are barren, a mare unable to catch."

And herself: "Are you certain I am the barren one—husband?"

"Of course!" Furious at this slur upon his manhood. "Of course—a wife of mine died in childbirth. I am proven, but you—"

Almost choking on her own rising anger: "Proven how? I do not see Rosa's belly swelling, nor any other of your mistresses great with child."

Hand clenching white around the handle of his quirt, he'd moved at her, *"Puta!* To speak this way to me—you *gringa* whore, I will teach you."

Her hand upon the gun butt. "Certainly, then, the last de Carboca."

Marilee opened her eyes and looked into the mirror. He was still waiting for her to come to bed. That time at the hacienda, he'd stalked out of her room, and later, in a mercurial change of temper, Alfonso had been charming at dinner, agreeing that perhaps both of them should be examined. There was no capable doctor in El Paso del

Norte, and since there was business upcoming with some people in Mexico, why not a holiday for them both?

They had traveled well armed and guarded, a long, hot trip to Guaymas, where he held careful meetings with men who came by night. It was a surprise to Marilee to go aboard ship with him there, to sail all the way around Baja California and up the coast. She'd thought he would return to the rancho, or go overland to Mexicali, if he meant to reach the north. But there were dialogues with the ship captain and discussions about the City of the Angels teeming with Juarista spies. San Francisco would be best, and also where excellent doctors might be found.

And a traitor general, gun merchants, smugglers' ships —and Joe Langston.

Alfonso said from the bed, "I have heard that certain diets, particular medicines will induce pregnancy."

"Perhaps," she answered. "And I have heard a woman should go cleanly to the doctor for examination."

In the mirror, she watched him pull up the sheet and turn his back to her. Marilee put down the hairbrush and went into the bath. Cold water didn't make her face any less warm, and she thought of what Alfonso had said, about a spark passing between her and Joe Langston. He was mistaken; it had merely been a certain shock of recognition, but she wondered why she'd never mentioned Joe to her husband before. Admitting to being wife to a Comanche chief, to other misadventures, she'd left out the time spent with Joe. Why?

When she went back into the bedroom, Alfonso was asleep, and she got into bed, careful not to awaken him. Sleep was a long time coming to her and twisted with dreams.

Breakfasting in their room with Rosa waiting against a wall, Alfonso said, "I must be put in touch with others and meet with the *gringo* lawmaker. Perhaps I will return tonight, perhaps not. Do not forget the doctors. A hired carriage awaits you in the street." Turning his head, he said, "Rosa."

Padding quickly to the table, the girl whispered, "I will care for her, *patrón*."

Alfonso didn't kiss Marilee when he left; he only did that when he was about to bed her, only kissed her hand in formal company. Oh, he still called her his darling, his love, his heart in flowery Spanish, but it was done with just a tinge of sarcasm.

She got up from the table. "Tía Rosa—Aunt Rosa, watching after the chaste wife. We're both so pure, aren't we? But for the sake of tradition, the mockery must be played out."

Rosa looked down and fumbled her hands. "I am sorry, señora."

Contritely, Marilee said, "I am, too—for both of us. Forgive me, Rosa—I know it is not your fault. Perhaps you would have been better off if your *madre* had not been rescued from the Comanches. Children are loved by them."

The girl looked up. "It is true I sometimes wonder how that would have been."

Marilee patted her cheek. "You look so mournful in that black dress, with your hair pulled back that way. But the proper duenna, prepared to keep the don's wife inviolable. Come—we leave the dishes for the hotel staff."

The Regency tried hard to be a first-class hotel, but it was too new for dignity, and its carpets were already tracked by miners' boots and wounded with spur rowels. It smelled of cigar smoke and careless tobacco juice as Marilee went down the stairs, Rosa trailing her by a step. She was halfway across the lobby when he arose from a chair turned absurdly small by his length and bulk.

Marilee stopped, seeing him in the broadcloth coat and soft shirt, the string tie, seeing him hold the beaver hat as he approached her, moving lithely in that aura of strength so natural to him.

He said, "Marilee Bradburn, the Señora de Carboca."

And she murmured. "Joe Langston, without a rifle."

"We've changed some," he said. "Maybe enough so that we can talk."

She was uncertain. "I—my husband hired a carriage. I have appointments with doctors."

"I know. I've already paid off the driver, so I can have the privilege of driving you myself."

Marilee choked back a near-hysterical giggle. "A gentleman coachman. But I have a *duenna*."

"I know a fine place and people she can visit, if she will."

Marilee hesitated, but she had no reason to fear him. To Rosa, she said in a low voice. "Must we always be

411

slaves, you and I? You are touched with the Comanche, and so was I. *They* do not bow to anyone."

The girl lifted her brown face. "It is dangerous, señora, but you are my friend, even after you saw—"

"If he even suspects, I will absolve you," Marilee said. "Come with me from the hotel, so none will suspect." And to Joe: "We will walk down the street—you can meet us there."

A block away, when she saw Joe driving the open buggy, she wanted to laugh. He was in shirtsleeves and bareheaded, his coat folded on the seat, his collar open— as if he could so easily disguise the look of himself. He passed money to Rosa and whispered to her in Spanish, pointing along the street.

Marilee said, "We'll be back by—"

"No later than three," Joe said, "and you two can ride in style with the regular driver. We pass the livery stable on the way back, and the doctor's office."

When he helped her into the buggy, his hand wasn't cold, but warm, warm upon her arm, and she said, "You're pretty good at intrigue—and, as always, sure of yourself. What if I didn't want to go with you?"

"I would have been very sorry, Marilee."

She couldn't resist. "No bending me to your will, no force?"

His eyes seemed just a little sad, those delicately shaded eyes. "I didn't always force you, but I know that sometimes the circumstances—"

He *had* changed, and she was immediately sorry. "Tell me what you've been doing, how you came to San Francisco, all of it."

Joe spoke slowly as he maneuvered the buggy through busy streets and north into gently rolling hills, away from the glut of people and jammed-together houses. She felt sea air fresh upon her face as he told her of his long overland trip and his business ventures here, and from the corner of her eye she watched his profile. Where Alfonso's was hawklike, Joe's was more calmly dignified: his mouth was hard, not ripe, and he wore no silver horns in hair ebony black. He hadn't yet mentioned two things: how he felt about her leaving him back there in El Paso and Mrs. Fitzhugh-Morris.

"The harbor is lovely from up here," she said, glad for sun on her face, for a sense of freedom almost forgotten.

"And you," he said. "I can hardly see the Comanche warrior woman in you anymore, or the girl wearing a castoff uniform and an eyepatch. It's good to see your hair like that, too."

"You—you haven't asked about my husband," she said, as he drew the buggy into the shade of a windblown cypress.

"No," he said.

"And I haven't wondered out loud about your lady."

"I'm glad you said lady," Joe murmured, "because that's what Martha is."

"It was a dirty word to you once."

"I've learned a few things."

Seabreeze whispered over them, and the scent of the tree was clean; greenbrown grass rippled in tiny waves across the hills. She got quickly down from the buggy and walked to the top of the knoll, staring very far out to sea, where ocean and sky blended. She could feel him standing close behind her, the fanning of his breath against her cheek a different kind of zephyr, and she turned naturally into his arms.

There was a special taste to his mouth, and a surprising gentleness, but she remembered the hungry power there and sought it with her tongue. Joe's hands touched her lightly, even though his strong body strained to her own, and she didn't remember sinking to the grass, didn't exactly know the moment when she was released from her dress and other confinements, but her flesh leaped exultantly at the kiss of the sun.

Her mouth wandered his throat and across his breastbone, roamed into springy hair, while her back arched to lift her body to him, open and unafraid and unashamed. She felt the shudder wrack him, and the tightening of his hands. Gladly, she gave herself up to the hard thighs of him, to the covering chest that flattened her aching breasts. Happily, she surrendered to the slow but insistent penetration and coiled her legs eagerly about his hips as their bellies joined.

Their rhythm was steady as the pounding of blood in her veins, speeding with the drumming of her heart; her flesh urged him to hurry, demanding that he give ever more of himself, but stronger, more fiercely. With a gasp that broke against her teeth, Joe did just that—the power thrusting from him into her velvet gloving, hammering, while a storm rose in her mind and a whitehot thunderbolt hurled its lance. Impaled upon sweetsharp heaviness, she cried out and burst.

Blown from the bay, a gull wheeled overhead, calling harshly; the tree rustled; the horse shifted and leather creaked—mundane sounds for Eden.

There was no need for talk as they came apart but not entirely; she held to him, and he to her, reluctant to let go. Her lips could not get enough of his flavor, and moved down his chest, tasting his rib cage, the smooth skin of his stomach; her teeth bit at his hips in turn and nibbled the flesh of his muscular thighs. Then she was with him once more, giving, giving, until suddenly there was a taking, also, a reversal of earth and sky so that the meshing became complete.

Melting ages passed, honeyed eternities spangled with cottonboll clouds; it was a gorgeous day, one created especially for making love, and Marilee thought that love should always be made beneath such a smiling sky.

He was sitting up then, cigar angled between square teeth. "You've been to school, too. Is the Spanish don your professor?"

The wind was a little cool. Marilee drew her dress across her thighs. "And your *sponsor* also? She's been here long enough to know all there is, I'd imagine."

"That's unkind, Marilee."

"We've never been kind to each other. I don't know why we thought that could change now." She held back a shiver as she dressed quickly, her back to him. "There's only a black need in us, something that makes us deserve each other."

"Maybe not—there might be more."

"No," she said. "Because I—did what I did, you cut at me with words, and you might as well have used a quirt." A silver-mounted one?

"And you come boiling right back."

"Why not?" She whirled upon him. "You never did understand that I'm not some piece of baggage to be used whenever *you* want, wherever *you* want, without any thought of *my* feelings. I'm not some nameless, faceless wench—I'm Marilee Bradburn—"

"Señora de Carboca," he corrected, and she could have

slapped him. "It seems you got what you wanted, another feudal kingdom to rule, another big house and more slaves—only now you call them peons. Whatever happened to that dream about building a horse herd through your stallion? Was it easier to just *marry* for it?"

She tried combing her hair, but it was tangled. She said, "About as easy as being a rich woman's stud, I should think. It seems you also got what *you* wanted— gold without working for it, and no thought of tomorrow. At least what I have is more permanent. Hacienda de Carboca is huge, magnificent, with thousands and thousands of acres. It's Cienegas, the place of a hundred springs, and when the New Mexico Territory becomes a state—"

"You'll secede from the Union?"

Jerking the comb through her hair, she said, "Perhaps I'll never get back to Bradburn Plantation, but it's not impossible. And if not me, then my—my son. It's not over. I won't let it ever be over because I can still live with *my* dream, Joe Langston. How about you? What happens when she gets tired of you or dies? How many businessmen will still trade with you, how many senators will shake your hand then? Your Mrs. Fitzhugh-Morris might be a great lady, but you're still only Joe Langston."

She expected him to rage at her, to blaze forth in that familiar anger, but there was only a tightening of his jaws, only the paling of the scar at the corner of his mouth.

"I'll drive you back," he said.

Chapter 44

A week later, when they left San Francisco behind and drove southward to El Pueblo de los Angeles, Don Alfonso was in no better a mood than when they'd started. Playing the hidalgo all the way, he'd insisted she ride in the coach—certainly not *astride* a horse instead of sidesaddle—like a respectable married lady.

And in Los Angeles, he left her for more clandestine meetings with Mexican representatives, but never unwatched. Now she found herself guarded by a real duenna, a humorless crone with a hairy mole on her face. Tía Francesca was a remote cousin of the de Carbocas, a maiden lady of indeterminate age who never seemed to sleep. The harridan was fiercely loyal to her illustrious cousin, the don, and grimly happy to be of service to Alfonso; beyond that she showed no inclination toward anything but duty.

The trip across a dry and searing desert was cruel, the coach surrounded by armed riders, evil-looking Porfiristas from across the border. But at least Marilee was allowed to leave the stifling coach sometimes, even though the gelding she was given to ride wasn't much of a horse. Day after stifling day the cavalcade moved east, its outriders sighting nothing more than jackrabbits and vultures, a few deer.

Alfonso shot at everything within range, his dark face set, lighting only when he scored a kill on some inoffensive creature. And he came to Marilee at night with the same kind of hard, merciless intensity, seldom bothering even to talk to her within the tent, using her body in a silent, driving savagery that seemed more determination than hunger.

The only person she could speak with was Rosa, and that usually in whispers. "The revolutionists, señora—they are more like *bandidos* and speak of defeats in the south, of a General Sostenes Rocha who puts them against the wall fast as they are taken."

And Marilee hissed back, "I wonder how much Alfonso has given them already. He's picked the wrong side this time, it seems."

At last they came to the village of Tucson, where Marilee could bathe properly, where even the fiery food was a welcome change from the diet of the trail. But Alfonso moved them out next morning for Nogales, and they made the rest of the wearying journey to the rancho along the Mexican side of the river.

"He's worried," Marilee said to Rosa when the duenna was out of sight. "He's sent men to search for his cattle down here, to look for his herdsmen."

"Señora," the girl murmured, "he is very angry also. I—I still hesitate to tell you, but in San Francisco, that day we came back to the hotel—there was a leaf in your hair, a single green leaf, and I could not hide the brush quickly enough."

Marilee frowned. "I could have picked that up anywhere, who knows how?"

"It is what I told *el patrón*, señora, though he beat me."

Squeezing Rosa's hand, Marilee said, "You are a good friend, too good—the man was not worth it—to either of us."

So that was the reason for Tía Francesca, for the sullen quietness of him; Alfonso suspected she'd had a tryst, and probably with whom. But all he'd asked was the doctors' opinions, and she'd told him that as far as they knew, nothing appeared wrong with her. Each had suggested certain exercises.

"For me, also," Alfonso had said. "I am virile, of course. I never thought otherwise. So we will produce an heir, in time."

Never a word about his jealousy; only Tía Francesca ever present, always watching. And because of her presence, Marilee could not help but think of the cause, of Joe Langston.

When they recrossed the Rio Grande, Alfonso's face was a thundercloud. Riders had been coming and going all day, and more Porfiristas dropping off to be replaced by de Carboca *vaqueros*. He flung from his horse in the courtyard and stalked into the hacienda without speaking, brushing past servants drawn up for a formal welcome.

Stiffly, Marilee climbed down from the coach, shook out her skirts, and headed straight for Bradburn's stall. Puffing behind her, the old woman jerked at her sleeve. "A proper wife follows her husband."

Marilee flung the hand away, her eyes hot. "Listen, *tía* —I am at my own home, and *I* am mistress here. Understand that—do not follow me or I will lose you in the desert for coyotes to pick your stringy flesh."

Bradburn neighed at the sight and smell of her, and she ran her hands over the great stallion, buried her face in his mane and told him how much she loved him. "More than any man," she whispered, "for you're worth more than any of them, all of them together. You're always here when I need you, and you—you love me back."

Hearing a sound at the stable door, she turned to see Manuel Venegas leaning there, quirt scar across his cheek. "Yes?"

"I had hoped *el patrón* had left you," he said. "You are bad luck to him, a woman who cares more for a stallion than for her husband."

Marilee stroked Bradburn's muscled neck. "It is none of your affair. If I speak to Don Alfonso of your words, you will carry other scars."

"He is a de Carboca, as was his father before him, and *his* father. It is his right to beat me if he wishes. You have no such right, *gringa*—even if you had not slept with Comanches."

Moving away from the horse, Marilee said, "They are fighters, the Comanches. Not one of them would accept the whip, much less lick the boots of the man who struck with it."

Below the ragged moustache, his teeth gleamed, and his eyes were black marbles. "You will never understand us, never know the traditions, the ancient laws. It is why you will not be accepted here, no matter what name you wear."

Standing very straight, she looked at him. "Do you know the de Carboca motto, *vaquero?* Those words in Latin beneath your don's coat of arms? No, I suppose not. Tradition and ancient law hasn't taught you to read. The words are this: Let them hate, so long as they fear. And the name I wear is de Carboca. You will never address me again without using it: *Señora* de Carboca. For I will not merely have you lashed for your impertinence—I will face you *myself*, out upon the land, so you may discover *all* I learned from the Comanches, as the Apaches discovered."

Venegas stiffened, then slowly backed up as she walked at him, but as she slammed angrily away, he said, "A *pistolera* is not a wife, nor a *caballera* a lady, Señora de Carboca."

By the time she got upstairs and into her own bathroom, Rosa had cool water ready, and scented soap, a wondrously fluffy towel, and Marilee had stopped shaking. But the soap's odor was cloying and thickened in her throat until it made her ill.

The sudden illness surprised her, embarrassed her when it came boiling up from her stomach and left her weakened, her coldsweat forehead pressed against the tiled wall. Rosa wiped her face and guided her to the sitting room couch.

"Perhaps now *el patrón* will be in better humor," the girl said.

Marilee rubbed her head. "What do you mean?"

"The signs, señora—the morning sickness. You are *never* sick, *es verdad?* So it must be that you carry his child."

At first, Marilee refused to accept the idea, but morning after morning proved Rosa correct; she was pregnant. Word went out over the ranch, at first in whispers, then more openly to prove Rosa right about something else—the effect of the news on Alfonso's humor. For a while, he was the man Marilee had first seen—attentive, graceful, the attractive and perfect gentleman.

It might be all right, she thought. Just possibly, she could make her luxurious prison into a real home, help turn the ranch into even more than it was, make it known for magnificent horses. And someday the pines and mossy oaks, great white columns, and a marbled ballroom with the scent of Cape Jasmine drifting. . . .

Before she was showing much, Marilee threw herself into the ranch work, handling and caring for the crop of Bradburn's foals in the Comanche method: breathing in their nostrils so they would know her scent, stroking and gentling them so they'd be without fear and wouldn't ever have to be broken to the saddle. Brought along with kindness and care, the babies would take the saddle without bucking, moved step by thoughtful step through their training.

They looked very good, Bradburn's muscle and power crossed onto wiry mustang blood, onto fiery barb blood. To the mustangs he passed his size and strength, to the barb mares a stamina and calming of flightiness.

"Oh, foolish woman," the *vaqueros* whispered, "treating those foals as if they are children, when she should be looking to the don's heir. Anyone knows horses are meant to be mastered, not pampered." Nodding sagely, they added, "Someone else, a man, must have broken the great stallion, not this one. Because a woman can ride, this does not make her a trainer of horses. Will she do any better with Don Alfonso's son?"

"Of course, it will be a boy child," Alfonso said over dinner. "The first children of all de Carbocas are males. And, señora, you are to take more care of yourself. Tía Francesca tells me you spend too much time with the horses, especially that stallion."

"Tía Francesca has nothing more to do than carry tales," Marilee said. "I feel fine."

His brow furrowed and the hard look gathered around his eyes. "Do not endanger this child, woman. It will mean your life, too."

Irritated by her swollen belly, but a lingering fall heat, by Alfonso himself, she said, "The baby is mine also. Do not threaten me, Alfonso."

Pouring more bloodred wine into his goblet, he drank it off rapidly. "Understand, woman—I grow no younger, and this might be my final chance to sire a—" Flushing, he reached again for the decanter.

At that moment she knew he had lied to her about seeing doctors in San Francisco, realized his male pride would not allow even the chance *he* might be the one at fault. Feeling movement within her belly, Marilee knew something else: this new life within her might not be her husband's child. Oh, God—Joe Langston!

Alfonso read the distress in her face and slopped wine over the rim of his glass. She had never seen him quite so drunk. He said, "Thinking of Rosa and the others, are you? As a dutiful husband, I should stop dallying with my mistresses? Not so! And do not look at me in that fashion, woman. Perhaps an hidalgo's sperm does not find fertile ground in lesser breeds—a wolf does not cross with a mongrel."

"I've told you, I don't care how many girls you bed," she said carefully, "so long as you don't involve me in your perverted games."

As if he hadn't heard, he said, "But you, my dear wife, have just enough *good* blood in your background to qualify as a dam." His eyes narrowed and the too-rich mouth was wet. "That is how it is, señora—that is how all here will accept my son. There will never be a word breathed about a green leaf caught in the hair of an adultress. This is *my* son!"

Marilee rose from the table. "I'm going up to bed."

His voice followed her, thick with drink, with an angry, sullen pain. "And stay away from that stallion until you have my permission!"

She sat on the edge of the bed, staring at an arched window and damning herself for having been so stupid, so weak as to think Joe Langston could ever really change inside. Because of their dark need for each other, that urgency that welled up from so deep within them both, she had made a foolish mistake.

And in a way, she had only proven Joe's low estimation of her, a married woman so eagerly, so easily leaping into a quick affair on a hillside. If she'd actually loved Alfonso, she would never have gone with Joe that day, but Marilee had never considered herself truly married to the man, either. That forced ceremony, the tame priest, herself surrounded by girls who had seen her tied and ravished only minutes before. . . .

The baby might *not* be Joe's.

After all, he hadn't made her pregnant through all the months they spent together; neither had the first man to rape her, that leering, vicious Yankee trooper. And Little Buffalo of the Camanches—two years of being his wife; and before him Timmy Santee and Gilmore Frazier, a gambler who went out to die so Marilee might escape. None of these men had made her body thicken and her breasts swell, and she had been thankful for it.

Perhaps she had been lucky, her body never ready for pregnancy because she was mentally rebelling at all the enforced intimacies. But so many women were forced, and so many of them had babies. And why *now*, for her? The child could be Alfonso's, one chance in millions that succeeded, the right moment in time.

Or gambler's luck.

She would never know.

Candles guttered out and the lamp flickered low as Marilee slept restlessly, waking often in the night, once hearing thumps and muffled cries. Alfonso was at it again in his own apartment, rutting with girls who didn't dare say no to him. She covered her head with a down pillow and courted dreams again. They came sorrowing and grotesque, gibbering at her, and among them a tall child with hair glossy as a crow's wing and eyes like wintery sky. Did he wear silver horns?

Marilee snapped up as her door flung back with a crash. Dawn was pale gray through the windows and she rubbed at her eyes. "Rosa—Juanita—and little Paloma! What—why—"

Rosa was crawling; the others swayed in the bedroom doorway. "Señora," Rosa groaned, "*por Dios*, señora— help us. He has gone mad."

They were all naked and sweaty, trembling. A trickle of blood seeped from the corner of Rosa's mouth, and brutal welts crisscrossed her full breasts. Staring, not fully awake, Marilee saw Juanita's doesoft skin marred with scratches, bruised by blows, and small, terrified Paloma: that delicate child's body had also been lashed. It looked as if a spur rowel had been dragged across her thigh, leaving red tracks behind.

"Insane, señora," Rosa panted. "He kept us with him all night, and started over this morning. *Borracho*—he has never been so drunk, and nothing we could do to please him. Oh, señora—he spoke wild things, *loco* things. He accused us of spreading gossip about him, of whispering that the child is not his. He said we laugh at him because he has made none of us pregnant. Señora, for the love of God, do not let him kill us!"

Clumsily, Marilee got out of bed and went to the dresser where she kept her Colt. Paloma whimpered, and Juanita tried to soothe her sister; Rosa came to her knees, trembling, mumbling a prayer.

The girls glanced over their shoulders and ran to the bed, to huddle upon it with their arms around each other. Marilee drew the pistol from its holster, holding it balanced as Alfonso strode booted and spurred across the sitting room, slapping the silver-mounted quirt against his calf. He wore no shirt, and his hair was tousled, his eyes swollen and bloodshot. Wine had stained his breeches and matted the hair on his heaving chest.

"Ah," he said, "the gathering of bitches, but only one with milk in her dugs. Now why is that?"

Marilee said, "They came for my help, and they have it."

Alfonso's mouth was ugly, smeared. "The *pistolera* threatens? *Gringa* fool—if you shoot me my *vaqueros* will drag you to death behind their horses and leave your body to the vultures."

"Your son's body, also," Marilee said.

Face contorted, eyes glaring, Alfonso swayed and caught himself. "You have me, wench—for now. But when the colt is weaned, what then? The mare is alone, yes. *Yes*, I say! No more vile, lying gossip, no more shaming of my name."

"Alfonso—"

"A pistol in your hand, a baby in your belly. I cannot touch you now, cannot punish you as you should be punished for what you have done to me, for the many times you have defied me. But—ah—there is always a method, ever a way to repay injustices."

Swinging around, staggering, he plunged from the room with an irate slash of his riding crop against the door. Behind Marilee, the girls cried softly.

Rosa mumbled, "I said nothing, nothing."

Marilee lay down the pistol to get a robe and put it on. Sliding her feet into leather slippers, she said, "He won't hurt you now, and when he is sober, perhaps he will forget all this."

An edge to her voice, Juanita said, "Not that one—he never forgets. He will make us all suffer for this—even you, señora."

"Believe me," Rosa groaned, arms crossed over her hurt breasts, "I said nothing, and Juanita, Paloma—they knew nothing. It is all inside his head, señora."

"And in his black heart," Marilee answered, wondering what convoluted plot was working in Alfonso's drunken mind, how he meant to take revenge upon them all, for real and fancied sins.

When the outraged squeal lifted from the stables and broke against her window, she knew. Heart caught in her throat, she trotted heavily to the door and down the stairs. *Bradburn!* He was doing something to Bradburn!

Running as best she could across the patio toward the barns, she remembered she'd left the Colt behind, but she couldn't go back for it now. Bradburn was bellowing in pain and furious surprise. She had to reach him, had to stop Alfonso. . . .

They were behind the stall in the small corral, Alfonso atop the saddled and bridled stallion. Bradburn was rearing, tormented by vicious rakings of sharp rowels into his ribs and across his bleeding shoulders, by the savage rise and fall of Alfonso's quirt. The stud's mouth was opened wide, jerked sideways by a punishing hand upon the reins, and Bradburn's eyes were rolling white.

"Alfonso! Don't—don't hurt him anymore! *Alfonso!*" The cry keened up from the very core of Marilee's soul.

"*Bastardo!*" Alfonso snarled. "Defy me, *me?* I will break you, beat you down until you grovel—there, there!"

"No!" Marilee was at the corral gate, tearing at its latch

with her hands, screaming. "Oh, no—let him alone! He never hurt you."

Somehow the stallion got his head down, neck muscles bulging, froth whipping from his tortured mouth. Alfonso sawed upon the reins with both hands, and his bloody spurs worked back and forth, back and forth. Bradburn fired both hind feet, and when they came back beneath him, vaulted into the air, twisting as he climbed. He slammed down with a stiff-legged jolt that snapped Alfonso's head forward, then back.

Marilee got the gate open just as the big stallion wheeled, shaking his entire body, spun faster, and got the bit in his teeth. Crow-hopping, he plunged across the corral and thundered into the rails. Alfonso lost a stirrup. Bradburn wheeled again and leaped. Alfonso went out of the saddle and across the horse's shoulder to hit the ground hard. Backing away and shaking his head, the stallion blew through his spread nostrils and watched the man.

In the corral, Marilee spread her arms. "Easy, boy—easy."

At her feet, Alfonso sat up, the side of his head scraped and dirtied, his eyes dulled.

Marilee kept talking to the horse, trying to quiet him, soothe him by the sound of her voice.

Alfonso staggered to his feet, and she saw too late that he was wearing his gunbelt. She snatched at his wrist, but he slapped her across the mouth with one hand and lifted the pistol in the other.

"It is the same as killing your lover," Alfonso panted, "perhaps better."

She fought him, lowered her head and rammed it into his chest, clutching at his arm, raking clawed nails at his face. Gasping, she fought him for more than her life. Their feet stamped dust, stumbled, and he cursed her, got one hand knotted into her hair and flung her aside. Weakened by the child in her body, Marilee caught at a rail and almost fell.

The pistol came up. Early morning sunlight winked dully along its barrel.

"Bradburn!" she screamed. "Oh, my God—Bradburn!"

Bellowing, the big stallion threw himself across the corral, shoulder knocking Alfonso away like a *piñata*. Alfonso landed upon one knee and aimed the gun. Bradburn's towering bulk seemed to fill the sky as he went up on his hind feet, and now it was Alfonso who screamed when the ironshod forefeet struck downward with all the great weight of the stallion's maddened body behind them.

Wet crack of a hollow gourd being crushed; damp breakings of bone; the scream suddenly choked off, stamped out. Bradburn quivered and drew back, coiling his hindquarters for another lifting, another strike.

"No!" Marilee called. "No, boy—back, *back!* Easy, Bradburn—that's right—back."

She tottered toward the still, mangled figure on the ground and stood above it, seeing it broken and ripped and stained. "You shouldn't have," she whispered, holding her stomach. "You *know* you shouldn't have hurt him."

And Marilee knew Don Alfonso de Carboca could not hear her, that he was dead.

Chapter 45

Joe Langston made another checkmark on the shipping list and shook his head at his warehouse foreman. "No," he said, "I know the money is tempting, but there's too much risk to it. If I mean to gamble, it'll be at a card table, where I can *see* what's going on."

Stanger followed him past the casks of tobacco, the bales of cotton, and sacks of corn. "But these Mexes swear they got the money in gold—"

"Once the arms are delivered in Mexico, right? Once the guns we pay for are loaded and shipped—at our cost—to some deserted spot on their coast. But what if they just take the guns? What if the other side finds us first? No, Stanger—I've been in Mexico while a revolution was on, and I'll stick to staple goods and stable customers."

Leaving the man behind, Joe stopped to inspect baled cowhides, checking the tanning process and finding it good. The smell of new leather always did something to him, reminded him of far places, traveling places. He turned and looked out to the dock where a merchant was taking on cargo, coolie laborers and Mexican peons working together to get it loaded. He had yet to walk up one of those gangplanks and stow a sea trunk in a cabin on a sturdy ship bound for China or Africa or around the Horn and across the Atlantic to Europe.

"You would love Paris, I think," Martha had said. "My husband took me there once. But, no—perhaps Spain would suit you better, for there's much of the matador in you, Joe."

Someday, he kept telling her—when the business can just about run itself; when you're feeling better, because I wouldn't enjoy going alone. And the somedays stretched into months, into years, while the farthest he ever got from San Francisco was that trip to Monterey with Martha. She wanted to visit the missions there; Martha had become interested in the old churches of late.

"She just kind of runnin' down," Marcus said.

"No," Joe insisted. "She looks better than ever—her cheeks are pink and she laughs a lot. You have to admit that, Marcus."

" 'Spect I do. Know one thing sure, and that's Miz Martha is happier'n I ever seen her, even when she was a bride."

Joe had looked at the big man. "There's not a touch of gray in your hair, man. You must have been a youngun when she married."

Marcus laughed. "Coachman then, coachman now. Difference was, I belonged to *him* then. I'm gettin' on, Joe— I just don't show it so much, I reckon." He was quiet then, driving the matched pair of gray geldings up the hill to the Fitzhugh-Morris mansion. "Reckon I shouldn't of warned you about her bein' a true lady, away back when you first come to her."

"You did right, Marcus."

"Well, you was so much younger and full of vinegar, and I seen a gamblin' man with an itchy foot. So I used you to get back her ranch, 'cause I seen somethin' else— the need you got to pay a debt. Tell you the truth, I figured you might even get yourself killed out yonder."

Joe grinned. "And you didn't much care, so long as I got the others."

"Not back then," Marcus said.

Walking out onto the street, Joe looked up and down it. Speculators were already talking about building more houses off to the north, where he'd driven Marilee Bradburn that hurtful day. Not Marilee Bradburn; Señora de Carboca, lady by blood and with a fancy title to go with it now, mistress of vast lands in wild country, married to a cold-eyed don who grew his own army of *vaqueros,* just as plantation masters in the old South, the gone South, had grown their own slaves.

But how quickly she'd forgotten her marriage vows to be with him. She might have done the same with any man who asked her. Joe took out a cigar and bit hard at the end of it. Maybe she'd been right when she said that all they had in common was a certain dark and driven need for each other's body. Once that hunger was filled, they were like strange wolves, circling and looking for tender places to sink their teeth.

It was never like that with Martha. With her, there was gentleness and ease, a softened caring, an understanding each of the other. He would have liked nothing better than to marry her, because that would have been the final step, the closing and locking of a door to shut Marilee away forever. He could never do to Martha what Marilee had done to her husband.

A coolie hurried by, baskets swinging on a pole; two bearded miners staggered along with their arms locked; a cowhand stood against a wall, out of place in all this noise and action, looking trapped. Joe continued to walk uphill, needing the exercise, needing to move among the ever-changing people of this city he'd come to know perhaps too well.

Barbary Coast shanghai groups didn't stray this far from their foul dens, although he would have welcomed them happily now. He was supposed to be civilized, but that was like putting a coat of whitewash on an old fencepost; he'd been out in the weather too long, and the marks of storms would always be with him. So he carried the heavy cane with the ivory handle that twisted off and turned into a two-barreled derringer; he kept the faithful Walker Colt tucked into his waistband, its worn butt hidden by his coat. They were solid, familiar things.

He was making money, but when he didn't hold gold coins clinking within his hands, money didn't seem real to him. It was all on paper, figures listed in a bank. The ranch and its cows were real; land and men were; but not this ever-shifting empire of profit and loss. There were few losses, because Joe was conservative, content to steadily pile up small gains instead of plunging, of putting too much into a ship that might sink or a government that might never be born.

That trait fooled some people, the big-bellied men who sat at poker tables with him, drinking excellent brandy and smoking the best cigars. For the fat men were money-fat, too, and played only in private clubs, among their peers. They had let Joe in bit by bit, because he was friendly with the senator and because he had enough money to make his play worthwhile.

Then the caution left him, and he played by instinct, slashing in with a raise, shilly-shallying when he should have been bluffing, and often taking their bank drafts home with him. A wild man, they gossiped, on an unbelievable run of fool's luck; if he does business the same way. . . .

Martha would laugh aloud when he came home in the dawn, propped up in bed with her cheeks drawn but her eyes bright. "I should think you'd be ashamed to play such charades with them."

"They want it to be like that," he'd say, leaning to kiss her chestnut hair, heavily silvered now, to kiss her eyelids. "They're so powerful and wise, and I'm only an upstart. Sooner or later, they just *know* I'll trap myself."

She had gone sober then. "And you don't feel trapped? Because of me, I mean."

"Never, Martha, but I'd gladly put my paw into your snare and have it closed with a ring."

"Please, Joe—"

She didn't want him to mention marriage, and after a while he didn't anymore. She knew how he felt about it, and that had to be enough. Joe didn't like to have her bothered by anything and indeed was sparing with his love-making, tender as could be and careful that she shouldn't excite herself too much.

There was the house on its hillside, iron picket fence protecting flowers beyond, set where it could catch the sun and where ocean winds could find it. Somehow, she'd gotten honeysuckle to grow here, but the orangegold flowers never poured forth sweetness as they did in the South. Joe thought perhaps all things transplanted were never quite the same.

He saw the black buggy, the horse anchored to a ring in the post, and began to hurry, pushing back the gate, cold against his hand. It had been many months since Martha had had need of a doctor; she'd been so well, so happy.

Marcus met him at the door, and there was someone else in the darkened sitting room—a brown-robed priest. Joe pointed. "What's *he* doing here? She's not that sick, and even if she were, Martha is no Papist—"

Big hand upon his shoulder, Marcus said, "Easy, man, easy," as if he were gentling a horse. "Miz Martha asked him to come. She—"

"Damn it," Joe said, "don't block my way, Marcus. Where's the doctor—what does he—"

"She waitin' on you," Marcus said, dropping his hand. "Go ahead on."

Pale against the pillows, wan as the sheets themselves, she tried to smile at him. The doctor hunched in a chair, a nurse stood nearby smelling of astringent; curtains were drawn.

"Martha—"

Her hand was cool in his fingers, dry. "It's all right, Joe—it's all right."

"You—" he saw her eyes, not bright now, dulled over in pain. Not resignation, only pain.

Voice reed-thin, she said, "Do you—do you still want to marry me, Joe Langston?"

His throat was full. "You know I do—I always wanted that."

At the door, Marcus said softly, "I brought him, the priest."

"You don't mind a Catholic ceremony? I—I converted while we were at the missions, Joe."

"Any way, Martha. I never was a churchman. But shouldn't we wait until you're better?"

"It's time," she murmured. "Padre? Doctor Nelson, Nurse, dear Marcus—where's Sissy?"

"Right here," Marcus breathed.

"All my friends and my lover. It's time, padre. P-please hurry."

Intoned Latin phrases; brown hand making a sign, moving in benediction; drylipped Martha saying yes, yes, and Joe forcing the word from teeth that wanted to clench, from a throat that tried to close. Sissy muffling a sob; something glistening wet upon the black cheek of Marcus.

Joe kissed her mouth and found it hot, dry as desert sand. "Martha, Martha—"

Shrinking before his eyes, folding slowly in upon herself, she whispered, "I could not, before—not and tie you to a dying woman, Joe. But you—you're my husband now, and I—I have never been more proud, nor ever more alive—"

He held to her hands, fought to hold her back, and all he could say was her name. Her lips moved, and he put his ear to them, touched them as her breath slid out and away. He only heard *love*.

"No!" he said then. "Goddamnit, *no!* She wasn't that sick—"

"Always been that sick," Marcus said. "Come away now, Joe—let the doctor man—"

Her hands were so thin, so fragile; Joe put them carefully upon her breast. "Doctor—what kind of damned doctor doesn't know when a lady is near to dying?"

"I knew," Doctor Nelson said, "and so did she. Mrs. Fitzhugh-Morris—ah, Mrs. Langston didn't want *you* to know about her heart."

Coming off the bed, not able to look at her, Joe whirled on Marcus. "And *you*—all this time, these years when she could have stilled the whispers, quieted the snickers. Damn you for a black bastard! Why didn't you tell me?"

"You want to hit out at somethin', do it," Marcus said. "Won't change nothin', but you can hit me."

The padre stirred. "Not here, not now. The last rites —I must perform—I must bless—"

"You son of a bitch," Joe said. "She was born blessed."

"Joe, Joe." Huge hands on his arms, turning him, stumbling him to the door and through it. Black hand pressing a glass into his own; the welcome bite of brandy, but no numbness from it, no real teeth to it.

Marcus said, "She hung on long's she could, never wantin' to bother you."

Joe drank again. "I could have made her happy."

"She was happy, man. You was good for her."

"Not good enough, not long enough."

"She was happy," Marcus repeated. "Once you get yourself real good and drunk, and real good and sober again, you're goin' to see the truth of that. And I'm to tell you about the will she drew up at the lawyer's, and how can't nobody even try to break it, because you and her was legally married up."

"Don't talk about it now," Joe said. "Don't talk about anything now." And he took the brandy bottle with him when he went hatless into the street, shouldering aside men and going blindly somewhere, anywhere as he drank.

On the Barbary Coast, he got into a brawl and gloried in the pain in his hands, the pain of his beaten face. He swayed out of the wrecked saloon and looked for more trouble, seeing Marcus behind him and shouting, "Get away, get the hell away." He flung money at startled Chinese, and broke his cane over the head of a hairy miner who tried to take a coin by force. Stupidly, he looked down at the derringer handle remaining in his hand and then lifted the short gun to shoot out a pair of windows.

Only conscious of bumping and movement, he felt himself being lifted and carried, and when the massive arms lowered him again, the heavy, unfeeling cloak of darkness was a friend.

In the morning, there were duties: the hearse, the burial to be arranged, things to keep him busy; flowers—she liked all flowers, and Joe sent people to scour the city for them. He was surprised to find she had already bought a plot and chosen a coffin. He fretted when her friends came, paced the shaded parlor like a caged wild animal. Damn it, death on the plains was so quick and simple, so soon done with and put behind. Here it lingered on and on, feeding upon tears.

It rained when Martha Langston was laid to rest, and Joe stood bareheaded in the rain until Marcus urged him away. In the coach, he said, "Marcus—the stone."

"Soon, soon."

"A bridegroom and a widower at the same damned time. The house still full of people?"

"Will be, I reckon. Everybody liked Miz Martha."

"I wish they'd go home."

"They do, you just get drunk again. Best let 'em all pay they respects. Then you do like she wanted—see the lawyer man. Workin' helps stop hurtin'."

"Damn it, I never even got to tell her I loved her. I never said that, Marcus."

The coach rolled slowly to a stop before the mansion where so many others were drawn up, and Marcus said,

"Could be you never said it because you didn't. Now wait up, man—don't lift your hackles at me. I know you respected her and cared for her and took right good care of her. *She* loved you for it, and that was good enough for Miz Martha. Let it be good enough for you."

Joe thought about that, and said yes, thank you, to women in black; yes, thank you, she was a fine lady, to men uncomfortable in the residue of death. He smelled lavender and the funeral perfume of calla lilies, surreptitious whiskey, secret cigars, and dishes of food brought as cooked offerings.

They murmured sympathies and whispered of the Lord's will, and he was glad to slip away from them into the study where Senator Littlefield poured drinks. "To Martha," the senator toasted. "One of a kind."

"Yes," Joe said, and drank.

"She wanted me to lend a hand if you need it."

"I'll get by."

Littlefield looked into his glass. "With your own property, yes. A shrewd move on her part, marrying you at the end—the husband inherits."

"I don't give a damn about that."

"She wanted you to have it, and I happen to know there are no other legitimate heirs—all gone in the war, you know. Martha chose well this time. Her first husband was a fumbling bore—never could understand what she saw in the man. Only shrewd move he ever made was when he turned all their properties into cash and sent her west. But you, now—a good businessman, from all I hear; wise enough not to invest in gun running to Díaz. Do you remember the don from the New Mexico Territory, the one with the silverblonde wife? Striking young woman."

A cold-eyed don and Marilee; even strangers would not forget that pair. Joe nodded and refilled their glasses.

"Well," Littlefield went on, "his gamble on General Díaz cost him dearly. Understand that he lost all his land south of the Rio Grande because of it; still considerable holdings in the Territory, of course, but little good it will ever do Don Alfonso de Carboca."

Proffering a box of cigars, Joe held a match for the senator and said, "Why not? She—the señora seemed capable."

"Oh, I didn't say *she* didn't profit. That is, if she can

hang on to the land. Wild country out there. But the don
—word is he got himself killed—by a savage stallion, it
seems. When a man makes one mistake, it seems others
inexorably follow."

Marilee was a widow.

"Don't mean to run on," Littlefield said. "All water
under the dam. Just wanted to say, in the memory of
Martha Fitzhugh-Morris—ah, Mrs. Langston, that is—I
am always available to you. Her attorney is a good man
—William Rivers."

"I appreciate your sympathy, Senator," Joe said, "and
all the good advice you've been so kind as to give me."

Littlefield rose heavily. "Any time, my boy. Bear up,
as I'm sure the beauteous Señora de Carboca is doing.
Different circumstances, though—you lost far more than
she did. Never did care for the arrogance of leftover dons
—always looking down their noses at white men. Bear up,
my boy."

"Yes," Joe said. "Thank you, sir."

And when the house was cleared at last, he sat with
Marcus and Sissy, drinking brandy; but the strong stuff
only made the girl whimper more, and they had to pack
her off to bed.

"Have to think on what to do, Marcus."

"That you have."

"This house is so damned empty without her. The
whole city is empty."

Marcus sipped his brandy. "You got a lot to do, runnin'
the ranch and your warehouse and all."

"Don't know as it's worth it. How much do you know
about stock, Marcus?"

"Some, but don't you go thinkin' of me and the ranch."

"You get along with the *vaqueros*."

"Ain't them worries me."

Joe said, "We'll think on it. I have to see the lawyer
tomorrow, and I'll know better then. Hell, I can't live in
this big house by myself."

"Your foot's itchin' again," Marcus said. "Ships leavin'
every day, I reckon."

Joe nodded. "Ships and horses."

Chapter 46

Don Alfonso de Carboca had been sealed into the family tomb for only hours when the trouble began, and Marilee was ready for it, ready as she could be.

They had wanted to execute Bradburn for killing Alfonso, but she'd backed them off with her dead husband's pistol, screaming wild-eyed at them until they muttered away. Now the horse was shut into his stall, safe for the moment, and he'd stay that way so long as she could sit guard with the Sharps and the Spencer, with the Colt upon her lap because she couldn't hook the gunbelt around her distended waist.

Chairback against the adobe wall, still in her widow's weeds, she listened to sounds from the little houses where the workers lived; voices raised in protest, mostly women; male voices rumbling, dominating; a clattering of simple furniture; horses stamping. And within her body uneasy movement.

She would fight if they came for Bradburn again. The stallion had only defended himself, striking out against unexpected and unwarranted cruelty; and maybe he had been protecting her, too. Alfonso had gotten exactly what he deserved, and Manuel Venegas could grumble all he wanted about ancient laws and traditions. A tyrant had fallen, and she was glad for it. *When the colt is weaned,* Alfonso had said, *what then?*

Once he had his son and heir, nothing would have prevented him from carrying out his threat to rid his stable of the brood mare—her. The señora would die in her sleep, perhaps, or of snakebite, or be thrown from a horse in the hills; so sad her head was crushed. Who would ever question Don Alfonso's version?

Rosa came barefoot in her shapeless dress, a black band about her upper arm. "Señora, some of them have ridden out to herd the cattle. They mean to take them south, señora."

"I thought as much. They will not work for me, for a *gringa* who caused the death of their master."

"Traitors," Rosa said. "Cowards all. They closed their eyes when he demanded their wives and daughters, but they steal from you now. Give me one of those guns, señora."

Marilee smiled faintly. "Your Comanche blood, Rosa? You don't have to do this."

"I do it for myself," Rosa said. "I have seen guns. What do I do with this one?"

Showing the girl how to reload the long Sharps, Marilee warned her to fire it from the hip, that it carried a heavy kick. "They may not come here—they may take the cows and horses and go away."

"And they may loot the house," Rosa said, "in the name of justice."

Then Juanita came, her younger sister trailing behind, both girls pale but determined. "Manuel Venegas is my uncle," Juanita said, "and was to look after me when my father died. He gave me, gave us both to *el patrón.*"

Marilee said, "Paloma, what are you carrying?"

Softly, the girl said; "A machete. We stand by you, señora—he would have killed us, but for you, and we will not leave you now."

"All right, then," Marilee said. "Here's the Spencer, Juanita. You know how to work it? Good. You and Paloma guard the house—stand at the door. Rosa and I will stay here to keep them from the horse."

"The blessed horse," Juanita breathed, "the instrument of merciful *Díos*."

Marilee rubbed her stomach; her breasts were uncomfortable. "The *vaqueros* are calling him *el diablo*."

Rosa held the long rifle carefully. "Not him—the real devil was buried in that tomb today. What he did to us—what he was going to do—"

"Here they come," Marilee said, and climbed awkwardly from her chair, the Colt held clenched in her right fist.

Venegas was walking unsteadily, and Marilee guessed he'd been at the wine cellar. Several other men were behind him—Lopez, Contreras, Garcia, sombreros cocked back on their heads, swaggering to cover their nervousness, big spurs clinking and guns at their hips. Beyond the men, at the corner of the nearest small house, lingered the women—and no children; the children were hidden away.

"Well, *jefe*," Marilee said, "do you come to brag of your thefts, to boast of stealing de Carboca stock?"

Boots planted wide apart, Venegas stroked at his moustache, small eyes flicking to Rosa, then across the courtyard to where Juanita and Paloma stood sentinel in the hacienda's door. He touched the quirt scar upon his cheek and looked back at Marilee.

"An army of women—I spit upon you. No, *señora*—" he accented the title with a mocking twist of his lips—"I do not brag, nor do I steal. We—" a wave of his hand—"we but take what is rightfully ours, now that no master remains upon this hacienda."

"No master, but a mistress," Marilee said, "and I say you are thieves, that you rob the de Carboca heir I carry in my body."

Venegas grimaced. "That is not what *el patrón* thought, and not what we think. We know you for what you are, *puta*—only a *gringa* whore. So we take what is ours, and we will cross the river to also claim the land there. We wil live as Mexicans once more."

"Only as peons," Marilee said, "and hear me, peon. Call me whore again and the only land you will ever claim will be that in which your body lies."

The man flinched and glanced around at his men for support. "We—we will be mericiful, and only kill the devil in that stall."

438

Lifting the pistol, Marilee centered its gaping muzzle upon his chest. "We, brave *vaquero*—*we?* I did not speak to Lopez or Contreras, nor to Garcia. I spoke to you alone. And I also will be merciful—I will shoot you in the heart, instead of your fat belly, so you die quickly."

Behind Venegas, the others shifted and began to ease away from him, hands carefully away from the pistols at their sides. At Marilee's elbow, Rosa cocked the long gun, and the metallic sound of its hammer going back was loud in the courtyard. Sunlight winked from the machete Paloma turned in her hands, from the barrel of the carbine held by Juanita.

"We—" Venegas spluttered. "*I* will not fight mere women. Keep the stallion then, but see how long you can hold on to the rancho with only a handful of *niñas* to fend off the Apaches. See how long it will be before the hacienda itself is in flames and all laid waste about you. No one to plant and harvest, señora—no riders to man the outposts and round up the cattle we have missed. And that devil horse—may he take you, all of you, to hell with him!"

Marilee said, "Scavenger, vulture, get off my land—now!"

Garcia broke first, stumbling hurriedly back; then Lopez, in haste to return to his wife, and Contreras, crossing himself and muttering an incantation against evil. Finding himself alone, Venegas touched the scar on his cheek and took a backward step, then another, turning finally to stamp from sight and roar orders.

Sighing, Rosa murmured, "That was very close, señora."

"Closer than you know," Marilee answered, lowering the pistol and placing her other hand upon her stomach. She watched them pull out, families that had lived upon this land for generations, leaving now in wagons piled with their possessions. To the south, a cloud of dust marked where cattle were being pushed across the Rio Grande, a goodly number of the ranch's horses with them.

She couldn't have stopped that. With the help of the girls, she'd been lucky to hold the pack at bay here, keeping them from Bradburn and from looting the big house. Marilee listened to the fading calls of children, to creaking harness and rattling wheels, to a faroff shout of a rider.

Going to reclaim de Carboca land below the border, Venegas had said. The fool; did he actually think the Juárez government would let them settle upon fairly good grazing land already expropriated, nationalized in the name of Mexico? *Bandidos* waited across the river, and *soldados* different only in uniform; the cattle would not last long among such, nor anything of value.

Apaches, Venegas had said; the *indios* roved those low hills, too, and when they discovered a moving herd, saw riders bound close by their women and children, Juárez's *soldados* might get to only pick over the remains.

Marilee didn't worry about Apaches coming here, even after they learned no *vaqueros* protected the ranch. They would all know it was home of the Moon Woman, and ride wide of her spirit. What did fret her was if Venegas and his men were driven back, with no place else to go. What worried her also was redfaced Jesse Flagg to the north, his land short of water.

But there was something more immediate. "Rosa," she said thickly, "help me into the house."

"Señora—oh, too soon. It is too early. Here, allow me to carry the *pistola,* to support you."

"The—the excitement," Marilee mumbled, "and so much strain. Alfonso flinging me across the corral—Rosa, *Rosa!*"

"Quickly!" Rosa cried to the other girls. "Prepare the bed and water—the towels—*pronto, pronto!* It is the señora's time."

Her legs gone weak and the pain slicing inside her belly, Marilee stumbled between them, her face suddenly turned wet with a chill sweat. She remembered stables and mares foaling, remembered being chased from the scene when she was small and gingham-skirted, only to sneak around back and peer through a knothole at the miracle of birth. But this was no miracle, this tearing agony in her abdomen, this cruel torture across the small of her back. This was the hell Venegas had cursed her with.

"*Ándale!*" Rosa's voice came dimly. "Juanita, you have helped before. Paloma! Bring the water and towels—"

Pain. How could a whiplash strike so deeply, cutting through her straining flesh and into the core of her being?

Pain. A grinding of her entrails; a savage hand twisting inside her.

Pain.

"Hold on to this sheet, señora. It is tied to the bed above you. Ah—just so. Hold hard and push, señora—*push!* Cry out, if you wish—there is no shame to it."

Comanche women never made a sound at birthing. Often they slipped off alone to have their children, returning only minutes later from the brush and holding a baby—or leaving it buried there if it had been stillborn. Marilee closed her eyes against the sweat and locked her teeth.

At Bradburn Plantation, she'd heard slave women screaming when they delivered, and the eerie chants of midwives. Only silence afterward, for those mothers had little to celebrate; their sons might be put on the block, their daughters sold for brood stock or, if light enough, as playthings.

"Push, señora—you are doing fine."

Alfonso wanted a son to carry on a name, a family line older than the *conquistadores;* he wanted the boy so much he was willing to claim him as his own. In a short time, the child *would* have been his own, and no sly whisper would have dared sully the proud old name.

"The head, señora—I see the head."

Old blood, blue blood gone sterile in the veins? Or a final spurting of power in desperation? The name of de Carboca, echoing emptily across so many acres of abandoned land, mocked by deserted hills, for the last of the de Carbocas was buried in that marbled tomb— or squirming here between her arching thighs.

"There, señora—oh, yes, I have it. Juanita, the cord."

If this baby had been born of rape, to a father shot dead in his own blood on the floor of a slave cabin, Marilee would have hated it.

"Lie back, señora. It is done."

And if its sire was dying Timmy Santee, she could only have pitied it. The beginning of life and the ending of life—so much alike.

"*Hola!* Careful with the water, Paloma."

Gilmore Frazier had been more afraid of life than of death. If he had fathered this child, it would have died with Marilee, when she was too ill, too tired to keep running. It would have been ripped from her by the blade of an Apache scalping knife.

"Señora, señora—"

Piava—chief of warriors, Little Buffalo would have held his son aloft for the tribe to see and admire. Drums would have welcomed him, and offerings been made in his honor. and in time, according to the spirits, the son of Piava would have been named, and named well.

"Are you all right, señora? Juanita—does she bleed too much?"

A hill overlooking the sea; grass beneath a whispering tree, open to the delight of the sun, to the caress of salt air—Joe Langston.

No.

De Carboca, but without the blackness in his blood, without cruelty. De Carboca, soon to be without inheritance.

"He lives, señora. He breathes."

A mewling, a cry that fluttered against Marilee's closed eyelids.

He lives and breathes and cries.

Marilee opened her eyes and held out her arms. Rosa put the boy into them, and Marilee held him lightly, not too close. He stopped crying and nuzzled blindly, like a newborn foal, driven by an innate need for survival. Rosa and the other girls had cleaned him, sponged him off, and tied the navel cord.

His face was wrinkled as a monkey caught out in the rain, the thick mop of hair was truly damp, but shiny as a raven's wing. Marilee couldn't see his eyes or much else of him. She winced as the baby began to nurse.

"A fine boy, señora," Rosa said, "very strong and loud."

Juanita leaned above them. "Greedy, also—truly a man."

"She looks so pale," young Paloma whispered.

"But she is also strong," Rosa said proudly. "Did you not see how she defended us, how she faced that pack of curs? Already she has stopped bleeding. When the *niño* is finished drinking, we will bathe her and put her into a fresh, clean nightgown."

Marilee felt the baby tugging at her nipple—strong, loud, and greedy. She was supposed to feel—what?

Tremendous accomplishment, overwhelming pride, a wave of magic tenderness called love?

She said, "Thank you all for standing with me against the *vaqueros* and for helping me here. I would have been very afraid without you."

Accomplishment, pride, love? Perhaps only gratitude that it was over.

"Not you, señora—you do not know fear."

"I do, and I fear for the hacienda now, for us all. Did they leave food? Were they able to get into the house from the back?"

Rosa shook her head. "All seems well. Those mongrels had not the courage to come boldly into the de Carboca home. We will manage, señora—we will care for you and the child until you are well again."

"And then? There are no men here, none to do the heavy work."

Juanita made a spitting noise. "Men—I do not care if I ever see one again."

Small-voiced, Paloma said: "I am afraid of the Apaches."

Stronger now, even though she was very sleepy, Marilee said, "I will see to the Apaches. Don Alfonso did not kill that brave last year—I did. And they know me well as one who rode with the Comanches. I think they will leave us alone. You are right, Juanita—if we have pride and work hard, we have no need for men." Her words began to trail off, and Rosa took the infant from her arms.

There was money, Marilee thought, sinking into a darkly feathered softness; Alfonso had not poured it all into Díaz's coffers. Some would be hidden in the house, and if there was no gold, the jewels—the magnificent emeralds. The *vaqueros* had not had the time to gather all the cows, and some horses were left; when needed, men from El Paso could be hired to drive them. She would see.

"There is one man here," Rosa said from far away, "one who does not have the cruel black eyes of his father nor the calm green one of his mother. This *niño* has eyes the color of the sky."

443

Chapter 47

It had been a while, but a man never forgot how to be careful, once he learned. Hunkering in a little cave which smelled of wild things that had also used it as refuge, Joe watched his smokeless fire flicker low and ate jerky with his beans. The food tasted better than anything in years, better than oysters in lemon sauce, more flavorful than meals prepared by imported chefs on Telegraph Hill.

Maybe it was because he wasn't carrying things on his back, heavy things like the warehouse and the ranch, Martha's mansion. And it could be he felt more free than he had in years, since he first set foot in San Francisco. Finishing his supper, he cleaned the tin plate with sand and dusted it with his kerchief, then leaned back and cupped hands around a light for his cigar.

In gathering night, he could hear the hobbled mare pulling at bunch grass, a big, strong mare with good lines —all he had left from the ranch stock. Rolling smoke in his mouth, he knew that wasn't quite so, but it was near enough. Technically, he was the major partner, and that was on paper in lawyer Rivers's office. But Joe figured he'd never see the place again, and the paper had been drawn up just to keep wolves off Marcus's back. Never could tell, though; he might just go riding back someday and see how old Marcus was doing with his wife, Sissy. Until then, people around the city would know enough to not mess with Joe Langston's representative.

Grinning, he remembered the black man's reluctance. "Joe," Marcus had said, "I don't hanker to be no target. We been more'n a hundred years gettin' this far, and it's liable to be a hundred more before a black can really be free to walk where he wants and own what he can pay for."

"Best you fret about handling Sissy there," Joe said. "The partnership's already made out, so it won't do you any good to grumble about it. You can run that ranch as well as me, but Cissy—are you sure you're not too old for that?"

Marcus grunted. "Take a stick to her, she be right smart, like a mule when you get his attention. Cissy the one to worry can she keep up with *me*."

Joe got them married in a civil ceremony, because he couldn't stand the sight of another brown-robed priest. Not for a while. It was funny how he came around to asking Marcus the priest's name, the one who'd pronounced a dying woman and a shaken Joe as man and wife.

He had so much time now, he walked the streets a lot, wandering along the docks and in alleys where he'd never been. There they were, grimy, ragged boys who scuttled away at his approach like so many packrats—suspicious and defensive. They slept where they could find a hole for the night and scavenged garbage; they stole; they existed.

Blinking at them, Joe Langston recognized every one of them, for they were him, a long time back. Some were even younger than he'd been when he prowled the dank byways of New Orleans, and most were skinnier, more desperate. At least he'd had a strong body to start with, but there were many sickly ones here, children with drawn white faces and eyes too big in them, rags fluttering around bony legs. They belonged to nobody, and nobody gave a damn whether they lived or died.

"Yeah, I know where the priest is at," Marcus had said, surprised. "Thought you didn't want nothin' to do with him."

"It wasn't his fault," Joe had said. "It was the whole thing, her passing away and him there like a big brown buzzard. But, hell, I was mad at everybody, I guess—myself most of all. Find him for me."

Padre Castillo had been surprised, too, when Joe told the man what he had in mind. "But señor, such a project—"

"Can you take care of it?"

Gravely, the priest had nodded, a light beginning to glow in his sunken eyes. "To think, after all these years. It is true that the good Lord works in mysterious ways."

"Nothing mysterious about it," Joe had said. "I don't want to stay in this big old house—not even in this city. And I figure Martha would have wanted it this way."

"A home for the homeless," Father Castillo murmured, "a light in the dark."

Joe had grunted. "A full belly and a warm place to sleep counts more. Her part of—Mrs. Langston's share of the money will go to keep it up for a while, but the house is yours anyhow. I imagine some mysterious way will show up to keep it running after a while."

"It will," the priest had said, running thin fingers through his beads. "I'm certain it will, my son."

"Not me, they're the sons," Joe had said, half angry. "Just be sure those younguns feel like *they* belong to somebody, belong somewhere."

Closing his eyes, the padre had said, *"La casa de merced."*

"Yes," Joe had said, "the Home of Mercy. She would like that."

His head pillowed upon his saddle, wrapped in a blanket, Joe listened to the night around him, the soft, chewing noises of the mare grazing. Martha would have approved of what he'd done; she'd understand why he couldn't wander those big, silent rooms, and why he didn't want to sell her house so another woman might sleep in her bed and look into her mirrors.

"You continue to amaze me," Rivers, the lawyer, had said. "I mean, your reputation and the gossip—then that business of making the black a partner, and now this."

"I amaze myself," Joe had said. "You can arrange it?"

"Of course." Rivers had nodded his white head and

adjusted his spectacles. "If you will just affix your signature here—"

Joe slid the Walker from its holster and lay it across his belly beneath the blanket. There'd been a time when he would have had to make his mark, scratch an X on the paper, shamed because he couldn't write.

"No," he'd told the priest. "No brass with my name on it. If you feel there should be some commemorative plaque, have her name inscribed, the Lady of Mercy."

How much she'd taught him, filtering so very many quiet lessons into his mind; not only books and art and the theater, but also things Joe hadn't even realized he was learning: how to be gentle when that was called for; how to taste the full flavors of life and sort honey from vinegar while knowing both had a place. Without seeming to, Martha guided and directed, and no man had ever had better to scout the trails for him.

Only embers were left of his cookfire; across the hills, an owl called a lonely cry, and a coyote answered in kind. Joe smelled sagebush and leather, sniffed the wide, dark night.

In his own way, he had been teacher for Martha, too. He'd shown her how to be a woman proud of her woman's hunger and proud of her body. He'd tried to make up for all the years she'd missed, and Martha had bloomed for it.

But there had been no desperation to her, even though she was older than his other teacher, Elizabeth, schoolmarm with a wagon train. Turning in his blanket, hand upon the Colt, Joe remembered Elizabeth's neat, smooth body and the fire in it, the woman's gasping and twisting. The trouble with Elizabeth had been her demands, her threats, the way she wanted to dig her fingers right on down into his blood and hang on.

Eyes closed, Joe watched the image of Elizabeth fade and he replaced by another dream shape, one he never quite got out of the corners of his mind. She was tall and slim, the flesh of her firm and silken to the hands; her breath was sweet, and there was a fierceness within her that no woman ever matched.

He could almost feel the globes of her high, rounded breasts in his palms, the slow, insistent thrusting of her hips, and Joe's body stirred restlesly at the memory of

Marilee's long, sleek legs coiling, crossing at the ankles, clinging, moving, tightening.

She could never lie passively, never simply accept; the need was hers also, and Marilee Bradburn reached to feed that deep-seated hunger with every fiber of her being, not giving a damn what was supposed to be ladylike. And that last time, spread nude and shining in the sunlight upon a hill above the bay, the wind rippling that polished silvery hair, those willowgreen eyes locked hotly into his own, soft red mouth dampened by her passion. . . .

Joe changed positions again and pulled the blanket up around his shoulders. He had no right saying what he had to her afterward. But she had startled him so much, doing those things with her hands and her mouth, dominating him at times, avid for all he could give to her. Warmly sated, drained of any urgency, he had kept thinking of the Spanish don she was married to, kept seeing the man with Marilee, accepting the same favors, knowing the rich rioting of her perfect body.

So the cutting words had just popped out, and of course, being Marilee, she'd chopped right back at him. Damn it; they couldn't be together more than a few minutes without looking for a throat hold.

"I was jealous," Joe whispered against his saddle. "I was jealous of the other man, and that's the truth of it."

Although it had taken four years to face it, the admission cleared his mind, but didn't do much to ease his body, so he slept uneasily the rest of the night and was awake to watch the first light of dawn come fingering pink across the dry hills. By the time it had changed to gold, Joe had eaten, grained and saddled the mare, and was on his way, long rifle under his left knee, carbine under the right.

When he had cleared the city and started southeast, it had all come back to him, the constant watchfulness, that feeling out of alert senses that would keep him alive on the plains. He'd found the place on an old Spanish map—Cienegas, the hundred springs that formed the center of de Carboca's sprawling rancho. Or once had, before the don had started pouring money into guns for the wrong Mexican army. Chewing on the end of an unlighted cigar, Joe checked the skyline, then looked over the ground ahead. De Carboca didn't know the *Juaristas* as Joe did;

they'd hang on to their republic like so many snapping turtles, and no other revolution would have a chance until old Benito himself was dead.

Crossing Arizona Territory, he'd asked himself why he was riding so long and far just to see her, just to say howdy and pass on. She had always proved herself capable of standing to any threat, stronger than any woman he'd ever known. She probably didn't need his help and would slap away the hand that offered it. But just in case, he carried letters of credit on the bank of El Paso and gold coins sewn into his saddle skirts and along the fringes of his buckskins.

Her place lay along the route he meant to travel, and it wouldn't do any harm to stop by. When she started jawing at him again—and she would—he'd move right on. For certain, he hadn't lost anything in Alabama, but he'd been thinking of taking a look around there. It would be ironic, if he'd decide to buy the old Paisley Plantation and play the lord and master in that big white house. But the house was no doubt burned to the ground, and the yard where he'd been held to be whipped had probably been scuffed over by Yankee horses. Even the creek where Susanna had seduced a willing boy—that had no doubt changed its course over the years, and there was no use looking for a certain glittering sandbar anyway. He would never find the boy again.

A hill loomed ahead, and Joe dismounted with the Sharps to lead the mare so far, then ground-tie her so he could belly up to the crest and take a look beyond. The telegraph in San Francisco still carried word of Indian raids and futile army pursuits, even though the stream of settlers coming west grew every month, trains of Conestoga wagons so long and heavily armed that few invited attack.

But the Apaches had to fight, and the Comanches would keep at it until the last brave fell, and meanwhile a lone traveler was fair game. So was a woman on a ranch in the middle of Indian country and set right next to the border where *bandidos* could hit it so easily. With the don dead, it might be his private army had dissolved; Mexican *vaqueros* were funny about working for a woman, unless she was one of their own, and a patrician to boot.

The valley beyond was clear, but Joe eyed the next low

ridges for a while anyway. Before long, he'd be coming to land almost flat, sandy and hard, baked by merciless sun. It would be better to hurry across it and reach the Rio Grande, because thirst could kill him and the horse just as easily as Apaches who might prowl the riverbanks.

It was a long way, a far piece to that muddy, shallow trickle, and he ran out of water before reaching it. Dried out as his mare, sun-blackened and with his lips peeling, he held back the horse until he was sure no squatty brave lurked in ambush among the little clump of willows ahead. Slowly, they approached the impossibly green trees, the mare snuffing and flaring her nostrils at the scent of water. Joe eased her into the willows and climbed stiffly down, hearing nothing, seeing nothing.

He let the horse drink first, but not enough to swell her belly, then backed her off. She could have more later. Disciplining himself in the same way, he swallowed brackish water and dipped his head into it. Water felt wonderful down his neck, down his chest when he sat back upon his heels.

Soft as the warning hiss of a snake, the voice said behind him: "I see you, white-eyes."

Joe didn't move a muscle. He waited for the impact of the bullet that would smash between his shoulders and hurl him into the muddy water. When it didn't come, he said in Spanish and without turning his head, "I do not see you, Apache. I have been careless."

"That is true, white-eyes. When I was young, I took scalps from men less careless."

Above and behind him, to the left, Joe thought; if he threw himself to the right and rolled, the Apache might miss. It was a slim chance, but all he had. Joe said, "And I have lifted scalps from the Apaches. One of us will not leave here, *nantan*."

Dry, whispery, the voice said, "I am not a chief, only a very old man. Tell me, do you have it in mind to jump to your right?"

Frowning, every fiber of him pulled tight, Joe said, "I did."

The Apache sighed. "Then I still think clearly. When you turn, shoot straight, white-eyes."

Something was out of place, wrong. An Apache killed without warning and never with a discussion. Catching his breath, Joe turned very slowly. The old man sat among drooping willow branches, leathery hands upon his thighs. His hair was gray and his scarred face heavily lined by time. He had no weapon.

Joe stood up. "Your tribe left you to die."

"It is the custom," the Apache said. "If they had not taken my rifle—but guns are worth more than old warriors. So are good knives."

"You would have had your last victory, Chiricahua, a prize to take to the hunting grounds."

"I think not, *pinda-lickoyi*. My victories are long forgotten, and I remember other things. It would be fitting to enter the hunting grounds with my own knife between my ribs, but the young ones would not leave me even that." Shrunken, tired, the Apache stared up at Joe from rheumy eyes. "But the gods sent me an enemy. Shoot, white-eyes."

Walking to the mare, Joe felt in saddlebags for a slab of cornbread, a handful of jerky. He let the horse drink again before retying her and placing the food in the old man's lap.

"Once I would have killed you without thinking," he said. "But like you, warrior, I remember other things. I am not old, but I am older than I was."

Shaking hands fumbled for the bread and meat. "Yes—sometimes it is so. There are those who remember fights—I think of fresh buffalo liver and a woman's soft eyes. I remember my sons, and when all this land belonged to the Chiricahua." Bread crumbs dribbled from the corners of an almost toothless mouth; the tired eyes blinked. "Like the summer sun, we could shrink the river of white-eyes as that stream is shrunken. But the river grew again each spring, wider and deeper, until we were swept away. Now we are only grains of sand, rolled over and over until we too shall be gone."

Joe watched the Apache gum the hard beef jerky and said, "That is true, grandfather. Still, each grain must resist."

"You are older than your years. If you are not careless again, perhaps your journey may be safe."

"I will remember your lesson, grandfather. I travel to Cienegas and the hacienda of de Carboca."

Nodding, his jaws working on meat, the old man said, "I know the place. It is where she stays—*Tson-tsose*, the Moon Woman."

Joe stared. "You—you know of her?"

"All Apaches know of her spirit and respect it. But the *mejicanos*, the *tejanos*—they know nothing of spiritual matters and try to catch moonlight in their hands. Such fools."

When the old man fell asleep, Joe refilled his water bags and canteen, unbrided the mare and hobbled her so she could strip willow leaves and sample marsh grass. Marilee, the Moon Woman of the Comanches, whose image had somehow taken on a superstitious aspect for the Apaches, too; but his hunch had been right—she was in trouble—not from Indians, but from her own kind.

He was putting the bit into the horse's mouth when the Apache whispered again. "It is much to ask, but if you would spare me your knife?"

Taking the blade from its boot sheath, Joe approached the ancient warrior and bent to place the knife on the sand beyond reach. "You are still Apache, grandfather. When I am gone, you can reach this."

The faded eyes crinkled and stubs of teeth showed briefly. "A fine boast for an old man to take with him, that an enemy still feared."

Joe mounted his horse and looked down once more at the shriveled brave, then squeezed the mare's barrel and moved her along the river bank. If he met no more like the worn Apache, maybe he could catch moonlight in his hands.

Chapter 48

Jesse Flagg hadn't directly bothered her for months, but his cows were encroaching upon her water once more. She'd warned him about that, but Flagg had only laughed and wiped at his sweaty red face.

"You ain't got enough cows to use it all," he said. "I have, missy—and I got the men to watch 'em."

Marilee stood just beyond the courtyard and looked about her, knowing that acre by acre Jesse Flagg would keep right on coming, that already some of her cattle were wearing his brand and there was damned little she could do about it.

She looked at empty adobes, at a line of sagging fence, and across the once lush flower garden nobody had time to tend. She worked and the girls worked, but it seemed that for every chore they completed two more took its place. Rosa and Juanita had enough to do just keeping up the vegetable garden and stables, feeding chickens, and hauling wood and water. And one of them had to keep an eye on the boy. Paloma had turned into a horsewoman and was a great help out in the fields, equally good when she worked horses in training.

But there was just so much anybody could do. Marilee rubbed her hands together, feeling the hard calluses there, the grown-over rope burns. They had even swung a scythe for hour after backbreaking hour, but the cut grass was never enough for winter hay, and the horses had to make out as best they could.

Just as everything else, everyone else, until Lieutenant Jody Carleton sent back some hired hands from El Paso. It had been a marvelous stroke of luck when the patrol he was leading had stopped here. Even those hated blue uniforms meant contact with the outside world, a way to send out for the help she so desperately needed, for Jesse Flagg had blocked every other way.

Taking a deep breath of cool evening air, Marilee turned for the house, the lowslung Colt tapping her right thigh at every step. Jesse Flagg—he'd come calling as soon as he heard of Alfonso's death (had it only been three years ago? It seemed forever) to "pay his respects." Always sweating, he'd crouched like a big toad on the porch, his small, darting eyes missing nothing. And a week later, he returned.

Inviting himself in but leaving a pair of uneasy riders to go around to the kitchen, Flagg spraddled at her table and ate her food, drank her brandy, and came to business. "Missy, you're a woman alone, since I don't count them Mexes for much. Nary a man on the place, and that ain't good. Now I know you ain't got no more land acrost the river, but that's just as good. You still got the springs, and that's water for both herds. This here de Carboca land and the Flagg place, too—why, we'll own a fair piece of the whole territory."

Marilee watched the man wipe greasy hands on a napkin. "You mean *you'll* own it, don't you?"

"Man's wife is same as the man," he grunted. "Way I see it, you can't pick and choose."

"You're actually asking me to marry you," Marilee said.

"No, not asking, *telling* me."

The beady eyes sought her own. "You called the turn, missy. Without them *vaqueros* you can't stop the Apache, and there just ain't no sense gettin' a fine house like this put to the torch. Waste of womanflesh, too."

Hardly controlling her hands, Marilee said, "And what of my son?"

Pouring himself more brandy, Flagg dribbled some on the tablecloth. "Well, now—changin' your name ain't changin' his. Gets big enough, he can pull his weight, but I ain't too old to breed my own younguns. Had me three wives and twice that many younguns, but most was puny, and what fever didn't lay low the Apache got. But that's all ahint me, missy."

"But ahead of me," she said, her voice shaking. "I saw your kind in Mississippi—wearing out their wives and children, working them like mules. No thank you, Mister Flagg. *I* own this land legally, and I'll keep it."

He wiped his face and finished the brandy. "Long ways from law, out here. You think on it, missy—but don't take too long—I ain't a patient man."

Night was coming now as Marilee paused in the courtyard; another night, and no sign of riders. Lieutenant Carleton—Jody—had promised to send them as soon as he could. He'd wrapped the emeralds very carefully in his kerchief and promised upon his honor as an officer and gentleman they would be deposited in the bank at El Paso and drafts drawn on their worth. Trustworthy riders would be advanced part of their wages and the rest held in their name, since they couldn't spend money on the ranch anyway. Jody Carleton had been solicitous and breathlessly adoring. He'd seemed so young to her.

Inside, tallow candles guided her into the kitchen, and not many of them. She'd closed off the dining room years ago. Rosa nodded and brought a pot of stew to the table; Rosa murmured grace.

Wayne Bradburn de Carboca sat beside her, quiet as always, erect and tall for his age. She had named him for her father, for the family itself, but there hadn't been time enough for the boy, time enough for anything. Once in a while, Marilee had tried to get through that quiet, withdrawn wall he'd built around himself, and although Wayne listened politely, he seldom spoke to her, and she couldn't remember him smiling. She wanted to shake him, to shout at him that he didn't know, could not understand what she was going through, that she was tired of fighting, so damned tired.

But of course she didn't; not with those pale blue eyes of his looking at her but not really seeing her. Upset, Marilee would go outside to the only comfort she knew—

the big, silken strength of the stallion. The boy was cared for by three other mothers; Bradburn had only Marilee to watch over him.

"No riders," Juanita said.

"Not yet," Marilee answered.

Paloma dipped stew into Wayne's bowl. "Perhaps the patrol did not get through. The Apaches—"

Marilee slapped the tabletop. "No! They *had* to get through. The Apaches have done good for us."

Rosa filled Wayne's glass with goat milk. "Not with any kindness in their hearts, señora. Only because they did not wish to ride so far around your land—only because they begged your permission to cross it, so they could attack Señor Flagg."

The stew was bitter in Marilee's mouth. "There was no other way. He was about to take the hacienda by force, and the Apaches' coming just then was a godsend."

Rosa and Juanita crossed themselves; Paloma didn't. Rosa whispered, "Never from *Dios*—not the Apaches. Their god is death."

"I will do anything, use anyone to keep Jesse Flagg's greedy hands from this ranch. I only wish the *indios* had gotten him, instead of a few of his men and cattle."

They were quiet, eating, and Marilee rinsed her mouth with wine; there was still plenty of wine in the cellar, and little else. The Apache chief had come openly, humbly, making the sign of peace from afar, and when she allowed him to come closer, she could see his eyes rolling and smell his fear. But the man forced himself, hands open and arms spread wide, his head bowed; there had been no weapons upon him or his mustang. Brave enough against enemies he understood—and all men were enemies to the Apaches —he was shaken by having to expose himself to the spirit of a risen Comanche medicine woman.

He asked to cross her domain; his band's horses were already weary from travel. Mexican *soldados* had been stubborn.

She did not deign to speak with him, but stood regally while she used fluent hand-talk: *How many?*

Only twenty.

A war party.

Yes, but no tribe would ever make war upon the Moon Woman.

Who, then?

Horses were needed; the man with the burned face had many, and there was a blood debt. Had the Moon Woman's spirit been told of Apache maidens taken by Burned Face and used until they died?

Pass then, indio—paint your faces and pay the debt.

Paloma said, "The raid kept him from us for a long time. He did not understand why they passed by us and struck him instead."

"But he grows braver now," Juanita said. "That one has heard the whispers that say you control the Apaches. One of his men is a half-blood who sometimes visits his mother's people."

Paloma flung back her mane of dark hair. "Perhaps it is time for another raid, then."

"Por favor," Rosa breathed. "Please, no."

Marilee drank more red wine. "I cannot go to them. They must come to me, or they would not believe in my spirit anymore. And with the army patrols, the Mexican *soldados* after them, the Apaches are busy running and hiding."

"May it always be so," Rosa said. Wayne looked up at her, and she broke off a piece of coarse bread for the boy.

"I can ride by the water holes," Marilee said, "until our riders arrive."

"Flagg hopes you will do that," Juanita said. "His men lie in ambush for you, because with you gone—"

Marilee pushed back her bowl and brought the wine glass closer. "The *teniente* is honest—he will send riders to us. Until they come, we must hold on to all we can. Flagg wants us even more now, wants me to protect him from the Apaches, and he will not kill me unless he has to. He may have to."

She glanced at the boy. He caught her eyes and looked away. She said, "He is sleepy, Rosa. Put him to bed," and went to go through the breeding records, to sit alone in the chill room with its heavy dark furniture like so many brooding shadows in the light of a single candle.

There had been much left unsaid at the kitchen table, but Marilee was aware of how the women felt. They were *women*, and although their only experience had been with the cruel mauling by Alfonso, their bodies were ripe and overflowing with urgent needs. Rosa had confessed that at times she had been stirred by the don; Juanita was growing more restless without knowing why, and little Paloma—not so small now, more assured since she had become a fine horsewoman—had also to be feeling the pangs of being without a man.

Marilee grimaced. She felt them herself, too often in the night, waking startled to listen only to the beating of her own pulses. And when her son lifted those pale blue eyes, she flinched from the memory of other eyes so much like them.

Had she disturbed Joe Langston so much that fargone day upon a grassy hill? Had he felt less the man because she had taken the initiative, because she had taken *him* instead of allowing him to dominate her? Perhaps she should not have kissed his belly and drawn her tongue along his inner thighs; maybe she shouldn't have clenched his head so fiercely in her own thighs; but *no*. Why was it wrong in his eyes for her to be without false modesty, to be honest with herself and with him?

Marilee felt the straining of her breasts against the shirt she wore and the tremble within her lower body, a familiar and too-long-denied warmth stealing along her flesh. Too long, too *damned* long—and the others felt it, too. Paloma, Juanita—they eyed the Yankee soldiers hungrily, and Rosa with only a bit more shyness. Only Jody Carleton's strict commands had kept his troopers from them. Next time, the next men. . . . Marilee shook her head; so much depended upon the arrival of riders from El Paso. Those men could help solve all the problems, except her own.

She had been sorely tempted by the young Yankee lieutenant, but something held her back, and she'd fallen back into the habits of the plantation, those precepts of flirt and promise, seeming always on the verge of surrender, but recovering her senses at the last moment. It worked well with Jody Carleton, and perhaps that was why she hadn't given in to her own desires; Marilee was now impatient with shallow games, the traditional rules of courtship that belonged in another time.

Sighing, she carried the candle with her, climbing the stairs to her bedroom. Wayne slept across the hall with Rosa, and she didn't look in on him. Too worn down to bathe, she fell into bed, promising herself a good scrubbing in the morning. Worries didn't keep her from sinking quickly into a blackness untroubled by dreams.

But she still drooped when she awoke, and the bath didn't help much; breakfast simply made her more weary, but she forced down every bite, knowing she would need her strength. Marilee felt better after currying Bradburn and looking over the crop of weanlings in the next corral. Lieutenant Carleton had been much taken by them and by the fully grown horses Bradburn had produced; they would make fine army mounts, and he'd pass word to the quartermaster about them.

Had he even reached El Paso, that young, romantic officer who carried the hopes of her ranch with him wrapped in a kerchief? Apaches might have gotten the patrol on the way, or some desperately valiant band of Comanches trying for a final strike of honor.

Straightening her back, Marilee moved toward the tack room, and stopped suddenly when she heard Paloma calling out.

"Señora! Look to the north. They are coming—the riders are coming!"

The riders. Jody Carleton had gotten through and, true to his word, converted her precious emeralds into gold on deposit. He'd found working cowboys reasonably good with a gun, men not afraid of the hostile plains. Beautiful, wonderful Jody Carleton, gentleman in a Yankee uniform.

Marilee hurried into the house to run a comb through her hair, her mind buzzing with what should be done first, getting the adobes turned into bunkhouses, feeding men who had come a long way, letting them see what lay ahead of them. She would also have to show them that she was a boss worth working for, a woman who could hold up her end of hard labor, and one who knew as much about ranching as any man.

In the kitchen, the boy glanced at her and away. She said, "Rosa, they're coming. We'll need more tortillas, and —and anything else we can feed them. Tomorrow they can butcher a cow, and—"

Coming from the north? El Paso lay due east. As Paloma came leaping downstairs, Marilee said to her: "Is it Flagg? Can it be his men?"

459

"No—that one I can tell from a mile away. He sits a saddle like a sack of corn."

"Yes," Marilee said, but reached for the peg where her gunbelt hung, and buckled leather about her waist. "Where is Juanita?"

"Milking the goats, but what—"

"Rosa—keep the boy under cover. I'll go out and—"

Maybe they'd gotten off the trail, or been pushed north by Indians; they might have been lost. That would explain what took them so long. Or it could be something else.

Hoofbeats rang in the yard, and she heard Juanita call out cheerily. Marilee looked at her son, the blue eyes of him unstirred, his round face showing only the hint of high cheekbones to come. If he would only show some expression, *something*.

"Get him out of here, Rosa. Not into the patio, woman —upstairs!"

But the kitchen door crashed back and struck Rosa's shoulder. Staggering, she blocked Marilee's view for just a moment, but that was long enough for it to happen. She had the Colt out and was lifting, earing back the hammer with her thumb when Rosa reeled aside.

Marilee saw the man snatch up Wayne, saw the body against his chest, and the gun muzzle reaching around her son. There was a noise behind her—glass breaking, Juanita's throaty scream of pain, Paloma raging. In front of her was the hardface stranger guarding his body with her son's body, the pistol centered upon her.

"Put that iron on the table and back off," the man said.

Rosa began to sob as Marilee relinquished her Colt and edged back. Her son's face was still calm, and Wayne wasn't struggling.

The man said, "That's a smart heifer."

"Don't," she choked. "Don't hurt him."

"Won't have to now," he grunted, and let Wayne's feet drop to the floor. "Good thing you turned loose that iron, woman—gunpowder and females never did mix worth a damn."

"What do you want—who are you—why—"

Oh, God; she'd seen other faces like his, stubbled around a hard mouth, flat eyes hot and certain: The first one had been in a slave cabin. Stained teeth shone dully at her when thin lips peeled back.

He brushed Wayne aside and put up his gun. "Hell," he said, "they told me you was slick and mean. Don't look so mean to me, but you're slick right enough. Yeah, purty as a filly just come into heat."

Marilee took a step back, and another. There were others; they'd come in front and back, and her Spencer was out in the hall. Paloma, Juanita. . . .

An arm whipped around her neck from behind, and clamped across her throat. She was slammed into a thick body as she clawed at the arm with both hands, her mouth straining for air. Writhing, legs flailing, Marilee battled to breathe; an unshaven cheek scraped her face.

Air rushed into her heaving lungs when he let go her throat and hooked a hand into her hair instead. Dizzy, her eyes blurring, she was flung into the wall and to her knees.

"*Buenos días,*" he said. "Ah, good day—*señora.* Did I say your title with the proper respect, *señora?*"

Holding her throat, Marilee shook hair from her eyes and stared up at Manuel Venegas. He touched the scar on his cheek and smiled wetly upon her.

"I hope you will be very stubborn, señora, so you will be treated as the whore you are."

Wide-eyed in disbelief, Marilee was jarred by another shock then, for Jesse Flagg waddled into the kitchen, wiping at his red face.

Chapter 49

From a distance, three riders eyed him, sitting their horses across the river. Joe drew the long Sharps from its nesting place beneath his knee and let sunlight flash along its barrel. Not Apaches, he thought; they wouldn't bunch up like that. He waited, and after a while they turned their horses and moved south. Soldiers or guerrillas, but not interested in crossing the river after him, so he watched a bit longer to be certain, then put up the buffalo gun.

Moving the mare along a slope where spring grass was showing bright, Joe figured he must be getting close to Cienegas, nearing the de Carboca ranch, if he wasn't already on it. It was good land along here, prime for raising cattle—or even the horses Marilee had been so intent upon breeding. If *comancheros* and other assorted border riffraff could be kept on the far side of the Rio Grande, that was. Marilee evidently had cast some kind of spell on the Apaches, according to the dying old warrior, a superstitious image that held them at bay. But hungry *soldados* and greedy *bandidos* didn't care about the spirit world of Indians; they respected only accurate rifles.

Joe angled his horse up the slope, reaching a cluster of mesquite and sagebrush, where he drew up. On foot, he climbed to peer over into the valley below. The ancient Apache's ambush had sharpened all Joe's senses and made him exceedingly cautious.

He saw the hacienda: U-shaped redtiled roof, a walled patio, barns and corrals and adobe huts. He saw horses moving behind fences, smoke lifting from only one chimney at the big house itself, and nobody moving about. Frowning, he searched the entire area again, for it was early in the day, and there should be plenty of activity down there.

More horses at a hitchrack, another one ground-tied behind the house; maybe there was a meeting, Marilee holding a conference with her *vaqueros*. He could just see her, arrogant and regal, giving orders like a general in skirts. Sliding back from the hill's crest, Joe went to his horse, wondering what he would say to her, how the sight of him would react upon her. He even wondered a little at the excuses made to himself for being here.

Halfway to the house, there was a group of trees around water that bounced back the sun, and he walked the mare to them, watching the house. A lone rider coming up from the river could draw a bullet before a call for identification, but in daylight and coming openly, someone should challenge him first.

Something moved beside the spring, and with a swift motion Joe laid the sights of the carbine upon it. It moved again, and he saw it was too small for a rifleman—a big dog, a calf strayed from the cow? He walked the mare closer, Spencer across his thighs, and when he reached the trees, the boy stood up to look at him.

Swinging down, Joe looped his reins around a limb, smiling so the child wouldn't dart away. *"Buenas días, niño—qué pasa?"*

Slim and unafraid, the boy said, "Nothing passes, señor —*nada.*"

Something hauntingly familiar about this child, Joe thought; a different look to him that Joe ought to know, but couldn't quite recognize. Then he noticed the eyes and said, "What is your name?"

"De Carboca," the boy answered softly, "Wayne de Carboca, and I will soon be four years old."

Wayne de Carboca—Marilee's son, and the Spanish

463

don's; green eyes and black eyes—had they produced pale blue eyes?

Hunkering down, Joe brought a cigar from his shirt pocket. "Four years old, almost—a great age. Will you share my cigar?"

Solemnly, Wayne shook his head. *"Gracias,* no."

"Ah—because of your mother. Women do not understand the affairs of men."

The boy hunkered down too. *"Madre* would not notice, I think."

Joe thumbnailed a match and blew smoke. "Mothers see everything, but often they save up what they have seen. Are you comfortable in English, *hombre?"*

"Mother speaks it to me, but not the others."

Picking up a dry twig, Joe began scratching a design in the dirt. "The others?"

"Rosa, Juanita, Paloma," Wayne answered, not too obvious about looking for his own twig. "I like Rosa best."

"Then you are the only man in the hacienda?"

Wayne scrached dirt with a little stick. "Sometimes *he* comes—once some soldiers dressed in blue. He does not see me, either, and he has a red face."

Joe glanced off toward the house. "I know you are almost a man grown, and you know it, but does your mother realize this also? This spring is some distance from the hacienda and not too far from the river. Perhaps a man traveling so far from his home should be armed."

Drawing in the dirt, Wayne said, "She told me to go, to stay here."

Joe hid his quick frown with cigar smoke. Not quite four years old, this boy; yet he was self-contained and unafraid, with a good vocabulary for his age; an intelligent boy. Did Wayne have a certain watchfulness, something wary in him, like the orphans prowling San Francisco alleys? No reason for that; he was well fed and clean, but dressed in simple clothing and sandals, more like a peon than the son of a don. Black hair and light skin—from Marilee, of course—and lighter eyes that did not look away, but also didn't expose any thoughts.

Maybe the familiarity of him that kept pushing at Joe was Marilee's bone structure not yet matured in the boy's face, but underlying it with strong hints of the shaping to come. Joe had only seen the father once, there at Senator Littlefield's home, but this calmness, this pulled-in-upon-himself attitude hadn't shown in that cold-eyed don. It wasn't Marilee Bradburn, either.

Joe said, "Who is the man with the red face?"

Wayne held his little stick in both hands, considering its length and weight. "Señor Flagg—they do not like him. Do you come from Mexico? I have never been across the river. I do not go anywhere."

"Mexico is like this, but more dry, *hombre*. Someday you will see for yourself. Why do they not like this Señor Flagg?"

Losing interest in his twig, Wayne dropped it. "He is fat and talks loud and makes my mother talk loud. He is a *gringo*—are you a *gringo?*"

"To some, but others have different names for me. Your pardon, *hombre—I* have not told you my name. It is Langston, Joe Langston."

"Señor Langston." The blue eyes probed his own, and the boy asked, "Joe—José?" Gravely, he extended a small hand, and, just as seriously, Joe shook it.

"Joe," he repeated. "An *americano* name, as is Wayne."

"I was named for my *abuelo*, my grandfather. He was a *gringo*, I suppose—I never saw him. I never saw my father, either."

Joe looked at the house again, at horses hitched in front, the one out back sidestepping its dropped reins to nibble at a dry flowerbed. "The *vaqueros*—do they take you riding?"

Wayne said, "Mother and Paloma ride, but do not take me. Juanita milks the goats and works in the garden with Rosa. They let me help them."

No *vaqueros*, Joe thought, and counted the horses: one in back, four out front, and none of them the shining red stallion. He said, "There is a horse named Bradburn?"

"*Sí*—he is beautiful and my mother loves him. I have heard her talking to him."

More than she talks to you, Joe thought; she always thought more of that horse than she did people. But if she rode any horse, it would be Bradburn, and the big stud wasn't in sight.

"The man with the red face," Joe said, "this Señor Flagg who makes your mother talk loud. Is he in house now?"

Wayne nodded. "With other *hombres* I have never

seen. Rosa and the others were crying. I think that is why
mother sent me here to the spring. She does not like crying."

Slowly, Joe stood up. "A young *caballero* such as you
knows how to watch a horse. I would be glad if you cared
for this mare while I am gone."

The boy glanced over his shoulder at the house. "My
mother might call me."

"A responsible job," Joe said, "and one I would not
ask just any man to do. If you accept this job, I will be
grateful, and I will speak to your mother when I go to the
hacienda, tell her of your work."

The shadow of a smile crossed Wayne de Carboca's
face, quickly gone. "It is good to speak with a man. Señor
Flagg never talks to me."

Crossing to the horse, Joe took the Spencer out again.
"Then we will discuss other things, *caballero*, subjects
that only men understand. Soon, *hombrecito*."

He could feel the boy's eyes following him as he went
trotting across the open space toward the house, and it
was an effort to clear his mind of them. Crouching, Joe
reached a tree, then tall bushes that needed trimming and
were choked with weeds. Behind them, he stared at the
house and thought he saw movement at a rear window.
Four horses in the patio, only one behind the kitchen, but
their placement could mean nothing--or everything.

He darted for the open gateway, running low to the
ground with the carbine at his hip. Inside the wall, he
pulled up to watch and listen. Maybe he was being a
damned fool, but something didn't smell right, and the
boy said women were crying. Joe couldn't imagine Marilee doing that, but she had sent her son far from the house
for some reason.

Never troubled by our warriors, the old Apache had
said, but the Mexicans and Texans try to catch the moonlight.

Joe pushed off from the wall and ducked past the tethered horses. The main door stood open; a window beside
it was broken. He took a deep breath and slid into the
shadowy foyer.

Chapter 50

"You been a burr in my hide too damn long," Jesse
Flagg said, "and I'm about to dig you out."

Marilee sat stiffly on the living room couch, fingers
digging into her knees. Across the room, Rosa and Juanita
trembled in the grasp of two saddle tramps; Paloma had
been jerked into a chair, where a Mexican gunfighter
stood looking down at her, one boot cocked upon the
chair arm.

Venegas rubbed his cheek. "Señor Flagg, I am eager to
persuade her."

Flagg leaned back and put both elbows on the table behind him, laced his fingers across a protruding stomach.
"Just as soon run her 'crost the river bare-assed and be
done with her, but that won't git it. This here Apache
lover is my trump card for keepin' them red devils off'n
my back. Don't know what kinda deal she made with 'em
or how she does it, but it's fact they go by her and jump
me. Jump everybody else they can find around here, but
not her—not never *her*." . .

Venegas smirked. "This one whored for Comanches—
why not Apaches, too?"

Grinning, Flagg bobbed his head. "Must be some special kinda poontang, to keep Injuns hoppin' thataway. Been meanin' to find that out."

Marilee stared hate at them both. Manuel Venegas looked seedy now, his clothes barely hanging together, boots run over at the heels, and there was the smell of tequila about him. She glanced at the girls, then back at Flagg. "Let them go—they can't make any deals with you."

Leaning up and tugging a bandanna from his hip pocket, Flagg wiped it across his face. "Any one of 'em coulda warned me about them damned Injuns comin'. That raid cost me six men and twenty horses, nigh onto a hunnert beef. Spooked my riders so much they kept hangin' back from your water—wouldn't get outa sight of each other. No, them wenches can't make no deals, but they can tote their share of blame." He jerked his head at the Mexican across the room. "Hey you, Pedraza, git on down the cellar and carry us up some drinkin' whiskey. I'll keep an eye on that youngun."

"Paloma," Marilee said, "please don't try to run. They'll hurt you, hurt us all."

Flagg chuckled, his jowls waggling. "Smart talk, missy. But looka yonder—them new boys of mine ain't *hurtin'* your petticoat ranch hands none. They're just feelin' up the gals a mite."

Rosa looked resigned and stood unmoving as the man ran his hands over her body, cupping her breasts and fingering down her thighs. Juanita hissed between clenched teeth as one man pinned her arms and the other worked a hand between her legs. Over his shoulder, she spat at Venegas. "Tió Manuel—dear uncle! How well you protect my sister and me—first the don, and now these dogs."

"*Silencio, puta!*" he snarled back. "You were always ready to lift your skirts, and you sided with this *gringa* against your own. What do you know of the hell we met in Mexico—the Apaches, *comancheros,* corrupt soldiers, and even *policia.* We lost it all—everything, you hear? The cows and horses, the wagons, food, our women, and our lives."

"Not you," she said. "The rabbit flees."

Venegas took a step toward her, but the Mexican came into the room then carrying bottles. His spurs jingled, and

Marilee thought he was young, not cut from the same shoddy cloth as the rest.

"I survived," Venegas said, accepting a bottle and working out its cork. "And when the *teniente* asked about riders for this hacienda. I lit candles in gratitude that I was in El Paso del Norte to be chosen."

"The church must have burned itself in shame," Paloma said, and the Mexican turned to stare at her.

"No need to let their jawin' bother you," Flagg said. "We got us drinkin' whiskey and women, and all the time we need to make missy yonder see the light. Ol' Manuel was lucky to be johnny on the spot and smart enough to round up these here other hands and come straight to me. Smart fella, Manuel—knowed he could make hisself double wages and more. Drink up, boys—here's to the biggest damn spread in the whole territory."

Eyes glinting wickedly, Venegas lifted his bottle to Marilee. "And to the new bride of Señor Flagg. Snake, Johnson, Pedraza, drink to this fine toast!"

Marilee said, "Never."

"But of course," Venegas grinned. "Padre Villano is on his way—he was sent for. You remember the good father, the priest who wed you to the don? Whatever you have done to the Apaches, you also did to Don Alfonso, so that he honored you with his name. But you were never a de Carboca, only an *hechicera*, only a witch who blinded him, whose devil horse killed him!"

Flagg drank, belched, and drank again. "Manuel wants that stud pretty bad, missy—you think on that some, too."

At the fireplace, a man said, "I wanta *play* stud pretty bad. Let's get on with it, Flagg."

"Might's well show missy here what she's in for, if she don't learn how to get along with me. Go ahead, boys—but do it up right, both of you to one of 'em, then both to the other 'un."

Against the wall, beside Paloma's chair, the young Mexican stirred, and Flagg rolled his eyes in that direction. "Pedraza, any time you're ready."

Pedraza murmured, "Perhaps, señor."

"Hey, Manuel—what you got there, a gelding? He don't seem anxious as the rest."

"He is young," Venegas said, "or it might be he waits for his turn at the—señora. As I do."

469

Marilee wanted very badly to close her eyes, to wish herself away from all this. The ugliness, this degrading terror and helpless, trapped feeling; she had known it all before, but she'd thought it done with and behind her. God, God—was it ever behind a woman?

"Snatch off their clothes," Flagg ordered. "Let's get a good look at 'em."

Rosa's thin dress ripped down in front, and she tried to cross her arms over heavy breasts, but the man called Snake struck them away. Venegas strode over to shove his niece away from the action and stand guard over her lest she dart for the doorway. Juanita spat at him and got a backhand across the mouth.

They were both at her then, animals without shame or conscience, rolling the woman upon the floor and laughing at their own nakedness, the ugly, swollen organs they poked at Rosa.

"W-wait," Marilee said. "Don't hurt her. Flagg—all right, damn it. Let her go, let them all go, and I—I'll wait with you for the priest."

Flagg drank whiskey. "You goin' to wait anyhow, and you goin' to speak up real polite when the padre asks you. But you don't want me to deprive the boys of their fun, now. I mean, missy, you think you such a hard case, think you're good as any man, and this here's about good a time as any to teach you a damned good lesson."

Venegas chewed on a cigarillo. "A *good* lesson, *jefe?*"

"Maybe so, maybe so," Flagg said. "We'll see how sweet and femalelike she kin be afore I make up my mind."

Snake and Johnson had Rosa between them, one man moving between her spread unresisting thighs, the other with a hand twisted in her long hair, dragging her head into his bared and hairy chest. Marilee looked away, but Flagg made a sign to Venegas, and the man jumped to take Marilee's head in hard, grimy hands to force it around.

"Just so you get an idea what might happen to you," Flagg said. "All these boys is right horny—been in the mountains a long spell, and on the trail. Reckon they can do it all day and come back for some more tonight."

"Take your filthy hands off me!" Marilee said to Venegas. And to Flagg: "You'd see these saddletramps defile *me*, the woman you want to marry? What kind of man are you, Jesse Flagg? What kind of twisted mind—"

"Hell," Flagg grunted, piggish eyes bright as he stared at the floor where his men were ravishing Rosa, where they were doing all manner of dark and perverted things to her helpless body. "Hell, missy—I ain't marryin' *you* —I'm weddin' this here ranch to my own, and you just goin' to be right handy against them Apaches. 'Course, you and these other wenches have to earn yore keep the best you can, cookin' and cleanin' and spreadin' yore legs. I always figgered a mare to be more hotted up, once one stud climbs down off her, and gives the next stud a better ride."

"Then the hell with you," Marilee said. "I'll die before I say yes to that priest."

"No you won't," Flagg grinned wetly. "I let you send that youngun outa the house account of it ain't too good for a little stud colt to get ideas afore he's old enough to do anything about 'em. But he ain't gone far. I kin send ol' Manuel to fetch him back and set him down where he can see every bit of what's goin' on. Guess he'll be special interested in what four, five of us do to his pretty mama."

Marilee went cold, and a black, bitter hate welled up within her. It was all the more virulent because she was so completely trapped, and there was nothing she could do to let it come boiling out. Jesse Flagg had her helpless as a hogtied calf waiting the redhot searing of the branding iron.

"Don't—don't do that," she whispered. "Please let him alone—leave Wayne out there."

Tilting the bottle, Flagg poured more whiskey into his thick-lipped mouth. "Damned if you ain't gettin' some sense. Won't take long, and you'll be sayin' yessir, Mister Flagg, sir, what else kin I do to please my lovin' husband."

Paloma was in the chair nearest the door, and Pedraza close to her, standing stiffly with no expression upon his face. Beyond them, Juanita sat on the floor with her back against the wall, dark eyes gone numb, a bruise marring the side of her mouth. Flagg stopped talking to watch the rutting of his men with Rosa, and Venegas slid his eyes at them also, the front of his pants bulging, one hand still gripping Marilee's hair. Only she saw the shadow move in the hallway, and caught her breath, hoping against hope that her son hadn't come back to the house.

But the shapeless form was too big for Wayne, far taller

and wider, and when it moved it became a blur that hurtled the man across the room with blinding speed. The carbine butt caromed off Flagg's head and drove the fat man spinning from his chair, his whiskey bottle crashing. Whipping around like a good cutting horse catty on his feet, the man fired once, and Venegas' fingers were whipped from their grip upon Marilee's hair, Venegas was slammed across the room and into the wall by the sledgehammering bullet that drove his life from him with a single blow.

Beside Paloma, the young Mexican jerked erect, and the carbine muzzle centered upon him.

"No," Pedraza said. "I did not want this."

Marilee's eyes stretched wide. *It couldn't be!* He was a thousand miles away, wearing a broadcloth coat and squiring a wealthy woman; a businessman in San Francisco, polished and gone mellow.

But there was no mistaking those coldly hooded eyes, the eagle cast of his profile, that terrible gunman's eagerness: Joe Langston.

The scar white at the corner of his thinned mouth, he said: "You bastards on the floor—get off that woman and crawl away from your clothes."

"N-now, fella—"

The Spencer jumped in Joe's hands, and a bloody furrow leaped along Snake's bare shoulder. In the echo of the shot, in rolling gunsmoke, both men scuttled panicstricken away from Rosa, scrabbling at the floor with hands and knees.

Joe said coldly, "You by the wall, boy."

Paloma spoke up. "This one was whispering to me, telling me he would let me run before he tried to fight them."

"Drop the gunbelt, boy," Joe said, and Pedraza carefully unbuckled it, let it fall. "Stand aside from it. Marilee—"

"Oh, yes," she said, coming off the couch, "I can use that gun. How I can use it!"

Jesse Flagg mumbled and pushed himself up to a sitting position. Blood ran down his face and his eyes were blank, his mouth hanging open.

Marilee scooped up Pedraza's pistol and turned furiously, but Joe said, "Easy—this one the boss?"

"Boss coyote," she gritted. "Boss tarantula. They were going to rape us all, and if I—if I didn't do what he wanted, he was going to bring my son in to watch. Get out of the way, Joe."

In the corner, two naked men glanced across at their scattered clothing, at their discarded handguns. Joe said, "Try if you want," and they wrapped their arms about their knees, huddling in upon themselves.

"I'll kill him," Marilee said. "I'll kill you, Jesse Flagg."

"Not you," Joe said. "Flagg, you still have your Colt. Stand up."

Wiping at his bloodied face, Flagg shook his head. "Not with you holdin' that Spencer on me. Don't know who the hell you are, mister—or how come you're buttin' in, but you bit yourself off a mouthful. These ain't *all* my men."

"Enough to dig you a hole," Joe said. "Stand up, you pus-gutted son of a bitch."

Knees wobbling, Flagg climbed laboriously to his feet. Joe said to Marilee, "These girls with you?"

"Yes."

"Here," Joe said, passing the carbine to Paloma.

"Señor," the Mexican boy said softly, "I will watch the others."

Paloma said, "I trust him. He was going to help us."

"All right," Joe said, watching Flagg, watching the naked men in the corner. "You and me, fat man."

Again, Flagg shook his head. "Uh-uh—you got the look of a gunslick, mister. You kill me, it's goin' to be murder, and the rest of my ranch hands—"

"Let me," Marilee begged. "Oh, let me."

With his left hand, Joe pushed her back. "You plucked jaybirds yonder—get up easy and walk out the front door ahead of your boss. Flagg, if you don't move, I mean to blow off both your kneecaps."

Snake and Johnson walked hunched over, naked butts shivering; Flagg waddled after them. Marilee, the pistol shaking in her hands, stalked after, and the others. Manuel Venegas would never walk anywhere.

Beyond the tethered horse, Joe stopped them. "You two, start west and don't even think about turning around."

"Good God," Johnson said, "you don't mean like *this*, man? Ain't nuthin' out there but hard land—cactus and rattlers and Apaches, and us naked, without no horse nor gun—we ain't got a *chance*."

"More chance than you have here," Joe said. "I'm only

an inch from drawing down on you, because you weren't
giving those women a chance, either. Walk out right now,
or see how you make out dragging a leg, or gelded, maybe."

"Oh, damn," Snake whispered. "Oh, damn."

They walked gingerly, already beginning to hobble before they got far beyond the fences, getting smaller as
they neared the hills, and Marilee looked after them with
no mercy in her heart.

"Now you," Joe said to Flagg, and fisted the man in the
mouth.

Flagg fell and rolled over, got up on one knee. Joe put a
boot against his shoulder and threw him onto his back;
dust puffed up around the man.

"Any time you get enough," Joe said, and dragged
Flagg up to hit him in the belly. Wheezing, Flagg staggered back, and Joe stalked him. "Any time you want,
reach for your gun."

Every time Flagg went down, Joe hauled him up and
hit him again, in the mouth, over the eyes, in the chest.
Flagg was bloody and dirty, gasping for breath as his eyes
rolled wildly.

"Any time," Joe said, and drove him into the corral
fence, punishing the heavy man with short, vicious blows.

Clawing at a rail, Flagg slid down and dropped his
beaten face, his chest heaving, back half turned.

Marilee said sharply, "Joe—watch out!"

Flagg got around on his knees, the pistol lifting. She
could barely see the flashing of Joe's hand stabbing for
his own Colt, but it was there, the muzzle rock-steady as
he fired.

The bullet jerked Flagg into the fence. His head wobbled
and his arms flung out, but his gun fired, fired again,
wildly. Joe shot him once more, and Flagg fell over onto
his face, heavy legs twitching, boot toes making zigzags
in the dust.

Past the corral, in the stables, a horse screamed.

"My god!" Marilee cried out. "A horse is hit—one of
those wild shots—"

Dropping her pistol, she darted past Flagg's body, her
legs pumping hard, begging, praying as she ran. Don't let
it be, dear God, don't let it be him!.

She tore open the stall door and saw Bradburn throwing his head, saw the whites of his eyes and the widely flared nostrils. There was blood on his chest.

"No! No, no—oh, Bradburn—*Bradburn!*" She took a faltering step toward the stallion, holding out her hands. He blew through his nostrils and stopped rolling his eyes, lowering the velvet of his nose to sniff her fingers. "Bradburn," she whispered hoarsely, calling the horse's name over and over again, fearful to look closely at his chest, unable to explore the wound with her hand.

Joe's voice was at her shoulder. "How bad is he hit?"

Turning, Marilee buried her face in his shoulder and sobbed, "I d-don't know. Oh, my God, I don't know!"

Chapter 51

Rosa had hidden herself away, and Marilee slumped at the kitchen table, chin in her hands, while Juanita prepared something to eat. Outside, Marilee couldn't hear the chink of shovels, but she knew Paloma and the young Mexican were digging graves for two men who'd richly deserved to die. Those graves would never be marked, cows would be driven over them until all signs of them were obliterated. She didn't even want to know where they were.

Across the table, Wayne de Carboca sat in a chair beside Joe Langston, his face turned to the man, smiling more often than Marilee had ever seen. She curled her fingers around a wine glass.

"Can't wash it away," Joe said. "Food's better."

"But he looked so—so hurt," she said. "As if I had betrayed him."

"He's still on his feet—a strong horse with a lot of heart, and you know that. The bullet passed on through, and we've done all we could. It's up to him now. Try to eat something, Marilee."

"I can't. Oh, Lord—Yankees and Apaches and Comanches—all the times Bradburn saved my life, and I can't do anything to save his now. It's not right—it's just not right."

Her son looked at her. "I watched Joe's mare as he said, and she did not get hurt."

Marilee's lip trembled. "I should have killed that man immediately. It wouldn't have happened then."

"Things happen," Joe said, and put his hand upon the boy's shoulder. "You did a good job, *hombrecito*."

The wine glass rattled against Marilee's teeth. "Talk, *talk!* Bradburn may be dying out there, and we talk."

"Used up all your prayers?"

She frowned at him. "*You,* saying *that?*"

Joe said to her son, "Pretty good stew, isn't it? I lean more to a good venison roast myself, but a thick stew like this puts meat on a man's ribs."

With only a faint rattle of dishes, Juanita was gone, taking something to Rosa.

Wayne said, "I do not think I can shoot a deer."

"Never liked to," Joe said seriously to the boy, "but when it means me hungry or that deer feeding a pack of coyotes instead, I choose me. There are times a man has to do things he doesn't like."

"Such as *madre* wanting to kill that man?"

Joe refilled Wayne's glass with milk. "She didn't have to, because I was here. In a little while, you will be big enough to do those things for her. Let's see now, you're almost five?"

"Before too long," the boy said.

"Almost *four,*" Marilee said, "and all this chatter—I'm going out to the stall."

Joe stood up with her. "*Hombre,* can you guard the house until we come back? A man does not always need a gun—often his eyes are enough."

Putting a candle and matches in her pocket, Marilee saw that her son sat more erect in his chair, that his eyes followed Joe. "I understand," Wayne said.

In the patio, Joe took her arm. "He's a solid boy—nothing scares him."

"Nothing gets to him," she answered, "nothing scares him because nothing reaches him. He lives in himself.

477

Joe, why are you here—how did you come along at just the right time—again?"

"I know how you feel about that stallion," he said, tall and comforting beside her. "It was something like that for me when Martha died. She was a lady I cared for very much. Couldn't see much sense in staying around afterward, and I got word about your husband, a hint of trouble you might be in. Figured I could lend a hand, if you wanted it. If you didn't—well, it's been a long time since I saw Alabama."

"You never liked Alabama. You must have loved her very much, your Martha."

"Alabama might have changed—people do. And there are different kinds of love, Marilee. *Can* I help you?"

She stopped at the courtyard gate. The moon was rising, and with it a warming wind. "You already have. I was finished. Flagg had it all right in his fat hands this ranch and all it contains, what cows are left, all my horses, even me. Oh, Joe, I've been fighting for so damned long. The *vaqueros* left, and the girls and I have been trying to hold it all together but it's killing us. Those men with Flagg—I sent my emeralds to El Paso with a Yankee lieutenant to hire some riders. They came back, on Flagg's side. I—I was so tired."

His arm felt warm around her shoulders, and he said, "I know. Listen, I'm carrying gold enough and letters of credit on the El Paso bank. I can bring supplies, riders, anything you need."

Suddenly uneasy, she walked out from beneath his arm. He followed her to Bradburn's stall, and in her mind's eye she could see every rhythm of that catlike, graceful walk. He was offering to lend money and furnish workers the place so desperately needed. He was a gunman at a time when guns were law. He was—could be—many things, but he was also Joe Langston. Polished and with the rough edges worn off, this man was still Joe Langston, who at last had cared enough for another woman to grieve over her. Marilee struck a match to the candle and held it high.

"He's still standing," she said, as light played over Bradburn's glossy coat. "His head is up and the bandages are still on."

Soft-eyed, head proud, Bradburn looked back at her, but she just couldn't go in there and hold him, bury her face in his mane as she did so often. If she did, she would never leave him, and Joe was right; it was up to the stallion now. "You'll be all right," she told Bradburn. "You have to be all right, and you will, you *will*."

Taking the candle from her hand, Joe said quietly, "He has grain and water, fresh bedding. Tomorrow, I'll pour whiskey and turpentine into the wound again. Let him rest, Marilee."

She let him lead her back to the house, but turned from the kitchen where she could hear the others talking and held to his hand. "I don't want to be alone, Joe—not tonight."

But she didn't want to, couldn't be made love to, either. Marilee needed the warmth of someone close, to be held softly and gently in a man's arms without lust, without having to give back anything. Fully clothed, she lay on the bed, and he came to her the same way. She put her head upon his chest and breathed of him, almost tasted him, so glad for his comfort that she wanted to cry.

"Tell me about your Martha," she said, and he did, spelling it all out for her, what this other woman had done for him, what she had helped make of him. Marilee wanted to cry again, for she could not tell him in turn of Alfonso—not in the way he spoke of Martha. After a while, he fell silent, and the candle burned itself out. At the window, curtains stirred, and she thought of April and new grass coming up, of calves and foals and all the signs of spring in bright new lives.

Bradburn, she thought, and somehow sleep came.

Marilee woke alone, feeling out for the warmth of him and not finding it in the bed. She sat up, throwing off a blanket he'd placed over her during the night, and came off the bed quickly, before her eyes were well open. She was down the stairs and across the foyer, out into the patio with morning new upon her face, before she saw him.

"Joe—how is he? Is Bradburn doing fine?"

He stopped her, held her arm. "Marilee, do you know why I beat that man Flagg so, why I forced him to try for his life?"

"Not now," she said. "The stall—"

479

He held her fast. "I beat him because he was me, a long time ago—because he was a heartless, know-it-all bastard who thought anything in the world was rightfully his, if he was man enough to take it. That was before I learned a man has to give as well as take."

"That's all very well," she said impatiently, tugging at his hand, "but not now. I have to see to Bradburn."

"He's gone," Joe said, and her heart stopped.

"Dead? Oh, my God, no—don't say he's dead!"

"Just gone," Joe said. "He broke out of the corral sometime during the night."

"Then we have to find him quickly. Let me go!"

He said, "I have horses saddled. He won't be hard to trail—he was bleeding."

A sob caught in her throat as she ran for the horses, and her teeth were clenched so hard her jaws ached. She was up in the saddle before she saw her son in the other one.

One foot in the stirrup, Joe said. "Figured he ought to go along with us."

"I don't *give* a damn!" she cried. "Which way—"

Arm around Wayne, Joe pointed to the hills, "That way," and she was conscious of his mare loping behind her as she put heels to her own horse.

A spot of blood stained the earth, and farther along another one, and each of them could have been torn from the pulsing depths of her own heart. She pushed her horse faster, not feeling the same response Bradburn would have given her, not knowing that same leap of power and eagerness. Marilee's throat constricted and her eyes blurred. She had to wipe at them before she could find Bradburn's trail again.

"The hill over there," Joe said behind her. "That's where he headed."

She was shaken and confused. "I don't see any hoof-prints—why would he go there?"

"Because it's the highest one," Joe said, "and stands apart from the rest, tall and alone."

Staring at him, not wanting to hear logic, she saw Wayne hanging on to the saddle horn, his short legs tucked along Joe's knees. It struck her that Wayne was a copy of the man, the same calm, watchful face; the set of their jaws alike; their hair and eyes—most of all, their eyes. Marilee kneed her horse around and sawed its mouth because it would not move swiftly as it should. No horse reacted like Bradburn—not one.

Reaching the slope, she dropped the horse into a slow jog, peering down at the tracks in soft dirt. He had been wavering as he climbed; his tracks showed he staggered here. Marilee caught her lower lip between her teeth and lifted her eyes to the top of the hill, praying to see him standing there.

She walked the horse uphill, her eyes frantically searching the brush and seeing only where her stallion had broken a path through. How long had he been out here alone and suffering? Why had he left his stall, driven to use faltering strength to break out of his corral? If he had only called to her. . . .

Joe's mare was at her side, breasting the sagebrush, cracking small limbs. Then they were out upon a grassy knoll, a tiny plateau softened by green.

And in the little mesa's center, at the very top of this tallest hill, Bradburn lay motionless, his muzzle thrust to the west and into the wind.

The cry ripped from Marilee's soul, wordless because there were no words for her agony, because this sorrow could express itself no other way.

She sat her saddle until Joe helped her down and held her so she could force her legs to move. Sinking to soft grass beside the great stallion, she tried to lift his head into her lap, but his neck had stiffened. Tears came then, hot and spurting and salty, and she leaned her cheek to Bradburn's cheek, her arms spread across the mighty body as if she could rock him like a child, as if she could soothe him or somehow pull him back from that great darkness. For a long time, she cried, and when she at last lifted her head and turned her streaked face, Marilee saw Joe kneeling, Wayne standing erect beside him, the man's arm around the boy.

"He's gone," Marilee said. "His heart—his great heart carried him this far, and then he lay down to die. Oh, Joe—why didn't he neigh for me? Why did he have to—"

Softly, Joe said, "Some people and some horses are lucky—they can tell when it's coming. Bradburn didn't

481

try to run from death or cower from it. He went out to meet it, but in a place of his own choosing. He was a fine stallion, Marilee."

"The finest," she said, aching and dry-mouthed. "And now it's all gone with him—building the herd, some day going back to the plantation. All the plans and all my dreams died with him."

"Stand up," Joe said.

She only stared wet-eyed at him, and he said it again, harder. "Stand up, Marilee." And when she still didn't respond, his hand wasn't gentle on her arm.

Joe pointed to the valley below. "Look there—I see horses grazing, don't you? How many of them are Bradburn's get—twenty, thirty? He has sons on that grass, Marilee, other fine horses with his blood running strong in them."

When she didn't say anything, he shook her, and she didn't flare at him. So he let her go and swept up Wayne, lifted the boy and put him in her arms. "Hold on," Joe said. "Hold on to this boy, because he's a fine one, too. Put your face to his as you did to the stallion's, and if you have any tears left, shed them for him. And for God's sake, when you're done crying, see if you can't give him just a little bit of the love you gave to Bradburn."

Wayne's arms were warm about her neck, and the boy's pale eyes searched her face—somber little boy, withdrawn child. There had been so little time for him, so many vital things to be done that he had been put off into an unimportant corner of her life. She held him closer.

Joe said, "Good Christ, woman—Bradburn left his stall so he could die with dignity, alone on a hilltop—it's a dignity given to damned few of us. And you say everything's gone with him? If you believe that, you're a fool. What's gone, *what*? The plantation in Mississippi with its big white house and slaves? Your family and friends? Hell, they've been gone for many years.

"And Bradburn himself isn't gone. There are other Bradburns down in the valley, just as proud, just as strong because they're his sons and his daughters. That's the only kind of immortality any of us are ever likely to have, man or horse. A plantation isn't immortal, and big white houses fall down—death comes and we can't shoot it or run from it, but if we have half the courage of that stallion, we walk out to face it. And if we're half as lucky as he was, to know love and honor and to pass himself on in his get, then we're fortunate, too."

Marilee stared at him and held her child. "Wayne may not—may not be your son. He could be, but I'm not certain. I can never be certain, and neither can you."

His voice was lower, and Joe put out a hand to touch the boy's shoulder. "I'd be proud to claim him, to call him mine. But I'm just as proud of him because he's yours."

"Alfonso was a cruel, vicious man," she said, "and Wayne wears his name."

Gesturing at the valley, Joe said, "And this hacienda isn't your old plantation—this Territory can never be Mississippi, but you fought to hold it. Take a good look, Marilee, a good long look at a new land and a new life. Feel your son, *our* son, in your arms—he's new life for old. So am I, if you'll have me."

"If—if I'll have you?"

He put his arms around them both. "It's April, and down by the springs willows are green as your eyes, those eyes I could never forget. Feel the warmth of the wind? It's what your memory has always done to me, blowing fresh and kissing my face. I guess what I'm trying to say is that I love you, Marilee. I have always loved you and needed you to make me whole, to make me into what I can be. It just took me a long, long time to see the truth of that."

She lowered her son, their son, to the ground but held on to Wayne's small hand. "It's going to be so good to have someone to lean on. Joe, Joe Langston—I've hated you and missed you and—and loved you. I love you now."

Gently, he held her, and the scarred mouth he touched to her lips wasn't hard and cynical now, but tender with promise. There were eternities in that pledge, fierceness and strength, gentleness and giving, and her heart lifted in exultation.

Joe stepped back and took Wayne from her, swung the

boy into the saddle of his mare and smiled up at him. To Marilee he said, "I'll come back and bury Bradburn here, in the place he chose to lie down. Feel the wind, Marilee —see it ruffle his mane. Here he can always know it. Here we can come to stand beside him and know it together. We can, we *will* drink the spring wind."